THE DARK
CIRCLE

THE DARK CIRCLE

CIRCLE

LINDA GRANT

virago

VIRAGO

First published in Great Britain in 2016 by Virago Press

3 5 7 9 10 8 6 4 2

Copyright © Linda Grant 2016

The moral right of the author has been asserted.

A CIP catalogue record for this book
is available from the British Library.

Hardback ISBN 978-0-349-00675-8
C-format ISBN 978-0-349-00676-5

Typeset in Goudy by M Rules
Printed and bound in Great Britain by
Clays Ltd, St Ives plc

Papers used by Virago are from well-managed forests
and other responsible sources.

MIX
Paper from
responsible sources
FSC® C104740

Virago Press
An imprint of
Little, Brown Book Group
Carmelite House
50 Victoria Embankment
London EC4Y 0DZ

An Hachette UK Company
www.hachette.co.uk

www.virago.co.uk

To Sara Marsh, my oldest friend,
from the time when we both learned to read

PART ONE

Each Breath You Take

1949–51

|

London. Big black old place, falling down, hardly any colour apart from a woman's red hat going into the chemist with her string bag, and if you looked carefully, bottle-green leather shoes on that girl, but mostly grey and beige and black and mud-coloured people with dirty hair and unwashed shirt collars, because everything is short, soap is short, joy is short, sex is short, and no one on the street is laughing so jokes must be short too. Four years after the war and still everything is up shit creek.

Top deck of the number 19 bus with sun coming in and out and the passengers' coats steaming with earlier rain. Smell of damp gabardine and nicotine. Lenny in his new suit and his Italian shoes looking sharp and young and on his mettle and a woman's voice jabbering at him from the seat across the aisle as they lumbered down Blackstock Road.

'Doesn't London look dingy? I remember beautiful shops; they sold everything you wanted and the meat was lovely, great rosy rashers of bacon and the rind like white marble. But you won't remember any of that. You're too young.'

Blah blah blah, working her way through hams and briskets and racks of lamb. All anyone talked about these days was food, the national obsession. There was even less of it than there had been on VE Day – how did that work, he thought. You'd need to read the newspaper to understand it, and who had time for reading?

The woman got off at the Angel and he didn't have to hear any more about meat, thank God. In a month he was supposed to be going into the army because as soon as one war ends, another starts. A future of Nissen huts and itchy uniforms. A world of Blanco, webbing, Brasso and pointlessness. Marching, saluting, scratching your arse and here, the bus turning from New Oxford Street into Charing Cross Road, were birds.

All the birds of Soho, Italians with little gold crosses round their necks and olive skin and nipples like raisins. They showed you what a cup of coffee was supposed to taste like. They gave you a meal of macaroni and sausage that was to die for. Heaven was an Italian bird in her half-slip standing by the window of a flat in Dean Street with the light on her hair and turning round to give you a big smile before she said her Hail Marys.

Give that up for a parade ground and beds full of farting men?

Cambridge Circus. Raining again, this quality of English rain to continue on and off all day so you never got a chance to dry out, your clothes steaming, your socks damp, rainwater down your neck, holding out your palm to feel for the drops and the momentary deception of dryness before the sky, having taken a breather, went at it once more. He got off and walked down to Trafalgar Square. Clouds of starving pigeons circled Nelson's Column. In the East End it was rumoured that a flock of them could carry off a small child if you took your eye off it for a minute. He was a few minutes early and stopped to watch a group of wet men in light jackets and open-neck shirts begin to file into the empty space. Some wore campaign medals across their chests. Most had flat caps. A woman built like a wartime pillbox was by their side barking directions as they crowded around the stone lions. One contingent marched in a disciplined column with placards tied across their chests, a sodden sandwich-board army.

Lenny wanted to know what was going to happen next, who they

4

were and why they were gathering. A microphone was set up and a man, a leader of some kind, began to speak into it.

'I'm really just about fed up of it. I was so fed up of it—' But the words were broken and then swallowed in a sharp gust of rain blowing in Lenny's face.

The speaker was fed up of it and why the fuck not? It was reasonable. There was so much to be fed up about. The crowd applauded wildly. They didn't seem to mind being wet, they were hardy, tough types. Even the few women with turbans on their heads looked like they could go a round or two with Freddie Mills.

He stood for longer than he had intended watching the speaker who had had enough and it seemed to him that he spoke the universal thoughts of everyone he knew. Fed up. Fed up with bad meat and girls with bad breath and long queues at the pictures if anything good was on. He turned away from the crowd, to his date with the army, looked up at the church clock and noted, pleased, that he was late. What were they going to do about it? He was here, wasn't he?

He was eighteen. He had slept with three birds already, including the Italian. He had his own London drape with two pairs of trousers. In the neighbourhood he was part of a gang of boisterous Jewish lads who thought they were on top of the world. They were apprentice bakers, cabinet makers, pressers and cutters; they all had jobs and girls on their arm. They were emerging Teddy boys.

'And if there weren't so many Yids swarming in, demanding to jump to the head of the queue, getting houses and . . . '

The crowd was packing in now around the speaker, they were applauding and some pointing their forefingers at him, as if they were acknowledging the correctness of his point. The Yids, the Yids, the bloody Yids who come over here and are loud and flashy and were shirkers during the war . . . never lifted a finger to help their own kind . . . didn't do their bit when everyone was doing their bit . . . running the black market stealing the food from the mouths of innocent kiddies . . . And Lenny thought, Fucked if I'm going to let him get away with that, felt in his pocket for a missile, found

5

the packet of sandwiches his mother had packed for him together with a slice of honey cake wrapped in paper, and in an overhand shot lobbed it at the orator.

Chopped fish on rye assaulted the speaker's cheek. The smell of the herring barrel was all over his face and collar. Minced onion fell down his neck. Cake crumbs got inside his nostrils. There was a meal all over him. His supporters rushed to help. Others thought he'd been shot by a silent gun. Find the bastard, cried the crowd, give him a good hiding, the cowardly little—

Next to him a muscular individual in a pea jacket, as if he'd stepped off the deck of a merchant vessel, was raising his arm. The arm had a fist at the end of it and something bulging beneath the fingers. '*The fucking little Jew-boy swine the kike-nosed prick let him have it.*'

2

And oh it is piercing cold when you have had your hands in a bucket of water all day and the shop is kept icy on account of the flowers because the sensitive little petals don't like to get too hot, poor darlings. Then they will wilt and Mrs Brascombe the sour bitch will pull a face and say, 'Not quite *fresh* today, do you have any others?' So you must freeze and shiver and get the sniffles and have snot stream from your nose because there are not enough hankies in the world.

'Mimi! Can you *please* take care of that runny nose of yours, it's so off-putting to the customers. Do you not have a clean handkerchief?'

'Sorry, Miss Haynes. It's all wet through.'

'Well, then you must try to make do with some newspaper.'

'I used that yesterday, I got all black marks round my nose.'

And she does not even know whether she *wants* to be called Mimi, which is a chic Parisian name suitable for a girl working in a florist's shop in a nice part of London and the moniker Miss Haynes gave her when she first started because, 'While there's nothing wrong with Miriam, it's a little too Hebrew for our clientele. Not that they are prejudiced, but they expect a level of service and certain standards from us.'

The van broke down this morning. The parts to fix it are not easily available so the deliveries must be done on foot or, if strictly necessary, by bus. A huge bouquet of bronze chrysanthemums and mixed fern must be delivered to a bone china shop on the Strand where she has to arrange it in the window to the satisfaction of the picky manageress, another old bitch-and-a-half who was the type who has sort of seen what she wanted but has no idea how to describe it, so is completely useless and impossible to satisfy, because even if you did it identical, even if you took her back to what she had in mind and showed her, she'd say, 'Oh, well, I suppose I was thinking of something different.'

Miriam loves flowers, adores them, is arty and good at grouping colours and all the arranging you have to do, choosing the right size vase and keeping everything in the right proportions. She knows what lasts and what dies as soon as you turn your back for five minutes. It's her trade and she's nagging her uncle to get her her own shop once she's learned the business but the bouquet this morning weighs a ton, scentless and knocking into her face. She stops for breath in Trafalgar Square where some people are marching around with sandwich boards on their chests and someone is ranting about how he's had enough, which was stating the bleeding obvious because everyone has. Misery piled on misery, just without bombs and bomb shelters.

The wet wind chases the speaker's words. Apart from having had enough, that was all there was to it. The protest is incoherent to her and without a point. She begins to walk away towards the Strand when her eye is caught by an arm rising into the air and lobbing something.

Now I see who he is, she thinks, blow me down it's *him*, old Jeffrey Hamm of all people, large as life and twice as ugly. Hit by a sandwich and a slice of cake, which you had to admit was the funniest thing ever, but whoever's done it is never going to get away with it, poor sod.

What she has are reflexes, they're like a tripwire. As if a camera takes a photograph she sees, burnished on her eyeballs, that fist raised towards her *brother* of all people, a fist walking ponderously towards him and him backing away, trying to break into a run.

Even burdened by flowers she makes a quick advance, reaches his assailant and swinging her bouquet, rams it hard round his head.

Blinded by petals, by pounds of chrysanthemums and knife-sharp ferns, the assailant is knocked off balance, walks back a step or two and stumbling on the kerb, falls into the gutter.

'Ha ha,' says Miriam and kicks him in the nuts with her brown-leather brogues, her shop shoes, her standing-all-day shoes, not the dainty things she wears at night when she goes out dancing.

The crowd starts laughing. 'Look, she's only a *girl*. Done it too with a bunch of flowers!'

Miriam takes her brother's arm, they run across the square to Charing Cross Road and stand panting on the corner, out of sight of the sandwich board men. 'Oh, blimey, that's torn it. I'm going to get sacked for those flowers. Fifteen bob they cost. It was worth it, though, wasn't it? Did you see that chopped herring on Hamm's face?'

'Was that *Hamm*? Never! Not Hamm himself.'

'Didn't you recognise him?'

'Nah, I just heard him going on about the Yids.'

'I clocked him straight away, nasty old piece of work, honestly, I thought he was finished. But that's him all over, Hamm by name, ham by nature.'

Lenny is still getting his breath back. 'Darling, I gotta get a move on, I'm late for my appointment.'

'It's not far, is it?'

'Nah, just round the corner. I'll see you later back home and tell you how I got on.'

'It's not going to be a problem, though, is it? They won't take you, will they? I'm not letting them lay a hand on you.'

'Yeah, you and whose army against their army? But not to worry, Manny's got it all sewn up.'

'We're never going to be separated, are we?'

'Not on your life, Beauty.'

And she is beautiful, to him, with her big bosom, slim hips, good legs, and a mound of blue-black hair enhanced by a rinse she puts on it, all in curls and kept away from her face by pins when she is working on the flowers. Boys are mad for her, he keeps an eye on that and vets them according to how he interprets their intentions. By next winter, he expects to have bought her a fur of some kind and not a stinking old coney either. Like an archer focusing on the bull's-eye, a mink is what he eventually aims at.

Flesh of his flesh, his twin sister.

3

After he'd handed in his chit and had it stamped and been given another chit and had that stamped and had his name checked against a list then another list and given one more chit he was standing in front of a doctor in a white coat who said, 'Why are you late? Were you held up by the agitators? Anyway, you're here now. Give us a cough, lad, it's just a test for hernia. We need to see if you're fit for heavy lifting.'

Lenny cleared his throat. He felt his testicles tighten and rise. They always did that when he coughed. He didn't know if this was a good thing or a bad thing.

'You passed,' said the doc, 'but I don't like the sound of your chest. Do you get bronchitis a lot? Have you had pneumonia?'

'Yes, a couple of years ago but I'm right as rain now.'

The doctor wrote something and then directed him along the hall. 'They'll see you down there.' And Lenny waited for an hour, nattering with the other boys who made dirty cracks about the nurses, told jokes everyone had heard already, and there rose up the universal lament, *I've just about had enough. I've really had enough.*

They were waiting to be X-rayed. No one he knew had ever had an X-ray. The general principle, as he understood it, was that the machine could actually see inside your body and take pictures that came out in black and white, but the wrong way round, like a photographic negative. He had been assured that the procedure wasn't going to hurt, but he wasn't entirely convinced. He imagined a series of knives penetrating him at different points. They told you any old rubbish to make you do things. But the nurse was smiling, she called out his name.

'L. Lynskey!'

Up he got. The nurse had the blondest hair he'd ever seen. She looked like an albino apart from traces of pink lipstick round her mouth. She had a spiel all ready and she was used to his type, there was no getting round her, she had a patter.

'Now you look like the strong silent sort, which of course I tell all the boys, so I won't expect any babyishness from you, though I've seen massive young fellows run screaming when they see the apparatus. It's just a big old metal box with a film inside. Think of it as a camera, because that's what it is, really.' And she opened the door to reveal something that looked like a gun emplacement in Normandy.

'All you have to do is stand still,' she said. 'I'll do the rest, and if you're very good and do like I tell you, the whole thing will be over in two ticks.'

He stood where he was told. The machine clanked. Waves of science passed through his body, then it was over.

'Off you go,' said the nurse. 'Down the corridor. Chop chop.'

He was in another room where an older nurse with an up-and-down-and-all-around-the-houses Irish accent offered him a large round flat metal dish set with red jelly. 'Just spit,' she said. 'This is the easy part.'

He coughed. He tried to raise some phlegm. Nothing came but a few flecks of spittle.

'Sorry,' he said, straining now.

'Is that all you've got? No more?'

'I don't think so.'

'That's all right then. You'll be hearing from us. Off you go.'

So that was it and all he had to do was wait for the letter.

Trafalgar Square was empty. Whatever the assembly was which wouldn't put up with it, they had dissipated back into the city. Which was funny ha-ha because it had stopped raining and the bastards had got the worst of the weather.

Uncle Manny was waiting for him by the big lions. All the beef in the family had gone into him, he got the muscle, the sinews, the balls and the brains; his younger brother, Lenny's father, had been made up of leftovers. Manny wore a Homburg hat and a coat with a velvet collar. No matter how small the ration, he looked as well-fed as a sleek house cat. He was said to have the best-looking moustache in all of Manor House and he took great care of it, looking in the mirror and giving it a little trim with the nail scissors. He used a special oil. Every girl likes a man with a nice moustache, he said, and Lenny didn't tell him they had gone out of fashion.

'How did you get on?'

He loved his nephew, the boy was special to him. His own son Max died of diphtheria aged six and was buried in Golders Green cemetery. For years his heart was ash then Lenny came up, so promising. A lovely boy, pure gold. No one was going to take another kid away from him. Sons, we are nothing without sons! Lenny's poor dad had done nothing for him except die before he could do too much damage, toiling over his religious books night and day in his junk shop in Stepney, and his mother was neither use nor ornament.

'Same as everyone else. Drop your pants and cough, X-ray, spit. Clockwork. No special treatment.'

'That's what I heard. It's when the papers get passed up that you'll get the wrong stamp. Sixty nicker, I paid! But my boy is worth it. I'm investing in you.'

'Thanks, Manny. I won't let you down.'

They strolled down into Soho in search of coffee. Manny had a high opinion of the Italians who were starting to come out with slimline, narrow-lapelled suits and he liked their grub, the spaghetti bolognese, the minestrone soup, the Chianti wine when you could get hold of it. He knew Lenny had a girl here but didn't mention

13

it. The boy could have his fun. The streets were full of foreigners, Eyeteye boys back from the internment camps full of resentment and elegant curses, Maltesers with black eyes and strings of girls on the game, refugees from Europe in clothes with faint traces and outlines on a lapel or a pocket of once having been expensive, the occasional figure of a coloured gentleman looking chilled to the bone and in need of directions to an incomplete address scribbled down on a piece of paper, the ink smudged in the rain.

Manny laid out his plans. He had been up north of Finsbury Park to a road where the V1 bombs had left an awful mess near the railway line into King's Cross. The place looked like mouths that had been in a fight and lost the argument and a few teeth. He described a plan to build a small modern block of flats for young families, with gardens at the back. He showed Lenny a rough drawing of what he had in mind.

Lenny looked at it.

'You know you could squeeze a couple more flats in.'

'How?'

Lenny quickly drew a rectangle at the rear of the building. 'See? One on top of the other, they extend out into the garden and they're facing the back not the street, quieter.'

'Smaller, though?'

'Yes, they'd be a bit smaller, but still give you enough space to have a kid in there. They'll come up with folding prams one of these days.'

'You're a marvel, son. You're going to make me thousands. You're worth every penny.'

Lenny was thinking of his bird Gina. If he could get away from his uncle there would be time to tell her that he was not going away to the army and was going to live and prosper here in London. He'd have everything in the palm of his hand, including a rum baba if he was lucky and her momma had been baking, and what came out of the oven had more sugar in it than most people used to see in a week.

*

Food, food, food. He was always starving. And he'd thrown his lunch at that fascist so he was even hungrier than usual. That morning Mrs Meltz next door had been out in the backyard strangling hens. Every Friday she selected a few victims and wrung their necks with her bare hands. Sinews stood out like metal wires in her scrawny arms. The children in the street were terrified of her, the angel of poultry death, but their mothers were all smiles and, 'Oh, Mrs Meltz, oh Dolly dearest, have you a nice hen for me today?'

When he got home Lenny's mother had roasted her bird and served it with boiled carrots and boiled kasha, a grey grainy mush that Miriam wouldn't touch. Unmentionable chicken parts were turned into golden soup. The livers were pulped and served on best bread. The hen was an opportunity in ingenuity – how many aspects of another species could you turn into food? In these women's implacable hands the humble chicken lost the battle with the human race.

Mrs Lynskey was not a fastidious plucker. She did her best but sometimes a few small feathers stuck to the skin. Once, on the evidence of these wisps, Lenny had recognised his favourite bird, Snowy, who marched up and down the yard, its head bobbing, flapping its useless white wings and looking as though it thought it was special.

When he was a kid he'd have cried his eyes out at seeing Snowy on his plate at dinner, but eighteen months of evacuation in Wales hardened his heart. You had to eat and he was ravenous. If he didn't scoff it right away, if he pushed the drumstick around his plate a bit, his sister would have it off him, not even put it down to cut it up with a knife and fork but straight into her mouth. She wasn't soft on animals. She never noticed hens. Or cats or dogs. She didn't even look up when a horse came clopping down the street pulling the totter's cart. They went to the zoo once and saw a zebra but after a glance she took out her powder compact and did her face. Lenny thought the zebra was something else. A pony with a statement.

'Where is Malaya, exactly,' his mother said, 'that place they want to send you?'

'Africa, I suppose. Or India. It'll be one of the two.' He had never got round to asking because he knew he wasn't going. His mother had not been informed. There were too many *yachnes* on the street, gossips who would never turn you in but would leak out too much information until it reached the authorities under its own steam.

'And what are we doing there, again?'

'It's the empire, Mum, something to do with that.'

'I don't know what we need one of those for.'

'Goods, they send us stuff.'

'Well, where are they, then? I don't see none in the shops.'

4

The ambulance carrying the two patients left behind the city. The girl said she'd never been south of the river, let alone to Kent, and didn't feel she'd missed the experience.

'There's nothing here,' she said. 'I mean, look at it, just houses and little shops. What would you come *for*?'

'You've restricted your outlook,' said Joe Hart, the ambulance driver, who was used to a wide range of personalities and life stories. 'I bet there's lots of things of interest in south London.'

'Doubt it.'

Then they passed the last house in the last suburb and there was nothing but green fields and the boy and girl looked round, as if they had been abducted.

'This place we're going,' she said nervously, 'nothing but sheep, I suppose. We hate sheep, don't we, Lenny? It was all sheep in Wales.'

'Evacuated?'

'Yeah.'

The year and a half of their imprisonment in the countryside gulag had fomented in them a hatred of Nature. The farmer had expected them to help out with various chores in the yard and offered to take them on rambles across the fields to put some roses in their sallow cheeks but however fresh the air, they stayed indoors with their comics, reading and talking to each other in a garbled version of their parents' native language, a child's illiterate Yiddish designed not to be understood by the adult occupants of the house. Later they agreed that the family had not actually been unkind, let alone cruel, had tried their best, but their homesickness was so intense – for familiar food and their mother's favourite wireless programmes – that nothing could console them. They had refused to learn the names of trees or flowers or pick up any useful country lore. They felt themselves to be amongst barbarians.

'Still,' Hart said, 'they'll make you better where we're going. Then you'll be well and fighting fit. As long as you can put up with a few sheep.'

'Do you think so?' said Lenny. 'Does that usually happen? Do you bring people back as well as taking them?'

'Of course not, they don't need an ambulance when they're leaving, do they? They travel by train or bus or motor car.'

Hart did not know if anyone ever really left. There were patients he'd taken and re-taken three or four times, on each occasion weaker and more hopeless. These poor kids, lucky for the boy to have been too young to fight, then this gets him.

In the back they nattered away to each other. It sounded at times like a secret code between them. He had no idea how they would fit in once he had dropped them off at the sanatorium's door. They were rougher than anyone else he had driven there, giving off a cheap sexy glamour, as if they had thrown a bottle of strong women's perfume over themselves after they washed. And the girl did smell of some scent with one of those names like Paris Nights or Secret of the Orient.

'This place I'm taking you,' he said as they crossed the river at Rochester, 'you'll have seen nothing like it before. Just wait.'

'We haven't seen nothing anyway,' said Miriam.

'Apart from Wales.'

'Exactly. Nothing.'

He explained about the sanatorium, the Gwendolyn Downie Memorial Hospital for the Care of Chronic Cases of Tuberculosis, to give it its full meat and potatoes, known by everyone as the Gwendo. Named after the daughter of the local squire and his wife (a former stage actress), who had died of TB in 1937, aged only twenty. The sanatorium was commissioned at the personal expense of Neville Downie who was in the brewing trade and the owner of many acres of hop fields. The architect was a young German who had come all the way over from that country to build something completely modern, designed for purpose, not adapted, and described in the prospectus for private patients as 'a building which is a machine to make people better, a medical instrument, like an oxygen tank'.

Until last year, all the patients were middle class or better. They came from nice families and many were officers, poor fellows – young chaps who had survived the war but fallen ill with tuberculosis, which was terrible luck – but now the National Health Service had opened it up to anyone and the place was completely free of charge. New arrivals were starting to turn up, types with bad table manners and no taste for the genteel facilities the Gwendo offered its languid inmates: bridge tournaments, flower arranging, golf for the fitter ones.

The pair in the back were common as muck. Of course, Joe Hart knew he was common as muck too, but over many years of driving invalids to the Gwendo he had learned to appreciate a nicer class of person and to cringe when he came into contact with rougher types. Plus, they were Hebrews, and that lot were only out for themselves, particularly the refugees. You had to keep an eye on them, they were *swarming* these days like bees. And we all know what bees are famous for: stinging you.

Past Faversham the sun came out intermittently and through the rear window the twins saw their first oast houses and first coned hop poles in the muddy fields. A couple of miles beyond Doddington, they entered Lower Otterdown, driving past the large chemist which had been knocked through from the adjacent premises to supply the many personal needs of the private patients.

Some had their own solid-silver or silver-plated thermometers, purchased by relatives who had no idea what to give the bed-bound as a birthday or Christmas present. The shop had a whole section specialising in handkerchiefs. You could send away to have them monogrammed with initials but others aimed to brighten the day of the unwell with scenes of the Riviera, or Mickey Mouse and Daffy Duck being little tearaways across the cotton. Along the street a butcher, a baker, a general grocer's, an ironmonger, a newsagent, a pub, the Singing Kettle tea rooms, a small milliner's occupying half a shop sliced in two, the other section, cutely, a doll's hospital where little girls took in Polly whose head had fallen off and Daddy couldn't get it back on again.

When the letter first came, Lenny had let out a yell. Manny had done it! Unfit for service. Then the doctor sent for him. Normally he wouldn't have bothered going. You had to pay. Except now you didn't. The doctor said, 'You've got TB, I'm afraid.' Lenny said, smiling, 'That might not be right.'

The doctor said, 'Here are the X-rays, see for yourself.'

Uncle Manny couldn't believe it. 'I spent sixty quid for nothing? The *mamzer*, what I'll do to him, taking my money.' Dark clouds of Yiddish curses from a night land of persecution and suffering came in clots from his mouth. *Black sorrow is all that his mother should see of him. He should grow a wooden tongue.*

But the *mamzer* said he'd done exactly as he was told, declared Lenny IV, unfit for service. It wasn't his fault he actually *was* unfit for service. Anyway, the money was spent now.

So Lenny wasn't going to Malaya but he wasn't going to be going into the property business either or in any other way make his mark on post-war London. He had a lousy rotten chest, bad lungs. He was a reject. He'd panted hard enough in the past, his heart beating like the clappers as he did it with a bird. Once he'd coughed up a clot of blood onto the pillow and the bird had screamed, but he said he'd just bit his lip in a frenzy. The blood didn't even worry him, he forgot about it. And Miriam had TB too. He must have given it to her, but she said, 'No way, it's our old man's fault. He weakened us.'

Hart was saying, 'It is quiet, isn't it? You'll soon get used to it, I expect. People stay for years. They don't complain.'

'Is that how long it takes to get better?'

'For some. Others are as right as rain in no time.' He never told anyone the truth, not even the hard-bitten RAF boys who'd been through the Battle of Britain. Whatever medals they came with, the only one they would win here was the military cross for endurance in the face of lassitude and boredom.

'Stop!' Miriam cried.

'What you talking about? We're not there yet, this is just the village.'

'I want an ice cream. I gotta have an ice cream, any flavour, but I gotta have one.'

'*Ice cream?* In March?'

'Sometimes shops have it. There are fridges.'

'There won't be. It's not that sort of place. Maybe at the seaside, not here.'

'You never know, it might be the last chance I ever get.'

'Don't be silly, there will be plenty more ice creams for you, you'll be licking cones for a long time to come.'

'Come on, mate, let's stop,' said Lenny. 'Just for a minute. Let's see if we can get one. We can try, can't we?'

Miriam saw ice cream as her only hope, the chance that they might escape their fate as victims of tuberculosis and her life over at the age of nineteen. If there was ice cream available in this shop then they had a chance. *Do* I have a chance, she thought? I've *got to!*

They were not late. They'd had a wonderful run from north London despite the overcast skies. Hart had thought he might stop in at the cathedral on his way home and look at the stained glass, he'd always been meaning to. Perhaps find a tea shop. But this poor kid was probably going to her grave and wanted what she was not going to be able to find, ice cream in March in an English village. He didn't have the heart not to let her try even if it delayed their arrival by a few minutes. He understood that it was just treading

21

water before you drowned, but a few minutes more of freedom would mean the world to her.

He stopped the ambulance. They walked up and down the street, going from shop to shop asking about cones. At the Singing Kettle they said they were sorry but they only served ices in July and August. He watched them come out, their shoulders drooping in defeat. The boy put his arm around his sister. Hart thought they might get on better than most up there because they had each other but it didn't matter. TB was a losing game.

Miriam leaned against the glass. She heard a bird make a sudden flight onto the branches of an apple tree in the front garden of a house across the road, landing heavily. She heard the church bell strike the quarter. She heard the rubber tyres of a bicycle pass and the leather soles of a pair of ladies' shoes patting along the pavement. Other than these sounds there was no traffic.

Defeated, they got back into the ambulance. Lenny said, 'We'll be long gone before ice cream comes back into stock. I'll take you to Chalk Farm, they do lovely Italian ices there.'

'Yes,' Miriam said, 'long gone.'

The ambulance passed through the village in under a minute and began to climb the hill.

The road was strewn with semi-blackened leaves, vivid and deathly. They glimpsed a couple of young men in tightly belted beige mackintoshes rambling through the woods with sticks to feel their way forward. Another young man wearing a tweed jacket, Fair Isle pullover and a silk cravat at his neck was walking down the road on his way to the village. He stopped to let the ambulance pass. Was he a patient or was he an employee or visitor? Standing there, watching the vehicle, he held up his finger to his throat and made a sawing motion. He shouted something into the wind.

'What did he say?' Lenny asked her.

'I didn't hear.'

Finally, their new home appeared, a sweep of glassy verandas, the curve of the sun terraces reflecting back the skeletons of trees. They knew great buildings, they passed them in the street without paying attention. They had seen St Paul's, Westminster Abbey, Buckingham Palace – big houses for the rich and places for Christians to do their praying. But *this*, this was almost brand new, this was like what you saw in the pictures, it could have been in Hollywood; in fact, it reminded Lenny of photos of a film studio. Talk about luxury, he thought, but didn't want to say it in case he was disappointed when they got inside. You had to admit, the place looked nothing like a hospital, let alone a prison. Barts, where he'd been taken for a few day's exploratory tests, *that* was menacing, this was not menacing, it was all fresh air and plate glass.

Out on the balconies the ill lay in their beds, taking in the rays of light and breathing, breathing, breathing. Most were too weak to wave. A couple of hands went up and shakily waggled a few fingers.

5

Inside, the day room was busy. Patients were doing jigsaw puzzles and crosswords, were reading the newspaper and fashion magazines and books, embroidering, gossiping or listlessly staring out at the view.

A group of four were playing bridge, bent over their cards, and did not look up when the ambulance discharged its new patients. One was busy writing a letter and he also didn't see them. Another had a sketchpad on her lap and was drawing an imaginary cat (no animals were permitted in the sanatorium). A third, who did see them, was wishing he knew the football results. He supported Aston Villa and kept detailed notes of their progress through the season. The doctors thought that sport made him over-excitable and kept the Monday paper from him. He could ask these emissaries from the outside world the score.

One dogged individual was carefully constructing a model of Salisbury Cathedral out of used matchsticks. It was waiting for the spires to go on. He had been at it for eight months and was both admired for his tenacity and artistry and scorned for concentrating on such a monotonous imitative activity by the truly artistic who thought that one should create something new. The nurses thought the model of Salisbury Cathedral encouraged the other patients to smoke their pipes and cigarettes in order to donate used match-sticks to him, which made their chests worse.

Mrs Kitson, the art teacher, was gathering people together for her painting lesson. 'Pick up your watercolour boxes, everyone who's coming, and follow me,' she cried in a loud clear voice. She was trying to introduce a pottery wheel, but Matron thought throwing pots would be far too strenuous. She wore an actual smock in Delft-blue linen with cross-stitch pleats at the shoulders. A small group followed her through a door to the arts and crafts room.

But whatever they were doing, all the patients were never far from consciousness of their breath, their temperature and the state of their saliva.

To Hannah Spiegel, sitting watching at the window beneath a Scotch blanket, having earlier overheard Matron talking about two new patients coming on the national scheme, all her fellow inmates were potential members of an imaginary orchestra. She assigned to each of them an instrument according to the sound of their voices and their anatomy, for some had hourglass figures and looked like violins, or spoke like string instruments, high and trembling, or were potbellied and boomed like a kettledrum. Many were weedy and reedy and piped like flutes. No one, so far, had the physical or vocal range of the grand piano. Bassoons and double basses were missing.

She looked up at the stocky, dark, frizzy-haired new arrivals, nei-ther of them with the characteristic attenuation and enervation of the tubercular, and hoped that she might be able to fill some gaps. Sometimes she felt that her fantastical orchestra was all that kept her going. She considered that the boy could be an oboe and the girl a set of cymbals. She'd never had those before, but the girl had just the brassy look for it. She smiled, but to herself, into her chin. Miriam caught her smiling and mistook it for a welcome, waved at her. Hannah lowered her head further to her chest.

Mrs Carver, Matron you must call her, did not have to check her files to know that they were coming under the National Health scheme and wouldn't pay a penny out of their own pockets, they could hang around as long as they liked and it wouldn't cost them a farthing. And they *would* stay, she felt sure of that. They would burrow into the system like parasites and milk it for everything they could get. Clean sheets, wholesome food, all the leisure time in the world. It was a skiver's paradise, a sanatorium which had been built for a better class of persons, and there was nothing at all that she could do to protect the admirable Lady Anne from the sight of cheap loud vulgar people.

'That old bag don't like us,' Miriam whispered, as they followed her along the ramp to Unit C, where administration was housed.

'Well, we're going to have to schmooze her then, aren't we?'

'We know we're lucky to be here,' he said smarmily when they sat down in her office. 'Dr Flucke said it's the best place in the country, you don't even need to go to Switzerland, there's everything you could want.'

'Of course, you don't have the high mountain air,' Matron said, not recognising his cocky insincerity and taking it as humble gratitude, 'but we have the very best doctors and all the latest treatments.' She looked at their notes. 'Recurring bouts of bronchitis from the age of fifteen, one bout of pneumonia, fatigue, some night sweats, classified IV for national service, not responding to bed rest at home. And you, young lady? How has your health been?'

'Me? Strong as an ox. I was on my feet all day in the florist's, no bad chest like Lenny, just lots of colds, but when they gave him the X-ray and it came out bad, Dr Flucke said I better have one too since it didn't cost nothing, and then it turned out I was threatened as well. I never expected that, I felt fine and dandy but I've got lesions. Are you going to make us better? And do you have ice cream here?'

Matron ignored the ice cream question.

'I'm sure we'll have you on your feet again in no time.'

She went through the rules and regulations of the institution. Mealtimes, bath times, lights out, a list of the recreational activities available, including Mrs Kitson's painting classes, watercolours to begin with and oils for the more advanced.

Lenny felt the solid world of London dissolving. They'd only been there half an hour, and now the city they'd left behind felt like over the rainbow. Or was this over the rainbow? The dissolution made him feel nauseous. He had seen grown men in chairs with shawls round their shoulders. *Shawls* like old biddies in Wales. Everyone looked all-in, beaten, half-dead, skeletons in pyjamas and slippers. We're gonna have to make a run for it, he thought.

Church services were held on Sunday mornings, Matron explained. The more vigorous walked to the church in the village and for the weaker patients the art room became an impromptu chapel where the chaplain came once a fortnight and took communion. RCs could also be catered for. Other faiths would have to make their own arrangements and could use the art room but Lenny said they didn't bother with any of that, and would eat what everyone else ate apart from the bacon, if there was any. For there were certain rituals they took part in three times a year and the rest of the time they rubbed along as Englishmen and women.

After all the formalities they were taken to their rooms. It was the first time in their lives that they had been separated from each other.

A wall of glass with a sliding door let out onto the external veranda. The view over the valley was an indiscriminate mass of green wet fields, bare trees and, dotted about, the smoke from farm and cottage chimneys. It was deathly quiet out there, horribly peaceful, like the moments in the bomb shelter after the screaming stopped and you listened in the stillness for life to return, for breath from the body next to you.

'Isn't it light and airy?' Matron said. 'I suppose you're not used to that where you've come from.'

'It's different all right,' Lenny said shakily. 'Am I dead yet?'

'Now don't be silly.'

Standing on his bedside table like a skittle was a bottle of Guinness. 'What's that for?'

'To build up your strength. It's free on the Health Service.

Everyone gets it along with milk. A glass of porter is said to be of benefit if you can tolerate it. I've moved things around a bit. Mr Cox will be sharing with you, or rather you'll be sharing with him as he was here first. He was with Captain Biller but he's gone home. Mr Cox will be a help with the things you can't manage if you speak nicely to him. He's a good sort underneath it all, just take no notice of his nonsense. You have an appointment with the doctor in the morning. He will explain everything to you.'

'Okay, but where will I find my sister?'

But Matron had already turned and left him alone to examine his new home.

Lenny sat on the edge of his designated bed taking in what he could of outside. He had few words to describe it. Big trees, little trees. Hill. A pigeon – he recognised that from any London street – landed on a bare branch and cocked its neck about like a pickpocket looking out for coppers about to pinch him for loitering with intent. It flew off with a sudden flurry, dive-bombing insects on the wing as the door to the room opened behind him.

'Scary Mary gone, has she? Left you all alone?'

A sallow middle-aged man came in, dressed in a blue suit and saffron tie with chartreuse zigzags held in place by a gold pin, maroon leather slippers on his feet. He was holding out his hand. Lenny could see he was supposed to shake it, which was an unusual situation. For months no one had wanted to touch him. He held the man's very dry palm for a moment.

'I suppose you're Mr Cox.'

'Yes, I am, but you can call me Colin. They told me you were coming. Leonard, isn't it?'

'Lenny.'

'Okay, Lenny it is, but excuse me, I've come from the pub and I've got to take my temperature, they make you when you've been outside, even if you're feeling okay. Give me two ticks.' And he sat on his bed with a thermometer in his mouth for seven interminable minutes during which Lenny just had to sit there looking at him, the thing poking out like a little silver cheroot, then he removed it, examined the mercury and put it down on the bedside table.

'Good or bad?'

'Slightly high, it should drop after tea.'

He turned to his night table and picked up a deck of cards and began to automatically shuffle them as if his fingers were a machine.

'Do you play?'

'Just kalooki.'

'I know that one! Jewish game, isn't it? Pal of mine back home plays it, one of my best customers. Sold him a Riley. Well, I'll give you a hand any time you like, I'll try to find a couple more to make up a four and we're in business.'

He sold motor cars in Bristol. He had been in the Gwendo for five months.

'Do you feel any better?' asked Lenny.

'Of course not. Nothing they do here makes you *better*. You might feel okay, and take a stroll down to the village, and wander round till you've exhausted its pleasures in ten minutes. I'm just stringing them along while I'm waiting for the new treatment.'

'What new treatment?'

'Don't you read the newspapers?'

'Not really, just the racing and the comics.'

'Someone needs to take you up, educate you. Not in the ways of the world, you've got sharp instincts, your race, but the bigger picture. Look, you can spend your time here rotting or you can use it to advance in life. Now at my stage of the game I've done most of my advancing. I have a very good business. I can buy my wife anything she needs, my two girls, Daphne and Muriel, want for nothing. Muriel is engaged to be married. Daphne is doing a shorthand typist course. Then this. Stops you in your tracks. You're on a bucking horse, not that I've ever been on the back of one myself, but you see it, don't you? You're clinging with everything you've got to hang on and not be thrown.

'And why you, you ask yourself. None of us have much in common with each other here, apart from our rotten lungs, so when you ask, why me, you have to ask also, why Lady Anne who you will definitely meet, she's the sort of queen of the place, lords it over us graciously. And why all the young soldiers, doing their bit for the war effort, then struck down? And why poor harmless Foye with his matches? You'll meet them all in time, even if you never strike up anything more than an acquaintance with most of them. Now I can't see the connection between us. It's just rotten luck, even though when someone says "oh, bad luck" to you it normally just means losing a round of whist. But here we all are in the same boat.'

And don't you half rattle on, thought Lenny, another blah-blah-blah merchant.

'I'm private, and I'm guessing you're on the government plan and yet it doesn't make any difference at all in the treatment, we don't receive any extras. We can have things sent in from home, things which make your life a bit more comfortable, you can have monogrammed silk pyjamas if you like, but when it comes down to it, we're all waiting for the new injections, to find out if they will work or not.'

'What new injections? First I've heard of it.'

'Streptomycin. You've heard of penicillin, I suppose?'

'Yeah.'

'Well, it's like that, a kind of antibiotic. It's supposed to be as complete a cure as you can hope for.'

'That sounds—'

'The cat's bloody whiskers.'

'Why aren't they giving it to us, then?'

'Because we fought a war and we're broke, that's why, and now we're practically bankrupt. We have to buy it from America. We haven't got the exchange currencies. I've heard that penicillin and streptomycin are kept in the military wards under armed guard while the kiddies are dying off like flies of infections.'

A blast of cold air hit Lenny in the back.

'Why are all the windows open? It's freezing.'

'They never close them, only when it snows. That's the funny thing: we're not locked up here, we could walk out any time we liked. Just take off. Yet no one does.'

'I'm cold,' Lenny said.

'I know you are. You're supposed to be. They say it's good for us.'

'Righty. So we freeze while we cough. And what's there to do?'

'*Do?* Ha ha. We have a film show once a week but they're old as the hills, some of them aren't even talkies. We're not to be excited, you see, by American gangsters and cowboys and Indians. Let alone love stories. Don't want the ladies blushing. And you'll have already heard the bloody Strauss waltzes on the hospital radio; hard to get away from them unless you're in your room and can turn it off. The regime here is an incessant diet of drivel and occupations to take our minds off dying, like Mrs Kitson's art classes. Aren't you going to unpack, by the way?'

'I'm not sure we'll stay that long.'

'Who's we? Are you married? You don't look old enough.'

'No, my sister.'

'That's some company for you.'

'I think we'll get back home and sit it out until the drug comes.'

'That's a shame, I'd have welcomed the company.' No one, as far as he knew, had fled. Once the system had you by the throat you lost all will-power.

In Lenny's suitcase were two changes of pyjamas, a dressing gown, underwear, toothbrush, razor, shaving soap. A picture of Gina taken by a street photographer, some young con-artist who went out every day with no film in his camera, taking your money, writing down your name and address and promising to send the pictures. Gina's brother had got hold of him by the throat and taken him down to the chemist to get a roll fitted and there she was, leaning against the window of Maison Bertaux blowing smoke rings at him. She had promised to write.

He'd sort everything out in the morning when he'd spoken to Miriam. They would make a decision together, they always did.

6

One floor above Lenny and Colin, Miriam was screaming that she wouldn't get undressed. She would not take off her clothes, she wouldn't take off so much as her shoes if this was what they were going to do to her. 'And not a chance I'll take my knickers off.'

She was wearing a cherry-red felt coat and a cherry-red beret pinned gingerly onto the back of her head, not to disarrange her foam of stiff blue-black curls. Her lips were painted with postbox-red lipstick. In this room she looked like a giant strawberry frozen inside an ice cube. The clinical interior, the glacial whiteness of it, the prim hospital bed, the hospital odours, the sight of the chrome spittoon and the silence outside the plate-glass window gave her the heebie-jeebies. She remembered the young man who had made a cutting motion across his throat as the ambulance drove through the grounds. He had shouted *abandon hope all ye who enter here* and she hadn't told her brother. She'd stayed shtum for his sake. But wherever Lenny was, he would know now. The ambulance driver had been lying to them the whole time. No one left this place. It was where you came to die and if she was going to die it wouldn't be in a silent glass box.

'No,' as Matron struggled to take off her coat for her and lift the hat from her hair as if she was a naughty toddler. 'I won't stay. We'll get the bus back.'

'There is a bus,' said Matron, 'but only twice a day. I'm afraid you've missed the last one.'

'Then we'll hitch a lift and if no one will give us a lift then we'll walk. I don't care if we have to tramp all the way home to London, we'll find our way.'

'You *must* do as I tell you. I am in charge here; the doctors have decided everything and it is my responsibility to ensure that their orders are carried out. You are here so that we can make you well. Your prescription is unique to you and your particular diagnosis. You have been ordered complete bed rest and that is—'

'I've *had* complete bed rest, months of it.'

'But in a stuffy room without adequate ventilation.'

'It was *freezing*. The ice made little pictures on the window glass. The cold was howling down the chimney and when you put your feet down on the lino they nearly stuck to it. My nose was always running.'

'Sooty air, I thought so. Out on the veranda you will breathe some of purest oxygen in England twenty-four hours a day. This sanatorium was purposely built to treat this condition, the verandas were designed to obtain the maximum benefit.'

'It's freezing.'

'Don't worry, we will protect you from the elements.'

'But how do I do my business?'

'Of course you are permitted to come indoors for your *movements* and so forth, or a chamber pot if you are too weak to walk, but all meals will be brought to you in your bed. Now doesn't that sound deliciously comfortable? Is there any other time in your life, apart from after a confinement, when a woman can put her feet up all day long and be waited on hand and foot? And not pay a penny piece for the privilege, all free, all on the good taxpayer.'

'I *like* standing, I stood all day in the shop.'

'And much good it did you.'

'But all on my own I'll go bonkers, there's nothing to do out there, and nothing to look at, nothing at all.'

'Oh, you shan't be alone, you'll be sharing with Miss Lewis.'

*

Valerie, lying doggo out on the veranda under blankets, had overheard this conversation but was unable to see the new arrival without twisting her body round to look inside the room. She wished they would issue her with a periscope or some other piece of equipment which would offer three-hundred-and-sixty-degree vision, maybe a system of mirrors. Her previous companion, who left a week ago, was easily the most boring woman in England. Mrs Hetherington, of Tring. *Tring Tring Tring went the trolley!* she said, more often than was amusing. Mrs Hetherington was not a dimwit, she knitted and took an interest in the mathematics of the knitting pattern, which was erudite but extremely tedious to listen to. Other than that, she spoke mainly of the accomplishments of her children, and their lovely manners. She had been unable to decide if it was rather infra dig to have a disease that normally contaminated the lower classes or rather posh to have one that had claimed the poets, Keats, for example.

Valerie mentioned Kafka. She had temporarily forgotten that she was no longer amongst university friends and acquaintances who liked to show off their knowledge of obscure foreign writers. Mrs Hetherington had not heard of him and when she began to recount with great relish the plot of 'Metamorphosis', pointing out that Kafka himself had TB and the story could be taken as a metaphor for his condition (because that was certainly how it felt to her), Mrs Hetherington began to scream, quite loudly. 'A BEETLE? *No*, how disgraceful.'

The girl behind her was a completely different proposition. Nobody within Valerie's earshot had ever talked to Matron like that, it was galvanising, it made you want to get up out of bed and forget to put on your slippers and run outside into the woods to watch fireworks set off noisily with great showers and flashes until they sank back silently into the earth. Not even seven months ago life for Valerie had been parties and incessant conversation, those trills and cadenzas of speech, arguing about French philosophy and socialist town planning and the new Elizabeth Bowen and Leavis at the other place and has anyone been to Aldeburgh, is it marvellous? And how one felt about marriage and how one felt about motherhood, whether it was inevitable or avoidable, and if maternal rousings in a girl were the enemy within, a fifth column of treacherous emotions. The colour of Van Gogh's palette, Monet's view of Westminster, Auden's latest, etc, etc, etc.

She had written last month to her friend Elspeth to tell her that she felt as if she had been thrown overboard from an ocean-going liner and was in her life-jacket, watching it sail on towards the wide horizon, its lights blazing, its orchestra rattling out the latest tunes, and herself left behind, cold and alone in the water.

But she had not sent the letter. Any lifeline to the outside was simply self-indulgent at best, at worst artificial.

Her father had got her a bed here and at first she thought she would only stay a month. But seven months had passed and still she lay out on the veranda and companions came and went and she stopped writing letters to her friends and they stopped writing letters to her and she knew she would not live to see 1951. When the mist came down over the hill she was cut off from the landscape in a phoney heaven. Then her world was muffled, blank, terrified. She was too weak and depressed to argue with the nurses and anyway, too frightened of the consequences, for they were all-powerful and some days she could not even walk across the room and down the hall to the bathroom. They had to put her on the chamber pot, and what if they handled her roughly because she'd cheeked them?

She was losing corporeality. In a few weeks whatever was left of her would dissipate and seep over the edge of the veranda.

The girl kicking up a fuss behind her was screaming, 'Not a hope in hell, gerroff me.' Valerie was encouraged by her rebellion. Most were white-faced, accepting, as she had been.

After a short struggle, and a lot of yelling, the girl was led out to join her and settled into her bed by Matron. She appeared wearing a spectacularly vulgar garment, an artificial-silk nightdress and negligée covered in pink nylon ruffles. Her breasts without a bra pushed out ahead of her like a pair of off-white cats curled on a sofa. She was holding a scarf and a pair of sheepskin mittens that Matron had issued her with.

'Hello,' said Valerie. 'Come to join me?'

Matron left them to it. Miriam was startled by the appearance of the woman in the bed. She was in her early twenties, thin as a rake, and her hair was worn loose to her shoulders, a natural wave with no sign of having had the rollers in or the perm lotion on, and not a spot of lipstick or powder or anything else. And what was she wearing! What a sight, making a show of herself like that even if no one could see her, dressed in, of all garments, a pair of men's blue and white striped pyjamas buttoned up to her chin, the sleeves much too long and her pale fingers sticking out like twigs on the blanket. Her face above the collar was a white lozenge, the blue eyes the only point of life or movement in the figure in the bed.

'Is this where I've got to stay? It's freezing.'

'I *know*, isn't it vile? But you do get used to it.'

'What are they going to do to us out here?'

Valerie laughed. 'Do? They don't do anything, all that's happening is that we are resting our lungs in the fresh air to aid their recovery. They tried it out first on rabbits, apparently, and they improved.' She laughed again. 'Rabbits. Oh dear.'

Miriam found her difficult to read. Whose side was she on? Was she the type who even let on when they had picked sides? Sometimes you couldn't tell.

'So what do we do all day?'

'We take our temperatures, we take them several times a day; they'll issue you with a thermometer if you haven't brought one from home. We spit a lot, we drink an enormous amount of milk, it's supposed to be good for us, it helps us put on weight.'

'But I don't get it. How do you make the time pass?'

'Yes indeed, that's the issue, isn't it? Well, I can tell you what I do. I read a lot. If I have a congenial companion, I talk to them, I look at the landscape, I think, I scribble a bit, and so on and so forth. Time passes, of course, but very very slowly.'

Miriam looked out at the valley. The sky was darkening, it

was five-thirty and soon the light would be gone altogether, blackness and stars and a slice of moon as sharp as a knife to cut your throat. And when the sun came up there'd be nothing to see anyway. To her the outdoors was composed of trees, flowers and salad.

If she wasn't careful she'd burst into tears and she'd only been here five minutes. And I am not a baby, she thought, I don't go wah wah wah like a doll.

'I've come with my brother, he's a bit worse than me, I don't know how to get in touch with him, will they let him come and see me?'

'Oh, probably. Look, this place isn't all that bad, they try to do their best for us and it has all the most up-to-date facilities. At least it's not a converted fever hospital. Those are dire places, you really wouldn't want to go there.'

Miriam settled noisily into her bed. Valerie thought about what on earth she could do with the girl to turn her into an agreeable companion. All she had wanted was a cultured person, someone who read, who would stop her brain from rotting. Ideas were falling silently out of her mind like leaves dropping from a tree. It was becoming hard to remember what she had learned at university. Pope, what was the name of the poem ... 'The Rape of the ...'? And the first line of 'Christabel'? *'Tis the middle of night by the castle clock*, clock, lock, tick tock.

The medical director, Dr Limb, came by, a spectral, stalking figure in a white coat, austere, faint, his eyes tiny diminishing fish behind his oval, silver-framed glasses.

He explained the regime to Miriam, ceremoniously handed her her own thermometer, disinfected after the horizontal departure of a patient the previous afternoon in the undertaker's car.

In a compartment in his mind there was a strongbox which contained his initial impressions of each new arrival. Something (he would never find words to explain it, even if he had been willing to divulge the secret) allowed him to know at a glance if they would live or if they would die. There were very primitive sections of the brain inherited from our reptilian ancestors.

This third eye, or whatever it was, examined Miriam briefly and recorded its conclusion as it had already done with Valerie Lewis and Miriam's brother Lenny lying in the floor above. The eye was always right. This supernatural hocus-pocus depressed him. Last week he had looked at himself in the mirror and seen a woman laughing beside his own reflection, but when he turned round no one was there, though the door of the room was open and he supposed someone could have slipped in, but why had he not heard anything?

He diagnosed himself with hallucinations brought on by over-work and loneliness. He had lived in since the Gwendo was built, he had been there from the beginning and would at some point be transferred to one of its double rooms if his luck ran out.

'Miss Lynskey, we will do everything to keep you comfortable and in time we can expect an improvement, I'm sure. This is a very curable disease these days, you know. We have a number of new treatments at our disposal.'

'Some of which you're not actually using,' Valerie said in a pleas-ant voice, turning her head towards him, and her light blue eyes in the pale face giving him what he thought of as his funny turn.

'We've had this discussion many times before, Miss Lewis, and I can only leave you with the thought that we do *exactly* what we can do, no more but certainly no less.'

'But how long am I . . . ?' Miriam was saying.

He walked out on her abruptly. In the hallway he leaned against the wall. *Valerie.* He had never spoken her first name aloud. Not the most distinguished of patients he had ever treated, but the one who pierced him. He was sure it had been her in the mirror, he recognised her now. Yet she would not, and certainly *could* not, have left her room to walk to the staff quarters. Perhaps he was going prematurely senile.

'Blimey, I only wanted to know how long I've got to stay here,' Miriam said. 'It's a reasonable question, isn't it? I'm entitled to know.'

'Did no one tell you?' Valerie said.

'No.'

'Look, mostly we have the same prescription, rest, some treatments, and then hopefully we're out in a couple of years.'

'TWO BLEEDING YEARS?'

'There are new methods of accelerating the treatment, they're just not using them yet. We could be out earlier.'

'I'll never stand it, I'll top myself.'

'No, you won't. I won't let you. And you won't be out here on the veranda the whole time, you know, it's just to build us up for the next stage, or so they say. But let me see if I can entertain you for at least a few minutes. How would you like a game of snap, just to start? Or too exciting for one day?' It was the only card game she could be certain Miriam would know how to play, everyone could play snap.

'Okay, I don't mind that.'

Miriam didn't understand the person next to her, she had no experience of educated people, only girls like herself, who liked the same things she liked, hats, hairdos, frocks, how to straighten your own stocking seams from behind by looking in a mirror, film stars and in her case exhilarating games of ping-pong.

Valerie pulled out a pack of playing cards from under her blanket and laid them out as close to Miriam as she could reach. The cards went up, the cards went down. 'SNAAAPPP!' screamed Miriam.

'My God, you'll give me a heart attack if you shout like that. I haven't heard such a loud noise since the blitz.'

'Where was you?'

'Edgbaston, it's a suburb of Birmingham, terribly *nice*. Then in 'forty-six I went up to Oxford.'

'Is that where that university is?'

'Yes, I was at Somerville.'

'Is that Oxford or a different place?'

'It's a college.'

'So that's not the university.'

'Yes it is.'

'You said just now it's a college. Which is it?'

'I'll explain it all later or we'll be here all day and never even get onto first-name terms. Tell me about yourself. Out here you get awfully hungry for new faces and information.'

'Okay, but I still want to know the difference. We're Londoners, grew up in Stepney but our dad died when we were little kids and we got moved out with our mum somewhere nicer, quite near Finsbury Park. Then when the war came we got sent to Wales, I mean that was *demonic*. Honestly, I've never known anything like it in my life. Of course we ran away first thing, just a night under that roof and we were off, but when we tried to hitch a lift on a lorry back to London no one would take us. They all had black hearts, those Welsh, they brought us right back again to the farmer and the farmer's nasty wife. That's why I know what to expect here, from the countryside. I mean, how do you stand it, honestly? I don't think I'll last the night, or if I do I'll be gone in the morning.'

'Yes, it's true we have fallen off the wheel of life, but there are things we can do about that.'

'Like what?'

'You'll see.'

Such throbbing energy in the next bed a few inches away, such stamina and rage, Valerie thought wearily. Yet she would fall into lassitude and boredom, we all have.

7

Mrs Kitson the art teacher, Lettice Arthur before her marriage, a war widow (husband posted missing, presumed dead), was waiting for the sun to rise. She laid a towel over the window ledge and wiped away the pools of water draining down from the steamed-up panes. From her bedroom window in the morning the cross on the spire of Holy Innocents was sometimes touched with fire. Occasionally, in certain atmospheric conditions, it was the first thing to reveal itself in the sky at the end of night but in the winter the earliest sign of dawn was the light going on in the newsagent window, then lamps, coal fires, gas fires burning in the windows of all the houses until the blackness evaporated, as if it were dark vapour.

These moments by the curtains, smoking her first cigarette of the day, holding a mug of tea in her hand poured from her Clarice Cliff teapot, still dressed in her green rayon kimono, flapping sleeves, trailing hem, her feet bare and frozen, were those in which she felt most like herself, the girl leaving the village to get married and live by the sea in Brighton. (But my God, she was entirely middle-aged now, thirty-four! Though not inside, inside no more than twenty-two.)

The bed was dishevelled. The ashtray was full of smoking stubs, hers tipped red. These traces of Bob, the cigarette ends, the soiled sheets, the toilet seat left up, his sputum in a teacup, fell to her to tidy away. She did not mind. He had walked back up the hill in the dark. He was only strong enough to manage all the different, diffi-cult elements of the assignation once a fortnight. She had no idea whether or not he would ever get well. She kept a notebook with the details of his condition. Now Bob would be sitting up taking his temperature. He would not go down to breakfast. He would rest for days, recovering while she was taking the sheets off the bed, was making toast, was washing her face, brushing her teeth, dressing, combing her long soft hair, applying her lipstick and her eye-black and leaving the house with her art materials under her arm.

She'd had a little idea of something her pupils could do with clay, which would not involve a wheel. They could shape a map of Britannia and they would decorate it with flowers, plants, trees, thistles. They could call it *The Garden of England*, which Kent was. It was very nice and easy, not at all strenuous. The little Britains would be baked in the kiln, painted, fired. Yes, that is what she would do, she would ask to order in the clay.

The day was clearer than the one before. She walked up the hill and had her weekly meeting with Matron. There was a new intake. Two new arrivals yesterday. Was she to sign them up?

But Matron said not yet, the girl was out on the veranda and the boy was going to have a treatment.

She remembered the arrival of the German architect (German! An actual Hun) a few months after the death of Gwendolyn Downie, the sensation he had caused in the village in 1937, the meeting in the village hall when he announced the plans for what they still called the isolation hospital. Four tied cottages would be cleared from the hillside and replaced by modern ones in the village; her family was one of those to be rehoused.

There was a sense that the place was to be a shrine to the dead girl. In the planned ornamental gardens with a pansy clock in springtime, a marble obelisk was to rise in her memory, the word-ing was already being carved by the county's best stonemason in

Canterbury. Where once healthy children – Lettice herself – had played in the fresh air a morbid site was to arise.

Quite apart from the eviction from the cottages, the place was talked of at once as a leper colony. A large contingent of sick people desperate for a cure, some terminally ill, would arrive and there was no question that the disease was contagious, coughs and sneezes spread it. Their home would be a plague village.

Lettice went to the meeting with her mother. The young German had his plans pinned to a screen and pointed at them with what looked like a conductor's baton. The Downies were sitting at a long table smiling encouragement up at him.

'Four wings,' he said, jabbing his pointer. She was surprised that he spoke very good English. 'There, there, there and there. A building both symmetrical and asymmetrical, do you understand? Quite unusual. The appearance from the outside is that of a continuous ribbon of windows, a panoramic strip of glass. In A wing we have the accommodation for the patients, double rooms, two sharing. A patent bed available at the moment only in Germany, to allow the patient to lie or sit, and with wheels to be brought outside for the weaker inmates who cannot walk. A sink, a cupboard, they won't need many clothes here, they can be left at home, a bedside table at an angle to the bed so they can easily reach the drawer without the awkwardness of twisting their bodies uncomfortably. Along the front south-facing elevation, deep sun terraces with awnings for those for whom direct sunlight is unsuitable.'

'Yes, yes! How marvellous,' said Mrs Downie encouragingly, turning to the audience who did not care about the details of the building but wanted to know if some kind of high fence was going to be erected to keep the germs out.

'Thank you. In B wing, which is single storey and set at a forty-five degree angle from its brother, we have the common areas, a grand open-plan vestibule, a dining room, library, a room you might use for something like art therapy and behind this, of course, the treatment rooms and operating theatre. This wing should receive maximum sunlight because we would hope that the fitter invalids will spend much of the day here and it will give out to an attractive vista over the valley. By the front door are pigeon holes, but not for letters. It is where the patients can leave their slippers when they venture out into the grounds in their outdoor shoes. Then when they return inside they might feel that they are entering a home, not an institution.

'Now here is C wing, which fits onto the back of B and contains staff accommodation, the laundry and the kitchens. And smallest of all, D wing, which will house the boiler room and the heating plant. The entire building will have a concrete frame, which will make it quick and quite cheap to put up.'

Then he explained, as if it would reassure them, that the original plans had been made for a luxury hotel to be sited above a lake. For there was no reason why the design could not be readily adapted to different uses, that was the beauty of this modern architecture. Establish the underlying function: guests or patients who wanted sunlight, rest and the visual impact of their surroundings and they had more in common than one thought. The sunbathing terraces for the wealthy vacationers become the recuperation verandas, the sun chairs replaced with invalid chairs. The staff quarters become the sleeping quarters of the nurses. So if the village thought of the sanatorium as simply a hotel in which invalids recuperated, they would cease to consider it a leper colony. Then he smiled his nervous, charming smile and sat down.

The publican, considered by many to be the villagers' official spokesman, stood up. 'All our little ones are going to go down with it and when they do, they won't be convalescing there, will they? It's for rich buggers. Ours are just going to cough themselves to death in their own bedrooms, the ones they share with their brothers and sisters and even grandmas.'

'Now, don't be silly,' said Mrs Downie. 'When you think about it, doctors and nurses are employed in these sanatoria without ever succumbing, aren't they?'

'They give them special medicines, expensive stuff, we won't get none.'

'But there will be jobs!' Mrs Downie cried. 'Well-paid work, I can assure you.'

The audience were shaking their heads like a row of puppets. They did not want the sanatorium, but Lettice knew they could not stop it because the squire was the squire and their lords and masters always had their way, whatever they felt like. The meeting was what the lady who owned the wool shop called 'public relations'.

And Lettice was right, the sanatorium could not be prevented, only temporarily thwarted. Over the autumn and winter it inched upwards from the ground. Sometimes there would be a month-long delay as they waited for the rain to stop and the concrete to dry out. Unsavoury equipment started to arrive from a medical suppliers in London. Despite the modern bathroom facilities, there would be chamber pots and bedpans for those too feeble to walk along the hall to reach them. They were delivered one morning, and were unpacked on the lawn. From what Lettice heard it was all quite depressing.

But Mrs Downie, unstoppable, announced that applications were now open for a wide range of staff posts with preference given to anyone local. Applicants began to arrive at the house, hoping to be interviewed for positions on the medical staff. To the Downies' chauffeur, who picked them up at the station, some of them didn't really seem up to the job. 'They look a little, I don't know, sickly,' he said to Mrs Downie.

'Well, you see, many of them are themselves tubercular,' she told him. 'They seek jobs in sanatoria so they will not infect those without the condition. And of course they are close to all the facilities and treatments so they can avail themselves of what they need to prolong their own lives. It's very sad.'

'Poor buggers,' he said.

Then it was finished. The sanatorium stood empty and glittering on the hill. The first arrival was Lady Anne who settled in at once, with her Parisian silk pleated nightgowns and cashmere bed jackets, and established the Gwendo's reputation for being a modern, iconoclastic facility for the very best people.

8

Lenny was served dinner in bed on a kind of tray table. It was mince and potatoes and cubes of carrot. Under an inverted saucer a bowl held a sponge pudding with custard. He ate most of the meal and at eight-thirty fell asleep exhausted. Colin came back to the room at ten and read quietly, shading his bedside lamp with a shirt. Lenny looked familiarly waxen in the bed next to him. He hoped he would not decline quickly. The boy might turn into a useful companion, appeared to have interesting family connections in London, the uncle sounded like a right card.

The kid was putting up his front and trying to be brave, to be a junior gangster, but Cox could see he was terrified. He'd calm him down in the morning with a hand of cards, it was possible that he had money to play with, or the uncle could give him money. Cox liked the Jews, if he'd known the word he would have called himself a philosemite. He particularly liked the new type of Jew, raising hell in what used to be called Palestine, showing the world they'd had enough and weren't going to take it. The ones he'd come across were right up his street, good instincts and curiously, despite the stereotype, not tight with money at all, enjoyed a nice motor and a good suit, just didn't want to pay through the nose for it, and could you blame them?

He watched Lenny sleeping for a few more minutes, then turned out the light and thought of his wife at home in her nightie. He sometimes felt that life here was a hallucination, that the well-Colin in his showroom in Bristol was dreaming and that he would awake in the morning to pick up his copy of the *Daily Express* from the mat and take it into the morning room where a pot of tea was already on the table and the porridge bubbling on the hob. Or was the old life something he had once dreamt and this was all that was real? That was the most depressing idea anyone had ever come up with. It kept him awake for another half-hour then finally he dropped off.

In the morning Cox and Lenny (looking much rosier in the cheeks than when he had arrived) went down to breakfast. Lenny had not unpacked and still seemed intent on leaving. The dining room was arranged in a series of round light-oak tables each laid for twelve place settings. Lenny saw baskets of brown and white rolls, racks of toast, jugs of milk, pats of butter, egg cups each holding a speckled brown egg. He had witnessed nothing like it in his life, had never seen such abundance apart from Uncle Manny's black-market lock-up in Dalston.

'Bloody hell, what's all this? Is it just for us?'

'It is, we get double rations of everything. Isn't it good? If you feel like eating at all you can't complain about the grub, I mean the quantity, there's no stinting there, but the quality is variable. Apparently it used to be better when it was private, they had a proper chef, not a common cook who used to serve up slop in the army, but one who could knock up anything you fancied as long as you could supply the ingredients, so people had quail's eggs sent down and even pots of caviar. There was a smoked salmon omelette once, legend has it.'

'It's like a hotel!' Lenny had never stayed at a hotel but he had seen them depicted at the cinema. Uncle Manny and Auntie Tessie went once a year to one of the Jewish hotels in Bournemouth and came back full of tea and cake and chopped-liver sandwiches and tales of table tennis and ballroom dancing.

He looked round. An etiolated woman, long face, nose, chin, ears, loosely waved colourless hair, wearing a pearl-grey dress he could only categorise as 'classy', was eating her boiled egg, her hands and arms in long oyster-coloured satin evening gloves. A double-stranded pearl necklace was threaded round her throat, fastened with a diamond catch. She reminded him of one of those figures people make with pipe cleaners, all white, with a loop for the head. Every few moments she stopped to catch her breath, as if she were running a race instead of just sitting there. Her head drooped over the teaspoon held in her frail fingers.

'That's Lady Anne I was telling you about. She's an actual titled Lady, it's not just something we call her. She's got her own cashmere bed socks and a solid-silver thermometer she brought in with her and she dresses like she's going to a Buckingham Palace garden party, but those gloves aren't even an affectation, she gets terrible chilblains in her fingers. She's as sad a case as any that have been here for years with no improvement. In fact, she's the type I don't normally have much time for, useless really. No get up and go. What you and me have in common, I suspect, is that we want to pick this country up and give it a good kick. Long overdue. And I don't mean the Labour government. They're the impediment.'

Lenny had eaten his own boiled egg cautiously. He had sliced off the top and interrogated the interior with his spoon, looking for flecks of blood. His mother had told him never to eat a fertilised egg, once an egg had the blood in it, a chicken was forming, a chicken would, sure as eggs is eggs, come into being. And he had managed a roll with butter and a cup of tea when he looked around and saw that patients were leaving, they were getting up and going, having finished their breakfast, their place settings had been cleared away, and there was still no sign of his sister. His energetic sister who *bounced* out of bed like an over-inflated beach ball.

'Where's my sister? Where is she?'

Panic, because he did not know where Miriam was. There had been no time in his whole life that he could not reasonably account for her whereabouts. They had shared a bedroom all their lives. She was there, stabbing at her eyelashes with her little block of eye-black, running her hand through her stockings looking for ladders, painting her toenails, one foot raised on the edge of the bath, or sleeping with a light snore he had never told her about. And when she was up and dressed she was at work with the flowers, or she was at the pictures with a girlfriend or some boy he would already have sized up and given a warning in his shell-like about how his sister must be treated. She was at a hop doing the latest dance-craze, she was playing ping-pong at the youth club, she was looking in shop windows in Kentish Town mentally pricing up an outfit. So where was she? He had agreed to come here because they had told him it was the best place, his chance of a complete cure, and he had hidden his fears and anxieties from Miriam, he didn't want to be a sissy boy.

And she had said, 'Are you sure, Lenny? You don't have to go if you don't want to, they can't make you do anything you don't like. We could stay here in bed and sweat it out.'

She was very considerate. She would leave and stand outside the door when she knew he wanted a wank. He did the same for her when she took care of some mysterious things of her own, even though he felt faint standing upright and his legs would buckle under him.

'It's not a prison,' he had said, 'it's all for our benefit. And how could it be any worse than the army?'

'So we'll go,' she said. They had entered together and now he had no idea where she was. He might have thought she'd fooled him, slipped back to London in the ambulance, never had any intention of staying, but that was not possible. He would have known if she'd planned to do that. And anyway, she wouldn't.

Suddenly he stood up and made a slicing motion with his flattened palm, a gesture that Manny had taught him to show you meant business, and overturned the teapot.

'WHAT HAVE YOU DONE WITH MY SISTER? Where's Miriam Lynskey? Why isn't she down here with the rest of us?'

'Steady, old chap.'

'What have they done with my sister? Who's got her?'

'What's all this ridiculous fuss?' Matron said.

The officers sitting at their own table – nine of them, the captains and the lieutenants, a few of them still in their old battledress tunics not having bothered to acquire a new wardrobe for civilian life inside a sanatorium – watched this altercation with interest. Day followed day with no drama, no let-up of the monotony or their own lassitude. For a few years life had been horribly over-stimulating (and how!), now they wandered around in a fog. It was a greyish fog not the white fog of an icy day, it was more like the air quality when the light begins to fail on a mid-December afternoon near the solstice at three o'clock and the pollution from all the coal fires of a city turns the figures of shadowy men and women, your fellow travellers, into faint outlines, warped blackish shapes in hats and overcoats resembling sluggish carp at night moving below the surface of a lake.

Captain Iain Jackson, who had once had the energy to march up the boot of Italy to liberate Naples and very much enjoyed himself when he got there, had enough fire left in him to have mounted a petition to get a billiard table for those strong enough to stand. Now, from their position they sarcastically called the officers' mess, he watched the youngster in the reflection of the window. The blinds had been partially lowered against the morning sun. It was a fine day. The upper half of the boy's head was in darkness, a line drawn below his eyes, as if he was wearing a hood. He was banging his fist on the table and shouting something about his sister.

The room with its circular tables reminded him of partners at a dance or the floor of a nightclub, waltzing couples in perpetual motion. The lad was bunked up with the car dealer. The bed next to him had been empty since Captain Biller was transferred back to London, to King's where his parents could visit him more often in the final stages. Iain assumed that the boy had been given Biller's thermometer, they were always running short, many breakages.

Like a moving Old Master, one that shifted its shape day after day, the arrangement of familiar forms quietly erased until a chair was empty one morning. Then filled again a few days later. It wasn't like the war. He had seen Private Craig step out of his tank to light up for a minute and a sniper shoot him through the head. A healthy man with sandy hair and a sandy moustache and a picture of a fiancée in his wallet became a shape on the ground, a huddled bag of clothes and belt and boots. But here the sanatorium stealthily removed the last traces of the officers' youth if they had arrived with any. It did it day after day, they were a table of old men still in their late twenties. Look at Flight Lieutenant Jenkins in his shawl over his uniform and his eyes circled with black shadows and his white lips. The Gwendo was their autumn season.

This boy was young enough to have seen nothing much. He was only a kid. Iain thought he would take an interest in him. Because he had just got here and already he was rebelling, usually it took a few weeks before that phase set in, if it even did. But would this fellow simply prove to be aggressive and unruly? He had no time for the awkward squad.

Matron was standing over Lenny, wagging a finger in his face like Little Jack Horner's digit about to plunge into the pie.

'Stop this right away, please do not cause a commotion and upset the other patients, you cannot raise your voice, you *cannot*. What is wrong with you?'

'I don't know where my sister is. She's not here.'

'Yes, why don't you just tell him where his sister is?' said Cox. 'You can see it obviously matters.'

And from across the room, Captain Jackson stood and called out, amicably but with authority, 'Now why shouldn't the boy know what you've done with his sister? It's a perfectly reasonable question.'

The other officers nodded.

'Hear hear,' they cried, because they'd follow to hell itself the chap who'd got them a billiard table.

'*Where's the sister, where's the sister, where's the sister?*' The half-empty dining hall took up the chant, it was something to do.

Matron, looking round, thought she had an insurrection on her

51

hands. It seemed to her that there had been a sudden collapse of order while she was in another room, that some disruptive influence had been introduced into the regulated system of the institution which would threaten disintegration. Even Lady Anne was tapping her gloved fingers on the table as if she were keeping time with an orchestra at a dinner dance. They would all have raised temperatures in a minute.

'Stop this, I tell you! You will all have raised temperatures in a minute!'

Mouths closed, hands ceased to drum. Mercury rising. They all hated that. It was back to square one. Back to bed. The boredom of the ceiling.

'Now what is the matter?'

'I don't know where my sister is, we arrived together, you saw, she's not come down for breakfast with the rest of us. What have you done to her?'

'She is *resting*. That is her *prescribed cure*. She is outside her room on the veranda with Miss Lewis, in bed, taking the air, and there is no reason at all why you shouldn't visit her. I shall take you myself.'

'There you are, then,' said Cox. 'Nothing to worry about, she's just out on the veranda. Shall I see you later? Fancy a drink at the pub? We could walk down to the village if you like, I'll show you all the sights, ha ha. That'll take five minutes.'

'He'll be seeing Dr Limb for a consultation at eleven. Come.'

Upstairs, Lenny saw his sister through the glass door. She was lying beneath blankets, rugs, a quilt, a scarf round her neck. Next to her a thin girl in men's pyjamas was pointing out into the landscape. 'And over there, if you really crane your neck, there are a couple of palm trees.'

The back of Miriam's head, drooping over her chin, made Lenny wonder if she was a dummy they'd put in the bed or a waxwork imitating his sister. She was normally a bolt-upright person who led from the forehead, butting like a prize-fighter.

He and Matron came out onto the veranda. Lenny said, 'But why aren't you up? What are you doing out here?'

52

'You'll never believe it, we've been here all night. All night! What do you think of that?'

'You dirty stop-out.'

'I *know*, I've never stayed out the whole night long but at least I thought it would be at a nightclub.'

'Why wouldn't they let you back in? What's all this about?'

'It's the cure, it's supposed to be a cure.'

'We had the bed rest already.'

'But this is in the fresh air at low temperatures,' said Matron. 'It's a completely different experience. People pay hundreds of pounds to go to Switzerland for this, you know, and look at the Alps all day, but here, you are getting almost as good and for nothing.'

'So you keep saying,' said Miriam. 'We know what we're entitled to.'

9

Alone at her table wiping her mouth with a napkin and rolling it between her fingers to feel the texture of the linen, to make out the separate fibres of the weave because it pleased her to enjoy every sense she had, Hannah Spiegel had observed the outbreak of disorder. Rebellion particularly interested her because she had seen what it could lead to. In a place like this, when you rebelled it was to obtain small concessions such as the billiard table and access to the absent sister. These demands were always possible to achieve, the system was elastic enough to permit a little modification and the sudden collectivisation of the other prisoners in supporting the new arrival's demands came, she felt, from an understanding that the regime was benign enough to permit some leeway. Its intentions, after all, were not evil.

The young man was in a panic, he was new, he didn't know the ropes. He had arrived with the girl and now he'd lost her. Hannah had thought she was his young wife when she had seen them yesterday, now she knew it to be a different relationship, closer, actually.

In other situations, as she knew, the system had absolutely no elasticity at all; it did not operate under some specious higher purpose said to be in the interests of the inmates. In such cases, rebellion was generally futile yet it happened anyway, irrationally, perhaps even furtively, just so the rebel could prove something to herself. Or as a gesture, a provocation, a theatrical act on which the curtain would always, without exception, come down. Why was that? Unknown to her, in a year or two she would be able to read Albert Camus' book on the subject, *The Rebel*, but he was still in the process of writing it so she had to muse over these matters on her own at her seat by the window, staring out with what some saw as a vacant expression; a shop with the shutters down.

Like the clock on the wall in the dining room which reminded those without watches of the excruciating passage of time until the next section of their routine, she ticked through her thoughts. The orchestra was simply light relief, to take her into something entirely imaginary. Had she been well she would have gone to a concert.

Certain individuals she now believed seemed programmed to rebel even when they knew that death was the inevitable result. They'd just had enough. Some like Lenny were outraged from the very beginning but their outrage didn't last more than a few hours before it was beaten out of them. As she classified people according to which instrument of the orchestra they might resemble, so she examined everyone in the Gwendo to see how they might function in another environment. The sick officers implicitly accepted institutional life and understood the nature of orders and obeying them, and so adjusted easily to their environment. A handful of anarchists would not fit, would not obey, but some of those were really just primitive types, criminals, gangsters often, not true rebels. And there were the rare few who understood that in rebellion lies freedom, not necessarily from the constraints of the environment, but of the soul itself. She had met them in another life, another time when the personality was forced into its starkest manifestation.

She herself was not a rebel. That had been proven beyond doubt. She preferred to keep a low profile and pretend obedience, which was how she had made it this far. There might be one or two true radical types who were capable of actually changing the system, she'd be curious to meet one but it seemed highly unlikely in the Gwendo.

10

Dr Limb took out a cigarette from a silver-plated case engraved with his initials, a gift from the Downie family to mark his tenth year in post as medical director, and lit it. 'You don't mind me not offering you one. Later, perhaps, when we've got you fighting fit.'

'I'm not sure if we're staying.'

'Really? Why not?' Limb humoured him. Many of his conversations with new arrivals began with this brief tug of war over their future.

'The boredom, for one thing.'

'Oh, my dear young man, there's plenty to do if you make an effort.'

'It don't matter, we don't belong here.'

'And why do you think that?'

'Too many trees for one thing.'

Limb smiled. 'Oh, you'll get used to it in time. I assure you, you are in the very best place and the very best hands. You have an illness and we shall try to make you comfortable and send you back out into the world if not exactly fighting fit, ready to resume your new life.'

'And what if I want my old life?'

'Well, you are rather unlucky for that will not be possible.'

'Anything's possible.' Manny's motto.

'We'll see.'

Lenny looked at the cigarette smouldering in the ashtray.

'That's a nice smoke. I'd have liked to have tried it.'

'Before the war I favoured an imported cigarette but you can't get them now.'

'I might be able to get hold of them for you. I've got connections.'

One could always place this bet when you had nothing else in your hands.

'Really? We'll see one day if I don't take you up on that. We've got off to a promising start, haven't we? Now, tell me your family history.'

Lenny was still sizing up the situation, how to play it. Families were a funny thing, both ha-ha and peculiar.

'I don't know, I think we came from Latvia, somewhere like that. It's in Russia now.'

'No, no, no, I mean medical history. Are both your parents still living?'

'Our dad died when we were seven.'

'That's unfortunate. And how did he die? An illness? An accident of some kind?'

His father's death wasn't something they ever talked about. It was a legend in Stepney and Whitechapel. The taunts were never-ending. He'd had to take up boxing for a while to deal with the laughter.

Dad as he remembered him was always a weak man, physically full of ailments. After their evening meal one night he had stumbled out the door into the yard to use the lav. His bowels were boiling up like lava inside him. On the wooden seat he sat down and spewed forth an immense gush of shit and blood. He held in his hand four pieces of the *Daily Sketch*, torn up. One sheet had a story about a murderess on it, her face black in ink and about to be obliterated completely by his backside. He wiped himself. He stood up, he pulled the chain, and the cistern came down from the wall and brained him on the side of his head.

The children heard a muffled crash from the yard and added it to their fears. They were listening for something else, for the man who lit the lamps and looked through the window at them in their shared bed. A little bed, with not enough room for the growing boy. The lamplighter's face was hidden by a greenish cap, they could only see his nose and his trembling lip. He was disfigured in the war, their mother said, poor *schlemiel*, and no woman would look at him.

Lenny had his own unique way of shutting out terror unavailable to his sister. Miriam saw his hands moving beneath the blanket as if he had a glove puppet down there. She put her head below the covers to see what he was doing; suppose he had a *toy* he hadn't told her about. Once Daddy gave him a broken train and a couple of lengths of track. She had a dirty doll. Lenny's new toy had its own vigorous engine.

Miriam, trapped next to him against the wall, said, 'I'll bite that off if you're not careful.'

The cat yowled in the yard. The cat was their enemy, vicious, scratching, flea-ridden, it guarded the door like a dog, no one knew its obscure purpose. They could only leave when their grandfather turned off the cat, leaving an aperture through which they could walk up the back alley, into the short street that led to school.

In the morning, their father was still dead in the lavatory, his wife not missing him, because he'd been known to spend whole nights there vomiting and crying. She went in and screamed.

'Don't go in there,' she cried to the kids.

'But we need to do our business!'

'Use the potty and then get off to school.'

They returned home at four o'clock, and took in the new situation, as explained to them by their mother and their uncle.

The undertaker had already been and gone, taken their father away to prepare him to be buried in the ground like a gnawed bone. Their mother's face lost all form, her features slid around on it.

The cat had gone missing, must have smelt death and didn't like it. Lenny decided they needed to take advantage of the new arrangement and walk back down to the end of the alley. Miriam was holding her hand on the place on her chest where her heart beat slowly. Lenny put his hand on his. When that stops, you are finished. Uncle Manny had started talking about the soul in a sentimental way, recalling his late mother and her goodness. Miriam said she didn't know what a soul was. She thought it was fish eaten by rich people. Lenny had to say, 'Don't be stupid, you ain't got a fish in your top half.'

Uncle Manny rent his garments, a deep rip in the lapel of his suit and in his tie with a pattern of loud magenta explosions. 'My little brother,' he cried. 'I shoulda looked after him!' (These were people who naturally talk in exclamation marks.) 'But don't you kids tell anyone what happened to him, we'll be a laughing stock.'

He reached into his jangling trouser pockets and gave them a mint imperial and a sixpence each to console them, the most they'd ever had was five farthings. Rich! They were on the way to being millionaires!

In the absence of the cat, they slipped away from their weeping mother, onto a bus, and by the time the conductor came round they were all the way along Commercial Road. They were Red Indians with tomahawks in their hearts.

And all Lenny could say about these primitive, almost fairy-tale circumstances from the pre-war world to the doctor with the half-moon eye glasses on the other side of the desk, in the cold white coat with the cold eyes like poached eggs, was: 'I know he was ill but I don't know what of. Everything, I think. My mum says it was just one bloody thing after another. But it was an accident that took him, a bump to the head.'

'I see. Was your father diabetic, do you know? I'm afraid there's an unholy synergy between TB and diabetes, they feed off each other.'

'I don't know nothing about him. I was only a kid. His older brother, my Uncle Manny, now he's healthy, strong as an ox. Nothing the matter there.'

'Excellent, so perhaps not hereditary in your case.'

'I thought you're supposed to catch it in the air. Through coughs and sneezes and all that.'

'Indeed. Yes. You do, but some people seem more susceptible to it than others, their systems can't contain it like healthy people. And they come down with it as you and your sister have done. But don't worry, it's not the inevitable killer it used to be. Let me explain. On a certain day, impossible to know when, I'm afraid, we don't have a time machine to travel back and forth across the years, some bacteria has lodged in your lungs and from you the bacteria may have been passed by a cough to your sister. Of course, it could be the other way round, we've no way of knowing. Now if either of you happened to have had a more robust immune system it would have been contained, perhaps trapped in a calcified nodule, and you'd have felt perfectly well.'

'Okay, so what went wrong?'

'Think of the bacteria as rod-shaped, which is what they are.'

He pointed to some charts on the wall showing coloured, cartoon-like characters plunging through a salmon-pink lung.

'It travels first here, comes to rest in the tiny air sacs and begins to multiply in the cells, growing slowly, only dividing every twenty to twenty-four hours. It's unusually slow work for an infection. Now you won't know much about this, I expect, and if you'd been luckier you'd have never needed to know that bacterial division rates are *usually* measured in minutes so you see how slowly this infection moves? And this is what makes tuberculosis a disease with a slow onset settling into a chronic condition which weakens the whole system, knocks out its defences then, I'm afraid, eats the living tissue as it moves on through the body.'

Lenny watched the pointer in the doctor's fingers waver over the heart, the liver, the kidney, down to the testicles. It was like science fiction, little rod-shaped green men from Mars had invaded the planet of his body. He held one hand down on his trouser leg with the other to stop it shaking.

'Are you following all right?'

He nodded. His mouth was like the bottom of a birdcage.

'It can take a couple of years before the first symptoms are noticed, this is the period of primary tuberculosis. Patients go to the doctor with a sputum-filled cough, low-grade fever, mild night sweats, some weight-loss, laboured breathing, chest pain. In your case, it was discovered early on by your army X-ray so that is very encouraging. People do recover, you know, they go on to lead normal healthy lives. There's a great deal we can do for you. The main thing here, while you are my patient – and I am the medical director, you will of course see other doctors but they derive their authority from me – is to learn *how* to be a patient, do you understand?'

'Not really.'

'Obviously you must *be* patient, I'm afraid that's an occupational hazard with this illness, you'll know that already. But to get better you must learn obedience, you must surrender to our will, completely and absolutely. Only then will you be well. Not very nice but there it is, and doubly hard when you are young and beginning your life, but think of it this way – had you passed your medical and gone into the army, your life would have been *all* obedience, and you'll find us kindlier than some of those sergeant majors. I don't say there's the foreign travel, but this is a pleasant enough spot.

'What we will do is teach you how to cough properly and catch your sputum so you won't infect others. You will learn how to take your temperature, how to rest, and one day you will be released with your own towel, your own flannel, your own plates, your own cutlery. Then you can go out into the world, the world you came from, whatever walk of life, it's different for everyone in my care – I've had lords and ladies and now we have ordinary working men like yourself because of the new health scheme, and you will be well enough to work, to marry, even to have children. You may not be entirely cured, your system may well be weaker than others, but with care you will cease to infect them and function quite autonomously.'

'Now I've heard it all,' Lenny cried. 'I'm only nineteen, you're going to turn me into an old man. I won't have it, I've had enough. This place will do me in!'

It was all a mistake; this couldn't be real because if it was, then London and Soho and the lovely Gina and his mother with her cotton apron wrapped round her middle as she toiled over the stove frying and boiling, and even Uncle Manny with his suits and his cigars weren't real. The diagnosis was wrong, he just had a long bout of flu or something, and if they left him alone in bed all day with Gina and the fire lit and good grub coming up from her momma's kitchen, he would get better and go back to the old life. This place, this glass and concrete palace, was a dream he was having and if he thrashed around he might be able to wake up. He was shouting on purpose to dispel the hallucinations.

'Now calm down, calm *down*, you're a volatile young person. I heard about the incident at breakfast, next time don't be so excited, just ask, we're here to help you in any way we can. There are certain advances on the way in the treatment. I can't offer them at the moment, the thing is we're going to try a pneumothorax injection. To collapse the lung, a temporary collapse to allow it to rest. It's a very successful treatment if combined with bed rest.'

'I don't like the sound of that. How are you supposed to breathe?'

'Why with your other lung, of course! Nature has given us two of most things. If we amputated one arm, you'd still have another. Tricky to tie your shoelaces, of course, but people manage. The lung will return to full capacity in time; meanwhile, the other will be quite adequate.'

'And what about my sister? Is she having that or has she just got to lie there?'

'For the time being, yes. We are extending the rest cure. I know you had a few months at home, but in less than ideal circumstances. Now don't despair, you are both young and fairly fit. You can stand, you can walk, and after a few weeks or perhaps months, you can go to the village, have tea in the tea rooms, even venture further afield by bus if you're feeling strong. Just listen to all the instructions, pay attention to Matron, surrender your will, young man. Surrender!'

But Lenny didn't trust him, there was something going on here which was to do with them being in it for themselves, keeping you for as long as they could to make money out of you, but they weren't making any money any more so what was their angle? There had to be a racket. Uncle Manny would get to the bottom of it.

So let's try playing him at his own game.

'The cigarettes you fancy, how many packets and when do you need them by? Just give me the word. My uncle can get anything.'

The doctor stood up.

'We'll see each other again, I'm sure. I advise you to make the most of your time here, we will help you. I'm most assured that we can help you.'

When Lenny was led out, Limb thought how very typical he was of his age and class, nothing unusual or interesting about it and in the future they would all come, the working classes who had nothing to excite his attention. It had all been very different when he first came and Lady Anne had been shown her room and it was expected that many more like her would follow and he was to be the medical director of a fashionable sanatorium which the wealthy would flock to, as they flocked to Davos.

Instead, the government had opened the door of the slums. It was difficult to be discerning about such an undifferentiated mass of humanity. Apart from Miss Lewis whom he knew, as soon as he laid eyes on her, was special though he was unable to pinpoint how exactly.

11

The patients were passing the time like zoo animals, recovering from breakfast. They were all suffering from the binding sensation of a surfeit of extra eggs. They had swallowed spoonfuls of cod liver oil and malt extract. They wore pyjamas, nightgowns, old flannel dressing gowns, Parisian negligées or day-clothes: slacks, pullovers, open-necked shirts, tweed jackets, woollen dresses, blouses with Peter Pan collars, skirts. All were in slippers.

A group of ladies known as the Mothers' Union sat together. Over the years they had collectively devised a set of rules for themselves:

1 Never give way to self-pity.
2 Always appear cheerful, particularly to the doctors and nurses and visitors. Feeling low is generally of no comfort to anyone but yourself. Have a good cry in private if you feel like it, but put on a smiling face to everyone else.
3 Maintain an interest in the outside world though news-papers and the wireless in order to be able to chat to your husband when he comes to visit and do not bore him with your health.
4 Catch up on your sewing, embroidery and knitting, so

many useful garments and tablecloths and napkins can be made when you have all the time in the world.

5 Arrange to have regular snapshots taken of your children so it will not be too much of a shock when you return home and find them almost grown up.

They were clinging on as best they could to being mothers when they were not allowed to see their children, when their babies screamed when they came near them, when the older boys and girls had given them up as a dead loss and transferred their affections to an aunt or a grandmother or a housekeeper. One mother had been allowed home and spent a few weeks there before her relapse. Her son had not recognised her. Even though she could not risk kissing him, and though his little clothes were boiled after she left, and she sat in a chair a long way from his bed, he seemed to have understood that something about this woman was wrong and she shouldn't be there and he wanted his daddy and his nana and not her.

'Daddy, will you make the strange lady go away?'

The Mothers' Union talked to each other of boys' shorts and girls' school plimsolls and school fees and grammar school entrance examinations and teething trouble and whether breast was really best or is Ostermilk in fact more nutritionally complete, and time-tables for vaccinations and school reports and in this way they did their best to continue to be mothers when they were quarantined from their children and some had been for years.

Some patients were terribly ill, skeletal creatures whose resentful eyes were the only signs of life in their sunken faces. If you looked carefully you could see that they were hardly forty years old. Yet others were quite fat, Lenny supposed it was the double rations, the cream, the luxurious pats of butter by each plate, the cod liver oil, the malt extract, the Guinness, and the lack of exercise.

A tinny noise was going on above his head, some music that was already driving him round the twist. He didn't recognise it, but he wanted it to stop. This must be the sanatorium radio, it wasn't exactly *Workers' Playtime*. Surely somebody could do better than this?

A nurse came to find him. She was a girl with crisp blonde hair arranged in waves onto which her white cap seemed to have settled like an airborne serviette from Lyons Corner House. Nurse Chitty. 'Call me Chitts. Everyone does. We're off to the surgical block, don't be alarmed, they won't do anything beastly to you in there. Not if I can help it.'

'I've never had an operation before. Dr Flucke used to come to the house to see how we were getting on.'

'It's not a real operation, we're not putting you under or anything. It's more like an injection, I expect you've had those before, but with a bit more oomph to it, you'll see. But you'll feel miles better afterwards. The procedure is a bit stingy but a handsome young chap like you won't blub, will you?'

'I bloody hope not.'

'Between you and me I've seen grown men go white when they first lay eyes on the apparatus, but you'll do all right, I know you will.'

He wanted to devote his full attention to her, a little ray of sunshine in her tight white uniform with a silver buckle on the belt holding her waist in and the bursting buttons round her breasts.

'Have you been here long? Worked here, I mean.'

'Just eighteen months, but honestly I love it. I was in Southampton before that, this is lovely and peaceful, I mean the village and the countryside and nice people, too. I adore all my patients. You're all good eggs. You've the patience of saints putting up with your unwellness.'

He had never met anyone before with a such cheerful outlook on life. He only knew people who carried sacks of anxiety and neuroses and cynicism on their backs. Miriam was an outgoing extrovert but she still regarded the world as a place that needed to be tackled like a prize-fighter with two fists raised. Chitts was the kind of girl to whom, it seemed, nothing bad had ever happened, not even the war. Not even in Southampton. Though it must have done. There were docks, and docks are a birthday present for bombs.

They were walking along a white ramp. Gold-framed portraits of a ghastly pale thin young girl of an earlier era decorated the walls, simpering, and another of a theatrical-looking woman in ancient robes, her arm raised histrionically.

'Are those the ones you killed earlier?'

'Don't be funny, that's Gwendolyn Downie, who this place was named after. And that's her mother who still lives in the big house. Now look, here we are, nothing to be scared of. All white and bright and even sunny. When the sun is out.'

She opened the door. They stepped in. He saw a surgical table covered with a cotton sheet and light blanket. A stainless-steel bin held the debris of previous operations, waiting to be emptied and incinerated in the furnace next to the boiler room.

A new doctor awaited him. Lenny saw nothing at first but a set of large ears like an elephant. He said, without introducing himself, 'First time you've had this procedure, I understand.'

'Yes.'

'I can assure you it works if you obey our instructions. We're resting the lung to heal it, so make *sure* you rest, am I clear?'

'That's all anyone has said to me since I had that bloody X-ray. Rest. I don't even feel unwell, apart from when I got out of bed to come here and my legs had gone from under me.'

'Yes, that will happen. Muscle wastage. It will soon come back. Now take your shirt off, lie down on the bed like a good boy and hold your left arm above your head.'

The nameless doctor turned away, went to the sink and began to wash his hands. A line of black hairs rose like iron filings from the wrist to the little finger. He dried them vigorously on a towel and the cute nurse handed him a pair of rubber gloves which he eased on as if he were putting on a set of rubber johnnies.

'Here comes the birthday cake!' cried the nurse, wheeling in on a trolley a piece of equipment in numerous interconnected parts from a cupboard. On a slab of varnished hardwood stood a cylindrical chrome frame, like the gasometer at Battersea, holding a series of grey bags, concertinaed down. At the side of it was a measuring rod, which reminded Lenny of the hated thermometer which now ruled his life. A coiled rubber tube connected to a kind of clock face, a pressure gauge, he guessed. The whole thing looked hideous, scientific, and was going to attack his chest any minute.

'I know what you're thinking,' the nurse said, 'but it's not all that bad. The main thing is, you can scream if you like, but whatever you do, *don't flinch.*'

'And here you are,' said the doctor, holding up Lenny's X-ray. 'This is you. We're not just working blind, you know.'

Lenny saw his ghost, the ghost of his lungs. He knew that in this world, the world of his chest, the darkness was healthy tissue and the light patches were his illness.

'Ready?'

I could get up and walk out, he thought, I don't have to take this. But he was too tired to stand.

He felt the hypodermic enter his chest, an unpleasant sting of pain, then the feeling that he was being pushed hard, pushed right off the table, and something crunching. He looked down at his pale skin, the coming thatch of black hair which grew larger every year expanding horizontally and down to a vertical line beneath his underpants. Miriam said he was getting hair on his back. His raised arm was going numb.

Oh, God help me, he thought, he's going to murder me.

Another needle entered him, thicker and attached to the rubber hose.

'Here we go,' said the nurse. 'Pecker up, young man. It'll soon be over.'

He waited to black out and then die. There was no sensation. He assumed he must now be dead. He was convinced that the nurse, the doctor, the apparatus had all passed along with him into the world of death, whatever that was, and they would be together for all eternity.

'You'll start to feel a pulling sensation,' the doctor said inside their common grave, 'it should feel tight round your neck and shoulder.' The dials on the equipment rose and fell.

The doctor removed the needle. Nurse Chitty stepped forward quickly and attached a bandage to his chest. His arm felt detached from his body, as if he could rise from the table and leave it behind on the sheet.

'Want to try standing up?' she said.

'Is that it?'

'Yes, all done.'

The doctor said, 'You might feel some pain later, sharp, knifelike. The adhesions will start to tear loose from your chest cavity and it can hurt a bit. Nothing at all to worry about. Nurse Chitty will look after you now. Good day.'

He turned to the sink and peeled off his rubber gloves. Then the door was shut and he was gone.

'Not much of a bedside manner,' said Lenny, breathless.

'He's very good, you know, despite all that. He's done this hundreds of times and he's a real expert. Sometimes the trained surgeons do it and they don't have the skill and the practice. Now your lung is going to get a lovely rest and you can lie about enjoying yourself. Won't that be nice? I'll take you back to your room and tuck you up if you like.'

The lift rose, Chitts winked at him. 'Aren't these lifts slow?'

He thought for a moment of lunging forward and trying to kiss her. He could manage a snog at least before they reached the second floor. He might have time to grab a cop of her tits. Then his legs went, he buckled at the knees. 'Oh, deary,' she cried. 'You all right? Take my arm.'

So he touched her all right, like a fucking invalid. Like an old man. When he was a kid in school and they'd worn the boots of dead children his mother bought for them on the market, and he'd weed in them because he was too shy to hold up his hand to ask to go to the toilet. The rising smell of his piss coming from his feet and having to go to school next day with the smell still there, dried on – that was the shame he felt as he had to cling on to a *girl* to get out of a lift.

He made her leave him at the door of his room. He had to do

it on his own, he couldn't let her put him to bed. 'I can manage,' he said.

'You're a proud boy,' she said. 'You don't need to be.' But he shut the door in her face. And now he had to keep up his front for a bit longer, for Cox was reading his paper and he hardly knew him.

'How did you get on?'

'I suppose it wasn't too bad. Didn't hurt as much as I thought it would.' He took a few steps and collapsed on his bed. The pain had started, his chest was burning. What had life done to him, the swinish creature that was supposed to be on your side and turned out to be a pig like all the other pigs?

'Who did you?'

'What?'

'Who was the sawbones?'

'I don't know, he never said his name.'

'They treat us like animate lumps of faulty equipment, some of them. We don't really have names, just the numbers on our case notes. The name is there, they just don't attach it to us. Some of the nurses are okay, though. Did you have the little blonde?'

'Chitts.'

'That's her. Alison Chitty. There's a sweepstake downstairs on who gets into her knickers first. Your name will be added to the runners and riders, you'll see. So far no one has done it.'

'Maybe she has a boyfriend. Why would she want one of us?'

'There are some that do. You'd be surprised. She may be playing the field. A couple of officers have kissed her but that's as far as they've got and only for an instant because she swatted them away like flies, and they're officers with medals and war stories. But as for you, young Lenny, you'll be all right, you know. The lung's still there, you've always got another one. Think of this resting lung as your spare tyre you need in the event of a puncture. I won't turn the radio on if you fancy a kip.'

Out on the veranda, Miriam was reading aloud to Valerie from a film star magazine she had brought with her. The article concerned an actress called Linda Darnell who had starred in a movie of a few years earlier called *Forever Amber*, which Valerie had not seen but Miriam had, and she had recently been in a new one called *A Letter to Three Wives*. It had been released while Miriam was undergoing the failed cure at home and so she had missed it and how was she going to catch it now?

'She's absolutely stunning, isn't she?' Miriam said, holding up a photograph of a sultry dark young woman. 'If she'd been old enough they should have cast her as Scarlett O'Hara, I'm not saying Vivien Leigh isn't gorgeous, but Linda Darnell takes the biscuit. I'd love to look like her. My Uncle Manny says I do, a bit, around the eyes, and I have the same colouring. What do you think? Can you see any resemblance?'

Valerie turned to look at the photo.

'Why on earth is she pushing her chest out? It must really arch her back.'

'Don't be silly, it's just a pose. It's their job to stand like that.'

'I don't go to the cinema much, to be honest.'

'Really? I go twice a week, whatever's on. Wouldn't miss it for the world.'

'Here, you'll find, we have to entertain each other.'

'How do we do that?'

'I don't know.'

12

Breath of spring. Haze of pale green across the northern suburbs of London. Saffron-coloured pompoms in front gardens. Washing tentatively out in the back defying rain-showers. A city staggering back to its feet, wrecking balls, builders hammering, concrete mixing and pouring, windows re-glazed, municipal flats rising from the bomb sites. Everything old that has reached the end of its useful life is going, this is not a time of restoration or preservation, it's a time of tearing down and starting again.

Blinking out across London the television transmitter irradiates the air with moving images. Six miles away at Broadcasting House the radio people refer to them sarcastically behind their microphones as 'those picture boys up at Ally Pally'.

Up the hill a parliamentary delegation was arriving to inspect the operation. They were being shown round by the Director General himself who was trying to impress upon them that television was the future – a million £90 Pye sets had already been sold. Sarah Brooks, standing to attention in a line with the other producers, smiling stiffly through the lipstick she hated wearing, spotted Peter Lezard, amusingly done up in a House of Commons tie. She winked at him. He detached himself from the rest and said,

'*Hello*, what on earth are you doing here, of all people? Now where would I expect you to be, let me think.'

And he thought that actually, he couldn't place her at all, not anywhere in the post-war world, because he had always found her so enigmatic, even when he walked into the French House one evening and saw her sitting at a table on her own, reading an Evelyn Waugh and drinking a glass of Pernod while all around her men of his acquaintance, and some women too, were thrashing about like great big drunk fish showing off.

'Well, you see, Peter, I work here,' she said. 'I'm a producer. I make the programmes, and think of new ones. And what about you? Surely you aren't an MP of all things?'

'I am indeed. Got in in 'forty-five with everyone else. Someone had to, why not me? It's a career, after all. Lots to do and you'll know I'm not shy of hard work. Fancy going outside for a smoke? For the view and fresh air as much as the fag.'

'I'm sure I can slip away. Do look at your boys, they're like children in front of the cameras, so vain, some of them.'

'Don't be so hard on the poor buggers; it's an outing, after all. We get precious few of them.'

They left the studios and stood on the summit of the hill. He held out each of his arms and wheeled them about, as if he was a child imitating an aeroplane. His wristwatch glittered in the sun.

'God, it's good to get out of all those *rooms*, that's what politics is, you know, sitting around all day in rooms, or on trains, lots and lots of trains.'

The last time she had seen him was that evening in Soho. The place pulled her in, like it or not. There were tiresome nights of men who drank too much and women being sick in their handbags at closing time and too much sex and too much being pawed at by hairy chaps who smelt of oil paints and turps, too much tobacco and too much stale sweat and yet there, somehow, the mind relaxed, became less watchful.

Then Peter had turned up, her brother's school friend all grown up, who wore his clothes like they'd been made for another man altogether, one with different proportions: narrower in the leg and broader in the back, so he both sagged and chafed in his suits. He was untidy and his head was weighed down with his brains. She remembered how he had tried her like a door handle years ago, just to see if it opened, not minded the complete resistance moments later because he wasn't even attracted to her, just going through the motions.

'Have you *seen* any television yet?' she asked him.

'Good God, no. I don't have a set for one thing, I don't have the time for another but what *is* there to see, honestly? There's supposed to be a wooden mule cavorting around on strings, isn't there? It's not exactly Chekhov.'

'That's Muffin and he's for children. There's a lot more to it than that. Tonight, for example, we've a programme about making stained glass.'

'Then I must hurry to buy a set.'

'Now don't be sarcastic. People are waiting for more to watch, and I'm trying to think up ideas. Stained glass is part of a series we're doing on craftsmen, for example.'

'Oh, but don't you find this rather trivial, after all, dear? Don't you feel like a bit of a potato dreaming up quizzes and wooden mules?'

'No, Peter, I don't. If television is going to be any good it's people like me who will make it work. The radio types are terribly condescending. We're caught in a bit of a contradiction – the upper classes consider us a vulgar little peep show and the masses can't afford a set so no one is taking us very seriously at the moment.'

'But how did you get into it? I mean, I've no idea what you were doing before.'

'Oh, didn't you? I was with the Crown Film Unit, first as a secretary then just before the war ended I was allowed to make a picture or two. You probably wouldn't have seen them.'

'Sorry, probably not. Look, I don't mean to be disparaging but I meant it, I'm up to my eyes in work, you know. This junket this afternoon, ridiculous waste of time in my opinion when there's so much to be done. I'm just here because my senior couldn't come.'

'Your senior?'

'My minister, I'm a private secretary.'

'Is it interesting?'

'Fairly, it's a good department Health, the new national service is proving frighteningly popular. We thought the middle classes wouldn't bother signing up but they have.'

The outline of her lipsticked mouth had turned into something completely different. Her face seemed to jerk into a different kind of life. She had, he thought, cheekbones like apples that pushed up when she smiled, a Celia Johnson face, not bad-looking, but she brushed men off, she froze them out with her eyes. If it hadn't been for the war, he thought, she would have become one of those unhappily married women who had read everything in the local lending library and drank too much sherry before her husband came home from work. Then the war had given her something decisive and important to do.

'Look, Peter, I have a *friend* . . . '

She was rather fine in profile, he thought, like the back of a coin, but full-frontal her face was a shade too wide and her eyebrows were not as tidy as they might be. This was the kind of thing he noticed. No, she wasn't particularly desirable to him, she was just a nice, rather clever young woman of a type you knew not that much about, even though they could seem as familiar as an old sock. About to ask him a favour. Or be indiscreet. Could be either. One is curious, he thought, which it will be and he mourned the end of his cigarette, which was starting to burn his fingers.

The Members of Parliament were sitting on benches now, some had taken out packets of sandwiches and were eating them in the mild sunshine. Others were smoking, or smoking and arguing, or smoking and looking out silently across to where the city gave out to the hills of Hertfordshire.

'Yes?' He remembered Sarah was prone to breaking off her sentences, as if she was editing the rest for final transmission.

'...she's not well. In fact, she is in a sanatorium, in Kent.'

'Bad luck. Not too ill, I hope?'

'Yes, she's very ill actually. TB.'

'Oh dear, and is the rest cure helping at all?'

'No, not really. In fact, she's getting worse. I saw her on Sunday. She's coughing blood all the time now.'

'Hmm.'

'But the thing is, as you *know*, Peter, there's the new treatment.'

'Ah, that.'

'So you do know all about it?'

'Of course.'

'I'd like her to get it.'

We are in an age of miracles, he thought, and everyone thinks I can do the necessary conjuring tricks for them. Poor Sarah, her eyes full of hope.

'Oh, my dearest girl, you and everyone else with a consumptive friend or relation. I do feel for you. The bloody press has a lot to answer for. You've been cutting out articles from the newspaper and hoarding them, and reading them over and over again, haven't you? It's another case of antibiotics, yes? I wish it were quite that easy. Let me tell you what I know. And I do know a fair bit about it. The trials in America have been very, very successful, beyond anyone's expectations, frankly. But you have to understand it doesn't work for everyone, when it works, yes, superb, but we couldn't go around handing it out to everyone willy-nilly even if we had any to give and it's expensive. And it's not just that, our advisors here think there may be a problem about toxicity. Though Waksman, in the States, he's the fellow who discovered it, thinks we're over-reacting just because we can't afford it.'

'And is it toxic?'

'Not necessarily. We brought a bit over in 1946 and tried a batch on some kids with tubercular meningitis, and frankly the speed with which it returned those little ones from the brink was nothing short of miraculous. But you have to remember that children have far fewer bacteria in their bodies so the chance of mutations and resistance is lower. Then we did a trial with about a hundred patients, half got the drug and half got the usual sanatorium treatment, it's called a control group. But we only tested on the under thirties because the chances of resistance were much lower. Same thing, good results, but, and it's a big but, we found out that some people's bodies reacted badly. Particularly young people. Is your friend young?'

'Not really.'

'Ah, well that wouldn't apply, but take George Orwell, for example, not young either. Well, he got some but it turned out he was allergic, developed a skin rash then a fever, a swelling around the site of the injection and he went into some sort of shock. Ghastly. They tried again, to see if it might just have been a bad batch but same thing. He died a couple of months ago, horribly, I'm told. Then there are the patients who do see quite an improvement until their bodies seem to develop a resistance. The secret, though, and this really is a secret, because the trials are still going on in the States, is coupling it with another drug, shaking up a cocktail, if you like. There's work being done on combining streptomycin with isoniazid, that might be the right trick.'

'I see. And how long will that take? My friend is very ill.'

'They're going full tilt, is all I can say. A year or two at the most.'

'As long as that? Oh, but I don't know if she has that long.'

'Yes, but she's in a good place, she's being taken care of?'

'Of course, but she is rotting. From the insides.'

'It's a condition of the illness, I'm afraid.'

She remembered the curve of her cheek, the nape of her neck with soft hairs growing from it in spiral curls, the narrow feet slipping inside the cheap second-hand shoes, the heat of her sudden temperatures, her frantic fumbling for the thermometer, in bed pressed against Sarah's back, the sharpness of the hip bone. Hannah by the window feebly doing some callisthenic exercises, panting, bent over, trying to catch her breath. Blood from her mouth in the morning on the pillow. Hannah once, just once, trying to sing. And crying when she heard her croaking notes.

'My friend has this illness overlaying a lot of other health problems. Her constitution was severely weakened by the war. I haven't told you that she's a refugee.'

'Then she should go to Palestine, or whatever they call it now. The dry desert climate and the warm weather would do her the power of good instead of some damp valley in Kent.'

'She isn't Jewish.'

'Pole?'

'No, she's German. She was in a camp, you see.'

'Oh. I see. Look, if she had some record of being on our side in some way I suppose I could put in a word, and I've absolutely no idea if it would do any good, but some random German woman who had the bad luck to find herself on the wrong side of the Nazis, there's no case to be made and she'll have to wait it out.'

And then looking at her face, and how she was staring at him as if she was about to take off the human mask and reveal that she was a wolf that could go for his throat and tear it out to get what she wanted – quiet Sarah, educated and polite, sitting alone with her book in the French, he thought, Oh, I *see*.

All she had said was, 'But you *must* help,' not even in a raised voice.

He'd never himself felt this sensation, only heard of love, read about it with at first incredulity, then acceptance that these fairy-tale emotions did exist. Love seemed to him like a form of mental illness, full of pain and suffering and you lose yourself and then you die. And then on top of that to love the wrong people, and often for the wrong reasons? What a mess. What a pit you would have to struggle out of.

He wondered if her brother knew, and those rather gentle, as well as genteel, parents in Henley.

The MPs had eaten their sandwiches and were dusting the crumbs off their lapels. London seemed to be leaping to life, bushes and trees and flowers were going at it hard, the birds were out in plenty, pigeons dropping their white deposits on the backs of wooden benches, and he had the feeling that the new decade would

78

be his, in the sense that men of his age, in their late twenties, who already knew the ropes, could take it, take the world. And then there were these hopeless cases like Sarah's girlfriend who were probably not going to make it, thwarted by circumstances. And then what if you could actually get her the treatment?

He took out a notebook and a silver propelling pencil. 'How smart,' she said, looking at it.

'Here you are, write down her details, her name, when she came here, the place she's in. Everyone is pulling strings, or trying to. Personally, I think she'd do best to try to hang on, but there you are, if she can't, she can't.'

'Thank you, Peter. And you won't ... '

'No, of course not. What do you take me for?'

Later that evening she walked home to her flat in Muswell Hill. Hannah's green dress was in the wardrobe, and the shoes Sarah had bought her with small silver buckles and a Louis heel in place of the Displaced Person's charity shoes that were too big. The dress came from a shop in Highgate also run by refugees. The dress was waiting, at a time when everyone else had stopped waiting and was already starting the rest of their lives.

She made supper on the gas ring and then put on the green dress, sat in the armchair smoking until she fell asleep and the dropped cigarette burned a hole in Hannah's new frock, through to the thigh, and she woke in pain.

13

From the verandas the village was hidden by trees. A stand of holm oaks which had come into leaf three weeks ago obscured the low skyline of the shops but Lenny knew they were there.

'I'm off for a bit,' he said, leaving his slippers behind in the cubbyhole. He was washed over with a sweat of relief that outside was still there after all, and you could be in it instead of looking at it. Not that the sky counted for much, there was sky anywhere.

He had put on the same clothes he'd arrived in, his charcoal and white striped London drape and the pair of thin-soled Italian shoes which came to a sharp point and were fastened with gilt buckles. In front of the mirror he had re-established the part in his hair and the wiry curls stood up either side of it. He thought he looked a bit better, but didn't know in what way. More colour in his cheeks? No. Fatter? Yes, he was taking double cream on his pudding and eating four slices of bread and butter with every meal. Plumping up, no longer so hooded and haunted by coughing fits, he felt all right, almost well. Would *be* well once the other lung was fully back in operation.

Outside there were benches and lawn chairs above the ornamental flower beds. The floral clock told a fixed and certain time. Gwendolyn Downie's marble memorial rose to a sharp point from the centre of it and the weak sun glinted off the gold letters of the florid, lengthy description of her lovely charms. The old lady lived somewhere near here, on the other side of the woods in the big house.

Beyond the flower beds the gravel drive on which the ambulance had brought them led straight down to civilisation, or a scrap of it. Where there's shops, there's life, he thought. There's a café and a pub. I can buy a paper and maybe some sweets for Miriam and fags. He felt ready to play-act the everyday life of a normal healthy person because the schism between Lenny ill and Lenny well was killing him. He didn't know how to keep the earlier kid alive inside, the buggers were taking him over and he wasn't going to have it.

Nurse Chitty waved to him as she saw him leave. 'Now don't get lost in the woods.'

'I'm not going near the woods, I'm only going to the village. It's not that far, is it?'

'Not if you go down by the road. Walk down the drive then turn right, you'll come to it, no trouble, but watch out for traffic. I know there's not much but delivery vans call, and up here your instincts can get a bit blunted. Make sure you step off by the verge or they'll knock you over. We've had injuries before.'

'Don't worry, I can look after myself.'

'I know that, but just in case you get cocky.'

She stood by the door waving him off, like a mother seeing her little child take his first steps to school. And where does she get off treating me like a kid, he thought, cute as she might be. I'll show her. He picked up his pace until the drive bent and she was out of sight.

Under his feet the gravel rose in painful stony pricks, ow ow ow.

He didn't think the village was far, he'd put up with it, he'd put up with much worse since he'd been down in Kent. And the weather wasn't bad, quite warm. In London he barely noticed weather, he was only outside when he was walking to the bus or the Tube, he was an indoors kind of a guy who lived mainly under electric light.

Relatives and friends of the patients were allowed to visit on Sunday afternoons and for that day the institution acquired a hinterland, a relief from the same faces, the worn-out familiarity of the inmates whose condition waxily waned. On Sundays the place turned into a world of outdoor clothing, suits and hats and scarves and high-heeled shoes and handbags and the ineluctable smell of women's scents, Yardley and even, in the case of Lady Anne's visitors, perfumes from Paris. It was the breath of air so unlike the howling gales on the veranda that they all longed for.

Uncle Manny drove their mother down in his motor through the Kent countryside. 'Oh, isn't it empty,' she cried. 'Not a shop or a picture house.'

'It reminds me of my early years,' he replied. 'Before the ship. All fields like this and trees and we slept around the iron stove at night, dressed in all our clothes.'

'How horrible.'

'Yes, but still, you know, I miss it, and my little brother next to me, the baby. Who knew how it would all turn out?'

She brought them food wrapped in greasy paper bags, kichelach, potato latkes, a pot of chopped liver which they ate with relish not because it was good cooking but because it was home, the taste of London and of Mrs Meltz's hens. Nurse Chitty was offered a mouthful of the chopped liver. 'Ooh no, it does smell strong, I'd be worried it would have a flavour.'

'What are these people like?' Mrs Lynskey asked Manny as they drove home. 'They are afraid of their own shadows, the food they give them, you notice everything is pale, no colour, no *tam*, tapioca, rice pudding, what kind of a meal is that for a young person?'

'Yet he looks well on it.'

'It reminds me too much of a camp. I don't like the place.' She took a picture of her children posed years ago in a photographer's studio from her handbag, and kissed their faces.

'Don't worry, they're getting the finest treatment under the sun; nowhere could give them better, not even abroad in the mountains.'

'Mountains are just to persecute you.'

'True.'

Lenny's main emotion since he'd been at the sanatorium was extreme boredom. Fear had subsided a while ago after the rough stabbing at his chest and the collapse of his lung. The tedium of the days had numbed any sense of terror. You rubbed along, because that was the only option unless you sat by yourself like the German lady, or had your own miniature society like the officers' mess. He'd sized up the pecking order, how it worked, who was in with the doctors and nurses and who knew how to keep the others in their place. Mainly he played cards all day with Colin Cox. He visited his sister and her new friend on the veranda but they were forming their own little unit, the two of them, and he was left out.

Pals wrote him letters from overseas describing rubber plantations and tin mines and rice paddies. Eggy Sitz said they were bombing and shelling a swamp but he had no idea why. It was exciting but too hot and he missed home. He supposed Lenny missed home too but couldn't he get out on a day pass?

Gina wrote him lovely letters in broken English about how she missed him and the progress of her cousin's on-off engagement and sent a snip of fabric from the new dress she was making. A few more things were appearing in the shops, she said. There was a little let-up from 'osteerity'. She said she was planning a visit. He didn't know if he was looking forward to that or not. What would she think when she saw him here, in this condition?

The fresh air felt nice on his face. There were things to look at – trees shrubs flowers, some of which he recognised from the Welsh experience – but his eyes had difficulty distinguishing them because they didn't have names. Or he didn't know what the names were. He couldn't wait to get to the village; if he timed it right, the pub would be opening. He wasn't much of a drinker but there might be a barmaid to pass the time with. The company of girls was what he wanted, not sick girls lying in bed but big bosomy girls who smiled a lot. Which wasn't really his usual taste, dark, olive-skinned birds were more his thing, he'd never taken to the Anglo-Saxon type, but Colin Cox had lent him a titty magazine and that was what was in it and he wanted to see his night-time reveries come to life, dispensing pints of Double Diamond and flirting with him.

After a few yards, he came upon a *thing* lying by the side of the drive. Someone dropped it, he thought. A handbag? Hard to tell. A pair of fur ears poked up from a dead eye. The internal organs were spilling out and a crowd of flies were massing round the carcass. A black-and-white bird was pecking at the catastrophe.

What the fuck was it, a rabbit? Bugs Bunny was the closest he'd ever come to one. Dead and decaying by the side of the grass verge, knocked down by a van or a car or a motorbike. He couldn't even walk past it. Something about this dead thing had to be bad luck, it must be an omen, some message to remind him he was going to die and be buried in a box and become full of worms and germs and other horrors. Sick oh sick.

A wood pigeon thumped down onto a slender branch, rustling the new leaves. The flap and commotion startled the magpie and startled Lenny. A screeching started up in the air around him, normal country sounds but he didn't understand them. He heard an engine coming towards him and backed off the drive a few feet onto a path that led into the woods.

So this was woods.

The path was less sore on his thin-soled shoes. The earth was dry and powdery, crisp leaves from last year's autumn still strewn about. He kept going because actually, he had to admit, it wasn't bad, peaceful, the air slightly humid and warm on his shoulders and a smell he couldn't describe or name its constituent parts but he liked it. Nor was it bad to be off the radar of the world all by himself after weeks of always being with someone, with Cox in the bed next to him. Or in the day room at the card-players' table with Colin Cox wittering on about cars. Or visiting Miriam and Valerie and trying to bring to them the atmosphere and gossip of downstairs, the social whirl of the sanatorium from which they were excluded. Or just sitting amongst an expanse of waxworks at rest time.

Here in the woods, walking in the fresh air under the tree canopy, walking in the woods to the village, strolling, strips of high pale mottled sky above him, his body seemed to realign. The legs reconnected at the hip-joint after weeks of sitting, the knees oiled themselves with synovial fluid, his arms began to swing from the shoulders. *I'm a little soldier marching along to my own tune.* Come to think of it, maybe it was a kind of privilege to get ill and be sent away like this, to meet a different class of person, and to eat all the grub you wanted and do nothing all day and return with a different perspective on things. For a bit it might actually be okay but not as long as they wanted to keep him. They should definitely go soon, you could walk out, no one could stop you.

The woodland path forked. A frill of violently spotted orange, like a Tudor ruff, wrapped itself around the fallen stump of a tree. Which was interesting. There were no signposts. Large semi-circular holes appeared in the bank, like the entrance to the home of Jerry the mouse in the cartoons – inside there were always mouse-sized tables and chairs and pictures of mouse ancestors on the wall in old-fashioned clothes. He had no idea what lived in a hole in the woods. Foxes? How big was a fox? Not a clue.

The Italian shoes were frail. The soles were pitted with gravel marks and the gilt buckles were coming away from the stitching. Grass and leaves gathered in the turn-ups of his trousers. He began to feel both hot and chilly. Stupid trees.

A sudden thrashing sound to his left terrified him. A bird ran across his path, a giant thing with red round its eye and a white-coloured ring round its neck. Enormous tail sticking out the back.

He remembered the gaunt young men they had seen when they arrived in the ambulance, rambling in the woods in mackintoshes and carrying sticks. Maybe he shouldn't have come in here all by himself without preparation and special equipment.

But now the path began to widen, he was sure he was near the road. The big bird made another rush across him. He jumped, the buckle flew off his shoe, his heel came out, he went down over a tree root and lay, his trousers ripped at the knees and elbows.

Fucking wood, fucking countryside, fucking nature with no buses or Tubes or chip shops or cafés, you can fucking keep it.

85

He stood up and stumbled on, sweating, the creases behind his knees dripped with sweat. Ahead of him a patch of sunlight slanted through the branches to a more open arena. Walking towards it, the ground became very blue. Which wasn't the colour of grass, normally. Must be flowers. He knew the names of four of them: dandelions, daisies, roses and violets. Violets were little things you bought in a bunch and presented to your mother on her birthday. Dandelions were miniature suns then turned into fluff you blew at. Daisies were something girls made into chains. Roses lived in the shops behind glass, Miriam's department.

He waded in to the blue carpet and saw a foot. He saw a trouser leg. He saw the end of a walking stick. They extended obliquely from the side of a bush. Close up, reclining on a fallen tree trunk, was Captain Iain Jackson in a tweed jacket and regimental tie, leaning on his arm, smiling to himself, with the stem of a bluebell between his teeth like Carmen Miranda or a silly person, the sun shining through his blond moustache making him look diaphanous, like a fairy on the top of a Christmas tree.

'Hello, there, it's young Lynskey, isn't it? What's happened to your suit?'

'Bloody fell over.'

'Bad luck. Come and join me for a minute. It's rather a nice day, don't you think?'

'It was, until I went arse over tit.'

'Have a bluebell.' He reached out and picked a flower and handed it to Lenny. 'Be a bluebell boy.'

'Is that what they're called? I never seen them before.'

'Really? Never seen bluebells? How very odd. I can't imagine that, I really can't.'

Lenny sometimes took a rowing boat out on the lake in Finsbury Park with one of his birds. After a period of being no good at it, getting the oars tangled in the rowlocks, and uncertain about even stepping into the thing, a shifting surface, he started to enjoy the rhythm of the wood entering the water and his shoulders pleasantly aching, the reeds, the ducks, the swans, his own bird of the moment sitting opposite him in a sun-hat. Afterwards they would walk through ornamental flower beds, past a floral clock to the place that sold ice creams. Wherever you were in the park you could still hear the traffic and be in sight of the perimeter, which was nice.

Now here he was in a wood, with a meshuggenah who had a flower in his mouth. And him a decorated war hero with an MC, which he carelessly kept in his sponge bag, rusting and tarnishing.

Lenny had never spoken to anyone at the officers' mess table. He was Other Ranks, or would have been if he'd had to go to the army. But Jackson seemed friendly enough and a bit batty with the flower in his mouth.

'I was trying to get to the village.'

'Really, why?'

'Cup of tea, a paper, maybe a bag of sweets. Mooch around.'

'But didn't anyone tell you it's Wednesday half-day closing? The pub will be open, there's a morose public bar and an empty snug. The landlord can't make his mind up whether he wants our trade or not, he'll serve you, but he never asks if you want the same again. The village, I'm afraid, is not exactly Shangri-La, even if you can get there. They love us at the chemist but barely tolerate us at the tea rooms, I really wouldn't rely on the village to relieve the longueurs. I've been here about eighteen months, though I try not to count so it might be more. But then this is my third go. Me and dear Gwendo are old friends, like sex and the clap.'

'What did you come back for? Didn't it work the other two times?'

'Not really. I was invalided out of the army in 'forty-four and sent here, which was an utter pain in the backside because inevitably you feel like you've let your men down, lolling around at home on double rations. Then they *thought* I was fit to leave, the war had ended, and I went into my father's shoe and boot business as I'd always been supposed to, not exactly strenuous at my level, factory inspections once a week but mainly monitoring production and output and our relationship with the Board of Trade. Even light duties didn't last long before I fell ill again. I had another crack at it, just nine months and they thought I'd made a full recovery, but I was playing cricket one afternoon, only a village game, and I coughed up a bit of my lung. C'est la vie.'

'But how do you stand it? You're only a few years older than me and you've seen everything, I mean the war and overseas, and then rotting here, I mean, sorry, I didn't . . .'

Jackson wound the stem of the bluebell round his finger, pulled it off and examined the coil before throwing it behind the log. He picked another flower and touched his finger along the line of bells.

'Look, we officers, all of us, are one way or another suffering from a kind of war sickness, that's the only way I can describe it. We survived the war, but not really, and that's true not just of those of us with TB, but the ones who came out of it without a scratch. One way or another, out on Civvy Street we don't know how things are supposed to operate, it's a struggle, and here we find there's a respite from all that. You see every day here is the same, the same war with our lungs, the same battles and skirmishes, so we're not challenged by the unpredictable and as much as we hate that, I think many of us like it because essentially we're cowards.

'I suppose you've seen our table – the officers' mess, everyone calls it. Well, that's exactly what it is. Every evening after dinner we retire to the games room and have what we call our pub evenings, when we behave as if we *are* at the pub, hand round a bottle of sherry, talk about girls and cricket and the news. We read the paper every day, we keep up, we listen to the wireless and we're angling for a television set. We pretend we're living when we're not, not at all.'

It's worse than I fucking thought, Lenny realised. They're dead men.

'In February we held a mock election, I suppose you must have been too young to vote? We collected ballot papers from almost everyone, took the whole thing out onto the verandas, delivered election addresses and had debates on the in-house radio, the works. And we voted in the real election, those who could walk went down to the polling station in the village, those who couldn't were picked up by nice people from their party of choice. The veranda lot had to lump it, unfortunately. We're still recovering from that bout of real life.

'But the point is not who is the government, we barely care about that, it doesn't affect us one jot in here, the point is being able to *appear* to care, to go through the motions to deceive yourself that you're doing all right. We don't want to admit that we don't give a damn about politics, that our mock election doesn't matter, that holding it doesn't matter. We're half-dead inside. We like the place, we tolerate it because we're scared of leaving, most of us, scared of what the world is changing into and having no real place in it. You have to remember the whole aim of the good old Gwendo is to turn us into invalids, permanent patients, I suppose you got that talk when you arrived. Well, it suits some of us. We don't want to leave. And then new patients arrive, people from the outside, like you, from the new post-war world. We see defiance, which you did so admirably when you demanded to see your sister. But we don't have it in us. It's just the art class, really. Have you tried it?'

'No, why would I?'

'Ah. Well, we've all done it at one time. There are obvious attractions, if you're any good it gives you something to feel a little bit proud of, which is a help. Even if you aren't if you've made some progress you don't feel that you're just vegetating. You never know, it might suit you down to the ground.'

'I'm waiting for the injections.'

'To state the bloody obvious.'

'But it can't be long now, can it?'

'To be honest, I don't know.'

And if he doesn't, Lenny thought, then who does? It took some of the air out of him, this uncertainty. Later that night he thought about Jackson's strange words about not fitting in the post-war world. They frightened him as he might have been afraid of a ghost sitting at the end of his bed.

They sat on the log for a few minutes longer talking about Nurse Chitty. Lenny offered to work out the odds of the runners and riders who'd be into her knickers first. Iain said that was the spirit. He led them out of the woods back to the gravel drive.

'I saw a dead thing here, maybe a rabbit.'

'Oh, yes, you see those all the time. Hit by cars and vans and ambulances.'

'And another thing, I saw a massive bird with a red head and big feathers at the back.'

'Pheasant. We used to have them for lunch sometimes when I was growing up, my father wasn't a bad shot.'

'What's the taste like?'

'Very good, rich and meaty.'

'Do we ever get any here?'

'No, and I don't know why. I suspect they do shoot them and sell them, somebody has to be making something on the side. Now, are you all right, old chap, you look a bit pale and damp. Take my arm, not much further.'

Lenny limped back, leaning on Captain Jackson, his trousers torn at the knee, one buckle left behind in the woods, the thin soles of his Italian shoes ruined, his shirt soaking. What a sight I must look, he thought, what a miserable specimen of humanity, and Jackson kept pausing to let him catch his breath.

'Don't worry, we're not in a rush, we have all the time in the world, it's not like we're trying to beat the clock. You'll be all right, just take it easy.'

14

Hannah Spiegel observed him enter with a twinge of pity then went back to her book.

Captain Jackson asked if he'd like to be accompanied back to his room.

'What, and tuck me in?'

'No, no, but it can take it right out of you if you haven't left the place for a while.'

'I'm okay.'

'If you're sure, no need for false courage, you know, there isn't a war on.'

In the lift the life went out of him, he leaned back against the control panel. Ridiculous what that walk had done, all for nothing more than the sight of a few blue flowers and a chat on a log. The lift ascended. A brief darkness overcame him for a few seconds until he heard the sound of the doors opening and he stumbled out.

He could find his way back to his room with his eyes closed, turn left and then past the reproduction of Van Gogh's *Sunflowers*, two doors and he was there. Someone had removed the sunflowers and replaced it with a woodland scene in which bunnies walking about on their hind legs were having a tea party. Spotted toadstools formed seats. A wasp was eating a slice of cake from a plate. He blinked.

A midget was walking towards him, a midget in pyjamas and a dressing grown, holding an even more midget version of itself with glassy eyes and yellow hair. The midget had two plaits hanging down on either side of its little head and so did its small companion. The midget was trotting down the corridor, breaking into a run, tearing past him. He turned, the thing had got to the lift and was trying to reach the button.

He walked back a few feet. 'Hello, mate, need some help?'

He felt woozy, he was swaying as he reached out. The little dwarf didn't speak, it looked up at him like tiny kids he used to see playing on the bomb sites, climbing over the bricks scavenging for some poor dead person's bits and pieces, sometimes you could find an alarm clock or a good saucepan and sell it door to door. Little arms and hands could feel through crevices in the rubble for pearl necklaces and hardly charred books.

'Make it come. Please.'

He heard footsteps behind him padding up the hallway. It was a new nurse, he didn't recognise her and he thought he knew all of them.

'What are you doing up here?' she said. 'Why are you on this floor? And you, Jennifer Simpson, why aren't you in bed? If you go on like this, you know, we will tie you down, tie you to the bed so you can't move your arms and legs, then how will you like it? You cannot carry on like this.'

'Where am I?' said Lenny.

'Somewhere you don't belong.'

If he hadn't been so exhausted, so faint, so done in, he'd have seen it was a girl, a child tearing along past him with her doll under her arm, but the only children here were the ones who came to visit their mothers and fathers and few did. He now understood that this child was escaping, she was on a prison-break, the poor kid, with her beaky little nose in her thin white face and he saw on her feet slippers with woollen rabbit's ears sticking out of the toes.

The child was holding on to his trouser legs, she had attached her fingers to the rips in the knees and was tearing at them. She

92

glued herself to his body and he felt her tears run down his shins.

'Take me home, please, please, I want my mum. I won't stay here any longer.'

He bent down and picked her up and held her in his arms.

'Don't cry, I'll take you to your mum, where is she? Which room is she in?' For she must be a little visitor, though visiting day was Sunday and it made no sense for her to be in her nightclothes. The lamb. The little lamb. It was the first time he had held a child. When his daughter was born he would remember the girl by the lift: 'Just another minute, please, one more cuddle, I'll give her back in a minute,' he would say to his wife.

'Who are you?' said the nurse. 'Are you a visitor? You must be a visitor, you have no right to ... you have no right even to *be* here.'

He had forgotten to change his shoes. He was not in his slippers, which were still in the entrance hall. To the nurse he looked like a hooligan, a spiv from the town.

Another nurse came down the hall. 'What is this commotion?'

'Jennifer has tried to run away. *Again.*'

'Oh, Jennifer, this must stop. We are busy making you better and all you want to do is thwart us. You know your mother can't look after you. We've explained everything. Now please come with me, back to your room and the other children.'

'What other children?'

'Who *are* you? What are you doing here?'

'I'm receiving treatment, I'm on the rest cure like everyone else. I've just come in from a walk in the woods and was all in, and I came out of the lift and there was this kid.'

'Then I see you have had a nasty fall and you should return to your room, where someone will look after you.'

She pushed the button and the lift doors opened. Jennifer was prised from his arms, screaming. Lenny was pushed into the little moving room and the doors closed on him. He rode down to the ground floor where everything was normal, and began to make a noisy commotion about the kids upstairs until Nurse Chitty led him into the empty art room and asked him to calm down.

15

Valerie had decided that she urgently had to find a way to mould Miriam into an acceptable companion. The nurses had discreetly explained that now the sanatorium had been taken over by the National Health Service many more Miriams and Lennys would be pouring in from London while the better-off, assessing the situation, found that really they did prefer Switzerland after all despite the enforced separation from family, but that with a cure in sight, perhaps the absence wouldn't be all that long. Valerie realised that if she did not take matters in hand she was going to descend into an infantile state in which ideas became grey gassy shapes above her head, floating away from her grasp.

Linda Darnell had been followed by the faces and biographies of many other actresses, none of whom she was interested in or whose films she had seen. At Oxford there had been a film society and she had attended occasional screenings of pictures from France and Italy, had seen *La Belle et la bête*, *Rome, Open City* and *Bicycle Thieves*. Yet despite the cultural chasm she was amused by Miriam. Vulgarity can be, she wrote to her mother, a breath of fresh air and her parents must not mind, when they came to visit, the girl in the next bed or be too snobbish about her. For her mother and father saw no reason to hide their prejudices; after all, they would frequently point out, could you dispute that some people simply are better than others, have nicer manners, live in nicer houses and have nicer opinions? Her mother wrote back that one felt for the Jews, of course, after those newsreels but that didn't mean you wanted a family of Hebrews to move in next door and be seen walking along avenues of trees in their funny little hats and speaking loudly in a variety of German, or actually German. This was Edgbaston, after all. One had certain standards and if you let them slip beneath you there was the abyss: *council houses.*

But Valerie found that leaving aside the film-star gossip she quite enjoyed Miriam's strident complaints, her refusal to accept the patient role or the authority that had put her in this cocoon of stifling comfort. She made demands, sent back the food, offered to do the nurses' hair for them in the modern style, even incorporating the cap, if they smuggled in a few cigarettes.

Miriam woke up every morning and picked up her powder compact from the bedside table and examined her face. 'Courage, girl, courage,' she told her reflection. 'Let's make this one a belter.' And Valerie found this surprisingly admirable.

She slashed her mouth with red, brushed electric blue powder onto her eyelids, sawed the miniature toothbrush over the pad of her Rimmel eye-black. She spent a lot of time looking at her hands. 'When I worked with the flowers, they were red raw from the cold and the nails were all broken and terrible. The proprietor had beautiful manicures, but she could do, she was all charm with the customers while I was out the back trimming thorns off roses. Now I'm here I'm going to let my nails grow and have a different colour on them every day.'

Valerie was amused, it seemed like a good idea, and why not? Painting your nails, letting them dry was the kind of occupation they had more than enough time for.

Deeper she went into the lives of the Jewish brother and sister and deeper into a way of life in London that her degree in English Literature from Somerville had not even hinted existed or was possible, so Miriam's extended riffs became a sort of prose-poem,

Valerie thought. At least she would treat them that way and try to analyse out the cadences and rhythms of these speeches though she was too often carried away by the content and lost the thread of her analytical thought.

'I had a chance once to make *big* money, you know,' Miriam rattled on. 'Still could if I wasn't ill, the offer is on the table, though I never would even if I was a hundred per cent. It's a woman – I won't call her a lady, though if you saw her on the street you'd probably mistake her for one, well, maybe *you* wouldn't, you can probably tell class from paste in the blink of an eye, no fooling someone like you. ANYway, she's always done up, made-up to the nines, furs, film-star looks, reminds me of Rita Hayworth. And, guess what she does for a living, just guess.'

'I don't know; something dishonest, I suppose. Is she a prostitute?'

'Everyone who rumbles her thinks that at first. Nope, she's the queen of the shoplifters. She's got a team of girls all over London, my age and even younger, some of them just fourteen. If you can keep a secret, I used to be one of them, just for a few months when I was a bit younger. I didn't last, not because I was no good at it but my uncle didn't approve. Didn't think it was respectable. He's happy to fence the goods, just not steal them. He's more of a middleman, but he wants to be on the level now, got into property. I was a bit of a tearaway and you couldn't tell me what to do, I was my own man, as they say, even at that age. Bolder even than Lenny. And I've always looked a bit older than him, I matured young, you know what I mean. In that department. My monthlies started when I'd just turned twelve. What about yours?'

'Fifteen.'

'That's late. Well, this lady I'm telling you about, she was the one who taught me how to do my face, because you can't go into those shops as naked as the day you're born, you've got to have the lipstick and the powder and the eyebrows pencilled, squirt of perfume too she used to give us on the wrists when we were going in. I'll tell you how we did it, they call it hoisting, you wear your hoisting drawers – big old-fashioned bloomers like the old dears

96

wear – but they have to be *silk* so the gear doesn't catch as it goes down, just slips in. It makes you walk like a duck when they're full because you can get something as big as a mink stole down there.'

'But how on earth can you get a fur into a pair of knickers? It hardly seems possible,' said Valerie, astonished.

'There's a trick to it, it's all in the *rolling*. You can't just go into a shop and chuck a few *schmattes* down your drawers. You have to know how to roll the stuff, you roll it round the hanger or the shop assistants will see them empty on the rail and sniff out something dodgy going on. Then you slide it down and run outside, quick as you like, and there she is, in her motor, jump in and off you go, job done. As I say, I did it for a few months but it wasn't just my uncle disapproving, I lost interest, I had bigger fish to fry. I found out about floristry and that was it, I knew what my true calling was. Manny got me a job in a flower shop and then I was in clover. Now I'm not going to lie, when you're not well and it's cold, yes, it's a bugger, and when your proprietor is shouting at you all day long because petals are falling when they shouldn't and you've got to load the van for the deliveries when it's pouring out, and then the cold water all day long, that's the worst.

'But once you're over that and you're your own boss and some-one is working *for* you, then you're on top of the world. My uncle is going to set me up when I'm trained, because you can't just buy a lot of flowers without understanding composition and what goes with what and their life-expectancy. It's a *profession*, Valerie, a *pro-fession* like any other, not just putting some stems in a vase. They have Latin names and you have to be able to reel them off, but I suppose you know Latin already.'

'I see,' said Valerie to whom all this had come in a great rush like lava sliding down a mountain and she was keen to get back to the shoplifting story because that was just fascinating, more so than the familiar world of the florist's shop.

'And out of interest, where exactly did you carry out your trade, when you were hoisting, I mean?'

Miriam turned to her, winked. Put a finger to her painted lips.

'Only the very best shops, no rubbish, no sweets and lipsticks from Woolworths or anything like that. Stores like Harrods and Selfridges, because they sell the most expensive gear. It's obvious, isn't it? That's where the money is. And you don't want to nick from your own, little corner shops that are just trying to keep their heads above water and hardly have anything to sell anyway because of the ration.'

'And then what happens to the stolen items?'

'They get moved on. You must have bought stuff off the black market, everyone has.'

'I did buy a pair of shoes from a friend. They were brand new. I don't really know where she got them.'

'There you are, then. Anyway, I'll tell you the point of this story, the whole point. I see you looking at me in the morning when I'm putting on my war paint. That woman, I'm not telling you her name for obvious reasons, she came up from Elephant and Castle before the war, she had elocution lessons to make her sound posh, even now she spends a fortune on her hair because you can't nick that, and it's the way that she's taken for what she's not. Everyone judges you on what you look like on the outside, that's how this country works. If you want people to take you as a labourer, wear a cap; if you want to be taken for a gentleman, wear a Homburg hat.'

'That's a little superficial.'

'Oh, but human nature is, Valerie, take it from me. Why do people buy flowers when they die so quick? To have something nice to look at, to cheer themselves up, particularly on a depressing rainy day. A girl I know is a hairdresser. She sees the ladies come in with their grey roots and go out again looking twenty years younger. And she says then they *feel* twenty years younger so they act it, they don't go home and put on their old housecoat and sit and listen to the wireless and go to bed at nine with a cup of cocoa, they go out, they have fun, they live a little. Because they'd paid good money to have their hair done and they want to get the value out of it. She sees it every single day, it's what she knows. This woman I've been telling you about, she couldn't do her job without being taken as a lady. And you, lovey, if you don't mind me saying so, could do with taking in hand.'

Valerie laughed. 'And who is to see me?'

'Me. I see you, twenty-four hours a day except when I'm sleeping, and my brother. Aren't we entitled to have something nice to look at apart from these bleeding trees?'

That seemed to Valerie to be an irrefutable point, she didn't know how to answer it. So they decided they might take each other in hand, each in their own way, and she allowed Miriam to cut her hair and have Manny bring in a box of cosmetics for her to try next visiting day. Every morning Miriam did her up. Valerie thought, And what is the harm if it makes her happy? Though she only partly recognised the face she saw in the mirror with brilliant blue eye-shadow rising up her eyelids and rouge creamed on her pallid cheeks.

16

'You go tell that boy you have a baby, you go tell him now. Make him do right.'

'Okay, Momma.'

'How do you get there? You need money?'

'A train.'

'Is it far?'

'I don't know. How should I know? It's not London, that's for certain.'

'However far you have to go make sure you arrange *everything* with him, don't come back here without the date for the wedding. And a ring, so far I don't see no ring. Without a ring, nothing is sure.'

'How am I going to get a ring?'

'You write, his uncle arranges everything. The man is rich. He sends a ring to the boy and he puts it on your finger and you are engaged and we make the wedding.'

But Gina did not write to Lenny to tell him she was coming or to ask for a ring. She decided to see for herself what kind of situation she would find in Kent from where he wrote her letters with so little information.

In Soho the streets were full of foreign people talking in all their tongues and living above their shops and some like her daddy went to the internment camp and came back a different man nobody liked, bitter and complaining about everything. Outside this neighbourhood, she did not understand life. The English were mysterious and cold and white like snowmen and snow-women with pale eyes and bloodless mouths. Lenny was very different, more like an Italian boy, with black hair on his chest and hair on his back and ears with soft lobes she nibbled like jellies. She hardly knew how she got pregnant when he had said everything he would arrange, the little rubber hat he put on. But what happened?

She put on her spring coat which was glazed powder-blue cotton and her best pink crêpe dress and her high-heeled shoes and blew on the gold of her cross and polished it with her sleeve and brushed her hair and put it up in a French pleat. In the mirror the baby barely showed. Is there a baby there at all? She did not believe it and felt indifferent to the little thing inside her, looking they said like not much more than a fat comma. On the bus to the station she was silently singing, songs from the radio, snatches, scraps, lines, melodies.

The night is like a lovely tune
Beware, my foolish heart.

I like to sing, she told Lenny. I could sing all day long. You're a bloody canary, he said, sing your heart out, sweetheart, if it's what you want.

She hadn't even practised what she was going to say to him. She would find the words when she got there, it was easy, you just point to your belly and smile and he knows what you're saying and that is that. Then point to the finger. Life is not so difficult.

On the train she fell asleep. The ticket inspector woke her. 'Your station, young lady.'

She made enquiries at the ticket office and was directed to a bus. The bus wound through green country lanes. So this is England, she thought, this is real England like they show you on tins of biscuits and calendars. She got off outside the chemist and looked

101

around for the hospital. A woman was walking along with a basket over her arm and the church bells chimed in warm air scented by early rose petals from the walled gardens of houses with half-moon lights above their windows. How nice it is here, she thought. So pretty, so— But she had run out of English words.

She had in her handbag a cake her mother made. He liked her cakes. For a cake, she would get a ring. This seemed to her to be a very good exchange.

Mrs Kitson, who was returning home for lunch after a morning's overseeing of the Garden of England clay models, directed her through the village to where the hill started. She pointed up to the treeline and Gina saw the glitter of glass reflecting back the leaves.

'It's not far, only about ten minutes,' Mrs Kitson said. 'You can't miss it.'

Gina walked past the woods, which in early summer did not fill her with the horror that had maimed Lenny's heart. She heard wood pigeons cooing and the clatter of red squirrels chasing up branches. The birdsong was very sweet and nice and she was very well and light on her feet. The woods were full of strolling patients but she did not see them until she came out at the top of the drive to the lawns and benches, the Gwendolyn Downie marble memorial and patients in wheelchairs with shawls round their shoulders, blinking out their last sight of blue skies from under dusty eyelashes.

Terrible place! Prison!

She walked past them to the entrance and looking through the door saw Lenny sitting at a table with a man with papery yellow skin, Lenny in his dressing gown, slippers on his feet like an old man, hunched over a hand of cards. A grandpa not a boy.

I don't want him, she thought. This is not a father for my baby, ring or no ring. She felt sorry for him, but no. Who could expect her to marry an invalid and then he dies and you are a widow and finished aged twenty, have to wear a black dress for ever like all the other widows? She was already turning round and walking away and Lenny never saw her.

*

She got home to Soho and her mother said, 'Well? I don't see no ring. What did he say?'

'Oh, Momma, when I got there, he died already.'

'He died! Oh my God.'

'Yes, they tell me he is taken away and buried. No good.'

'So. We make a new plan. Sit down.'

Momma looked out of the window. Across the street Poppa was standing by the lamp-post smoking a cigarette and talking to one of the waiters from Bianchi's in a black waistcoat and a napkin stuck in his waistband.

'See that boy?'

'Yes.'

'Very nice boy.'

'Okay, Momma.'

'Go down and talk to him, Poppa will introduce you.'

17

'Now let's read,' Valerie said, feeling it was her turn to take control over the conversation.

'I haven't got a book.'

'I will read to you and then, if you like, you can read to me, we'll see how we get on.'

A well-meaning aunt had brought her in a collection of Somerset Maugham's short stories, which she had only glanced at, for they were both out of fashion and designed, she felt, for simpler minds than her own. The cover emitted a slight pot-pourri odour of the drawing room but they were supposed to be immensely popular so opening the volume at random she landed on 'The Three Fat Women of Antibes'.

It was all about idle rich old dames in the South of France playing bridge, dieting and eschewing cocktails, starches and fats. Miriam thought it was hilarious. 'I know bitches just like them,' she said, 'they moan about their figures saying how they never let a morsel of chocolate pass their lips and they never lose a bloody pound. You'd think there was no ration on, the greedy pigs. Well, they're getting their cakes from somewhere.'

After a couple of weeks during which Miriam, like the queue of recipients for cod liver oil, their mouths wide open in a perfect O, would say, 'More, read another one,' Valerie moved her on to the sensationalist classics, *Frankenstein* and *Dracula*, both of which Miriam said she knew from the pictures but this explained a lot more. Miriam would have requested *Gone with the Wind* and *Forever Amber* if Valerie had not forestalled her with some H. G. Wells (the science fiction). They moved on to *Animal Farm*, which Miriam saw in terms of the various jumped-up authoritarians she knew from the floristry trade. And she recoiled from the pigs. 'Dirty animals, they smell! We saw them in Wales, you know, they tried to make us eat rashers of bacon but we kept our mouths tight shut.'

Stories filled the long days. Valerie's throat grew sore from reading aloud, she would often fall back exhausted under her blankets. Once she started to cough and couldn't stop. She was coughing red. Her lungs were not healing. Dr Limb came up to see her and said they'd try another pneumothorax if she didn't improve. When he left, Valerie waited till Miriam dozed and then turning her head away, wept. Oh, she was going down, down, down into the long dark. Death, perpetual blackness, dreamless and she had had only twenty-two years in the world. When she had got the second opinion in Harley Street, the doctor seated in his white coat holding out his hands as if he were giving a blessing at the Last Supper (hers), she had stumbled out and crossing the road had walked into the path of a slow-moving taxi and was lightly knocked over. That was the moment her death warrant had been signed and she sometimes thought she would have been best out of it, quickly and cleanly, without this long rot from within.

Yes, the date of her death existed, like someone scheduled for execution by hanging. And would be carved by the stonemason on her grave. She didn't keep an appointment book any more, but if she had one, it would be there, and she would be searching for the invisible ink which had inscribed her own last day.

Unless streptomycin. This hope they were all afflicted by. This torment.

'You rest yourself,' said Miriam. 'I'll read, if you like.'

Valerie handed her a copy of Kafka's short stories in the Penguin paperback edition and asked her to start with 'Metamorphosis'.

'It's rather odd but now I'm getting a better idea of your taste, I think you're going to like it.'

'Meta what? What does that even mean? Say it again, I need to learn how to pronounce it.'

They settled back into their beds and Miriam began.

'Bloody hell, bloody, bloody hell, what a story,' she said after a few pages. 'I got to get my brother up here so I can read it to him.'

When Lenny came up to see her after lunch the next day, she said, 'Val, you don't mind, do you? I gotta start from the beginning cos Lenny hasn't heard it.'

It took a number of afternoons to get through the story. Lenny kept saying, 'But, hang on, how could that have happened? People don't just turn into insects, there's no explanation, it's not scientific. How can you go to bed as one thing and wake up as something else? I don't get it.'

'That doesn't matter, Len,' said Miriam, 'it's not the point. We don't believe in ghosts, do we, or pixies or any of that rubbish, but you don't tell the fairy stories they can't be true. It's like a dream.'

'I never had a dream like that.'

'You probably did and you don't remember.'

'That's true, I don't remember many dreams.'

'Mine are Technicolor. Before there even was Technicolor!'

Valerie said, 'When you approach a story, it's not necessarily just about one thing. Anyone else would die of fright but he is determined to adapt to it. Why? Does he have any other choice? His family are completely horrified, disgusted by their son, and from that time onwards they begin to shun him, he's loathsome to them. It's both Gregor's ordinariness before it happens and how he goes on being ordinary inside that makes the story so interesting.'

Lenny was thinking about how the letters from Gina had stopped. He hadn't heard a word. Other fish to fry, the little tart.

'Sounds familiar,' he said.

Since Valerie was admitted her only male company had been

the rather odd Dr Limb who had the unnerving habit of *lingering* by her bed and ineffectually patting her hand then withdrawing his own suddenly, as if, she thought, he was terrified she'd infected him. She had tried to decode its meaning, coming to the inevitable conclusion that he knew for certain she was going to die. He was normal and matter of fact with Miriam, which made his behaviour to her all the more peculiar.

As an only child, Valerie had never known the protection of an older brother who in other people's families just seemed to be bothersome, noisy, dirty creatures. She thought it was pleasant to have a young man in and out of the room, sitting next to them on the veranda, filling them in on the gossip from below. He was fairly good-looking but not in the tall, sandy, blue-eyed manner of the boys she had known at Oxford with their college scarves and bottles of sherry and toasting forks making her crumpets on the gas fire and the butter dripping down their chins that she had once licked off with her tongue. She had had boyfriends, not serious ones. She was not looking, as so many of her friends were, for suitable husband material, not yet, not until she had achieved something with her degree. Lenny was dark, his eyebrows met in the middle and gave him what she thought of as a caveman look. He had entered the Gwendo with a certain shoulder swagger but had lost most of that now, which she felt was a pity. He had told her the story of his getting lost in the woods and his rescue by one of the officers. It made her laugh. He was younger than her, just a boy, an uneducated semi-lout, yet look at the way he took care of his sister – made himself her eyes and ears of the world, rubbed her feet when they were cold and smoothed her hair from her face.

Her parents had passed him in the hall when they were coming to visit her and seen him closing the door of her room behind him, nodding to them, looking them over and her father had said, 'Who on earth was that hairy Jewish gorilla? Was he bothering you? We can put in a complaint, you know.'

18

Lenny had brought Miriam and Valerie news of the children's floor above them – the secret installation, he called it, as if he was thinking of a spy movie. It was horribly sad. And he was obviously upset when he talked about it. 'It gave me such a turn seeing that little girl in prison like that. I never want to see anything like it again. It's like those orphans after the war, parents murdered or disappeared. We saw them on the newsreel in their beds with no one to love them.'

He'd managed to get the truth out of Lady Anne of all people. Had been bold enough to go up to her and ask outright since she was the longest-standing patient. She'd twiddled her pearls at first, coughed, looked at him, then said, 'Oh, where's the harm?'

The children of the Gwendo, locked away on the top floor. No one liked to think about what was happening up there. Here, one could do what one pleased, it was impossible to be actively prevented from going out for a walk in the woods before one was ready, returning like him, with ripped trousers and bloody gashes in his knees, looking done-in. But there was, she understood, a duty of protection to the little ones, the sanatorium acting *in loco parentis*. She remembered when they first started to arrive and the delight amongst the adult residents that these small people would liven them up with their games and toys and sing-songs, but they vanished upstairs and were not seen again. Often bundles were carried downstairs by Tom, the odd-job man who was in charge of maintenance, and these blanket-wrapped objects were handed over outside to weeping parents.

As she understood it, the children up there lived entirely in their own world, one in which radical treatments were practised on their bodies in the belief that a harsh attack on the disease in its earliest phases could eradicate it. 'And the poor mites don't have it in their lungs like us,' she had told him, 'but in their bones and joints, and they imprison them in full-body plaster casts and traction. It's quite horrible.' The children were without independent will, they had not yet reached autonomy. Their parents had delivered them to the sanatorium and gone away, to prevent the infection spreading to other members of the family, their sisters and brothers. The kids were in a kind of germ-free vacuum designed to disinfect them so they did not contaminate others. No school work was offered. Five years was considered to be an effective stay. The boredom was so intense some of the children had to be tied down.

All the secrets of the sanatorium were opening themselves up to them now. Valerie had revealed something she had found out from one of the nurses. When they sent anything out of there – a letter, a postcard – it was autoclaved – put in a pressure chamber to sterilise it.

'We really are unclean beings,' she said to remind them of the metaphorical similarities between the TB patients and Gregor Samsa, transformed.

'But he doesn't turn back into a man, does he, and we could be cured.'

'Yes, we could be cured,' Valerie agreed. 'It's perfectly possible that that will happen.'

'And what kind of insect is he supposed to be, anyway? A beetle, a cockroach? The way the author describes him it's hard to be sure.'

Lenny was trying to get to grips with a story that brought the horror movies he'd seen with Boris Karloff in them to an uncomfortable proximity. Being here, he realised, all kinds of thoughts filled your mind, new ideas, and nothing of that straight path into the future built on the foundations of post-war property development that he had been counting on. Here he was, discussing a *book*. And Miriam was forging on ahead, had read more than him, had more opinions about what she'd read, was sucking up words like a fizzy drink through a straw.

'I don't know, because of course we are reading a translation from the German.'

'Yuck,' Miriam said.

'What's yuck?'

'German. This Kafka was a German, then? Nasty little Kraut, if he turned into a fly himself he probably deserved it, what they done to us.'

'No, no. Kafka was Czech, he just wrote in German.'

'There's a German lady here, bit of a sad character, always on her own,' Lenny said. 'I wonder if she's read it.'

'If she has it will almost certainly be in the original language. She might be able to cast some light on the matter.'

'She doesn't talk to no one, but I don't mind asking, if you're interested.' For he could sort of see Gregor in his mind's eye, mutated into something with wings and fangs and possibly human eyes looking out with such sadness from the horrible carapace of his new body, which was how he often felt himself and what he occasionally saw when he looked at Colin Cox in the next bed.

'Yes, I'd very much like to hear her interpretation,' said Valerie.

'Give it a go, Len. See what she says, mind you remember everything.'

19

Hannah Spiegel was tuning up her imaginary orchestra. She would have them play Beethoven this morning. It was just after the time of silent rest, the suspended animation before the electric bell announced they were free to resume their activities, and books and crossword puzzles and knitting and packs of cards were picked up again, and she was left to consider what instruments she had and which she lacked. The brassy cymbal girl who had arrived a few months ago had only been sighted once. Up on the veranda, she supposed.

No one spoke to her for several reasons. She knew that some assumed she was a deaf-mute; others gave her a wide berth because she was a Kraut; she expected that there might be rumours that she had been a spy, on our side, perhaps something to do with the SOE; she might have been part of the wartime listening station in Caversham; she could be a refugee. Perhaps, it was suggested, she did not speak English.

She had visitors. A woman came every single weekend, and they would go to her room presumably for private conversation. The nurses said she did not share with anyone, she had the whole place to herself but only the medical director could say why, they didn't know. Apparently she had some other medical problems apart from the TB, was a rather complicated case.

Now Lenny was walking towards her carrying a paperback book. She had not noticed him reading before, what was it he held that she could not see? He had asked one of the nurses her name to address her politely, but was she Miss or Mrs? No ring on her finger.

Now he was by her side. 'Miss Spiegel, do you mind if I have a word?'

She tried shaking her head. Lenny interpreted this as hearing difficulties so he sat down next to her and thrust out the book, saying loudly, 'Have you read this?'

She looked down at it. Was taken aback. Of all the books, *Die Verwandlung*!

'Yes, I have,' and her words surprised her and surprised everyone who heard them, who looked around at the unremarkable middle-aged German woman, blonde hair greying, two profound lines running from her nostrils to the chin, fissures dividing the cheeks from the main features, and faint blue eyes that lost their colour altogether on grey days and became one with the overcast sky.

And then, as if she was coughing up phlegm unavoidably, or spitting blood, as she did so often, she said, 'In fact, not only have I read it, I once knew someone, in another life, who was great friends with the author.'

Lenny was sideswiped. To *know* a writer, well not him, exactly, but that close? And a foreign writer, a dead one? Books were a mystery, they came out of nowhere, that anyone could make all that stuff out of their head was inconceivable. Books had been conceived, like kids, then grown in the dark. 'So you can explain it all to us?'

Her smile had rusted up many years ago or she might have considered smiling, examined whether it merited arranging her face to present the appearance of a person amused by a request both ridiculous and difficult.

'Explain? No, no one can explain, it's not possible to do so. You experience it in your way, it's a labyrinth you must pass through but the labyrinth is yourself.'

'A labyrinth, that's a maze, isn't it?'

'Yes, that is another word.'

'Me and my sister and the girl she's sharing with, we've been reading it. They're outside on the veranda with nothing to do all day so they keep reading things. What we want to know is what exactly he turned into. What kind of insect.'

'Where does the author say he is an insect?'

'Here.' Lenny opened the book and pointed to the first two lines. *When Gregor Samsa awoke one morning from troubled dreams he found himself transformed in his bed into a monstrous insect.*

'That is only an interpretation by the translator. The German says something different, I think it is *ungeheuren Ungeziefer*, which means an unclean thing, some horrible vermin. Kafka was simply trying to express Gregor's own disgust with what he had become, so yes, horrible vermin might be more correct, I never asked Milena, maybe I should have done, but you see, I did not take the transformation literally. I understood it as meaning a thing that has no real definition. Something horrible and repellent to human society.' She paused. 'And at that time we were all that.'

Lenny felt that he was out of his depth. He wished Valerie could have had this conversation, she would have understood better, and now he would have to go back upstairs and relay its details, as far as he could remember them, and was sure not to get them quite right.

'Has he written other books?'

'Oh, yes. Several. All as perplexing as this.'

'You've read them?'

'Some, not all. For a long period I had no access to books and no privacy to read.'

She did not know why she was telling the boy these personal things. So many of the young people here, and the not so young come to that, were the type who mean no one any harm. These individuals did not get very far, in her experience. All the ones she had known were now dead. There was a poor young man in the refugee reception centre who reminded her of her cousin Otto who would sometimes go into his parents' bedroom and try on his mother's hats. But this one, he was made of rougher material and that pleased her. Roughness can be quite a virtue in certain situations, and she was pleased that he wasn't afraid of her as so many were. He might be of no use at all in the woods, but in a city he would come into his own and she did not enjoy being outside cities.

'I don't know what's coming over me in here, I'm not cut out for this way of life, you know, but you got to adapt, don't you?'

'Yes, you are exactly right.'

'Adapt without letting them get to you. So when you go back to the real world you're still yourself, but you haven't completely wasted your time. Anyway, thanks a lot, I'll go back up and tell them what you said.'

'You are welcome. I enjoyed our little conversation. I am not approachable and I don't want to make an approach. It can lead to misunderstandings.'

'Like what?'

'I don't think I can even remember any more.'

'You sit here all day,' Lenny said. 'You just seem to stare out of the window. Aren't you bored out of your skull?'

'No. I am not bored. I have had far too much stimulus, enough for a lifetime. The banality of this place is very pleasant to me, I like how nobody here, I mean we patients, can do anyone any harm and the nurses and the doctors can't make us better but still they try, even when they know their schemes are largely worthless. I find it very satisfying. I do not expect to leave here. I *hope* I do but that's not the same thing. I am safe. To be safe is more satisfactory than a young man like you can possibly imagine. And you, I rather thought you might not stay after your altercation on your first morning, looking for your sister.'

'I thought that too but the fight's gone out of me.'

'I'm very sorry to hear that.'

(Which, it seemed to him as he made his way back upstairs, to be the kind of phrase Valerie would use, or Captain Jackson, and this place was starting to rub off on him in ways he hadn't expected.)

20

Weeks pass. The reading group on the veranda is making its way through the sanatorium's library and attempting to expand the dimensions of its incarceration. Lenny has been enjoying exotic foreign voyages in the company of Joseph Conrad. There has been an unsuccessful foray into Jane Austen. Miriam throws *Pride and Prejudice* off the veranda where it lands in a rhododendron bush. 'Them girls should just get bleeding jobs instead of hanging around fluttering their eyelashes at rich fellers.' Valerie agrees to give up on *Middlemarch* when she sees it is sending them to sleep. Lenny says, 'That bird is like our teacher, Miss Prickett, always droning on, lecturing you, loves the sound of her own voice.'

And reading is not enough, Valerie admits to herself. I used to think it was everything, it isn't. I'm so bloody bored. The hands of the clocks seem to have stopped altogether. What day is it, what month? Stupor.

To Lenny, too, the days seem mouse-coloured. The officers still in their old battledress jackets have become mouse-like creatures, timid and grey.

No one is discharged well, they leave secretly without goodbyes. New arrivals disappear onto the verandas. Stuck.

Lenny wonders if he died under the pneumothorax needle.

Upstairs Miriam has become if not a different person, then one whom her own mother on visiting Sundays finds disconcertingly calm, as if the gas has gone out of a bottle of pop, her hands resting quietly on the blanket, listening.

'They're in their own little world, those two,' says Mrs Lynskey, driving away in Manny's motor from their two hours in the Gwendo. 'Valerie is a very nice lady, but Miriam doesn't seem like my daughter any more. She's been changed. I don't like it.' She begins to cry, remembering Miriam now with her hair hanging loose to her shoulders and sometimes even forgetting to put on her lipstick – things have got that bad. And it seems to her that her son and daughter are losing their youth, they are jumping a decade every few weeks and becoming old. They are old without the experience of a life.

Lenny is always trying to shake himself awake, like someone losing consciousness behind the wheel of a car. He goes for walks, not in the formless woods with no landmarks to guide him other than trees whose names he doesn't know, but down to the village. He drinks a cup of tea in the Singing Kettle. He reads the newspaper.

Princess Elizabeth has had a baby daughter, called her Anne, this bores him. It's all meaningless. Who cares? The things he wants to know about they don't print in the paper anyway.

He plays cards with Colin Cox, he listens to the stories Miriam and Valerie are reading aloud and enjoys them. He has volunteered for the Wireless Committee, which broadcasts a diet of background music designed, he supposes, to cheer them up, but is just annoying wallpaper for the ears. They've told him there's a waiting list, spots come up infrequently because the station is manned by the Chronics, long-stay patients who never improve.

He feels no worse and maybe a little better, unless he's kidding himself, but the doctors tell him the same thing, he must be patient. He doesn't know if he'll be cured or not. Yes, the streptomycin is coming, but when a day seems like twelve months he thinks he might top himself before it gets here.

He talks sometimes to Hannah Spiegel, non-committal conversations on her part. She has noticed that he has let himself go, sartorially, content to wear a dressing gown over a jumper and old trousers he has half grown out of. His black stubble on his face is always there now, he shaves only every other day and sometimes the stubble begins to turn into a beard. The light has gone out of his eyes.

She has confided that she finds the choice of music on the radio station pretty dull herself and that it could be vastly improved, and he should try a little harder to put himself forward and not accept this immediate knock-back, which surprises him because he doesn't imagine they'd have the same taste but he supposes she's just being kind. Other than that, she has no verbalised complaints, in fact she's infuriatingly passive about her situation or if there is some spark of rebellion inside her it's not something he can understand or disentangle from her placid, timid exterior and calm conversation about matters he knows nothing about.

She has, however, told him a little more about Milena, the girl who once knew Kafka, but he still has no idea exactly how Hannah knows her. He has learned that Milena was the type of person who squanders life to a ridiculous degree, inexhaustible and profligate in her affections and kindnesses, including her own feelings. She had been in such a state of sympathy with the author that she imagined that she too had TB, and blood had actually flowed from her mouth.

'Everyone fell under her spell, she was a truly marvellous person, if exhausting, and if she was here, well, certainly you would know it,' Hannah says, 'for she never developed the personality of an inmate, you could not deaden her senses or make her indifferent to the suffering of others. She did not want to die, no, not at all, but she did die, three weeks before the invasion that would liberate us. She would have loved to have seen that with her own eyes, the ships sailing across to us, the soldiers disembarking, the sounds and sights of the battle and the push forward. Of course, I believe that for all this intensity she sometimes got on Kafka's nerves.'

And so to Lenny, the bitterness that rises in him is that at least the older patients, and that includes the officers and even this strange German woman, have at least *lived* for a while – the officers in short, extraordinarily exciting, often terrifying bursts. They have been everywhere, to France, to Germany, to Burma. They have flown planes, sailed in troop ships, directed infantry through enemy terrain.

To pass the time, Lenny, who has a good maths brain directed at the kind of fast mental arithmetic bookies possess, is starting to make a count of the patients who are left-handed and to calculate the odds of which the next new arrival will be. Then Arthur Persky walks in.

21

Arthur Persky. A name to shatter glass, Lenny later thinks.

He arrived like an explosion in a mine when flames shoot out from the earth, blocks of ground are projected into the sky, bodies are catapulted towards the sun. He had a Gothic look about him, pale in the face and a black widow's peak. He was tall and lanky, he wore blue trousers in a material Lenny did not recognise, held up by a studded belt. Persky came out of nowhere, he jitterbugged in and up to Matron and said, 'Baby, wanna dance?'

Then turned and winked at the waxworks.

A Yank! A Yank from the land of cowboys and gangsters and film stars and skyscrapers and hotdogs and baseball.

Matron looked at him with her assessing gaze. She had seen them all come through the doors. They arrived with spirit; a few days on the balcony and that had evaporated, for in her experience patients always succumbed eventually to the rules, which were not her rules or the rules of the institution but the rules of the disease itself. Well, the thermometer would soon show *him*.

Persky held out his arms as if he'd stepped onto a stage, like he was Max Miller or Danny Kaye.

'I'm A. Persky, Able Bodied Seaman without medals or distinction, and man oh man, what do we have here?'

No one asked what the A stood for, though everyone wanted to know. They were too shocked, they were still taking him in. This was no way to arrive, as if already he was the king of the place, or its president. And what was he wearing? What were those strange trews?

The question they were all asking themselves was: is Persky destined for the veranda? In which case they would not see him again for months. People such as Miriam turned up like characters with bit parts, spoke a couple of lines then vanished. They descended back down from the verandas meek and habituated, feeling that the liberation from twenty-four hours in bed was enough to be grateful for.

But a few hours later Persky was down for dinner.

Nurse Chitty, walking through the day room in her tight white uniform, giggled suddenly for no apparent reason. Lenny mentally closed betting on who was going to pop her cork. All the gentle creatures, the frail officers and broken war heroes, had *nothing* on Persky. He was the most vibrant consumptive anyone had ever seen.

On Radio Gwendo yet another Strauss waltz was playing, performed in a mediocre, tinny way.

'What *is* this shit?' Persky asked, looking round, his arms spread out, making jazz hands. 'You can't dance to this oldey-timey crap.'

'Language, language,' said Chitts.

Lady Anne put her hands over her ears but her eyes were peeking at him, her bloodless fingers hot against her face.

He attempted to take Chitts by the waist. She wriggled away but it was obvious that the Persky charm had already made inroads because two pink spots had appeared on her cheeks.

Metal trays of food were being delivered to the tables. A. Persky looked at the contents.

'Okay, grub's up, I see. What have we got here?'

'Today it's shepherd's pie.'

'Punishment rations?'

Lenny laughed. 'It's not that bad and there's lots of it.'

'Mind if I join you?'

'Go ahead, plenty of room.'

The table wanted to know everything about Persky and Persky was forthcoming, he didn't hold back. They learned that he was from a place called Brooklyn, over the bridge from Manhattan, though born in the Bronx on 28 April 1924 and thus was twenty-six years of age. That he had one brother and two sisters, both parents in what he called the garment trade and his father a union man, who had taught him never to accept anything, always to question, that this was how he had been brought up and as a consequence, it became apparent, he intended to 'rock this joint'.

No one knew what that meant.

'Shake things up!'

Lenny was fascinated by his unusual clothes. 'Those trousers you're wearing, what's the material?'

'These jeans? They're denim, man, you never heard of that? Made by the Levi Strauss company for America's cowboys.'

'I don't know what he's on about,' said Colin Cox, 'does anyone else?'

'You'll get used to me.' He laughed, a short howl of humour.

Then they wanted to know what he was doing here in the Gwendo.

'I started coughing. We were docked in London. I started coughing and before I know it, there's a ball of bright red blood on my handkerchief. Wouldn't let me sail back in case I infected the passengers. They brought me here. And then I found out there was nothing to pay. Incredible.'

He put a fork full of shepherd's pie in his mouth.

'This is not good.'

'You have to eat,' said Lenny. 'We have to build ourselves up.' And felt as he said it like a teacher's pet parroting her instructions.

'We ought to do something about this. We should start a food riot.'

Everyone thought that sounded exciting, if far too energetic.

They were served a suet pudding with golden syrup.

'Have you people never heard of chocolate, pecans?' said Persky, putting down his spoon after a tentative taste.

'There's rationing; we had a war on, you know.'

'C'mon, you can always get round that bullshit.'

'So what does the A stand for?'

'What A?'

'The A in your name. Your first name.'

'Oh, that. It's Arthur. A hero and a king in olden times, or so I hear. But call me Persky. Arthur is a name I only use in bed.'

22

Looking round at the day room, Persky saw a herd of nodding, whispering, sleeping sheep. He was fundamentally into this situation for himself, he could see that in a place like this you needed to put your shoulder to the wheel, you had to oppose the regime, you had to show it who was boss if you were to survive.

A few hours' observation had led to an emerging idea. That the Gwendo was a kind of experimental station for what could be done to tear down the individual self and rebuild it in the model of the well-behaved citizen. And this thought made him sick because there would be no greater power over Persky than Persky, which was what had led him to stand up to his father, to tell the old man that he would not come down to the picket line that day, that he would not march in a circle, carrying a placard, and so his father ran to the table and picked up a dinner plate and in rage smashed it over his son's head.

Young Persky wrestled his father to the ground and held a broken shard to his father's neck.

Mrs Persky screamed for the cops, she ran to the kitchen and filled a bucket of water and threw it over them, as if they were fighting cats.

Poppa said as they stood up, water dripping from their noses,

'You're rejecting real life! The only real life is amongst the Masses. There is discipline, there is sacrifice, what makes you so special that you think you can run away, can live without comradeship? Who are you *for*?'

And when his son said, 'I'm for me, Poppa, just me,' then it was over between them and he wangled a seaman's ticket and set out to conquer time and space, those easy targets.

He had had the Gwendo lecture on learning how to be a patient. He didn't believe a word of it. All he had to do was stick it out here until he got a little better and could ship back home to the States. Or the streptomycin arrived, when he would be cured. In the meantime, he planned to mould the environment to himself, not be moulded. He had not been to prison (yet) but this was a jail, no mistaking it, and though you could, for sure, walk out when you liked, he didn't feel like taking his chances on spitting out another scrap of his lung.

When he sized people up, he saw that Lenny was the one he'd take under his wing. Lenny would be Robin to his Batman.

'Listen, we have rights,' he said to him. 'And you and me, let's face it, we have these rights because we know exactly who we are, we're not the disinherited of the earth, we're not a people with no history, we have three thousand years of a Book and a story, we have a moral meaning.' (These were Poppa's exact words – learned verbatim in childhood – he was repeating.) 'And every time the bastards try to wipe us out, we get to push back at them and come out on top. I'll tell you, something cold and hard and sick needs to form inside you. What's that about? It's the realisation of the reality of the world we live in, you have to hate it, but hating isn't enough, you have to replace that feeling with your own power to change it. Are you with me?'

Lenny didn't understand at all but yes, he was with him. Persky took the ordinary fellow like himself and showed him that he could be bigger and better than he was. The doctors rarely made eye contact, they were always looking down at their notes or holding the X-ray films up to the light. To them, you were just a set of symptoms.

124

Persky was the type who has the trick of talking to you like you're the only person in the world.

For the first time since he'd been here, he felt he had a friend, as Miriam and Valerie were now friends. Colin Cox was just someone to play cards with. Captain Iain Jackson, kind as he was, was kind to everyone, and no potential soul mate. Hannah Spiegel you went to listen to and learn. Persky was something else.

He explained him to Miriam. 'Get him up here, at the double, Len. I want to meet him.'

The Wireless Committee had existed since the Friends of the Sanatoriums donated the equipment, not long after the Gwendo opened its doors. After the installation, putting speakers in each room, they'd asked for volunteers to run the station and a few of the younger patients had put themselves forward (but they were gone, cured or dead). The Chronics were a depressing company who ate at their own table and were shunned by the post-war arrivals, for the sight of those waxen individuals gave the young soldiers the creeps. David Hubbard was their leader, the origin of the Strauss waltzes. He had held the position since 1943. He had long since got sick of the records but an element of perversion led him to put them on as part of a routine playlist. If anything, he was taking it out on the staff in the most passive-aggressive way he knew, subjecting them, as the patients were subjected, to the deadening effects of a lack of variety. He had almost completely surrendered to the Way of the Patient, he was the ultimate submissive, apart from the waltzes, the small bead of revolution still left in his heart.

'We're gonna have an election,' said Persky, 'and you know what, let the nurses and docs have their say, they have to put up with this crap same as us.'

Hubbard laughed silently. Well, good for him and let youth have its day, Persky would come to the same pass as everyone else in the end. Hubbard had no belief that any miracle drug could cure him, he was damaged in both lungs, he was on his way out. So let the

Yank take over. And to everyone's surprise, he announced that he would not stand for election. He gave the Strauss records to his young nephew, who boiled a kettle, softened them and turned them into ugly black bowls and cups and saucers.

Advisory democracy was not unknown at the Gwendo. There were patients' committees, and food committees and recreation committees, and they were elected but with little interest and only a handful of the more energetic inmates put their names forward. It was often the case that there were too few candidates for the number of spots. Appointments tended to roll over, year after year. The committees didn't accomplish much but they provided a safe outlet for a dissatisfaction about which they could do little. As a result of their efforts food began to have a bit more variety and the range of social activities was extended, particularly to serve the young officers who were bored and restless.

To Persky, these stationary objects, people leading the life of a log, needed to be *raised*, raised by fire if necessary, and he aimed to be a gun going off in their minds. Or he'd raise a gun to his own head. He knew that the way to mould this place to his needs was by grabbing everyone's attention from the get-go. That *show* he had put on, his entrance, the dancing in, had knocked him out, he'd had to sleep like the dead to make it down to dinner. He had a dream of Rio de Janeiro, of Sugarloaf Mountain, and dark-eyed girls, beach bums drinking rum cocktails, gambling. He would make Rio, with the help of antibiotics.

The medical director, Dr Limb, agreed to administer the election and be the returning officer. The first whistly upbeat chords of Strauss's *Annen-Polka* reminded him of having a filling at the dentist, the high whine, the emphatic repetition – a never-ending merry-go-round of bullying insistence that one be happy happy *happy!* He saw now that he shouldn't have been so supine, should not have let things go this far with the Wireless Committee – had even authorised payment for the replacement of the records when the grooves simply wore out, subjecting them to Straussian torture until the end of time.

He proposed that candidates submit a manifesto stating the kind of music they would play. Then they would be invited to go *on* the radio to make their case in speech as well as in writing with a sample of their proposed output. There were two hundred and seventy-six enfranchised staff and patients and eight names put their hats in the ring for six spots.

Under the influence of Persky, Lenny and Colin Cox put in a joint proposal for a variety show involving not records, but live turns by the patients themselves. There was a man who could play the banjo, for example. Someone was bound to be able to sing, at least until they ran out of breath. And what about silly games and quizzes? Lenny saw himself and Cox as a double act, Flanagan and Allen, ringleaders in the circus of variety. Miriam was delighted. Valerie said, 'Oh, what fun,' so that was enough to go ahead and get on with putting in a manifesto and going round the day room soliciting support. Captain Jackson said, 'That's the spirit, old chap, now we're talking. I'm sure my lot will go for it.' Even the Mothers' Union thought it sounded quite amusing and were prepared to lend their qualified support – 'No smut, we hope.'

Persky's own proposal was incomprehensible to the patients and stood no chance of winning. He planned a playlist of country and western, boogie-woogie, doowop, jump blues, rock and roll. No one knew what any of these were but for his small group of devotees there was a sense that they were prepared for anything he could throw at them, even if, as some suspected, it was Negro music.

Up in his room, which he shared with Terry Ormerod, a bus conductor from Camberwell, Persky had unpacked a heavy suitcase full of records, which he called platters or discs. They lay in their paper sleeves, wedged in with sheets of the *New York Daily News* from 1948. In his wheezy state he had had trouble getting the case across the hallway from the lift, which he persisted in calling the elevator, and one of the brawnier nurses had had to take it for him. The suitcase was locked. He kept the key on a chain round his neck along with a silver medallion warmed by his black chest hairs. He wore a pinkie ring and on his left arm an obscure tattoo had been etched which changed shape when he flexed his bicep.

Terry Ormerod watched Persky struggle round their room, trying to do some exercises, bending and twisting. Terry had only been there a month longer than Persky and if he was honest with himself, he was enjoying the rest, they could do what they liked with him as long as they left him alone to observe the changing colours of the sky. He wasn't afraid of death, he welcomed it.

Outside the sanatorium, people's domestic lives, their work, their social activities were in three different places and under different rules and systems. If you hated your boss, at the end of the day you could go home. If you hated your wife, you could go to the pub. Here everything took place in the little modernist masterpiece designed to break down the barriers between these different spheres and bring them under a single monolithic authority from which there was no escape at all.

And this institutionalisation was what Persky rejected. On board ship was another total institution and he had found ways round that, he always had room to manoeuvre. He had brought to the situation intelligence, his poppa's skills at union organising, and a belief that a man will always get his own way if he knows exactly what he wants.

Persky took out of his suitcase his copy of Jimmy Preston's 'Rock the Joint'. He'd bought it in Baltimore the previous year. As a travelling man, a wandering man, a rambling man, he didn't always have a machine to play it on. His music went with him, but it wasn't exactly portable. Sometimes he would burst in, gate-crashing parties he'd heard about, just to put his discs on the turntable and listen to them.

'Rock the Joint' erupted in the Gwendo. To Hannah Spiegel, it broke above her head like the dome of the universe cracking. She hated it.

No one had ever heard a song with such a steady backbeat. The pace of it was relentless. The instruments were not harmonious. A tenor sax screeched, like the hens next door to the Lynskeys. It was an *anarchy* of sound.

128

A voice was not singing but what? Shrieking? Whoever he was, what Jimmy Preston and his Prestonians, almost certainly Negroes, had to say was perverse, immoral and horribly exciting.

We'll rock a bye baby in the treetop
Don't need no wind for Mr Blues to rock.

This was no lullaby, it would wake all the dead discreetly buried some distance from the Gwendo in a cemetery maintained at Mrs Downie's expense.

We're gonna blow down the walls and tear up the floor
Until the law come knockin' at the door.
Something something high as a kite.
Something something ball tonight.

Who knew what any of it meant? In their beds and in the day room many patients were covering their ears, crying to the nurses to make it stop. The dying deliriously thought they had slipped over to the other side and for their sins were in hell where devils eternally twanged terrible electric instruments.

Lenny, doing the odds for whether it would be jam sponge, treacle tart, spotted dick, egg custard or jam roly-poly for sweet at lunch, his idle mind making perpetual permutations, heard *We're gonna jitter-bug . . . every girl's gonna cut you up* and he also had no idea what the singer was on about. But the underlying beat, the vitality, the sexual energy of the song – a world of people dancing, smoking, drinking, stealing, fucking – the racing pulse of it, acted in the same way as the electric bell. The bell that called for silence was now the universal cry to *rise*. He thought of death as the darkness and unremembered silence of the universe before you *were*. He had been softly padding towards it. Death had ceased to matter. His father died young, he'd accepted he might die even younger. The great surprise to him had been being alive at all, when the odds of it not happening, of *his* unique sperm missing its target, were simply enormous.

Somewhere, there was a party going on. He now wanted to be at that party. Nothing would do but to be at the party.

And when he went up to see Miriam, before he could sit down, she'd said, '*Did you hear that? Did you hear it?*'

'I know!'

'What did you think, Valerie?' said Lenny.

'It's not really to my taste but I can see the essential appeal of it, in a raw kind of way. It's quite interesting.'

'She talks like that sometimes,' said Miriam. 'Pay no attention.'

'I think we're entering a new phase,' Lenny said. 'I think something is going to happen, I'm not sure what it is. He's got my vote, anyway.'

'And mine.'

'And I'll vote for him because it will make a change,' said Valerie, generously.

As if small bubbles were beginning to form and rise to the surface in the process of fermentation, a growing core of individuals were beginning to carry out petty rebellions against the lunch menu, the ceaseless temperature taking after each small exertion, the extreme age of the film selections. In this emerging climate of disobedience Persky went all-out, campaigning for his manifesto, he spoke to everyone, even the Mothers' Union table whose votes he knew he had no chance of winning. He explained that the music he was proposing to play was *modern*, it was the coming of the future and whether they liked it or not, leaving the sanatorium, as he assured them they would, involved adapting to the new decade with all its clamour and contradiction and vitality.

Years later, Lenny would tell his business associates that it was from his time in the sanatorium that he learned how to pitch a project – even the most radical, left-field idea could catch on if you put the muscle into it and if, like Persky's efforts, there was absolutely no let-up in your sales patter.

23

Mrs Kitson came up the lane singing, carrying a lumpy bag of shopping. She wore a green coat tightly belted and a pair of brown brogues onto which she had painted at the heel apricot-coloured bows. Cute, thought Persky who was waiting by her front door.

Day will break and I'll wake
And start to bake a sugar cake
For you to take for all the boys to seeee!

She laughed as she saw him. 'How long have you been here?'

'Not that long. They told me where you lived in the pub.'

'Well, don't expect any cake from me no matter what I was just singing, I don't have light fingers. My pastry is a horror, Mum always said, which is funny because I'm quite good with a paintbrush.'

'Where is your mom?'

'Oh, she died just after the war.'

'No dad?'

'Flu took him when I was four.'

'Crap.'

'I know.'

'And your husband didn't make it either?'

'No, Trevor didn't come back.'

'That's terrible.'

'Coming in?'

'Sure.'

'Have you had your lunch yet? I could do us a couple of poached eggs on toast, if you like. Don't worry, we always have eggs, my aunt keeps a few hens. And I've just been to the bakers. Look, a loaf of best white.'

Persky looked around at the chocolate-brown armchairs, protected with antimacassars. On the window ledge a row of china figurines played at being Cinderella or ballet dancers or flower girls. It was a nice feminine room with some reproductions of famous art he half-recognised in frames on the walls. It seemed to him a cosy nest for a gal who lived by herself and had occasional gentleman callers. The armchairs looked like they could take some weight. You might not want to get up out of them once you'd sat down. And then the little *chotchkies* to show you who was really boss in here. His mother had a few like this, were her pride and joy, dames liked this kind of thing, he liked that kind of thing as long as he didn't have to come home to them every night.

They sat down at the kitchen table and ate their poached eggs on toast. She asked him about America and whether he missed it and he said that he missed life at sea more so she understood him and didn't mind because he wasn't pretending anything he didn't feel. He talked about the ports he'd visited and conjured up palm trees and beaches and foods she'd never heard of that he'd tasted.

'Well, try this fruit cake, one of the neighbours made it, nothing exotic about it, but it's got plenty of dried fruit and it's moist.'

She cut him a large slice. He tried to masticate it but she could tell it wasn't to his liking. He had a mouth full of crumbs. He swallowed, then sneezed.

'Oh dear, are you cold?'

'A little.' He winked.

'We'll have to see about that.' And started singing again.

Picture you upon my knee
Just tea for two
And two for tea

'Do you want to sit on my knee?' he asked her.

'Oh yes. Shall we try it? To see if I fit comfortably?'

He sat down in the armchair and pulled her down into his lap, one arm around her waist.

'What about a little kiss?' she said.

He winked again, then pulled her face towards him, his hand manoeuvring beneath the hem of her dress. No stockings! And further until, expecting to come across a cotton gusset, he reached even tighter curls and the blood rushed to his head.

'Baby!'

He began to move his fingers into the crease. She held back her head and closed her eyes.

'Nice?' he said.

'Ooh, lovely. Shall we go upstairs?'

'For sure.'

In the bedroom a china doll in a dusty lace dress looked down at them from a shelf, the little voyeur. A dappled blue and yellow glass bowl suspended from chains concealed a light bulb. Next to the bed, a wooden candlestick lamp held up a peach-coloured artificial-silk tasselled shade.

'This was my mother's bedroom, it's mine now, I just had the little room before, I hope you think I've made it comfortable.'

She took off her dress. 'As you can tell I like to feel free, I hate all underclothes, everything really, stockings, brassiere, knickers.'

His long pale body unclothed inhabited a section of the pier glass on the chest of drawers.

'You're very white,' she said. 'White as a ghost.'

'I know. When I'm at sea I catch the sun but ashore I'm a night owl.'

'You're like marble.'

'That doesn't sound too good, like a tombstone.'

'Be careful, don't exhaust yourself.'

'I *intend* to exhaust myself. That's my whole plan.'

She laughed.

'I'll tell you what's going to happen, baby, we're going to do things a little different to what you're used to but I think you'll like it, I think you'll be surprised, but I think you'll be pleased. As they say on the submarines, Going down!'

When he came back up for breath she thought she was going to pass out with the *crash* of it – the *huge crash*. He said, 'Okay, so you're all done and can you just give me a hand, it shouldn't take long.'

'You don't want to . . .'

'No, takes too much out of me since I've been sick.'

She helped him. He wasn't very hard.

'Touch my balls.'

'Okay.'

That seemed to work. Wetness eventually gushed out onto her fingers, he was clutching her breasts plaintively, went red for a few moments then seemed whiter in the face and neck than when he'd first undressed.

'Are you all right?'

'Yes, yes. That was good. Good for you?'

'Didn't you hear me?'

'That's great, honey. No, that's really great. I aim to give satisfaction.'

'I've had perfectly competent lovers but—'

'I think I can do better than competent, I hope so.'

'I mean, I've never—'

'No, plenty of women haven't.'

He coughed.

'Are you all right? Oh dear, I keep repeating myself.'

'You know what? I think I got one of your hairs stuck in the back of my mouth. But I'm going to keep it there for a while so when I go on air and start spinning my platters you'll be able to hear what a great time we just had.'

134

She was in the art room helping one of the members of the Mothers' Union with her Garden of England when she heard him clear his voice with a conspicuous cough and announce his first disc and she understood that Arthur was going to remain stuck in her own throat and there was not much she was going to be able to do about it.

Persky had won votes by various means – flirting, reasoning and finally appealing to potential rebels who didn't even know they had the power to resist. When the results were announced he had managed to scrape a spot in one of the winning positions. Everyone was amazed that this really reflected the will of the constituents. Some demanded a recount, even a re-run of the election. Since the ballot papers were not marked with the names of the electorate it was impossible to tell how anyone had voted so no one knew that Mrs Kitson, who was in charge of the count, had artistically tampered with a few of them to put Persky just over the finishing line.

No need to do that for Lenny and Colin Cox who had won easily and were already planning their Sunday Nights at the Gwendo Palladium.

24

'Man, that is terrible,' said Persky when Lenny told him about the children's floor. 'Those poor kids. It's like a concentration camp.'

'I know, that's what everyone thinks.'

'What are we gonna do about it?'

'What *can* we do?'

'Go up there and liven up the little varmints.'

'It doesn't work like that. They won't *let* you up there, they chase you out. Parents only, then just on visiting days.'

'You know you think too much of the rules. They did something to you since you've been in here, fixed you, made you a gelding, know what I mean? What are you, a *girl?*'

'For fuck's sake, Persky, you can't say that to me.'

'How old are you, nineteen, twenty?'

'I'm nineteen.'

'You should be out balling chicks and getting stoned.'

'What do you mean stoned?'

'You never smoked any hashish?'

'No. I don't even know what it is.'

'Never mind, let's go find those kids.'

'Now?'

'No, we need to make them a party first.'

Persky got Mrs Kitson to bring in a bag of balloons from the village shop. They came in all colours, he liked the red ones best, anyone would, he said.

'Now we need to blow these suckers up.'

There were no balloons in Lenny's childhood, too poor. He'd never blown one up before. It turned out to be the most heroic thing he had ever done, stopping every few moments to catch his breath, squeezing the neck to stop the air escaping, the little rubber bags expanding in stages.

'Whatever you do,' Persky said, 'don't stop and take a breath when the thing is in your mouth, it'll go down your throat and kill you.'

Lenny looked at the balloon squeezed between his fingers, a potential murderer all of a sudden. He got his first balloon inflated and tied a knot in it. It bounced softly on the floor looking full of air and emptiness and promise.

'We got one,' Persky said, 'we made a start, let's fill 'em up.'

'This is ridiculous, we're weak as new-born kittens.'

'We got to persevere, the kids are counting on us.'

'They don't even know we're coming.'

'Forget about that, Robin, my man, they'll go wild when they see us.'

It took half the morning to get the packet of twelve fully inflated. It was weird to Lenny to fill the balloons with his tubercular breath. Anywhere else they'd take one look at what he'd done and puncture the first sample with a sharp pin and chase him out of there.

Persky took the wadded newspapers from his gramophone-record suitcase. He went for the funny pages, for Blondie and the Katzenjammer Kids and Goofy and folded them into sailing boats and upended one on their heads.

'How do we look?'

'Like nutters.'

'That's great! Let's go.'

*

The children were small, their beds were tiny, they were packed in eight to a room. Persky opened the first door he came to.

A child of indeterminate sex with a pudding-basin haircut looked at him.

'Have you come to give us cabbage?'

'No, I got no cabbage.'

'Have you come to take my teddy?'

'Nope, that neither. We got balloons. Look.'

The row of faces looked up at the explosion of mainly primary colours above their heads in the sterile white environment. Their little arms were under the blankets, they all wore brown calico uniforms, they seemed to Persky to resemble drowned kittens in a bucket.

A kid smiled. It took out its hand from under the covers. Lenny went over and handed it the balloon.

'What's your name?' he said.

'I'm Ronnie.'

'You're all boys then, hard to tell.'

'Yes. What's on your head?'

'Hats made of the funny papers. You like?'

'Yes.'

'You want one?'

'Yes, please.'

They went round the room handing each boy a balloon and a hat.

'Don't give Nigel one,' Ronnie said, 'he's got no hands.'

'What do you mean? How can he have no hands? That's impossible.'

'He's *got* hands, but they've been put away.'

'Hey, kid,' Persky said, 'show me what they done to you.'

Nigel was bigger than the others, and had ginger hair, he seemed more robust but his white angry face stuck out above the sheets, and he was shaking his head.

'I *can't* show you, they put my hands away.'

'Let me take a look.'

Persky pulled down the blankets.

138

'Oh Jesus, what is this?'

'It's what they call a straitjacket,' Nigel said, 'we get put in them when we're naughty.'

'What the hell did you do?'

'I kicked a ball at a window and I broke it. They went mad. You're not even allowed balls, my uncle brought it in for me and I hid it under the bed and got it out at night-time when we're supposed to be sleeping but I kicked it too hard and then that's what happened. They threw the ball away, which wasn't fair because Uncle John gave me that and it wasn't theirs to take.'

His ginger eyelashes had started to bead with tears, a defiant face crumpling into a fight with crying. Lenny couldn't take his eyes off the child, he felt all the weight of the world's cruelty and the helplessness of its victims in this body. He was furious with the regime, and why, he thought, should I let them do what they like with me because of what they say is their good will? What if they're all *mamzers* and Nazis? He wanted to touch the boy's face, wipe away his tears, but his heart was overwhelmed with hate.

'Let me get you out of that thing.' He picked up the boy and untied the cotton straps and pulled the garment away from his arms. 'Better? Just wiggle around, give yourself a stretch.'

Persky handed Nigel a balloon. 'Hey, look at this? You want?'

'Yes, please.' Nigel took the balloon by its string and with his other hand tapped it. The pink rubber reflected a healthy glow onto his white face like a sunrise. He smiled the smile of a slice of watermelon, a perfect curve.

'We got a hat for you,' Persky said, and jammed Goofy down onto the boy's ginger curls.

The children were squealing and laughing, looking round at each other with their paper boats upended on their heads. Persky began to do Donald Duck impressions, turning his lips into a beak, the children were screaming with laughter, some stopped carefully to cough between giggles, like old men, Lenny thought. And they were so young, done nothing seen nothing and might not even grow up to have their own bird.

'Hey, we made you quite a party here,' Persky said. 'Where's your toys?'

'We don't have any.'

'What?'

'They're taken away from us when we come here and put in with all the others then once a day we're given one to play with.'

'It's not your *personal* toy,' Ronnie said, 'not the one Mummy gave you, we have to share because some children have more toys than others. Or nicer ones. It's – what is it? I don't know the word they said.'

'Equitable,' said Nigel, who was slightly older and with a better memory for interesting new words, but unable to read his explorers book because his hands were tied down.

'Screw that,' said Persky. And he picked up Nigel, set him down on the floor and took his hand. 'Lenny, get the other hand.'

'Are we going to do swingies?'

'Sure we are. Let's go.'

'Aren't I too big for that? Mum says I am.'

'No one is ever too big for swingies. C'mon.'

They took a hand on each side, soft warm, not plump enough for a kid. Nor did he have a child's wholesome smell, Lenny couldn't work out what he smelt of, something medicinal and wrong, off.

Outside the corridor was empty. They ran with Nigel whose toes dragged against the floor then lifted him in the air.

'Hey, man! You're flying!'

And Nigel felt he was flying and could fly out of the window across Kent back home to Mummy and Daddy and his little sister Christine in Swindon and never see the Gwendo again, because he was in motion with his paper hat and the balloon tied to his wrist, up in the clouds where there was no TB and no nurses and then home in front of the coal fire playing with puzzles and planes while Mummy was fetching cake from the pantry.

Two nurses emerged at the other end of the hall like curses from hell and screamed. Nigel screamed too when he saw them. 'They'll hurt me, they'll hurt me.'

'Put that poor child down immediately. Who are you? What

are you doing here? You will kill that poor boy.' A crowd of them now emerged from doors up and down the corridor, shapes in blue uniforms, white starched hats like the sails of a densely populated rescue armada. One pulled a broom from a cupboard and began to assault the two intruders with the bristles.

'I've seen one of them before, he's from downstairs, he's trouble. Do you remember a few weeks ago he—'

'Oh, *him*. And who's the other one?'

'Alison's "beau", if you can call him that.'

The nurses thought it loose and immoral to have sex with a patient and it hardened their hearts against the invaders even further. The battle didn't take long.

'Let's beat it,' Persky said, with floor sweepings in his eyes.

'I think we did something there,' Persky said in the lift. 'What do you think?'

'I think we were heroes. Poor bloody kids. The state of them! This place needs taking down, it needs—'

25

The medics told Miriam that the rest cure was doing her the world of good. She was progressing very nicely. 'They're pleased with me,' she told Lenny, 'haven't I done well? And all thanks to Val here with her stories and books and whatnot.'

Her temperature had stabilised, her sputum tests were negative, her X-rays showed an improvement. From the relentless freezing fresh air of the veranda with its view of blackbirds and pigeons and wrens, those birdies she recognised from the back of the farthings, she was allowed indoors for a bit. They introduced a regime of sitting upright in a chair, short walks round the room, then she was on basins. She had been on the veranda, now she could wash at the sink and go to the toilet. Everyone was on something. They took her down one morning to be X-rayed. She was in the other lift, the back way, then across the covered ramp to the treatment block, to the X-ray room. She didn't even walk, they wheeled her like an old lady. Waiting for her X-ray she'd met a whispering woman. 'Can you hear me? I'm not allowed to raise my voice, I'm on whispers.'

Miriam realised that there was a whole world of tortures they could put you through here and not being able to talk was bound to be the worst of it for there was no meaning without talking, without expressing yourself, loudly and firmly. Lenny had suffered a lot of pain after they collapsed his lung, he'd said it was all very uncomfortable, but imagine not being able to talk to your own brother?

Under the improvement plan, she got up. She began to walk again, felt shaky, that passed, walked a few more steps, her heart was beating like mad, thunder in her chest, iron claps, but day by day more effort, more feeling well until the Doc said she could try going down into the big room with the others, a space she could barely remember, having only passed through it on her arrival. Now Lucy, one of the helpers, came to make her bed. 'Red letter day for you,' she said.

Miriam washed her own face and her body with a flannel. She sat in a chair and waited for Lucy to come back with her breakfast. She ate porridge, succumbed finally, sinfully, to bacon (lovely taste! Shouldn't eat it but it was for your own good so what was the harm in it, waste not, want not), fried bread, butter, marmalade, cup of tea, two sugars.

'I'll leave you to get dressed,' Lucy said. 'Ring the bell if you need any help.'

She was going downstairs in the lift to join the main party. She would put on her cherry-red polka-dot costume Uncle Manny bought her from his old pal Sam Bluston's gown shop in Kentish Town. She would sit at the table and pour a jug of cream on her apple pie.

The disembodied voice of Arthur Persky: 'Now before you even drink your *coffee*, how's this for a dose of medicinal jumpin' jive?'

She sat on the edge of Valerie's bed. Valerie held up a hand-mirror for her, Miriam applied eye-black to her lashes. Before the diagnosis, there had been mornings when she was too tired to reach back and fasten her bra and she'd left it off, the effort made her pant so. Now she watched Miriam resolute, fully concentrated on the task – she'd rather kill herself than go downstairs not looking the part. Valerie rather admired this. She thought it was courageous for it mattered so much to the girl and wasn't it true that life was better when something mattered, even if it was just putting on your war paint in the morning?

She could see that she was right, with all this stuff on you could hide yourself behind it and there were certainly days when that could be very, very useful. Her own face was pale and freckly, she had dark circles under her eyes, her lashes were fine, almost invisible, her eyebrows, fawn-coloured, didn't make much of a statement. She appeared rather indistinct and was that a good thing when, as soon as she was better, she wanted to make an impression in some way? For what was education for if she did not make a career out of it? In college the dons did without lipstick, but that was an all-female enclave and the same rules didn't apply.

Finally, Miriam uncurled her rollers and brushed out her hair. She took a comb with a long tail and began to push it up and down the roots in sections. The effect was to make the hair stand on end.

'What are you doing now?' said Valerie.

'Never seen backcombing? Never had it done at the salon?'

'No. I just have it cut and washed, a shampoo and set for special occasions.'

'Never had a perm?'

'Never.'

'Well, your hair already has a lovely wave in it so you probably don't need to. Mine needs all the help it can get.'

Miriam stepped into her cherry-red skirt and buttoned up the matching blouse. She clasped a string of artificial pearls round her neck and took from the small wardrobe a fox tippet. The fox's open mouth and glass eyes screamed.

'Honestly, Val,' Miriam was saying, 'I wish you were coming down with me, it won't be the same without you, we haven't been separated for months and your stories and books have been everything to me. You've opened my mind, you know, to bigger and better things, but it's time to get back to the *real* world.'

'I don't think I can remember it any more, it seems so long ago.'

'I'm not leaving you, you know I'm not. I'll be back in a few hours and we'll have another book, your choice. I can go to the library, see what they've got. Any requests?'

'Ask for Graham Greene. See if they have *Brighton Rock*, you'll like that.'

'Done.'

Before the war, Valerie had visited the zoo in Regent's Park with her parents on a Christmas excursion to London. In a pen a turtle had fallen on its back, shell-side down, and was unable to right itself. A second turtle had drawn in its head and with its horny carapace was butting the first turtle, trying to help it turn over.

'Now look at that,' said her father. 'Without assistance the turtle would starve to death, its unprotected underbelly eaten by predators. The shell is no use at all in this position.' They watched while the turtle *ran* towards its stricken partner which toppled back over, right way up, and walked away a few inches, as if to reassure itself that it could walk and normality had resumed. It was a measure of the evolution of the turtle, Valerie thought, remembering the incident now, that altruism had entered its nature. Without it there was just unending horror of a life lived alone without help or love. She was on her back, helpless.

'Socialism,' she had said, impudently, to aggravate her father.

'No dear, charity.'

Miriam of all people was the only one capable of rescuing her in the night when she needed to get up to use the chamber pot under the bed. The bathroom was too far, her legs were too enfeebled. She thought of all the girls she'd known in college and how they had made cocoa at the midnight hour and believed that this was living. She missed her friends. But here she was an upended turtle with Miriam saying, 'Don't worry, I'll be back soon.' She had thought she would be glad of a rest from her, but instead she just felt anxious.

Lenny, waiting outside the door while Miriam did her intimate rituals, wondered what effect her appearance would have on the drabness of the day room. The whole joint was starting to wake up as from an enchanted slumber with the arrival of Persky and the new regime imposed by the invigorated Wireless Committee. The rock and roll records were bringing the patients to attention, as if the somnolent half-life of waiting – waiting to get better, waiting for the streptomycin – was coming to an end and a new dispensation was arriving.

'Are you ready yet?'

'Coming.'

It was the first time he had seen her dressed since they arrived in March. The sight of her was a shock. Had this always been his sister, walking out in a trail of cheap scent masking the general odour of disinfectant, her lips pouting in a cupid's bow? She had refused to put on slippers, her withered ankles wobbled inside her high-heeled two-tone shoes.

This place, Gwendo, was all about plate glass, calm light blue paint, the stillness, the paths through the woods, the bells that rang to punctuate your day, the reading of books, the playing of cards, and above all the ceaseless measuring of temperature, saliva in the spittoons and the mysterious darkness inside your chest which the machine could see and you couldn't. Your skeleton which held you up and would be what was left of you when the worms had finished chomping at your insides. But he and Miriam were London people, the London of coffee bars and dance halls and smoky rooms and black-market nylons and Rimmel lipsticks.

That was what she was dressing for.

Few of the day-room denizens remembered Miriam from her brief appearance months earlier. They were not expecting her. Miriam, on her brother's arm, felt no twinges of uncertainty or lack of confidence or shyness. She knew you needed to face the buggers down. The Blustons costume was too tight round the bust and hips, she'd put on weight lying in bed, it was straining from all seams and she thought, I'm like a bleedin' peach, I am, all ripe and luscious, they'll love me down there, all the old sticks and them young soldier boys and particularly the crazy Yank. She felt light-headed and light-hearted, the storybooks had passed the time, she'd enjoyed them, she'd be lying to say otherwise, but here she was, back in the swing of things, about to show them what's what. She did not brood, Valerie brooded, much good it did her.

Life rose in you like the mercury on the temperature sticks they

146

were always jamming in your mouth. And in she walked on Lenny's arm, walked in to the sound of Big Bill Broonzy singing a song called 'Horny Frog'.

Persky did not see her arrive downstairs. He was in the converted broom cupboard that was Radio Gwendo's wireless station. He had two more discs to play before lunch, before the torpor of the afternoon rest set in.

In the day room, 'Horny Frog' was drowned out by wolf whistles. The girl was vulgar, her appearance was cheap, her blouse was too tight, it was splitting at the seams under the arms, and the wafts of scent she gave off made Colin Cox gag. Even her nylons were cutting into her thighs, you could see the indentations through her skirt. To Captain Jackson, she seemed like the cartoon outlines of Rita Hayworth which decorated the fuselage of a Yank fighter aircraft he'd seen on the newsreel. Or Betty Boop.

'I don't think she'll be welcome at our table,' said Mrs Jarvis, one of the members of the Mothers' Union.

'No, indeed,' said Mrs Pope. 'After all, what would we have in common?'

Tables and tables and tables of patients were turned in her direction like snowdrops to the sun. The pale ones, Miriam thought. All them pale ones. And aren't I better dressed than any of these sticks? They've hardly made an effort at all in their tweed skirts, what a dowdy lot. And aren't *I* going to be the Queen of this place when I've got my strength back? Yet her ankles shook and the high heels seemed bloody uncomfortable and she had to sit down quickly at the place set aside for her at the table, wave her hand around the room and blow kisses at the officers' table.

Hannah Spiegel, watching her arrival, thought suddenly of other entrances she had blocked from her memory, a deep and necessary suppression of the image, like a newsreel without cameras, of columns of haggard women with matted hair, dazed, frightened, some still believing that an error had been made, that this world was not the real world. They thought only the dregs of society, the criminals and prostitutes, belonged here and deserved their period of corrective concentration. They tried to explain the mistake and were beaten.

Occasionally there was a girl like Miriam, who turned up looking like she had once been a film star, some of the patina of glamour rubbed off like silver plate, back to the base metal below, but traces left of a hairstyle, an attempt to brighten the lips with something, perhaps her own blood. In a few days you had lost sight of them, because they had become one of the living ghosts in a place of women. All women. All the female gender in their extensive variety, the lady and the maid, the professor and the pickpocket.

Miriam was not her type, she preferred a more intellectual beauty, like Sarah with her glasses, her green eyes shaded beneath them, her tweed skirt, her untidiness, her chewed fingernails, the pink spots that appeared on her cheeks when Hannah kissed the inside of her wrists or lightly touched the nape of her neck.

The modest beauty of Sarah, her bare lips leaving a dewy mark on the rim of a cup, caring nothing for hats or backchat, and devoted to rescuing Hannah, falling in love with her over the sandwiches in the refugee centre. And Hannah, waiting, not sure whether love was possible. Because where she had been nothing at all had been possible. Sarah's boldness, her declaration, saying it straight to her face without preamble, so Hannah knew exactly what she meant, a sentence without nuance, leaving the speaker no place of safety. Their hands together under the table, Sarah's little finger lightly resting on Hannah's knee, shudder of shock, electric current, and before she left, Sarah kissed her at the side of the building, under the corrugated iron roof of the coal shed. The smell of bitumen forever associated with love.

26

'Whoo!' said Miriam when Persky came out of the broom cupboard holding his rock-and-roll records. 'This is him, this is the very feller! Come and sit next to me, dreamboat.'

In bed upstairs, next to fragile Valerie, waiting to move on from basins, she'd avidly listened to the Yank and his new music. It was full of noise and vitality and sex. It was *fully intentioned*, it *meant* for you to dance till you tore your precious nylons, and got drunk on terrible wine and worse whiskey and smoked too many strong cigarettes and fell in love with the wrong guy and threw away your heart.

Miriam did not know she was waiting for Elvis Presley, she had painful yearnings for America, for skyscrapers and movie stars, she wanted to be dancing in her high-heeled Minnie Mouse shoes, swishing the full skirts of her unrationed party dress whose net petticoats went *whoo whoo whoo*, like the sound she made when she saw Persky: his slightly cadaverous figure, and his own sideburns, which he'd begun to grow since he'd been in the Gwendo with time on his hands.

Walking in from the broom cupboard, seeing her sitting down next to Lenny and knowing exactly who she was because the resemblance between the two was strong – and who else in this place would dress like a Bowery hooker? – he went down on his hands and knees and skidded across the linoleum floor to kiss the hem of her Blustons costume as if she were a princess.

The table cheered, a few of the officers took up the applause. Now things would get interesting. It was common knowledge that Persky had overcome the modesty of Nurse Chitty, and obviously he was one of Mrs Kitson's protégés, so here was a complicating factor, for both those women were semi-detached from the hourly life of the patients with their own private quarters and different routines.

The Lynskey girl was on the same regime as him, she could and would watch him like a hawk. She was blowsy and common and over made-up like all the clichés about fruit – peaches, melons the whole bowl. It was undeniable that she was Persky's type in as much as anyone who turned on the sex-appeal neon sign was his type.

She took his hand, queenly, as if the folding chair was a throne, and pulled him to his feet. He bowed from the waist and came back up a little breathless and sat down quickly. She had heard so much about him, and heard his voice on the radio, that she had forgotten that he was like everyone here a consumptive patient, she was a little disappointed to see that he was not Superman as she had imagined, but ill, like everyone else. But still, whoo.

'I'm Mimi,' she said.

'I thought you were Miriam, have I got this all wrong?'

'Sometimes I'm Mimi, too.' She had decided she wanted her florist-shop name back, it was more up-to-date.

'Okay, I get that. So what do you think of rock, rattle and roll? You heard my records?'

'I love it. You can wake the dead with that sound.'

'Exactly.'

He wanted to say more, but found himself panting. The floor-slide had exhausted him. He didn't know how long he could keep it up, it was good to sit. He hoped he had done enough and he wouldn't need to repeat the performance, it had made him feel like an old man. There was no way he could keep three women in play – the art teacher, the little nurse and the sister – it wasn't possible for a person in his condition and one would have to be given the old heave-ho. It was, he understood, *expected* that he would become Mimi's boyfriend. Everyone in the day room was watching them, there was no way out of this situation and sure, she was luscious in her too-tight clothes. At any other time he wouldn't have had a second thought about *Oh baby-ing* her and burying his head between her big fat tits. But once you embarked on a relationship with a girl in here, a patient, it was going to be all hand-holding and comparing X-rays and he, Arthur Persky, did not wish to tie himself down to any girl when he was only twenty-six years old and soon to be cured and shipping back out again, not with a sweetheart in tow like some superfluous lifeboat.

But sometimes you looked at a girl in the morning when the face-paint had worn away, when the eye-black they put on themselves was smeared across the tender lower circles, and the lipstick had lost its stain leaving just a rosy outline. These traces of their masks always moved him. They were tender girls beneath the bravado, sleepy, the corners of their lids crusted with night-dust. He would put his hand on their hearts to feel the beating or watch the rise and fall of the lungs as they took in the ambient air.

There was too much of her, and she was too much in a way that he could not decide was a good thing or a bad thing. And then while he was thinking, What am I going to *do* about this chick, she started telling him some story about a group of dames in the South of France. She was laughing while she was telling it and the words were tumbling quicker and quicker, she was throwing soft snowballs of words at him, then on she went to another tale about a guy turning into some kind of bug, which he didn't follow exactly, not making any sense, until finally she said, 'And you know one night, when it got really freezing, we had to sleep out in the *snow*.'

'The snow?'

'Yes, I've been on the veranda for months with my friend Valerie and all we had was the bloody trees and each other, it was so cold, they gave us hats and scarves and piled blankets on our beds

151

because the air is supposed to be clear and pure but Arthur, I was so cold.'

'I'll warm you, baby,' he said, and took her hand. 'I'll wrap my coat around you, I'll burn a candle for you.'

Miriam felt tears. You lay out there and dreamed and the dreams could not come true, you dreamed of getting out of bed and lighting out for the city but you couldn't get out of bed, you couldn't walk any more, and you dreamed of a fellow who understood you were so cold you thought your blood was freezing and your heart was freezing and he cared that you were cold. Here he was. Arthur Persky was what she wanted. He was holding her hand. His little finger tickled the inside of her palm. He winked at her across the bread rolls and plates of mashed potato and cabbage and dry slices of beef.

The Mothers' Union was watching, everyone was watching. Mrs Kitson, arriving after her lunch at home to take the afternoon's watercolour class, saw them. She knew Persky was frailer than he appeared. She didn't know the girl, didn't remember her from her arrival months ago. Who was she? A green stick of jealousy erected itself in her heart. All her boys had been hers alone, except for Persky whom she had to share with the little nurse. Was this some kind of love affair blossoming here in the Gwendo? If so, it was unbelievable, nothing like this had ever happened before. Of course, flirtations, crushes, but love? Look at her eyes, what were they full of? *Moon.*

'I want everyone to call me Mimi,' she was saying, 'even you, Len. I'm Mimi from now on.'

27

Peter rang Sarah at work to invite her for a swim in the underground pool in the block of flats in Pimlico he had moved to when he became an MP. 'How very smart,' said Sarah, 'how luxurious.'

'I know, but don't think we're all grandees here, we have every type, businessmen, taxi drivers, even. Then let me take you to the House for tea on the terrace. It's fun, you might enjoy seeing where we're making everything right. You haven't been to the House before, have you?'

'No.'

'Excellent. I'll buy you a slice of walnut cake. It's very good.'

She had been relentless, phoning him, writing him letters, outlining in more detail Hannah's past circumstances and current situation. Peter had evaded, but he understood he was dealing with the ruthless force of love.

The real reason he asked her to spend the afternoon with him was because he was bored. The House was not sitting but he was unable to get away, to Italy, the Lakes where the light cheered him up and there were wonderful girls and plenty of fantastic food. Spaghetti and clams, he could still taste them. And a piece of veal with a sage leaf round it fried in plenty of butter. But he couldn't bunk off, duty called and called and called and there was not enough fun. Behind the scenes they were grinding through the bloody Allotments Act, abolishing the restrictions on keeping hens and rabbits on those patches of spare ground. And one hadn't imagined that the NHS would be so expensive, for how could one have known that the middle classes would use it, and with such enthusiasm? All his friends had taken up their numbers and were leaving old Dr Arbuthnot or whatever his name was.

For as his pal Charlie Keane said, 'Just gives you more money to spend on booze and girls and racing.' There was such a cash shortage, they were going to have to bring in a fee for spectacles and teeth, though Nye said over my dead body.

The information he was ready to impart could have been given over the phone but he thought she surely owed him *something* for his efforts on the German woman's behalf. In other circumstances he would have made it clear that a seduction was in order but that was out of the question so he would merely make do with her company. A girl is a girl after all, even when her heart has hared off in another direction.

'And have you got a costume? No need to bring a towel, I can lend you one.'

Yes, she said, she had a costume. It dated from before the war when she went on holiday to Cornwall with a group of school friends and they had bathed in stinging cold water in June off a beach at the Lizard Peninsula. She had not rinsed it out before she put it away and it smelled of salt and seaweed, a few grains of sand were still caught in the crotch: a modest garment in a very sensible navy with white piping. Picking it up and holding it against her she thought of the girl she had been who did not want to attract attention to herself, not from boys or from anyone, because she thought that if she was much as looked at by girls they would guess and she would redden and blurt out everything. Those days were long gone. Now she had armour and self-confidence and Hannah who had taught her how to endure. She turned the suit round. Two mammoth moth holes right across her bottom.

The building where Peter lived was only a few years old – astonishing place, she'd heard of it but never been. She was tethered to north London and the studios, she never came down here except to go to the Tate sometimes for exhibitions. Hannah had asked to see the Turners and she had taken her to admire the fluid world; from then on Hannah said she always looked up at an English sky and saw not weather but paint and brushstrokes, and this was for her remarkable for she admitted that she was not so visual and not usually moved by a flat thing on a wall.

She walked down to Sloane Square from Knightsbridge Tube, nipping into Peter Jones to buy a new costume. You could buy dresses and gloves and steam irons and sofas and refrigerators and diamond necklaces and clocks and books and monogrammed notepaper and all she wanted was a swimming costume. And perhaps she should buy stockings too. She felt the odd sense of exultation, ridiculous really, of being able to walk over to the counter and say, 'I'll have two pairs in Cinnamon, please,' and have them wrapped up without having to get permission to buy from a cardboard booklet. She ascended in the lift to the ladies' room to get changed into her new two-tone yellow and black suit, which made her look like a wasp but it was the cheapest one they had and she couldn't imagine herself swimming again for a long time.

Scent of soap and powder. Mirrors in which the reflections of women – fat, worn, wrinkled, buttery – anxiously peered at themselves. Weren't they angry, she wondered, about all this perpetual patching up of faces that were coming apart? Did they not wake in the morning and raise their heads with the weight of their metal rollers slavishly held in under hairnets and think that today they would not bother even to wash their faces let alone smear their cheeks with beige cream and apply a scarlet paste to their mouths, motes of powder flying everywhere? But Hannah had said, 'Oh, don't deny members of the female race their little pleasures. I can assure you, everyone rushed for a lipstick as soon as we could after the liberation. It made us feel human, like we did not belong to a horrible third sex set apart from other women. When our hair started to grow, we wanted to wash and set it. Even me. This is normal, my dear, normal.'

She lit a cigarette and leaned against the sink. Everyone smoked. You would go mad with nerves if you didn't and have to take a hot milky drink before bedtime to get you to sleep. Her clothes stank of nicotine and smoke. Hannah noticed but said nothing. The smell of Sarah was a complicated mixture of soap, tobacco, a hormonal musk and the ink of typewriter ribbons. Her fingers were indented with the marks of her pencils.

Then looking at her watch she brushed her hair, descended in the lift, came out onto the King's Road and walking along Chelsea Bridge Road reached Dolphin Square, a riverside fortress of a thousand newish flats. You tramped through endless corridors to reach your destination and she thought, This is where Hannah and I should live, because among such anonymous walkways nobody could possibly be interested in your affairs. No washing lines, front gardens, nets over the windows here. But would Hannah feel that it reminded her too much of an institution and prefer something more domestic, more vernacular and red brick and homely? Actually, she had no idea. She had tried to get her to talk about the life they would live when she was well, but Hannah had always resisted, said, 'Here we are, what more do we want?'

Lying together on a narrow bed surrounded by spittoons and thermometers with the thump of a bed on wheels being delivered out to the veranda on the floor above.

Peter opened the door in a maroon spotted dressing gown. 'Welcome! Would you like to change? I'm ready, we can go straight down. I've got towels for us.'

'I'm already in my costume. What a nice flat. Everything is so new.'

'I know, and I can walk to the House in twenty minutes flat. It's often the only exercise I get all day.'

A row of sketches in square black frames led through the hall into the sitting room.

'My Henry Moore collection. Good, aren't they?'

'Peter! They're all nudes.'

'Oh, ha ha, I suppose you're right. I hadn't noticed.'

They went down in the lift to the pool. She got in before he'd taken off his dressing gown and raced up and down doing competent, efficient breaststroke. Peter watched her arms like blades in the water. Funny old girl, he thought. We were all in this together, that was the purpose of his political life and of his party, the clearing of the slums, the building of five million new homes, the creation of the Health Service, ironing out difference, but could you ever, really? Wasn't life just made up of endless oddballs like her?

You tried to be fair, you tried to have no special preferences, everyone had their own set of individual grievances. They came to him with their tales of sorrow and injustice and you tried to help but God, he had had absolutely no idea there would be so *many* of them. The middle class was a thin lacquer overlaying a great sore of misery. He was middle class, wasn't everyone? He'd thought so until now. People like him had connections, they knew how to make things work to their advantage and that was wrong, but how the hell do you stop yourself? Are we not individuals first, members of society second? Nothing was fair, though you did what you could to make it fairer.

So he had stuck his neck out for the German woman, made some enquiries about her, how she had arrived in the country, sponsored by one of the Displaced Persons organisations. The camp she came from was not one he was familiar with, a peculiar place just for women, north of Berlin. Awful-sounding hell-hole. She'd been used as a slave labourer by an electrical company called Siemens; no wonder she was in bad shape. The thing about Sarah's friend was that she really wasn't a heroine of the Resistance of any kind, nor was she put away because she was Jewish. She was no more than a school music teacher. She was not a concert pianist or a violinist or an opera singer, she just taught girls the rudiments of notation and prepared them for their examinations and conducted the choir, singing, inevitably, *Lieder* which Peter couldn't stand, particularly Schubert, God how he hated *Winterreise*. Hannah was just an ordinary citizen of Germany (Stuttgart, he had learned, where they made cars), who was put away because she and one of her pupils had been found together, in the empty music room, kissing.

One knew queers. One felt both repulsed and sorry for them. Some made his flesh crawl with their simpering and lisping, others were such frail creatures, hardly equipped with any of the necessary resilience to live a normal life. Others seemed straight as an arrow. You were in the army with them, you fought alongside each other, they were killed, you felt a stone grow in your chest at the sight of the humped meat which was all that was left of a chap, then you heard later from the stretcher bearers that under their uniforms they wore pink silk and lace drawers with a Fortnum & Mason label! With women, the distaste was different, they were often butch types, aping men with their short back and sides and suits and ties and they gave him the creeps in another way, but Sarah was just a normal girl, you couldn't possibly have known. There was absolutely nothing odd or bohemian about her and he had spent enough time with her never to have had the least suspicion.

Look at her up and down the pool, her hair secured under her rubber bonnet, it was all a mystery. He knew he would have to marry one day because that was what was expected of you. Who wanted to be a confirmed bachelor in a fusty old flat with a cleaning woman coming in once a day to empty the ashtrays? He supposed he must get on and find someone, everyone was rearranging themselves in twos, like the ark. There would be a girl out there for him somewhere, though preferably not in the Labour Party, they tended to be hard work, intense and driven and opinionated. He was looking for a girl who was all laughter and straight seams and smelt nice.

'Aren't you coming in?' she cried from the deep end.

'Yes, just a minute.' And he dived splashily, overtaking a slow-moving Cabinet minister whom he pretended not to recognise. The place was crawling with Members of Parliament, God knows what plans were hatched behind those thousand doors.

An ineluctably Tory face (he could never have stood for another party, whatever his convictions, no one would have believed him with that Colonel Blimp ginger walrus moustache) puffed past. Peter recognised him from the Opposition benches. A total reactionary and hypocrite with a Cheshire seat, using the flat to screw his two mistresses, a blonde girl from the Westminster typing pool and a shop assistant from Gamages whom he'd actually waited for at the staff entrance with a bunch of cheap flowers, like a stage-door Johnny. Pulling himself out, the fat fellow looked Sarah up and down as she stood shivering and drying herself off after twelve neat lengths.

Peter gave him the evil eye, a gimlet glance he'd learned from his grandmother.

'Oh, sorry, old chap, does she belong to you? Bit plain, anyway. You keep her.'

They were scum. Utter scum. He hated them.

Sarah said, 'I don't really like this place, I'm sorry. I don't really know if people are showing off or hiding.' And it seemed unbelievable to her that wherever she was in London she somehow seemed to be at the heart of the Establishment, if that was what the BBC was, and this certainly was, and where she was going next was its very beat.

I pass, she thought. I have that knack. I don't know myself how I do it. If she wore a mask, then the mask was made up of her tweed skirt and cream blouse and gold locket at the neck, her new stockings, her mouse-coloured hair brushed in waves on each side of a parting, her green eyes. A mask made of her own body skin.

After they'd dried off and dressed they walked to Westminster. He took her through the panelled halls where she recognised this face and that from the newspapers, famous visages of important men with briefcases, scornful or worried or laughing at some parliamentary joke – talking as they walked, quoting figures and statistics and graphs and targets and in such gibberish that it would make her head ache to listen to it for more than five minutes, which was why she took so little interest in politics. Those ties and bow ties and polished shoes and the important sense of purpose of those who wore them, which eluded her altogether, apart from her little television programmes, which seemed to her now to be small and inferior compared with the vastness of Empire and wars and house-building and hospitals and schools. But it was a man's world and no wonder she felt so little for it.

They passed a man in a frock coat, buckled knee-breeches, a white bow tie and buckled shoes. How ridiculous, yet *Hannah*, she thought, might actually love it, delighted with the fancy dress, for what harm could possibly come, she would probably say, from such innocent ritual? She made a mental note of the man's attire to describe to her at the weekend.

And then they were out through a door and returned to the sunshine and sat down on the terrace under Big Ben at that place where power expanded outwards, across London, across England, reverberating to the edges of the British Empire, the iron gongs of Parliament and the law and the war.

Coal barges trawled the river. They were building on the opposite bank. All kinds of concrete structures were being erected, palaces for the arts. At work the other producers argued about the value of the site so far from the West End, who on earth would want to trudge across Hungerford Bridge to reach it unless you were coming south from Waterloo and who would be? The zealots among them thought that television would simply wipe out the need ever to go to the theatre or to a concert again, you would just sit at home and everything would come to you.

But Sarah quite liked what she saw. It was nice being in a new decade with a pleasant number, the curly 5, the fat 0, no longer the sharp points of the 4, which could rearrange themselves into a swastika if they felt like it, and had done. They were exactly halfway through the century. War was in the process of becoming a memory, not a situation to be endured and survived. Anything new had to be a good thing. She sometimes had a vision of all the red-brick Victorian houses of London being flattened to make way for unassuming beige and white boxes in which everyone could live calmly, with central heating and fitted kitchens.

'Huh,' Hannah had said.

One didn't know what that meant.

Peter began to talk about the rehabilitation of the opposite bank and the festival site, which was coming along quite nicely, but Sarah said, 'Look, I don't want to be rude, but do you have anything to tell me or not? If you can't help why not just say so? Time is running out and I need to be certain one way or the other.'

'You really are a terrier, aren't you?'

'That's what Daddy said.'

'The old boy was right. Well, skipping the pleasantries, I do have good news. A new shipment of streptomycin and the PAS pills you take with it has arrived and I've arranged to have some doses sent to the sanatorium your friend is in. There will be enough courses of treatment for six patients and I've been in contact, though not directly, with the medical director, instructing him to make her one of those guinea pigs. The implication being that we owe her something on account of some unspecified assistance during the war, which he seems to have swallowed, and I understand she'll start the treatment in the next couple of weeks. It's the first lot of batches they've received and they have to have some training in how to administer it but after that it should be plain sailing.'

'Oh, thank God.'

'Look, Sarah, you must understand, it might not work, it doesn't always, some people have adverse reactions apparently, others are too far ... never mind. Just don't get her hopes up too high, please. I did what I could, now you have to wait and see. The other thing I need to ask you is to keep this completely to yourself. Don't even tell her, just let her think it's random that she's received the treatment. It could cost me my job if it came out that we were giving preferential treatment under the NHS, especially to a refugee. Well, you know what I mean. People are heartless and unkind. Particularly in these times, they don't like pushing to the front of the queue.'

'Oh, I won't tell anyone; there wouldn't actually be anyone to tell.'

'Ah. Of course not.'

'But it will work, I'm quite sure of that.'

'Why are you certain? How can you be? The doctors don't even know, if they did they wouldn't waste the stuff on the hopeless cases.'

'It's Hannah herself, she can overcome anything.'

'Look, you're just speaking metaphorically, but I understand the need for hope.'

'It isn't hope. She'll be fine.'

'Whatever you say.'

Something had broken in the world. A vast crack had appeared caused by the end of the war and she and Hannah were on one side of it and everyone else was on the other. A new continent was forming, an original landmass rising from the sea in which she and her love would be normal people leading ordinary lives. It was to be the rule here that women loved women and men loved men and no one would remark on it. For the moment, this continent existed only in spots above the waters, such as inside Hannah's sanatorium room and the wardrobe where her dresses hung at home in Muswell Hill, but soon the sea would subside and the new reality would emerge. It wasn't a dream.

'Cake?' Peter was saying. 'The walnut is definitely the best. Don't know what they put in it but it's very moist.'

'What do you want me to do in return? There must be something, I'm incredibly grateful.'

'Just promise you'll vote Labour in the next general election. Will you do that?'

'Of course I will, is that all? But isn't it a long way off?'

'I don't know, we have such a little majority now. We increased the popular vote but it just piled up in all the wrong places.'

'But you'll be all right, will you?'

'Probably not, to be honest. Touch and go in my seat.'

'And what will you do then?'

'I don't know. I'll find something.'

'Try television!'

'You know the awful thing is, it might have to come to that.'

When she said goodbye, Peter continued to sit, smoking on the terrace watching the coal barges and thinking about his own future. How odd it was to have, while still only in your late twenties, the power of life and death as if you were God, simply by writing a note and making sure it was in the right hands, was not intercepted and interfered with. In what other job could you make something of yourself and of your country? He wanted to carry on, finish the task they'd all started five years ago, but he felt that it wasn't going to come to that. There was what he could only describe as an odd *mood* in this new decade, of not surrendering to a higher purpose but just being in it for yourself, wanting fun and holidays at the seaside, and who the hell could blame them?

He threw his stub into the river. She was almost certainly right. Television was the coming thing, he'd just have to burrow his way into there one way or another.

28

It was 12 September 1950 when Dr Limb sat down in his office with a packet of cigarettes and the files of every single patient in the sanatorium. It was 5711 in the Jewish calendar and the day was Rosh Hashanah, the new year, when God sat down to do his annual accounts like a tax officer but with much heavier penalties. In the Book of Life God was inscribing the name of everyone who was to live and everyone who was to die in the twelve months to come, an arduous task since each required careful consideration of their good deeds as well as their evil thoughts. God was the Law.

Well aware of the situation and superstitious, in Dean Street amongst the market traders and the theatrical impresarios and the actors and the shop girls, Uncle Manny had his head bent over his book and was rocking madly under his prayer shawl, hoping for the best. There was a ten-day grace period between now and Yom Kippur when with a heavy bout of atonement and fasting you might be able to talk God out of it, as Moses had once persuaded God to back off his plan for a total genocide of his children when they had got on his nerves once too often and enough was enough.

Not that you would have immediate confirmation, you had to wait and see what the next twelve months would bring. God was completely unpredictable. For example, from Manny's point of view, in a year, anything could happen. There could be another general election and the socialists could be out on their ear and a time of opportunity would arise for entrepreneurs like himself.

In Kent, Lenny and Persky had set up a makeshift shul in the art room and held a scrappy, abbreviated service. They gabbed long and hard in Hebrew. Persky actually took a yarmulke and tallit from his room wrapped up in a velvet bag with the sign of the star on it. His mother had given it to him before he went to sea. It was one of those items that you never knew whether it might serve a purpose, get you in with the right crowd or at least a free hot meal from some religious types who liked to take in young strangers and feed them up.

Miriam did not take part. Learning Hebrew was for the boys, a necessary accomplishment on the road to the bar mitzvah. She would sit with her mother in the ladies' gallery, gazing around at the hats and the outfits and down on the velvet-covered heads of her brother and uncle. She emerged from her room on the Holy of Holies to sit outside on the lawns in the mild afternoon sunshine, Persky holding her hand like a couple.

'In a year,' he said, 'we'll look back on this place and think, *Are you kidding? Was I really there?*'

'Where will we be?' asked Mimi.

'Anywhere you like, baby.'

'As long as it's with you, I don't mind.' She adored him; it was worth coming here and staying in bed to meet the wondrous Arthur.

Lenny was also thinking that in fact coming here had not been such a bad thing. He had read books, and some books! He was making inroads on the wireless and enjoying it. When he got home maybe he wouldn't work for Manny after all, but strike out on his own, though doing what he had no idea. Upstairs, he and Valerie were spending afternoons together chatting while Miriam and Persky canoodled or whatever it was they did in Persky's room, having sent Terry Ormerod away to play billiards. Valerie, who needed help just sitting up, had started to rely on him to reach her cup and her handkerchief, it was the very least he could do for her. They got on. He didn't really understand how it had come to this, couldn't explain it to himself. Valerie, with greater self-insight, thought she was simply starved of male attention and he would do as well as anyone. And if this upset Edgbaston, well so what?

Dr Limb looked at every file. He filled the ashtray and drank five cups of strong sweet tea to give him energy for the exhausting task. Halfway through he understood he probably needed a new pair of spectacles, one of the lenses had a long scratch he had squinted past for months. His skin felt dry as he turned the pages, he wasn't as well as he would like to be. This colossal reading effort tired him terribly, he would start to run a temperature if he wasn't careful.

He was familiar with the initial results of the trials that had been carried out three years earlier. They had tried various treat-ment times for injected streptomycin. It had been planned that all patients in the trial would be treated for six months but this was moderated after it became apparent that the ones who recovered best needed less time. Some patients would do well and treatment was stopped because the disease appeared to be arrested – arrest not cure was the modest goal. In other cases it was stopped because the patient became worse. It might have been due to resistance among bacilli, or other aspects of their individual condition. During the trial all the patients had been kept on bed rest, allowed up to use the lavatory only if they were well enough. Others just got the bed rest and it was against that which streptomycin was tested. It did rather seem that the streptomycin was winning.

And it was quite possible that whoever received one of these courses of treatment could be going home for Christmas, never to return.

He understood that he had some leeway, he might make his own decisions. Streptomycin alone, streptomycin combined with the PAS pills, streptomycin combined with bed rest or pneumothorax, or even thoracoplasty. It was largely in his hands as long as he faithfully kept notes and reported them back to his superiors at the Medical Research Council.

Only six, and who on earth did you choose? One course had already been allocated to the German woman, he had no idea why, the letter had come with a handwritten note from someone in the Ministry of Health requesting she received one of the first doses. Her file contained the referral from the doctor at the DP organisation in London explaining that the tuberculosis had been contracted in a concentration camp in Germany and she had survived many privations but the actual cause of her incarceration had not been explained. So why was the Ministry taking such an interest in her? The only possible explanation was that she had been a member of some kind of Resistance group and perhaps now they had an urgent post-war espionage assignment for her in the Soviet sector. She was a nice enough woman, silent, watching, but placid. The perfect patient in many respects, she behaved with meticulous attention to the rules, never complained. He wished there were more like her.

Moving on, he faced an impossible choice. So many, so sick, so desperate in their individual ways and each one perfectly deserving of a cure, he wasn't treating venereal disease, after all, they had done nothing to bring this condition on themselves; it was just bad luck or poverty or a weak constitution.

After a while he decided to arrange the files into various groupings to give him a sense of how to weight the various demands. In the first, of course, were the members of the Mothers' Union, those poor women deprived of their children, missing them terribly. So many little ones being brought up by harried incompetent husbands, housekeepers, grandmothers and maiden aunts. 'And now I'm completely forgotten by Roger,' Mrs Turner had said to him, on the edge of tears. 'My husband told me he'd said he doesn't have a mummy any more.' One candidate must certainly come from this pile.

Then the officers. Many here to choose from, all serving their country with honour and bravery and coming home expecting to start new lives, youth still on their side, and then afflicted with this. There was no doubt that Captain Iain Jackson would be a top contender, a very nice young man, energetic in representing others and doing so in a perfectly reasonable, common-sense, matter-of-fact manner. They had done their best with him but he did keep coming back, poor fellow. He deserved to make the cut, but on the other hand, didn't that unruly bunch need someone like him to keep them in order, enforce discipline? He would be sorry if Jackson left, cured, he was a useful intermediary.

He considered next the young people, those who had endured the bomb shelters or evacuation and were now at the stage where everything should be girlfriends and boyfriends and dances and tennis parties but instead were wasting their best years in bed. Valerie Lewis was, of course, at the top of this pile. He would have to come back to that decision last.

The children, oh the poor children. One's heart went out to the mites, away from home, frightened (there had been two new cases of little ones trying to escape after the absolutely disgraceful incident of the invasion and little Nigel Coomb's parents were livid when they found out), but from what he had read, they were the ones most likely to have an adverse reaction to streptomycin, so one would have to leave it to the parents to make the decision for them and it would have to be a truly *informed* consent. And how informed could they really be, without medical training? Would the sanatorium survive the probing over a child death from experimental treatments?

The Chronics. Those who had been there many years surely deserved the injections under the rule of first come, first served? Without even looking at the files, he knew that at the very top of that list was Lady Anne, the pinnacle of their little society, the first, the original patient at the Gwendo, who had moved in only a few days after the builders had finally left and before the grand opening. He recalled the ribbon cut by one of the Downies' actress friends who had starred in an Alfred Hitchcock film and turned up in marvellous furs, drenched in a French scent and disappeared off again to luncheon on the arm of the mayor of Canterbury. A photograph of the occasion hung on his office wall.

There she was, the Lady, waving a handkerchief at the camera, and himself beside her. Only thirty-two years of age and his hair dark in the sunlight. It was a long time since he had considered Lady Anne's case, not, he thought, since the beginning of the war. He couldn't remember the last time she had been X-rayed. She was a recidivist, who seemed happy enough and with few remaining skills to cope with the outside world. In many ways she, not him, was the pinnacle of their little society, kind, gracious, enervated.

In the summer she allowed herself to be wheeled out to the gardens where she raised to the sun whatever part of her face wasn't covered in hat brims and veils. The other patients regarded her as a source of society gossip for she was one of those types who said they knew a woman who knew a man who had danced with Mrs Simpson and been surprised to feel her hand on their bottom. Lady Anne had been invited to the royal wedding. She was unable to attend, of course, but still ('they are so good, they have not forgotten me') she was pleased to have received the card, the stiffie, she called it, and had sent christening presents when little Charles and little Anne were born. Darling matinée coats from the children's department at Fortnum & Mason.

And then the rest, the odds and sods. Colin Cox, the bridge player chap, all the middle-aged bus conductors and shopkeepers who had become entitled to this treatment because of the Health Service, individuals who did not really interest him, except as bed fillers. Would one necessarily have to choose one of those? The American might be pushed out, he was nothing but a troublemaker. And the Hebrew boy with the black-market connections who was spending too much time with Miss Lewis. His sister – he was unsure what her actual condition was at the moment. She would need further examination.

For Miriam had done very well for a few days after she had been permitted to come down to the day room but then her temperature had soared, she had developed a fever and been returned to bed for a week. He had not attended her himself but Matron had advised him that another set of X-rays might be in order. Then she rallied, her temperature fell, and he had cancelled the appointment. These relapses were common and one had no idea where they might lead.

Finally, himself.

It could be argued, he thought, that he should receive the most experimental, earliest dosages, for were he to be permanently cured, would he not be better able to serve his patients? On the other hand, if the cure was indeed permanent, what exactly would become of him who had imbued all those under this roof with his perennial maxim: learning to be a patient? He was frightened. He had not married because of TB, he had not made friendships beyond the small inner circle of doctors and Matron. He had tea with Mrs Downie, that was all, never went to the theatre or the cinema or took a holiday. He lived in his double suite composed of two rooms, one adapted as a sitting room with comforts such as a sofa and bookcases and footstools and a personal wireless. All his meals were taken in the staff dining room. He had nowhere else to go.

No, he would stay, would stay until the bitter end, when all there was to do was lock the door for the last time. But this supposed that streptomycin really was a silver bullet, and he doubted it. On the other hand, he was hearing that the socialists wanted to give every single child the BCG vaccination, which was supposed to protect them against TB and other illnesses.

Morally he disapproved, for was it not, like pasteurisation of milk, merely papering over the cracks of underlying problems of public health? Armed (literally) with a shot in the bicep, the youth of the nation, he read in the *Daily Telegraph*, would almost certainly revert back to the kind of slovenly living that had weakened the resistance of their parents and grandparents. Though one found it hard to square what he thought of as the 'healthy-living propagandists' with individuals like Valerie Lewis who had grown up in a nice home and seen nothing of the sordid world apart from her Oxford college.

He made his selection. He would give the benefit of the doubt to Captain Jackson who deserved to be offered the chance. From the

Mothers' Union, Mrs Clarkson who had five children and needed to get back home to look after them. Of the Chronics, he chose Desmond Foye, the builder of matchstick models of cathedrals purely because the craze for collecting matches was driving the staff mad. The young person was Denise Edwards, a charming and lively young lady with a fiancé in Hove and a postponed engagement. For the sixth course of treatment, he decided to leave the decision in the hands of Mrs Wright, matron of the children's floor, as to whether a course would be allocated and discuss the matter fully with the parents. There was to be no place for the odds and ends.

And having done his duty he called for Matron to come and take away the files and smoothing his cuffs, lit another cigarette. Not his beloved pre-war ones but Player's. A less than adequate smoke.

Once, a very long time ago, he had had a girlfriend, but she had sacked him when he was diagnosed and that was the end of that aspect of his life. There was no other patient for whom he had felt what he called a *tendresse*. He loved Valerie, couldn't say why. In a film or a novel, the age difference would not matter, or at least it wouldn't if he was handsome and distinguished, but he was neither of those. He was short, stocky, a little pigeon-toed, wore pince-nez, had let his clothes grow shabby beneath his white coat, his skin was yellow and his eyes bloodshot. Why should a man who looked like this be entitled to love, let alone be loved? He had no right.

Yet he could imagine a future in which, during her long recuperation, Miss Lewis could grow to love him, in an affectionate way, and he would court her appropriately, with flowers and small presents, and intimate that she was special to him and when she was recovered . . .

Look, why not? he thought. Knowing at the same time that it was rubbish and he should get a grip.

29

Persky said, 'Do you know if there's a track round here?'

'What sort of track?' Lenny said. 'The station is—'

'A *race* track.'

'I think there's one at Folkestone, I've never been there but I can find out. You want to go?'

'Sure.'

It was a big idea, it was huge. It meant returning to the actual world even just for a day and the joy of it was that no one could hold an arm out and stop them. What punishment could the Gwendo mete out to people who were not actually prisoners? Other patients did go out, they went to the golf links and returned looking pink and bright. Golf was considered an improving activity, a halfway house between the sanatorium and a return to normal life, but Lenny and Persky, neither of an athletic type or disposition, preferred to watch sport not play it, to follow teams with the devotion of fans. Lenny supported Spurs, Persky, having been born in the Bronx, retained an allegiance to the Yankees. They liked their games fast and preferably violent.

Horseracing was the ultimate in spectator sport, you watched and if you were good at understanding the form you won. It was all over in a few minutes then another rush of speed on its way right behind. There was something arbitrary, dangerous and wayward about betting because it could change your life in either direction, make or ruin you, leave you feeling exultant, able to reach out and grab a handful of stars from the sky, or wanting to slink into a hole and slit your throat. And at the track there was life, every kind of person – the lords in their top hats putting a thousand nicker on one gee-gee and the railwayman with five bob in his pocket spread-betting. Lenny loved the races, he'd been going since he was a kid before the war. He knew the characters, he liked the life. The smell of the turf and horse flesh gave him a lift.

He tried on his London drape. He had filled out since he wore it last in the woods, even the sleeves were straining and a tubby little belly had appeared under his ribs. A barber came in once a week to cut the male patients' hair but often Lenny didn't bother. His wiry bush was growing straight up from his parting. He looked like Groucho Marx. He shaved and tried to resemble a human being. The problem with this place was that you let yourself go because they allowed you to, they didn't know who you were before you arrived, so if you sat with a shawl round your shoulders that didn't matter to them as long as your fucking temperature was stabilised.

At the last minute Miriam decided she was well enough to join them. Her temperatures had subsided and not requiring permission to leave, they were not in prison, after all, she would not be stopped. Persky had suggested the excursion as a chance to get away from the intimate twosome that had been imposed on him and her sudden insistence that she would be coming along took some of the air out of his excitement.

They discussed how they would get there. Lenny said, 'I reckon we can do it on buses, what do you think?'

He asked Mrs Kitson who was local. She said yes, it could be done by bus, she had the timetables and she wrote it all down for them. She would have liked to go herself but was not invited. Persky winked at her and said he'd come back with something nice, if he could find anything.

She had accepted the Miriam situation. The girl was a force of nature who got what she wanted.

'Oh, you little ray of sunshine, you do cheer me up on a wet day.'

'It ain't raining yet.'

'It will.' For the sky looked to her country girl's eye like it was going to tip down later. An iron-grey wall of cloud was advancing from the south and the air smelt to her of rain, no one who can smell rain can explain it to someone who can't. Cattle, she observed, knew when it was going to rain, they didn't even need the sight of the sky to tell them.

'Good luck with your adventure.'

'An *adventure*? Are you serious?'

'You'll get more tired than you expect.'

He shrugged. 'So we'll sleep.'

Miriam came down in her Blustons outfit, her fox tippet slung over the shoulders of her forest-green felt overcoat, which no longer buttoned up. 'I'm fat as a pig, I am, look, Arthur, I'm *bursting*.'

'You're a peach, babe, gimme a kiss.'

They waited for the bus outside the village hall. Miriam was looking round at the village as if it was a film set, a picture she had once seen starring stiff-upper-lip actors like Ronald Colman and Celia Johnson. They had seen *Brief Encounter*. 'Why don't you just fuck her?' a voice from the row behind had jeered and the sight of the stolid husband in his armchair had made Miriam snort pop through her nose. It was terribly funny, this place, bound to be full of people like the staid old hubby who took silly ideas like honour seriously, childish because they belonged only in books.

And the village looked to all three of them now like a film in which they themselves were actors standing there without the lines for parts for which they'd been miscast. Lenny the stockbroker, Miriam his Women's Institute wife, Persky the spectacled librarian.

The bus was single-decker, cream and green. They all laughed when they saw it come up the road, for it was nothing like a London bus. It seemed to want to disappear into the hedgerows.

'We got buses in the States that are silver,' Persky said, 'like bullets, and they go that fast.'

'I'm going to go on one of those one day,' Miriam said.

'Sure you are, baby.'

They trundled through the villages, which looked like a succession of calendar pages, January, February, March, all thatched roofs and cottage gardens and stone war memorials on the green. Lenny fell asleep. They alighted in Canterbury and found the next bus. They waited. The queue behind them grew longer. 'This always happens,' said a woman with the beefy furious face of one who had just about had enough under a hat with what seemed to be a small stuffed bird near the crown. 'It's a bloody disgrace, this service, has been for years. You'd think there was a war on and they couldn't get the drivers but that's finished and I'll tell you what, I'll swing for them one of these days, not even a proper bus shelter and we'll be soaked to the skin in a minute, you mark my words.'

'It's broken down on the hill,' said a late arrival, sauntering towards the stop and stopping everyone in the queue to impart his news with the satisfaction of one who saw the world as a permanent veil of tears. 'They've cancelled it, we're going to have to wait for the next one and here comes the rain, wouldn't you bloody know it.'

The rain started off as English rain often does with a fine dew-like drizzle that refreshed tired skin and then turned into glancing arrows it was impossible to avoid. They got on the bus when it eventually arrived, steaming like wet cows. The sun came out. The bus passed very slowly through verdant lanes. Housewives going to market towns to do their shopping got off with empty string bags and on again with full ones containing tins of peas and loaves of bread and paper parcels wrapping the meat ration.

Folkestone was by the sea. It smelled different. Persky raised his long nose and sniffed. He looked to Lenny like a wolf that has come across fresh meat. Colour flooded into his face. Miriam could see he was in his element and it made her nervous. She had never seen him outside their shared environment, here it looked like he could easily make a run for it and leave her high and dry, just disappear like a person who was well (and he was recovering fast, everyone said so, he was doing okay).

The race course was a couple of miles out of town, they had to take yet another bus. The sun was coming and going like the door of a tart's boudoir, Lenny thought.

'Make your bleeding mind up,' he said, looking at the sky.

The rain started up again. 'It's just mocking us now,' Persky said.

When they finally got to the racecourse they were wet and Miriam was starving. They went to the restaurant and ate pies with gravy and mashed potatoes. While they were eating the sun came out and lit up the emerald swathe of turf, the stands turned from shadow to tiers of men and women in hats that were lifted or dashed. Losing betting slips littered the course, some crisp, some in sodden balls. They smelled green turf, horseshit, sweat, perfume, potatoes and pies. To Lenny it was intoxicating, not an antiseptic note in the whole reeking perfume.

Miriam was looking around at the clothes. The hats were a different shape, like petals hugging the head, the waistline was still wandering around, bosoms were starting to come to a point. If I don't get back I'll have fallen behind, she thought, *right* behind, and then where will I be?

Lenny took his thermometer out of his pocket then put it back again. He was trying to remember who he was a year ago before he got sick (or was found to be sick all along). He had to remember how to shove. The crowds frightened him, everyone was well, or looked like they were.

Don't panic, he told himself. Whatever you do don't panic in front of the others.

The bookies were on their ladders screaming the odds, the tic-tac men were tapping their arms in code, which Lenny could read as Valerie could read and understand difficult books. An outlandish figure stood out from all the others dressed as an Ethiopian prince in a waistcoat decorated with stars, a cummerbund and a headdress from which rainbow feathers rose like a Red Indian warrior.

'Who the hell is that coloured guy?' said Persky.

'It's Ras Prince Monolulu, he's a bit of a character. My uncle knows him. He's not really a prince.'

I got a horse! Ras Prince Monolulu cried. *I got a horse to beat the favourite. God makes the bees the bees make the honey the soldier does the dirty work the bookie takes the money. Why does the bookie take the money? Because you bet favourites.*

'That's true,' said Persky, 'gimme long odds any time. Let's go down and see the gee-gees.'

They strolled along to the paddock where the horses were being paraded round in a circle by their jockeys. It was a fine sight, so many pinks, lemons, scarlets, acid blues on the silks after months of the monochrome interior of the sanatorium. The horses were huge and charming, 'Like velvet,' cried Miriam. 'Can I touch one?' But the buff-coated officials wouldn't let her anywhere near the beasts.

'One day I'm going to have a horse.'

'What, to ride? You on a horse?'

'Nah! To race, I'll be a racehorse owner in a hat and they'll give me a big silver cup when my horse wins and the King will bow to me.'

'You got it, baby,' Persky said. 'We'll get you a horse.'

'Maybe I could ride one anyway. Yeah, not one of these great big fellers but a pony. I'd like that.'

'When have you ever seen a pony before now?'

'The coppers ride them, don't they? I'm gonna have a horse and one of them velvet hats and them trousers with the sticky-out bits at the side. Yeah, Manny will take care of it, won't he?'

And this ambition seemed to Lenny to be fair enough, after all that they had been through.

You heard them first, a dull throbbing on the turf, distant thunder growing louder, then an overwhelming sensation in the ears of excitement, anxiety, the horse's reins in your own hands and your feet in your high-heeled red shoes digging spurs into the sides of the thin air between them, *Come on.* COME ON. And then the pack was on top of you, a rainbow flashing for seconds and your horse out in front not on its own but nudging nudging to the finishing line. This dream of winning and Miriam's horse came in second and she had won ten bob and was screaming and crying and shouting *I only bloody did it, didn't I, you darling horsie I'd give you a cuddle what was its name again, Len?*

Ras Prince Monolulu gave Miriam her winnings. 'What you going to spend your money on, young lady? Bottle of gin? Fancy perfume? New hat?'

'A suitcase,' Miriam said and winked at Persky. 'A fine leather suitcase with my initials on it in gold.'

'What's those initials?'

'There's an M, don't know about the rest yet.'

Persky thought, So that's the way it is. What do we do about this situation? He looked around and felt he'd had a shot in the arm of some vitamin cocktail they took out in Los Angeles to make them perky, it was a grand day, and he didn't feel like going back. There was some opportunity to give them and the Gwendo the slip, head to the city and find a ship. But without a doctor's all-clear no captain would take him on board.

Everyone felt low and out of spirits when they got on the bus and they sank into the silence of melancholy.

Miriam let out a volley of sneezes, Persky counted eight.

'I don't feel good,' she said. 'I want to be in bed but I don't, if you see what I mean. Not that bed, my bed, at home with Mum and you, Len. Not that place.'

'Nothing much we can do about it. Val would miss you, anyway.'

'I know she would. Still.'

And she hung on to Persky's arm, he put it round her shoulders and kissed her hair.

'You never did dry out, did you, from the rain. You're damp and cold, particularly on your front.'

'Am I?'

He put his hand on her beating heart.

'You're still living, babe, that's all that matters.'

They toiled up the hill to the sanatorium in silence, Miriam let out small moans every minute or two. 'Oh, these shoes, these shoes, my feet aren't half killing me, I feel like an old lady.'

Between them the two men were half dragging her along and she was not light in their arms. She began to cry, 'I want my bed, I want my bed!'

'We're here now, just a few more steps, come on, darling, not much further,' said Lenny. Her sudden deterioration frightened him. The whole idea had been a mistake or they should have done it in the spring but that was months away.

30

Alone on the veranda while the others were at the races, reading the new Elizabeth Bowen which her cousin had sent her for her birthday, Valerie felt a cough coming on. She tried to stifle its arrival but it erupted in blood, gouts of blood on the sheets and blankets, and another cough, and more blood. She was haemorrhaging. Her lung was full of moth holes, months of bed rest had not healed them. Pain and sputum.

She rang the bell, Chitts looked at the sheets. 'I'm going to call for Dr Limb.'

He came very quickly. He had broken off a consultation with a member of the Mothers' Union when he heard he was needed by Miss Lewis. She smiled at him when he came in. 'Oh dear, I have got worse, haven't I?'

He sat on a chair by her bed. The sun was shining on a triangular section of the bedclothes. Which was not good for her. 'Nurse, will you draw down the blind, please?' Then he asked her to leave. 'I won't need you any more.'

'Miss Lewis . . .' And then, with his heart lurching, 'Or can I, since we are old friends, call you Valerie?'

'Of course.'

'And I am Gerald.'

'Gerald.'

She had no idea what these intimacies were all about. Was he trying to thwart the anarchic authority-defying influence of Miriam by befriending her?

'I can't tell you how sorry I am that there has not been the improvement we hoped for. I genuinely thought that in your case prolonged rest, and of course, the pneumothoraxes we've already performed, would help, but they don't seem to have done.'

'I see. Am I going to die?'

The urge to reach out and take that thin hand in the blue-striped pyjamas was overwhelming, like an alcoholic's thirst for a drink. Was there any harm in touching her for a moment?

'No! Of course not,' he cried and impulsively he darted out, took the hand, squeezed it, let it lie there for a few moments, his heart pounding, managed to resist raising it to his lips and kissing it.

How kind he is, Valerie thought, most doctors are so remote and uncaring when they're not being avuncular or patronising. His hand was soft, it was sensitive, it had to be for it performed minor operations every day.

'Valerie, there is an operation you may have heard of, it is quite a ... radical measure, it would put the lung permanently to rest so hopefully you would have no further trouble from it and you can live perfectly well and happily on your other lung.'

'How would that work?'

'Well, you see, we would have to ... remove some of your ribs.'

'*What?*' Her mother might have told her off for this vulgarity, reminded her that 'Beg your pardon' was the polite phrase.

Miriam would have cried *Fuck*.

'It's not a new procedure, we've done it several times here at the Gwendo, we call in a surgeon from London to perform it, it's rather specialised, there's a man at St Thomas' I have a great deal of confidence in. It's a long recovery but ... '

'Remove my ribs? How many?'

'Up to eight. Probably not all in one go.'

'But surely I'd have a concave chest.'

'Oh, I'm sure you would still look very pretty and—'

'What's it called, this operation?'

'It's a thoracoplasty.' Her dictionary was beside her bed.

'Could you please hand that to me?'

'Very well.'

Plastic operation on the thorax, as excision of portions of ribs to close an abscess; Estlander's operation. Origin, 1891.

'I see. And that's all you can offer me? A visit to the abattoir?'

'Oh no, it's not as bad as all that. I realise it sounds drastic but you can live comfortably without a few ribs, and think about being well, wouldn't that make it worth it?'

'What about the convalescence?'

'Well, there will be lots of pillows to prop you up, it's imperative that you stay quite still and we will put a mirror at the end of your bed, here, you must keep looking in it to make sure you're not getting lopsided. We'll weigh down the other shoulder to even things up a bit.'

'My God. Nobody will look at me after that.'

'What an earth do you mean?'

'A deformed creature, one breast sunk in, how horrible.'

He remembered one poor girl who had cried, just as Miss Lewis had, 'But no man will look at me now, what have you done?' Yet she had told one of the nurses a shocking story which had reached him through the usual channels, about a young officer trying to teach her billiards, his front pressed in against her back as he explained how to hold the cue correctly, and she felt something quite *hard* protruding into her lumbar region and blushingly admitted that perhaps she was an object of attraction after all.

He knew that whatever happened *he* would look at her, but that was no reassurance, she meant the young officers downstairs. If he could he would quarantine her from all young fellows, she might come to love him, it was possible. She had not arrived with the aura of death about her, the sense he had of some people who were goners, who couldn't survive. But she had got worse. The operation suited his professional and private interests, it had worked wonders before, and bedridden for months, something might deepen between them.

But then she said, perhaps under the influence of that girl she shared with, the troublemaker, 'What about streptomycin? I'd rather wait for that.'

'Yes, yes, the wonder drug, or so we've all been told, but is it really? It's too soon to tell. The trials are promising but do you want to be experimented on with something that may not be safe?'

'Why can't I just wait until we're sure?'

He cleared his throat. 'I would advise, Valerie, if I may still call you that after bearing not very pleasant news, that you consider this operation seriously, talk it over with your parents. Seek the wise counsel of your family doctor, I'll write to him and advise on what I am planning to do. Older heads may prevail.'

I'm buggered, thought Valerie. If I don't do this, I'll die. That's what he's saying.

31

When the news leaked out that the streptomycin was coming, would actually be here in a week or two, and the first guinea pigs had been selected (some thought in the interests of democracy that it should have been put to a vote with others arguing that it wasn't a popularity contest) the residents of the sanatorium roused themselves from their torpor. Languid souls whose faces were permanently disfigured by a handkerchief felt that maybe they might live after all. To be an invalid was no longer a permanent way of life but a condition to be snapped out of. A kind of hectic cheerfulness arose, like people who have booked a holiday long ago and having half-forgotten about the beach, the hotel, the sites to explore, the packing for a different climate, as the date approaches are now crouching by the letter box awaiting the arrival of the tickets.

The chosen few disappeared up to their rooms for complete bed rest, streptomycin injections and the large, foul-tasting PAS tablets, four at a time, which they struggled hard to swallow and keep down, like swallowing a crow. On the top floor one of the children had been selected secretly, for Matron said there'd be a riot if the other parents found out this child was getting the miracle cure.

Iain Jackson, one of the chosen, procrastinated about starting his treatment. He saw that since the news all discipline was beginning to break down, a refusal to obey orders was rife. In the army there were always members of the awkward squad but you could count on the rest of your men to keep them in line, usually for their own self-preservation as well as an instilled respect for order during training. Those who couldn't swallow it spent most of their service in the glass house. Here, the rebels were starting to gain the upper hand.

Do I care, he asked himself. Should I? He was entitled to use his military rank for the rest of his life and be addressed by it, all the officers were still doing so, not only here but in the outside world. They went on being managers and motivators and leaders of men when there wasn't even a war on but why should I, he thought. Why the hell do I have to have this burden of responsibility?

Perhaps when he left he would just drop the title, become plain Mr. In fact – radical thought – perhaps he would not after all go into the family shoe and boot business keeping the nation shod in serviceable leather and protective polish which his father regarded as a higher calling for we all have to put something on our feet. And yet, apart from his father's crushing disappointment, and his mother crying and his older sister lecturing him about loyalty, he could, he supposed, do anything he liked. If the streptomycin worked on him he would never see the inside of this wretched place again, or walk in the wet woods, or eat another slice of dry Madeira cake at the Singing Kettle or be on the receiving end of the usual looks in the pub or take his temperature or spit or retire after dinner to the company of men of his own class once who had long ago worn out any stimulating conversation.

Limb had explained everything, what the course of treatment would be and how it was expected to proceed. He'd have to go back to bed for three months. He had tried to hedge the information about the excellent results coming from America with his worries about toxicity, to which Jackson had replied, 'Well, sir, if you don't mind me pointing out, all the sawing and hacking and lung punctures aren't exactly without their side effects and all they do is turn you into a perpetual invalid.' Limb said, 'I wouldn't say that exactly.' Jackson replied, 'I disagree. That is it, exactly.' And was surprised at his own chippiness. Hope, concrete hope with experimental data and clinical trials behind it made you a bit bolshie. But what about his responsibility to his men – not *his* men, of course, he reminded himself, but the officers whom he had cheerfully and calmly represented out of a sense of duty and of being the most familiar with the regime and its management. Trusted not to rock the boat, to make reasonable representations on others' behalf.

Streptomycin seemed to him now not just a cure, but almost a form of immortality. I could reach the age of eighty, he thought, that would be the year 2002, what a thought, time *racing* instead of a sluggish dribble. But my God, he thought, How will I adapt? I must marry, I suppose, be a father, go to parties and dinner parties and watch my hair disappear in the mirror. Is it really worth it, this *life* business?

The more he considered taking the treatment the more conditions in the Gwendo began to deteriorate. The patients were questioning, demanding, revolting, not forming committees as they had before, but acting as atomised individuals, only out for themselves, grasping at the drug, their elbows sharpening, knocking others out of the way. He found it all quite depressing that human nature should be so self-centred. Why couldn't they be more altruistic?

He went down into the woods with his stick and thrashed away at nettles. He didn't even like the woods, found them claustrophobic and depressing, preferred the sight of open fields. By 1943, before he was invalided out, he had got to Naples and adored it. Went up to take a look at Pompeii, took the boat across to Ischia and Capri. The slash of blue of the Mediterranean had become encoded inside him as a strip of longing and discontent with this monotonous life. He could just go, go back to Italy, see Venice and Rome, it might be as little as three months in the future. Yet somehow, without him in any way asking for the position, he had become the de facto leader of the officers' table.

He considered Grimes, a recalcitrant former lieutenant in the tanks, had no idea how he had managed when he was commanding

186

men. The fellow loved to argue, to point out flaws, all in a calm, reasoned manner, but it was exhausting to deal with his constant dissent. 'I am a man of principle,' he had insisted, 'I cannot go against my conscience.'

'Look, we all have to do our best to just muddle along, don't you see?'

'No, Jackson, you're quite wrong there. Muddle and mess is the exact problem we've got.'

Grimes looked sick. He had grown a short beard which, at the age of thirty-two, was starting to come in white. His hands shook when he tried to shave, and his old dressing gown was covered with stains. Still he kept up his debating society tricks over lunch. Jackson couldn't stand him. The thought of never again having to deal with his carping was a refreshing pleasure but then if he didn't keep Grimes in line, who would? Oh, this wretched sense of duty one had, which weighed you down with its heavy thoughts.

A squirrel raced up a tree and disappeared amongst the branches. The canopy of leaves rustled.

He'd never seen young Lynskey here again, the boy was terrified of the woods. The insertion into the Gwendo of these working-class characters, plus the arrival of the American merchant seaman, had disrupted the social order in a way that Jackson thought was probably for the good. Some kind of new age was being born, one in which duty and patience and respect didn't matter. The whole business of learning to be a patient simply wasn't taking with them for some reason, they placed no trust in doctors, possibly because they had too little experience of them – they didn't lead lives where there was any room for all that fussy attention to their own physical state, they just had to get on with it. Whereas before, everyone was *waiting* for the cure, now there was no patience at all for waiting. They had no intention of putting up with it and Limb had no idea how to cope.

Lynskey, that first morning creating a fuss because he had no idea where his sister was. And me, he thought, so obedient I won't even take my trousers down in the art teacher's bedroom. What have they done to me? What have I let myself become? Do I even deserve one of the first places on the treatment plan?

He was disgusted with himself, with his cheerful reticence. Maybe Grimes had it right after all, maybe he should start to moan a bit more. That would wake them up all right.

He walked back to the sanatorium having decided. The first thing he was going to do when he got back to his room was shave his moustache off. That would be a start. It would show others that he meant to part company with the familiarity of his own face in the mirror. He had had a moustache since he left school and was allowed to grow one.

Persky saw him, starting to take off his outside shoes and replace them with his slippers at the cubbyholes, then with his laces half undone, putting the slippers back, and walking through the day room, fully shod.

'Do you see that? Look what comes over a man when he knows he's going to get the drugs,' he said to Lenny. 'We need that streptomycin. We're going to have to figure out a way of getting it.'

Upstairs Valerie saw Captain Jackson, a figure slightly familiar to her but without a name, returning to the sanatorium from the woods. Miriam was dozing in an armchair, her chin was slack on her chest, her mouth open. In her sleep she was humming.

32

Life for Hannah Spiegel in bed was little different apart from having nothing to look at any more. She found scenes of nature generally quite calming with their muted tones of green, brown, blue and grey but of no more interest than that.

As a child she had grown up in a Stuttgart apartment with a piano and two brothers who both played the cello, Sundays were for walks in the park like little soldiers swinging their arms then home for torte and conversation. Ernst, the youngest in the family, worked for Volkswagen as an engineer. Viktor, the elder brother, was killed in 1917 at Messines. The family had gone downhill after that and even the excursions stopped. In her teens Hannah went to concerts by herself and fell in love from her seat with a beautiful contralto. Then home became for her even more silent, always watchful. Eventually there had been a genuine love affair, consummated, with a bookshop girl her own age and that had lasted for several years, discreetly done until Monika's mother came upon them holding hands and nuzzling each other's necks in the empty powder room of a department store. Monika had broken off all communication. Hannah later heard she was married and saw her in 1931 wheeling a baby in a pram and her heart was punched.

The schoolgirl had been such a risk. The girl was attracted to her, mooned around, sent her poems and handmade presents. The kiss had been their first physical contact, it only lasted a few seconds then someone blundered in, a cleaner, who reported them. Apart from the embarrassment, apart from feeling sorry for poor Lotte who was withdrawn immediately by her parents and Hannah never found out what happened to her afterwards, she had thought that she would simply leave Stuttgart, would move to another city and find a new position. If she could not find work in a school she would take pupils. She did not think it would be so hard to find employment. So in the immediate aftermath she did not care about the brief kiss, did not foresee its consequences. How could she have known what was going to happen to her, where she would be sent? The camp. The place for women criminals and prostitutes and later the Jews.

If she had understood any of this when she was still a music teacher she would have followed Monika's example and married some useful prop, buried herself alive for the rest of her life, been content to lie in the darkness next to a snoring husband thinking of smooth skin, a soft mouth, blonde down on a young girl's neck. Yes, it would have been better than what happened. Disowned by her parents and surviving brother. The arrest, the camp, the situation.

And now she missed her watchful activity of the comings and goings in the day room. This state of observation was what she had used to hold herself intact at home, at school, in Ravensbrück. Her orchestra would have to tune up now, play out its overture with some incomplete sections. So she read more, listened to the wireless more, began to be mildly amused by Lenny and Colin's twice-weekly variety programme, or at least she was attempting to understand it and why it might appeal to those of a more demotic cultural taste than herself.

For Sarah was always explaining to her what they were up to on the hill above London. They had filmed, for example, a troupe called the Windmill Girls doing a dance called the cancan involving an awful lot of attractive leg.

33

Now the period of waiting grew far more intense. Winter fell on
the landscape. Fewer patients rambled in the woods, they were
confined to their verandas or the day room where rumour and
gossip spread about how it was working out for the guinea pigs,
all of whom were imprisoned in the languors of the rest cure as a
condition of the prize of being part of the clinical trial.

Iain Jackson said he was feeling better but Nurse Chitty said that
didn't mean anything, only the X-rays would say for certain if he
was cured. Hannah too felt an improvement, but Desmond Foye
was said to have suffered an allergic reaction and been taken off it.
When that was found out a clamour arose as to who was to have
his unused medicine. Dr Limb shut himself up in his office and told
Matron that this new cure regime would be the death of him, it
turned patients who had once been placid into agitators. Only dear
Lady Anne uttered merely the usual well-bred sighs.

Miriam was back in bed, pale, sweating, coughing, tired.

Valerie was alarmed. Miriam had been a cartoon girl up to now,
yet she realised that brother and sister possessed an internal emo-
tional life which felt as real to them as her own did to her.

Lenny's comb, which he kept in his breast pocket as others put
their pens there, was a red plastic affair which was as familiar to

her now as her own hand, for he was always taking it out and trying to restore the parting to his hair. There was something slight and vain about this gesture but she thought she might prefer it to the sad sacks who wandered about in shawls. At least he made an effort. Both of them did and it was unusual and interesting to her to watch two people you could hardly describe as 'slaves to petty convention' (one of the remarks she had made about her mother and which she now felt ashamed of) take such care of their appearance.

She was developing a slight crush on Lenny, which she recognised as no more than a temporary emotion rising from the unusual situation she was in. He was a friend, a kind of brother, but the sight of his lips, quite full and red, and the eyebrows that met in the middle and the glitzy charm he gave off when he walked in induced a twang in the head, a guitar string, a reverberation like the sound waves in the air when a bell has stopped ringing. He was so ridiculous in some ways in his silly suit and his Italian shoes but also unselfconscious. As students they were all up-in-arms about this and that injustice and joining societies dedicated to the cause of anti-colonialism or decimal currency or comprehensive education but he had thrown his packed lunch at a fascist! So funny. And not a political bone in his body, just an angry boy in Trafalgar Square expressing himself, quickly, without consideration of the consequences. She liked that. And his sheer recklessness. He was knocking what remained of Edgbaston out of her and who could complain about that?

34

In the next bed to Lenny, Colin Cox was deteriorating, they'd put him out on the veranda again. He begged for the treatment but was told, 'Sorry, old chap, you're not on the list.' And what a short, short list it was.

His wife arrived in a mink coat one day. 'I'm so cold,' he told her, 'I can't take the icy draughts, come here and give me a cuddle.'

'You know what,' she said, when the electric clang rang out and she had to go home, 'I'm leaving you my coat.'

'I can't wear a lady's fur, what are you thinking?'

'I don't mean wear it, just keep it over you when you're in bed. I can't bear to see you like this. Your toes are like blocks of ice.'

'Oh, sweetheart! But what about you? You'll catch your death with no coat.'

'I'll take your tweed overcoat, the one you came in. Is it in the cupboard over there?'

'Should be.'

'There you are, then, I'll be warm as toast.'

'In a man's overcoat? You'll look a sight.'

But she laughed and said, 'Who will see me behind the wheel of the car?' She was an excellent driver, fast and confident, could drive already when he first met her, unusual in a girl of her class.

Snow fell in the night, it fell in flakes on his sleeping face and iced the hair of the mink so that when he woke at three in the morning his body had been transformed into a cocoon of brightness under the moon. He looked up at the storm in the sky, still falling in drifts across the woods and the surrounding hills. It was all so strange and so like death that he was frightened for the first time. When he was a kid there were fairy stories his mother had read to him, things that happened in forests in other lands, Germany, maybe, and wolves and witches and goblins and out here it seemed to him that that world was real not imaginary and any moment now an eagle would descend from the sky and pick him up and carry him, wrapped in the snowy coat, to some mountain top where he would be devoured by its ravenous beak.

A few days later, he felt better, his temperature had stabilised and Dr Limb allowed him to go downstairs for an hour or two where he found a couple of new arrivals who enforced a new lease of life in him. They were poker enthusiasts and what's more had the money to play. He rose from his bed and managed to make his way to the day room each evening for a couple of hours after dinner, promising to go back to bed after breakfast the next morning to recover from the excitement. Lenny watched him become more and more reckless. He understood that it was boredom which made him agree to higher and higher stakes, even when he lost. As a man who knew the turf Lenny was not interested in placing his own bets; even if you studied the form, the odds were in general against the punter and in favour of the bookie. You never saw a poor one. The law of averages favoured the person taking in the money and only handing it out on the winning bet. Lenny had done all the sums in his head and concluded that Colin Cox was an idiot.

By Christmas, Cox had lost £75. That was a lot of money, particularly as his brother-in-law was running the motor business in his absence and taking a fifty per cent share of the profit.

One evening after dinner he bet the last thing in his possession, his wife's mink. He lost it to Cyril Barrie, who gave it to his wife Veronica. Mrs Cox had to endure visiting days seeing her coat on the back of some vulgar little woman from Penge, strutting in smelling of toilet water and showing off the lining when she took it off. Cox had had his wife's initials embroidered on the satin, Veronica Barrie had unpicked them and inserted her own. Her possession was complete. And what was worse, Cyril Barrie resolutely refused to fall sufficiently ill to be banished to the veranda so the coat was always ostentatiously slung over the back of a chair when Mrs Cox arrived.

'She'll never forgive me,' Colin said to Lenny. 'Sooner I get that streptomycin the better.'

Colin Cox worsened very suddenly over the course of a few days. Lenny watched him go under. This was what death from tuberculosis looked like. Coughing, wasting, haemorrhaging – and the smell.

There was a stink in the room, a terrible pong, a sweetish odour. The smell came from the next bed. It was Colin Cox who stank.

Lenny caught Chitts in the hallway and pushed her against the wall.

'You can't do that,' she said. 'Take your bloody hands off me.'

'What's wrong with Colin? What's the smell?'

'Oh dear, is it upsetting you?'

'Of course it's bleeding upsetting me. It's horrible, but what's the matter with him?'

'Well, you know it's his lungs.'

'That's obvious but what's the smell?'

'The lungs decomposing, I'm afraid.'

'Can't you do anything?'

'Not for him, not at this stage. But I'll talk to Dr Limb. I don't think you'd like watching him die.'

'No, I don't want to be there – I can't.'

'Only a saint would, to be honest. It's not a death like in the operas.'

A few hours later they came to move Cox to the surgery block. 'I doubt if I'll see you again, old boy,' he said to Lenny. 'I've enjoyed our little chats about cards and what have you.'

195

'Rubbish, you'll be back up here in no time.' Lenny had never had any trouble lying.

'We'll see.'

He followed the wheelchair out to the lift and waved him good-bye. He went back to his bed and wept.

The next day Lenny tried to visit him, but a nurse barred his way. 'No, I'm sorry, he is very weak, no excitement.'

'I could just sit for a few minutes, cheer him up.'

'His wife is coming to get him; he is leaving the day after tomorrow. They'd like him to be back in Bristol so she can be by his side when—'

'He's a goner, isn't he?'

'We don't like to—'

Now he could see the future, his own and everyone else's. This could be his sister in a few months if she didn't pull round from that day at the races, the day which had been the turning point in her health, just as she was on the up and up and now she was back in bed worse than she'd been when she came in, worse than him. He was full of fear and rage.

Lenny watched Colin shuffle past the pigeon holes with their outdoor shoes and slippers, out into a waiting Daimler. 'I'm going out in style, at least,' he whispered. 'Rented for the day from a pal. I'll go with my head held high and on the finest upholstery. I'll miss you, old chap. As I say, I enjoyed our little chats, and our wireless turns, keep up the good work. And don't let the Yank boss you around, you're the one with all the ideas, he just plays records. But anyway, television's the thing, radio will be shut down, who'll want to bother when you've got the pictures as well?'

And then he raised a very cold, very dry hand and Lenny took his own from his pocket and shook it.

'Look after yourself,' he said hopelessly. 'Have a good journey.'

England in 1950 was a country without motorways. They headed west on the A road to Bristol and Glenys Cox, who was a keen and confident driver, navigated the Daimler through Hampshire.

It was a cold bright day at the end of the year. Colin dozed for half an hour in the back seat, and woke to the sight of his wife's head, her blonde hair curling round her new hat, or at least he had never seen it before. What did she want a new hat for? She never went out anywhere, or did she? He didn't know any more about her life since he'd gone into the sanatorium. Her hands gripped the wheel in beige leather driving gloves. A faint noise came from her, a hum, yes, she was humming, a tune he didn't recognise, some new thing. And out of the window he saw hills, clouds of crows rising, skeletal trees and bushes, road signs, other cars, many from before the war, and he thought how he would never find out what the future of the motor car was to be, what new designs they would come up with, because they were taking him home – no, not even home – but to die in a hospital ward of tubercular men on their last legs.

He could no longer remember how long he had been at the Gwendo. The regime discouraged calendars, they made the inmates think they were enduring an indeterminate prison sentence. They were supposed to take each day as it came, the day, the day, the bloody day.

A small bump in the road, a pit, or a small animal the tyres had crushed and he noticed his wife's pearl earrings rock against her neck. Like the hat, he didn't recognise them. Had he bought her a pair of pearl earrings? He might have done, that was the kind of gift he would give her after a good month in business, or for their wedding anniversary. But he had no recollection of ever seeing them before. Was he losing his mind? Going senile, soft in the head? Or did she have a fancy man? Was someone waiting to step into his shoes? His slippers, more like it, the leather mules he'd bought when he was first admitted, thinking he'd hardly get any wear out them.

And then he thought, *Oh, what is the bloody point?* For he was going to be knocked off his perch soon, and he might be going mad or his wife was being altogether previous taking a lover on board before he was even in the ground, and why wouldn't she, she must have been lonely enough and he had lost her fur coat at cards and been a complete disappointment to her since he became ill. He wasn't a man, he was a sack of bones and decay.

But don't cry, he thought. No point in crying, just get on with it. And he opened the car door, as they travelled at fifty miles an hour, and with a weak push threw himself out onto the rushing road, the A34 to Bristol.

35

To the nurses and medical staff, the patients were always occupying points on a calendar closer to or further away from death. Colin Cox, when he left, had had no more than a week or two to live. Captain Jackson, under the influence of the streptomycin, could easily survive a normal lifespan, reach a hale eighty. Miriam Lynskey, on the other hand, was waxing and waning in health, sometimes her symptoms were alarmingly severe and Nurse Chitty was frightened for her, on other occasions she seemed to rally and return to normal. She might live on to any age or last only a few more months, it was hard to tell and Chitts had asked Dr Limb to keep a closer eye on her. He was unworried. 'I've seen many cases like hers before, a few more weeks' bed rest is the answer, I'm sure of it.'

Valerie, he insisted, when he spoke to Matron, was almost certainly dying. Without radical intervention she would not last until Easter and so after consultation with her parents the surgeon had come from London and sawn her up. They put her under with injections and she went down into the blackness of insensate death and surged back up in a state of physical shock, blood pressure plunging, her whole body shaking with cold, hearing the panic in the recovery room as they piled blankets on her, then stabilised, hearing a voice say, '*a nasty situation there for a mo*—' and thinking that she had probably died and like a human-shaped balloon floating upwards to heaven had been pulled back by a nurse catching hold of her ankles.

They kept her in the surgical block for a week. There were no other patients there, and she was left alone with an unfamiliar nurse who came to check on her, first every fifteen minutes to test her vital signs for life, then every half-hour, then every hour until she was left alone between mealtimes to feel the concavity in her chest beneath her right breast where three ribs had been amputated. She had never been a large-breasted girl, 34B bra size. Now the breast lay sunken, the chest abnormal, flaccid. Her nipples lay indented beneath the jacket of her pyjamas. They were far too big for her now, even though she'd bought them in the boys' department, not wanting the fuss of the nightgowns her mother had wanted her to wear to 'look nice for the doctors'.

Pain, tears, self-pity. The surgical-block nurses were efficient and practical and not particularly friendly. The patients didn't stay long enough to develop relationships with them. She was not permitted visitors. She was allowed to listen, if she did not become over-excited, to the sanatorium radio and she heard Lenny and his silly games, the voice she thought of as cockney with those guttural inflections and a slight lisp.

Her parents were due to visit. She was looking forward to their arrival more than anything, for the company and for the comfort of their presence, feeling that she had every right to return to early childhood since she was as incapacitated and helpless as a baby. But leaving the house, her mother slipped on an icy patch on the path, went down clumsily onto her shoulder and broke her arm. Her husband had to drive her to hospital where she was admitted overnight. He found a phone and rang the sanatorium to pass on a message that they would be unable to come. This did not reach the surgical block until the following morning.

Valerie thought, I've been completely removed from the world. This is just the waiting room for death, isn't it? And what have I accomplished? Got a good Upper Second, kissed a few boys, been to Paris and seen the Eiffel Tower and eaten snails, and that is all. How paltry and worthless. She didn't realise she was talking aloud. A nurse, passing the door, heard her and called Dr Limb, who arrived with a frightened face and said he had no idea why her mother and father had not turned up but would she like him to sit with her for a few minutes?

'After what you've done to me?'

'I haven't—'

'Bugger off.' And she turned her head away, feeling a touch of triumph that she had resisted and so rudely. It was the first pride she had felt since she graduated.

Returned at last to her room, Valerie lay propped up on five pillows with miniature sandbags strapped to the other shoulder to even up the two sides. A mirror was leaning against the end of the bed in front of her in which she had to check every few minutes to make sure she wasn't slumping.

These were what she would always call the torture months, the months of the rack: 'The doctors and nurses were my persecutors and Miriam and Lenny were the angels of mercy, I know, such clichéd language but that was what I had fallen into, I couldn't even remember a time when I didn't speak in these commonplaces, and much good all my education had done me.'

She knew that she suffered from a gap, a different gap to the one where her ribs had been. There was an empty hollow occupied in other patients by religion. Even Arthur Persky, of all people, prayed. But she seemed to be alone in not believing in God or mercy or salvation or life after death, only a Manichaean duality dividing the living world into clearly defined sectors of light and dark with the latter usually maintaining the upper hand.

Dr Limb, for example, a man of her own class, was of the devil's party. She hated him and wished he would perish. *Gerald*. The sight of him made her flesh crawl. Her father, coming to visit her alone, his wife still laid up, turned his head away to hide a wetness in the eyes, said nonetheless, the doctors knew best. But after he left her, he demanded to see the medical director, asked him what the hell he thought he was doing to his daughter when everyone knew that streptomycin was no longer on its way, but actually here, and from what he'd been told, in use in this very sanatorium.

He became less and less satisfied with Limb's equivocations. Murmured something about a letter to the Ministry, there would be investigations. And when he got home he did indeed sit down to write a letter to the Department of Health, which unusually was taken account of by a civil servant who noted in the Gwendo file a letter concerning the request to administer the doses of strepto-mycin to one Hannah Spiegel and passed it up to his superior for his attention, there being, he thought, something slightly unusual and perhaps even fishy about the document.

If Dr Limb was Lucifer, the Jewish sister and brother from the East End, with bad manners, who talked too much and dressed too flashily, were the ones who kept up her spirits, who willed her to stay alive by making her laugh with their stories of the *shtarkers* and the *nebbishes* of their world, the strong men and the weaklings. Those who stand and use their fists and those who are on their knees, praying. These thieves and holy fools populated their lives in London.

Their Uncle Manny arrived on Sundays with their mother. Valerie had met both these characters now, the mother who wrung her hands at the sight of her two children as if she was squeezing wet laundry, then ran at them with parcels of food in greasy paper. The uncle with fleshy lips, wet-tipped cigars and the Homburg hat with his initials ML blocked in gold in the sweatband which he twirled round his forefinger as he stood by Valerie's bed and wink-ing said, 'Now is there anything I can get for you, sweetheart? Just name it, never mind the ration.'

Yes. She wanted something to take away the pain of endless suffering so she asked almost brassily, she thought, for a bottle of French perfume. And got one. A vial of L'Air du Temps, acquired, she imagined, through the medium of a pair of hoisting knickers but was beyond caring. A few dabs rising from the papery skin next to her bandaged chest was enough to alleviate for a few moments her suffering, as if the bottle contained scented spirits which warred with the underworld of terror and agony and paralysis.

She sent Lenny to the library for books and he returned with them and sat by her bed as if she was a little child who felt in glancing surges the safety of Mummy's head bent over the pages by the nightlight, telling her a story. She didn't understand why he was willing to go this far for her, apart from the idea that everyone had far too many hours in the day to fill. He didn't know either. He imagined it was merely a rest from the energetic presence of Persky who demanded of a man his full exhausting attention.

He had been straight with her and told her he didn't have the advantage of an education like she had, left school at fifteen with no certificates and gone to work for his uncle.

'So a lot of the time I don't get what you're saying, or the words I have to read out in the books. It's like being a kid again when I dropped my sweet down the back of the sideboard in the junk shop and I was crying because I couldn't tell Mum, not having the word yet for sideboard, and I had to nag her to come with me into the shop and point. What I'm saying is I ought really to buy myself a dictionary if I want to get on in life.'

Valerie had had one of those by her bed. She used it quite a lot. Lenny had said it was the word police, but Valerie replied, 'Well, it would *like* to be, but you see dictionaries are much more like the Keystone Cops, clumsy, ineffective types who are always falling over themselves running after words that are so much quicker and cleverer and adaptable and more cunning. Words don't come from the dictionary, they aren't born there, they come up from the streets, from humans like you who make new ones or change the use of ones that already exist. *You* are the origin of words, not books.'

Now that, he thought, that was something to think about, him a boy who thought of school as a place of useless torture, once they had taught you to read and write and do sums in your head. He was not attracted to her terrible damaged body – how could he be? – but her humour, what was left of it, and her intelligence, were for him an unusual combination in a bird. These sanatorium characters, her and Miss Spiegel, were types he would never have met in a million years had he not been threatened in the lungs. And he found he was drawn to them with some fascination he didn't really understand. He liked their company. They were different. And it wasn't as if you had to see them again when it was all over, when you were well.

Valerie, in bed, closed her eyes. Lenny promised her he would let her know if her body shifted. Sometimes she drifted off and dozed for a few minutes, and when she woke his voice had gone silent. She thought how bored he must be with all these *pages* but he was looking at her, at her face and the other side of that bandaged chest.

Is he sweet on me, she asked herself. It wasn't possible. She was a skeleton with hair and stretched skin. Not even a whole bag of bones.

When Desmond Foye was taken off the medicine Valerie told Dr Limb that she would not succumb to the second part of the operation, the removal of two more ribs. Not until the streptomycin was at least *tried*.

'I know you've got all those unused doses. Why not me? Why put me through this further torture? I *want it*. Give it to me.'

'Now, Valerie—' said Dr Limb.

'Now, *Gerald*,' she replied. 'If we are on first-name terms as you wish, I think we both know that I'm not going to come out of here alive if I don't get the injections.'

'And the pills, there are the PAS pills, you know, they can be very uncomfortable to swallow.'

'And you think I'm comfortable lying here, with a sunken chest and a wonky shoulder and a collapsed lung? Give it to me, I want it.'

'This is not you, I don't recognise—'

'No, of course you don't. I am indeed no longer myself. And I'm glad that I'm not, because the person I was when I came here believed everything you told me and was prepared to submit, and now I won't. I've had enough, I've just about had enough of you and your experiments on me. Am I an animal? No, I demand you give me the treatment.'

'But you're not in a position to—'

'Demand?' No, I know I'm not, but I'm doing it anyway. To make you see. It's the cure everyone has been waiting for, you know it, I know it. If we had more of it everyone would be getting some. That old man who had the allergic reaction, he was unlucky. Maybe I'll have the same thing, but that's no reason not to try. You know it isn't.'

'Valerie!'

'Oh, stop that, stop trying to get round me. I don't know what your game is. Are you sweet on me, is that it? Me, the wreck?'

'You are becoming hysterical. I am leaving now.'

'Yes, go, but tell me, are you giving me the treatment or not? *Tell me*.'

'I shall make my decision and inform you in due course.' And he almost ran to the door and slammed it behind him.

Miriam said, 'I'd call that geezer a cunt but he ain't got the warmth or the depth.'

36

The short-term impact of Victor Lewis's letter to the Department of Health was the request for a formal inspection of the premises, which Dr Limb would later say, 'unfortunately brought the house down, so to speak'.

Unlike the many years in which he had only been answerable to Mrs Downie, he was now the servant of the government – those hard-eyed socialists who were keen on breathing down everyone's necks and making trouble if you didn't toe whatever party line was in vogue this season. They saw things very differently from him and did not buy his philosophy (for it was one) that the patient must learn not only to be patient but to *be* a patient. For in their eyes this might do for the leisure classes, but not for the working man (or woman) who would be driven into poverty by chronic ill-health. The point of the Health Service was to make people better at no cost to themselves, not to indulge malingerers.

They were starting to talk about introducing a mass X-ray campaign, mobile units, machines on wheels, which would travel to the big cities and encourage people to form orderly queues outside to have their chests filmed. Some hyperopic visionaries were saying that if you could locate all the cases of TB and treat them with the new antibiotics, then the disease could be eradicated. Which seemed to Gerald Limb, being of a conservative disposition, almost blasphemous, for TB was as old as time, as least as old as the human race, and its longevity must be respected. One might as well say one was prepared to allow the Classics to go out of print so that no one knew any more who Odysseus or Achilles were. He thought of TB as he did the old gods, one of Zeus's emissaries on earth bringing with it flashes of divine inspiration to a selected company. The tubercular were often those whose bodies held a more sensitive and discerning mind, convalescence taught them to lie quietly, to read and think, and this could produce art of the finest quality. Keats had had tuberculosis, so had Chopin. It was a distinguished disease, in many cases, and at the Gwendo there were, and had been, some distinguished inmates over the years.

But the inspectors were coming and would inspect him out of a job and out of a properly conducted life if he didn't watch out. He had been advised to have, ready for external examination, the files and case-notes of every patient. This presented a difficulty since he couldn't put his hands on Lady Anne's notes. As she had been the first arrival, a filing system had not yet been established and when it was set up, somehow her particular paperwork had not been transferred up the hill to what the villagers were still calling the isolation hospital.

Now *she* was the perfect patient, the ideal exemplar of his regime. Some people would say to hell with it, and prefer to burn out fast in waves of *activity*, and he could see the reason in that if you were one of the restless young officers, but a person like Lady Anne would have only lived a life in the drawing room anyway and what was the difference between a salon in Mayfair and the stainless-steel and concrete interior of the Gwendo, with its bridge, embroidery and watercolour classes? Only the company had changed, was no longer of the finest, though she seemed not to mind and would talk to anyone, having become very democratic in her ability to tolerate the presence of what would have been for her the servant class and now less than even that, the scrapings of the slums. And because she was the perfect patient he had stopped treating her, or X-raying her, or thinking about her health at all.

But the Ministry of Health would not see it that way. The place was to move over completely to the NHS with no beds at all for private patients. They had their own deities, equality was one of them, whatever that was supposed to mean. Eventually, like everyone else, once the supplies properly arrived from America Lady Anne would be tried on streptomycin, and sent off home well, or she would have to come to some other arrangement, perhaps involving private nurses, which he assumed she could easily afford. What she would not be allowed to do under this ruthless regime with no fat in its system was linger. Linger gently but *beautifully*, as Mrs Downie had once put it.

Dr Limb walked past the empty flower beds, the ghost of the summer's ornamental clock, and bowed his head at Gwendolyn's marble obelisk. Poor girl. He took the short-cut through the woods. It was January and the sun was very weak, a pale lemon disc in the sky trying to burn off a mist that lay on the lawn. Crows alighted and cawed noisily, their voices echoing right into the kitchens where the cooks were frying bacon and stirring porridge and toasting bread.

An English morning in the fog. All sounds muffled or echoing.

But have I led a *cramped* life, he thought, as he pushed through the frozen brambles. Should I have gone abroad and served the Empire in some capacity, seen palm trees, parrots, girls in cool white linen dresses? Provincial Englishness sometimes seemed part of his own sickness with its quiet comforts and suppressed nerves but then were we not all put on earth to be thwarted in our dreams?

He didn't much like the woods with their fairy-tale qualities of the supernatural and was pleased to get out of them as quickly as he could by following a path which wasn't obvious to most of the patients, ending up right beside the clumps of azalea and rhodo-dendron bushes of Mrs Downie's drive.

Once you got to the front door it was all stained glass and mahogany staircases and sulphurous yellow velvet curtains with tassels and fringes and scalloped pelmets and in the middle of this, Maude Downie in her wheelchair who suffered from terrible, excru-ciating arthritis in what seemed to her to be every bone in her body. But he had once said, unwisely, that there were two hundred and six in total and it was quite unlikely that every one was arthritic. 'In fact, it is the joints not the—' But she said very sharply, 'Don't tell me where I hurt, young man.'

The housekeeper greeted him at the door and took him to a small, not particularly grand room which Mrs Downie had retreated to for its lack of draughts. A fire was lit. She was as close to it as she could get without scorching herself.

'Oh, and there you are at last, and will I ever see another spring?' she cried confusingly, as he entered.

'Am I late?' He looked at his watch. It was a minute after nine, so he had been exceptionally punctual reaching the front door and the housekeeper must have seen him come up the drive because she was hovering behind it when he rang.

Silk shawls had been draped over the sides of the wheelchair to disguise its unattractive utilitarian function. This was a woman who had once strode about on the stage waving her arms. He sup-posed that if she wanted to move she would have to take away the shawls and that they were just for display, probably for his benefit alone, as if she could disguise as an armchair her apparatus. She was a doll in a pram, that tiny twisted body, the joints of hands like knobs and her ankles carefully concealed beneath blankets. Apart from money, the poor woman seemed to lack everything that might make her crippling condition more bearable, such as visits from lively grandchildren.

The face remained vivacious, the only part of her which was not a source of pain. Her features lay beneath a mat of artificially waved and coloured hair in what he thought of as a period style. In the corner of the room was a large new piece of furniture in varnished wood that he didn't quite understand at first, not a sideboard or a cocktail cabinet, surely?

'It's my new television! It's completely marvellous. Just open the doors and it will reveal the screen, go on. And see below, the drawers, they are to store my copies of the programme magazine. I cannot *wait* for it to start up every evening. I've seen all kinds of plays, oh, I tell you, the plays are absolutely marvellous.'

'Do you think we should get an apparatus for the sanatorium? Some of the patients have been requesting one quite forcibly. I've been rather reluctant, I fear that they might become excitable, though I haven't seen it myself yet and I'm not sure if I'm worrying about nothing.'

'Oh, you are such a fusspot. Television will perk them up, and they need perking up, some of them. I know my darling Gwendolyn would have loved a television, and I can assure you we would have bought her one the moment she asked.'

'I see, well, I shall speak to Matron later today and ask her opinion. You will authorise the cost?'

'Indeed. I don't suppose the Health Service will purchase a set, so let it be my personal gift. Those civil servants are tiresome, don't you think?'

'Yes, they are very tiresome.'

'You mentioned when we last spoke that the streptomycin has arrived. What is your opinion? Or is it too early to tell?'

'No. Not too early. As I expected, it works on some people, but not on others. One of our patients had an awful allergic reaction, you might remember the chap who built cathedrals out of matchsticks? I'm afraid he died. A massive final pulmonary haemorrhage leading to shock and asphyxia. We were unable to save him. Such a pity. We had to dismantle his cathedral, we didn't really know what else to do with it, just a lot of spent matches in the end. On the other hand, one of our young officers, Captain Jackson, is doing terribly well and I'm sure we will soon see his departure to a new life, he has really *bounded* back to health. As for the others,

I'd say a slow but steady improvement. We're not out of the woods yet' – and he remembered for a moment his walk under the bare trees that led to the gravel drive to this claustrophobic house – 'but I do think that streptomycin, provided it is teamed with the PAS tablets, is terribly promising, yes. I certainly believe we might well see a complete cure in my lifetime.'

'Oh, my poor Gwen, we were just a few years too late.'

'A tragedy.' The housekeeper wheeled in a trolley bearing silver pots of tea and coffee and a tiered stand of various cakes. Mrs Downie took a cup between two distorted claws. Dr Limb selected a slice of seed cake, which was the only specimen that did not appear to have spots of bluish mould on its surface. Mrs Downie waved the cakes away without taking anything.

They ran through the week's business and he cleared his throat and made a rapid advance on the subject, or as rapid as he could manage.

'I'm afraid I have an unpleasant request, well, perhaps not unpleasant as rather insensitive. As you know, we are to be inspected. It's a difficult affair, one of the patients became rather distressed and as a result her father wrote to the Ministry and while those problems have, ah, been ironed out, so to speak, nonetheless, the letter has triggered what I've been told is simply a routine assessment of our position, which would have happened anyway, as we go over to full Health Service. As part of the inspection I have to surrender the files of every patient.'

'Oh dear, do you keep them in good order?'

'Very good order, there will be nothing to complain about. But, you see, I don't have, indeed have never had, Lady Anne's file. I think it was never transferred.'

'Was it not? Oh dear, well, I'm sure it *should* have been. What a muddle.'

'I will need the file.'

'Of course, But well, really, do you know I shouldn't think I'd be able to put my hand to it. This is a large house and things got moved about all over the place during the war. Does it matter?'

'I'm afraid it does.'

'Then you shall have to tell them it is lost. Perhaps you kept your own notes, I imagine you must have done.'

And yet, when he thought about it, he had not kept any notes on Lady Anne, because he had not had her file and because, from the very beginning, she had followed his precepts so accurately that there seemed nothing to remark. Some were terribly sick, would die, others could be sent home after some resting of the lung. He had done nothing for her, he realised now. And could not quite remember ever deciding that. As the saying went in his branch of medicine, the disease just took its course.

And it seemed to him now that something must have been said by someone, if only he could remember what or when it was, about her case, which had caused him to, as it were, *put the Lady to one side*, to regard her as a kind of ornament to the new sanatorium, a permanent fixture whose role was to draw wealthy patients with the cachet of her long stay. For if she was perfectly happy there and always to be relied on to speak of how marvellous the staff and doctors were, what a comfortable environment, the best of care, etc etc, and all this was in the promotional brochure put together by the management committee which consisted of local dignitaries, and friends of Mrs Downie's, then the others would come. And they did.

And now it was all ruined because of the foolish socialist government, practitioners of interference. But the dereliction of duty was all his. He had been impressed by her title and her manners and her willingness to surrender to his method. Though he felt oddly that he hardly knew her for she breathed along a continuous equilibrium between health and sickness, never getting well or declining. She was probably the vindication of his theory and yet he had paid her no attention at all apart from pointing her out as a model for later arrivals to emulate.

'Perhaps your housekeeper could take a look,' he said. 'I'm sure it will turn up somewhere.'

'I'll certainly ask her but don't hold out too many hopes.'

Then she began to talk about television programmes again, and he would walk back through the woods with the resolve to have Lady Anne X-rayed the following morning and ask her who had been her referring doctor. For he must be a Harley Street man and would have kept his own records.

37

'And so it turns out,' said Nurse Chitty, 'that she was never even ill in the first place. Lungs as clean as a whistle. No sign of any lesions, even healed ones. When he really pressed her, Mrs Downie just said, "Well, I do remember she had a heavy cold when she arrived." A heavy cold! Thirteen years in a sanatorium for a runny nose? Mind you, she always *looked* ill. What in the old days they called delicate. Delicate, my eye. She was putting it on the whole time, and what for? A quiet life? I don't know, but I'm sure we'll never get to the bottom of it.'

They were in the Singing Kettle, eating slices of Bakewell tart. Alison Chitty had said the jam was very good, she'd never tasted anything like it. The waitress had explained that it was locally made, Kent was known as the garden of England, their raspberries were renowned.

'But what on earth does her file say?' said Mrs Kitson.

'Well, you see, the file isn't there, maybe there never even was a file in the first place, because there would have had to be a doctor's referral and what would he have said? There used to be something they called nervous exhaustion, you know, cracking up, but why send her here when they've got funny farms for that? If you ask me she's just a bit touched and Mrs Downie knew all along. But you would know better than most because you must have been here when she first came, setting up the art room and all that. Do you remember her arriving?'

'Oh yes, I can see her now getting out of the car in her beautiful furs, you've no idea how glamorous she seemed to us.'

'Dr Limb says the inspectors are going to go mad when they find out, it will all come down on his head, make him look like a complete quack. He's getting rid of her the day after tomorrow, not that she's got anywhere to go, they're arranging some kind of hotel or boarding house, I understand, but at the double, so she won't have a chance to go and have a look, like it or lump it, poor woman. I do feel sorry for her, what about you?'

'She's a very nice lady, it's a pity it's come to this,' Lettice said.

'Didn't she do your painting class?'

'From the start. I think it was her favourite thing.'

'How did she seem when she first arrived? Apart from the cold?'

'Oh, very much the same as now, rather relieved to be here more than anything else, I'd say.'

'I meant her health. What did the X-rays show?'

'I really can't say I remember any X-rays, but I wouldn't, would I? It wasn't my department. I'm occupational therapy. I've never had anything to do with that side of things. At the beginning it was all very new and things just happened as they happened. People were arriving all the time, and anyway, Lady A had answered an advertisement in *The Lady*, so—'

'So?'

'You don't have any experience of what it was like to work in a private clinic. There wasn't the same – interference. It was the way they did things. It's probably better now.'

'Of course it is.'

It seemed so tranquil to Alison, so very pleasant to be sitting there gossiping over pastries. Still, she wondered, in a very basic way, whether the place was all it seemed, and if the government inspectors were going to find out all sorts of irregular carryings-on leading even to dismissals just at the time when everything was getting exciting, with the streptomycin starting to trickle in and being able to watch dramatic improvements with your own eyes.

Upstairs in the children's ward, the parents were clamouring for the drug, they were battering down the decision to not treat the little ones just yet. They did not know that one child was being secretly treated. The children's floor nurses had kept their mouths shut. She had heard that they had formed a committee and were corresponding with each other by letter, telephone and even telegram during the week and were meeting up as a group just before visiting hours started to take their case to Dr Limb in person.

For they thought, indeed she thought, that you really can't teach children to be patient, it simply isn't in their nature. And for that miscalculation on his part he was going to be *hounded*. It seemed like the very glass and concrete of the place was cracking around his ears, poor man. The medical advances alone were going to make him redundant, like a blacksmith in the age of the motor car, which was not a condition you expected ever to apply to a member of the medical profession but power was already being stripped away from him, he had started to resemble a fawn mouse scuttling through the halls.

Lettice lit a cigarette and tapped her short crimson nails on the tablecloth and said, 'If you ask me, being thrown out like this will kill her.'

'You think she's really ill?'

'Oh, no. She doesn't have TB, we know that now. But she's institutionalised, isn't she? Because that's what Dr Limb is trying to do to them – not on purpose, he's not a nasty man – but he wants them to be so dependent on the system they'll be too frightened to leave. Everything they have and know is under one roof. Now how is she going to manage out in the world on her own? She won't cope.'

'It's more a matter of what she is going back to. I'd have thought a hotel would suit her down to the ground, plenty of long-stay guests like herself. And she has friends, doesn't she, I've seen them on visiting day. It won't be too bad. I mean, she's not exactly an old lady. Only in her early forties, she could have a whole life in front of her if she wanted, do something useful, make something of herself for once in her pampered existence. When you're a nurse and you see people every day who are *really* ill it's hard not to get cross.'

Lettice turned to the teapot. 'Can we have some more hot water?' she asked the waitress. 'I'm sure we can squeeze another two cups out of these tea leaves. But tell me, Alison, how is the American getting on? Any improvement in his X-rays?'

'Oh, yes, *he's* coming along nicely. He'll be right as rain whether he gets the streptomycin or not.'

'I understand he's taken up with that rather blowsy young girl.'

'Didn't have a choice really, she completely threw herself at him.'

'And do you still ... ?'

'Still what? I really don't know what you mean.'

'No? Just gossip, then.'

Alison leaned forward across the tea strainer and crumpled napkins and said, 'Did he do that ... ?' And felt the blood supply rush into her face and into the roots of her fair hair.

Lettice blew a smoke ring and winked.

'So he did it to you too!' said Alison. 'And is that normal? You see, I don't have the experience, it was my first time.'

'Well, I'd never heard of it before, let alone—'

The two women began to giggle.

'We won't forget him in a hurry, will we?' said Alison.

'I'd say not. But he's not someone to count on, you're *not* counting on him, I hope?'

'If you mean do I think he'll put a ring on my finger, never. I knew that from the word go. Now that poor girl, Miriam, *she* thinks he'll marry her and take her back with him to America. She hasn't got a clue. Her brother ought to have a word, he should be looking out for her. Her last couple of X-rays weren't too good at all. He'll be off before she is, you mark my words.'

'Who? Her brother?'

'No, Arthur.'

It was the first time she had spoken his name aloud to another person. As soon as she did, she felt that she had somehow leached out of herself the specialness of their relationship, had made it ordinary, a thing to be shared with all his other women. Before she had agreed to go with him to the radio cupboard she had imagined sex to be a very serious thing, something solemn and accompanied by vows. He had sat her up on the desk next to the turntable and undone her suspenders, rolled down her nylons, removed her knickers with one finger, gently parted her legs and then kneeled down on the floor, taking his time, doing it delicately with butterfly flutters of his tongue so as not to get out of breath. And then having to come up for another gulp every minute or so and willing her to get there fast while he still had the air left in his tyres.

But the downside, as she would come to understand in later years, was that he'd spoiled her for sex for the rest of her life, not ever daring to suggest it to her future husband, so Arthur would remain forever also stuck in her throat.

'Oh, Arthur, isn't he a one?' Lettice said, laughing now. 'Makes a nice change for once.'

'From what?'

'The usual.'

'You see I haven't really had the usual, to be honest.'

'Well, don't take any notice of his nonsense. He's a chap, after all. The same as the rest.'

'Not your husband, though, he must have been different or you wouldn't have married him. Still heard nothing?'

'About Trevor? Of course not. He's dead. I know he's dead. I don't need a letter to tell me that. Not everyone has a marked grave, you know. My poor man. He was only doing his duty, why do men do that? I've never really understood. We were living in Brighton by the sea in such a lovely little flat and then the war came along and he just *had* to step up and say, "It's my duty, dearest." I can hear him saying it now. Brighton was so nice. It was the light, you see, such big skies and the great white houses like wedding cakes along the sea front, that's where we were, in one of the Parades. Then when he went off, I came back here, it seemed like the right idea at the time, to look after Mum.'

'Oh, Lettice, chin up. I'm sure someone will come along. Just not Arthur.'

'Him? I'd forgotten him already.' She laughed again.

'Listen to us, talking about *that* and in public. It's not what nice girls are supposed to do, is it?'

'It's hard to be too nice in our line of work.'

'Yes, that's what I tell my mum and dad, you see it all, you can't have any blushes left in you by the time you've finished training. Anyway, we've got two new patients arriving to take up Lady A's room, must press on.'

'Poor woman, I honestly feel for her. She brought me a box of chocolates before she left as a thank-you for the art classes. I'd never seen anything like it. Charbonnel and Walker, they're called, from Mayfair, I'll keep the box for ever. I hope she's all right.'

'Nothing we can do really, is there?'

'She said she'd write when she's settled. I wonder if she will.'

When they left the tea rooms Lettice walked home, took off her stockings and suspender belt, changed into her green rayon kimono and sat and smoked. What now came to mind was the day Lady Anne arrived, driven from London in the back of a Daimler, and getting out all furs and kidskin gloves and a hat with a veil. Her brother who had travelled down with her held the door of the car open. He was a somebody, he was in the government in some capacity, an advisor or a lord. His suit smelled of cigars.

She had paused for the photograph with the Downies, Dr Limb and the civic dignitaries and then was taken straight to her room where a maid unpacked her clothes and went back later in the afternoon with the brother to London. There was a certain amount of curtseying and genuflecting at first, but she had waved all that away.

Lady Anne had come down the next day, with her handbag in the crook of her arm as if she was in a hotel but with the most beautiful silk embroidered slippers on her feet, of which Lettice had never seen the like, small and elegant in scarlet and gold thread on midnight-blue velvet. But how pale and wan she is, she had thought, for she herself had only known robust health, exposed to every kind of village germ and building up a hardy system.

Lettice would have liked to have been an art teacher in a school but she didn't have the qualifications, she knew she was just a shop girl with a flair for the visual and a hunger for greater experience than the fields, the hops, the hills, the trees. When you have seen the sea, when you have watched the tide boiling on the Brighton shingle, when you have witnessed storms blow in from the Channel and try to rip the roofs from houses, the ships wavering on the horizon as if they were going to sink any minute, then you know the safety of the land is not be taken for granted.

Trevor saw the jungle. His bones lay under some rubber tree. She'd never even seen the coast of France, however long she looked out of the window of Marine Parade through binoculars.

Something had gone wrong with Lady Anne, she was not wired right, or the wires had got crossed somehow. She must have feared she'd spontaneously blow up if she didn't find some kind of sanctuary but it would take cleverer heads than her own to work out what it was all about. Yes, sex was bound to be at the bottom of it, because in her experience, it always was. She'd had a bad experience in a taxi or something.

In his office, Dr Limb was considering the medical nature of blushing. His mother was a blusher, there was no minor social shame which would not cause her cheeks to turn suddenly rosy. When he qualified as a doctor she had pleaded with him to find out if there was a cure for her affliction, but he had told her that as far as he knew there was none. She was simply too sensitive, not only to the crudeness of everyday life but to the imagined criticism of others, such as when she ordered a nicer cut of meat than usual at the butchers and felt another customer look at her the wrong way with some implied disapproval about extravagance and waste which really was entirely down to her imagination. The blood ran to the face for absolutely no physical cause, there was nothing the matter apart from a sudden attack of embarrassment. There were, of course, he considered, other aspects of the body doing things to you when you were perfectly well, butterflies in the tummy, for example. None were signs of sickness but of the psyche bearing down on the soma.

He had read his Sigmund Freud, which is to say he'd read a few newspaper articles and thought them tosh. Paralysed arms and legs, sleepwalking, migraines, fits, someone who forgot to speak her native language. He was half-convinced the Austrian charlatan had made the patients up for publicity. In the matter of Lady Anne there was no question that she was, in some way, unwell. Her pallor, her temperatures, her wasting body all indicated chronic consumption except the underlying medical condition simply wasn't present.

And what, he asked himself, if she was not a conscious fraud, but like his mother's blushes caused by anxiety could not control her body which had reproduced the symptoms of the disease without actually having it? Why? He had no idea. There was this word *neurosis*. He took down his dictionary from the shelf, his old friend, a present from his aunt when he went up to the Varsity.

A functional derangement arising from disorders of the nervous system, esp. such as are unaccompanied by organic change.

Looked at that way, he supposed there must be something the matter but it was a problem for a psychiatrist, not a TB specialist. The manifestations of whatever was wrong had led her, rightly or wrongly, to be placed here and she seemed to have seen no need to leave. His treatment had not improved her mental state, except perhaps to give her a place of safety in which she could operate on a daily level, managing her symptoms perfectly well within a narrow sphere.

He was sorry to have hustled her off, but what was he supposed to do? When the inspectors arrived they would demand answers about her missing file and he would have to explain his theory that she was either a hypochondriac – a person who had fooled everyone because of his carelessness and Mrs Downie's snobbishness – or she had been misdiagnosed and suffered from some other complaint. Or that, like his mother's blushing, her symptoms were real enough but generated by something inside her mental condition which it was far too late to get to the bottom of. Freud would have said it was down to sex, but he frankly doubted it, for where would a young lady like her have come across that exciting activity in her own elegant home?

Anyway, she was gone now. To a hotel in Edinburgh of all places. Her choice. She would find it terribly cold, but then she would be used to that. There was nothing more he could do.

38

'Let me tell you the situation,' said Uncle Manny. 'The kids are down in Kent in that godforsaken place in the middle of nowhere. Miriam is not doing so good, Lenny heard the nurses talking about her and it terrified the living daylights out of him, what they said. I can't repeat it, tears come to my eyes. Maybe it was all from when they went to the races and she got soaked to the skin and went downhill, I don't know. It could have been a contribution, who can tell? Lenny, on the other hand, is on the up and up, him, I'm not so worried about. And is that fair when she wasn't so unhealthy to start with and only went because you couldn't separate them? Everyone knows you can't tear those two apart so you do what you have to do. You understand my meaning?'

'Of course,' said Ronnie Sprince, 'anyone would do the same. But what *needs* doing, boss? If I can help you, I'll help you.'

'Have you tried the salt beef sandwich? It's better than Blooms, in my opinion. Are you hungry?'

'I can always eat.'

'Waiter, bring us two salt beef sandwiches. Nice cut, no end pieces, no gristle. This time of day they serve you quick. You come in later and the showgirls are arriving and the service collapses, I saw one, she still had the plumes in her hair, just ran out from the dressing room for a quick nosh. The boxers don't even wash sometimes, still in their sweaty singlets.'

'Terrible.'

'Now listen, the question is not – do you do this? Of course you do it! Your own flesh and blood, the future! I have invested a lot of money in my family, I paid for my boy to get out of the army, this time it's the girl needs my help. I promised her mother I'd set her up in a florist's shop and I'm as good as my word. What I'm talking about, to make myself clear' – he looked around to see if anyone was overhearing their conversation but there was only a sallow waiter leaning against the wall licking his finger and applying it to a spot on his shirt – 'is—'

'A heist!'

'Oy, are you out of your mind? No way. I don't get involved with that kind of activity. I'm talking about the art of persuasion, you understand?'

'Ah, a bribe!'

'Now you're getting the picture.'

'It'll cost a bomb.'

'I know. But what can I do? Your hands are tied when it comes to the kids, your own brother's boy and girl. You were born here, weren't you, Ronnie?'

'Yes, I was, in Whitechapel, my mother and father came over, young marrieds, no kids, I never knew the other place.'

'I remember everything, I remember the ship, I remember the rigging and the harbour and sky like a lid of a box over us, the brine smell of the sea to inland people like us who knew only muddy lanes and fields. It smelt of salted herring and pickled cucumbers.'

'The sea smells of pickled cucumbers? I never knew. I've only been to Southend.'

'No, no, I mean it *reminded* me of pickled cucumbers. The salt. I was born in a place called Varaklani and I don't say that with reverential memory but a curse. I was nine years old when we left, huge white birds in the sky screaming, losing sight of land – nothing all around us, just water in motion with ridges, never blue always

224

black, under it maybe the fishes, but I never saw a fish, not once on the voyage. My little brother had snot on his face, always with the runny nose, the sores, the boils, the blisters, like Job himself and all his afflictions. Me, I was hearty and robust. We had a sister, Gittel, her I hardly remember, she died of meningitis, a bow in her hair, that's all, just a piece of ribbon, and left behind in the old lands under the ground.'

'Terrible, bad times.'

'Here comes your sandwich, let's have a look. Go on, pick up the bread, make sure the meat is okay. Fatty meat wraps itself round your heart, it's no good for you, always ask for lean. Our family, every one of us is cursed, we're feeble nags that fall at an early hurdle, I thought I was a success but lost my son. My brother's kids both sick in the lungs, what do you have to do to save them? The question is the eleventh commandment, how do you do it without getting caught?'

'Yeah, how? An inside job?'

'This is it. This is it exactly.'

Manny called for two glasses of lemon tea. A few lemons had started to reappear in restaurants after a long gap when citrus fruits had become curiosities and he had had to drink his tea black and tasteless. The showgirls would be getting up now, bleary, their arches and hamstrings aching. Up the street at Jack Solomon's the boxers were hammering away at each other, seven bells, what for? He didn't understand it. He was never a man to use his fists, violence was for the *goyim*, start a fight and you tear your suit, they knock your hat off into the street, a beautiful hat you saved to buy, how do you roll up sleeves that have cufflinks? You put them in your pocket, in five minutes you've lost them.

'What we are going to do here is what the doctors should be doing, give her the medicine she needs only we have to get the medicine from where it is, which is under lock and key in the hospital.'

'I don't know nobody who works in a hospital. I try to keep away from those places. I don't know if I'm the right—'

'That's not your business, this is in my hands alone. Trying to find a bent doctor or nurse is not going to be easy. These people think they have a vocation, they're like rabbis, what they do is holy. They're not going to walk out with the goods and hand them over, the best you can hope for is leaving a door or a cupboard unlocked. After that, it's a matter of getting the stuff out. This is where—'

'I'm with you now.'

'Good. Are you finished? Food okay?'

'First rate.'

'Okay, let's drive over there and take a look. The motor's parked outside.'

The streets were getting a little busier, there were more cars than there used to be a few years back and they drove about for business and for pleasure, not war work. And still the city was black and ruined, though judging by the noise they were doing something about it.

'Very nice,' said Ronnie, settling into the calf-leather seat.

'It's beautiful, isn't it? I paid a lot of money for it. But I sold three of the flats I built, the rest will be gone soon, made a good profit.'

'Up Finsbury Park?'

'A bit further north, a bomb site it was, on a hill, very high, you can see St Paul's from one of the flats. I planted cherry trees in the garden. In the summer everyone gets to eat.'

'I didn't know you was interested in gardening.'

'No, true, I'm not, but Lenny had the idea. He's a diamond, what he thinks of. And never held a spade in his life or not if I could help it. But an aristocratic lady in the place where he is told him about the cherry tree in her garden when she was growing up and how the birds would come to pinch the cherries and they'd wave them away with sticks.'

'Who did?'

'How should I know? Now listen, do you know anyone who works at the meat market?'

'A few.'

'I heard a rumour during the war, things happening underground.

I heard of secret experiments deep in the cold store for the meat. Is it true, do you think?'

'I also heard that, and from the horse's mouth and not a dead horse either. The way I heard it they was mixing ice and wood pulp to make something, I don't know what it was, but it was supposed to be tougher even than steel.'

'To do what with it?'

'They were going to build floating airstrips in the middle of the Atlantic.'

'Why?'

'Refuel cargo planes.'

'No kidding! Well, you live and learn.'

'From what I heard the scientists were hiding behind frozen hanging carcasses with their test tubes or whatever it is they use, and the meat porters above them slinging pork trotters over their shoulders and no idea what was going on!'

'And what came of it?'

'Nothing in the end, it turned out they built better planes that could get across the ocean under their own steam.'

'But it goes to show, this town is full of strange incident and here we are, the hospital.'

They passed under an entrance guarded by a statue.

'Who's that?' Ronnie said.

'The Englischer king, Henry, the one with the wives and the executioner's axe, not a man to get the wrong side of. A *shtarker* in a gold crown.'

They both laughed.

Beyond there was some kind of church and then a fountain and Manny thought of himself, born far away in Latvia, and none of this history meant a thing to him. The place was named for a saint, his name was Bartholomew but everyone called the hospital Barts. What was it supposed to say to them that it was founded so long ago, and by monks and what have you? What did it matter that the Christians built such a place and kings and queens did or said something about it? They only knew a couple of Georges and the *chazzer* Edward who was spooked by a seductress and never got over it.

'The king we have at the moment,' Manny said, 'he's a solid fellow but in the wrong job, he's not up to it, never wanted it and no one to take over the family firm but the young girl, and she's a mother of two little children, a lady who ought to be at home taking joy in new life.'

'I heard he's sick, I heard he had cancer.'

'I heard that too.'

'We had queens before, I believe. On the back of the pennies, you can see her face.'

'Victoria.'

'That's the one.'

Beneath their feet, the ghosts of cattle and sheep and pigs were seeping out to run off down Cowcross Street, back to their fields.

Manny couldn't go in. He couldn't even force himself. The stench of antiseptic and disinfectant and wounds and blood was too much for him to handle. In the war he'd had to dig out an old horsehair sofa to see if anyone was still alive under there, sometimes there was an airpocket, they could survive a long time if they could breathe. He had picked off the fallen rubble with his bare hands, a chintz cushion with a pattern of roses was still lying there beneath the bricks and plaster dust, he'd hoisted up the couch, upended it and seen a head of hair, a child's. He touched the head gently, it was wedged in by a fallen tabletop. He called over another fellow, the little girl's eyes were open but the head rolled from side to side. That was all that there was of her, the rest was somewhere else, probably a few feet away. He went home and Tessie couldn't get a word out of him for two days.

So he would not go inside the hospital. It was enough to visit the young ones in their sanatorium, he wouldn't step foot in this house of carnage.

They sat down on the edge of the fountain and lit cigarettes and Manny thought about what was going on under their feet. The cattle used to be herded down Caledonian Road from the countryside but according to his information they now came on special trains and the trains went underground into tunnels in the bowels of the market where the experiments had been conducted. Beneath there must be a different city, like the Tube lines. Anyone who went down there was bound to be a character, a person not normal like those who lived in sunlight, or at least the fluorescent light of cafés and billiard halls. An individual amenable to interesting propositions.

Suppose there were tunnels under the hospital. There might be. How did they get rid of the bodies? They couldn't cart them out through the front door, surely, and the bits and bobs they amputated, there must be a boiler room, a furnace for disposing of limbs.

The thought of it made him sick. It was a dark business he was getting into, when all he'd ever wanted was to make a few bob, quite a *few* bob. For the family, to secure their future in this new country, in this city which enclosed him comfortably like an overcoat and he felt in all its pockets.

39

Both sides of the road leading to the hill had been struck by a doodlebug in 1944 killing nine people, four called Gould – a whole little family wiped out early on a Sunday morning as they pulled back the blackout curtains, put a kettle on to boil for tea, swept last night's cold ashes from the grate. Eleven houses had been demolished and a collection of temporary one-storey dwellings went up in their place, constructed out of the latest materials, concrete, aluminium and asbestos. Already the resourceful and tenacious occupants had created gardens front and back. One had dug a pond with a miniature bridge across it, and sticklebacks had mysteriously taken up residence.

Here below Ally Pally Manny felt he was close to nature and was not surprised to see rabbits gambolling along the perimeter fence behind the prefabs, freed for an hour from their hutches. You could still, if you were a countryman, smell the remains of old farms and their crops and animals. Manny had met an ancient feller in a wing collar below a face with two livid spots like dabs of rouge who stood on the street and called out at him in a fluty voice, 'I remember when I was a boy it was all fields. And dairy cows! Imagine that. Then the non-conformists built their chapels and the clerks came and some of them wouldn't even fight in the war.'

'Very interesting,' Manny had said, who had a meeting with Harry Pike, the jobbing builder from Bounds Green.

Now it was finished, more or less. He had financed the project and it was coming good. The flats looked modern, different from what else was on the road, houses less than fifty years old, some of them, but looking terribly shabby with dirty net curtains and peeling front doors and cracked steps, quite a few still lit by gas mantles. The whole neighbourhood was getting slummier. His flats were properly built of bricks, traditional London stock; the bays at the front were steel casements, which was the coming thing, and inside all-electric. There was an air of confidence about the structure, he thought, in a couple of decades the whole street would be pulled down with its stained-glass panels and floral ceiling roses, and replaced by up-to-the-minute architecture.

Three flats had been sold already to young couples waiting to move in when the snagging was finished. Another two he was hanging on to to rent out. The last was still for sale. Once he'd found a buyer he could start on the next development. Across the other side of London no-good shysters were buying the leases of mid-last-century houses for a fiver with only a couple of years left to run on them and letting them out to the coloureds, a whole family in one room, which was not a respectable way to behave and he would have nothing to do with it.

He walked up the stairs and let himself into flat four. Everything was clean and white and empty. The kitchen with blue Formica worktops stood waiting to be used by an eager housewife. The cooker was straight out of the showroom and the drawers of the cupboards glided freely. Manny's wife Tessie had chosen everything, knowing, she said, what the post-war housewife wanted. In the living room a built-in gas fire was surrounded by a mottled beige tiled fireplace, no sweeping out the cold cinders in the mornings.

He went into the kitchen. From the window he could see the television transmitter slowly blinking, it was a hell of a view you had up here of the palace, slightly shimmering as if it was a mirage rising from the green of the hill. Breathtaking, he thought. What a city! What opportunities this town offered to a person like himself, whose own father was just a rural middleman in a bog in Latvia dealing in grain in a small way. Who can touch me, he asked himself. Who can lay a finger on me now? Those days are gone, we are kings here, *kings*.

The TV transmitter like a finger beckoned him into the future. This was something Lenny had started to talk about, television, maybe working in television, and Manny had said, 'What? You don't come to work for me when they finish with you?'

Lenny had flinched. Backtracked. 'Of course, Manny. Of course.'

'You're my investment.'

'I know I am.'

But something happened to him in there which Manny didn't know what to do about. He was exposed to a different type of person who had given him ideas, thoughts and feelings that were outside Manny's range of experience, the narrow road you stepped on and walked forward, like you were building that road under your feet and every day it was a little longer. The boy was turning into something Manny couldn't put his finger on. Like he'd developed a new kind of brain in there, the soft kind that dreamed and had no grip on reality.

But I have bought him, I have invested, I know my rights.

The troubling sight of the television transmitter irked him, he felt his bladder pressing in and he went into the bathroom to take a piss. He raised the toilet seat carefully and when he'd finished he flushed, standing well to the side of it even though he'd installed the modern low-lying cistern with no chain. In memory of his brother. Life was full of danger, a toilet could kill you, never mind TB.

He walked back into the empty living room. The prefabs across the road seemed humble in the sunlight, as if mankind was stepping back to the time of hut-dwellings, yet a fellow in his shirtsleeves and, of all things, a beret on his head like a Frenchman was cutting back the grass with shears. Next door a woman was doing what women everywhere do – hanging out her washing on a line strung between two wooden posts. Manny sang out at them.

232

Down in the jungle, living in a tent, better than a prefab, No rent!

The other bomb site lay abandoned. A small wilderness had overtaken it in only a few years and turned it into an impenetrable tangle of saplings and rose bushes gone very woody, with whitish blossoms struggling up to find the light beneath an over-canopy of eager ash branches.

He should find out who owned that plot. Sometimes the council took them on, sometimes they didn't have the cash. His empty land had gone for a song, a bent planner and some insider information.

He heard a van pull up. Ronnie got out, holding a suitcase. Manny moved away from the window, he heard Ronnie's usually light tread come up the stairs, his feet landing awkwardly.

'Come in, come in, so you got it.'

'Nice place, boss. I come here straight from my lock-up, what a change of scenery. Mind if I put this down? Weighs a ton.'

'Wherever you like. No problems?'

'Not that I know of, boss. You can't be too careful but I think it was okay.'

'You think? You just think?'

'No, it was fine, no hitches. I'll tell you what, it's something else down there, the stench! Put me right off my dinner. I'll never look a lamb chop in the face again.'

'You'll get over it.'

'Nice Welsh rarebit I had last night instead.'

'Still comes from a cow.'

'Nah, grows in bottles, everyone knows that.' They laughed. They were happy to relieve the tension, the knowledge of what they'd done.

Manny picked up the suitcase. 'Blimey, this is heavy.'

'I told you.'

He set it down on the Formica counter in the kitchen. There was no furniture in the empty flat. 'Is there a key?'

'Got it here.' He took it from a piece of string round his neck, it was still warm from his chest under his jumper, and Manny recoiled slightly at the idea of touching the little man, one of those runts that their tribe sometimes produced, like skinned cats.

The contents of the case were smothered in balls of newspaper, he felt his hand in and reached the neck of a short fat bottle with a metal cap. He pulled it out. So this was what it looked like, the famous streptomycin, the very miracle which people would kill for so as not to die.

'Calcium chloride complex,' he read. 'Merck. What is Merck?'

'No idea, boss.'

'There should be instructions what to do with it, but I don't see nothing.'

'I suppose the doctors get told that.'

'Then they'll have to go on what they already saw.'

'Okay.'

He had pulled it off, him, a man who always stepped only a few inches on the other side of the law so he could dodge back, was not what he thought of in his mind as a criminal.

Pride and discomfort. Suppose he was caught. Was this what he was going to be famous for, in the papers, him and a lowlife like Ronnie Sprince together in the dock?

'Okay, the job is done. Here's your money. No debts between us now.'

'Of course not.'

'We might not see each other again for a while.'

'Lie low, boss, that's right.'

'I meant, the association.'

'Oh, I see. You don't know me, never met me.'

'Exactly.'

'Well, if I don't see you again, I wish you plenty of mazel.'

'You too.'

'Very nice flats. Any chance—'

'Did you not hear what I just said?'

'I done myself out of something there, didn't I?'

But Ronnie Sprince was not the type of tenant Manny had in mind, he was thinking of young couples, the husband who took the train to Moorgate with the other commuters, a good war record, honest, tip-top payers, aiming eventually for a house near the Green Belt. Ronnie did not fulfil any of these requirements.

He left it fifteen minutes after Ronnie had gone, walking round the garden inspecting the junior cherry trees which would, he'd been assured, give fruit in around four years. The red fruit hanging from the tree and families sitting under the branches, maybe watching television sets in the evening with the signal from the Palace streaming sharp and brilliant into the screen.

40

As Sarah entered Maison Lyons she saw the fleshy man she recognised from her Sunday visits to the sanatorium raising in his hand the *Daily Express* as they had agreed, his gold signet finger bent over a photograph of the two-year-old Prince Charles in a delightful little coat walking with his hands behind his back in imitation of his father. And the incongruity of that fat digit half concealing the royal child's head struck her with a frisson of what she thought of as a sneaking pleasure – that the royals, to whom one must pay such respect, could be covered with a forefinger and smeared with the grease stains from a buttered toasted teacake which he was already eating.

She held out her own hand and he put down his newspaper and gave her his own, wiping it first on a napkin, warm raised mounds at the base of the fingers on his palm and the heated gold of his ring. He raised the metal dome under which the teacakes were being kept warm. 'Eat!' he cried, and poured her a cup of tea.

There was something both boastful and proud in the way he spoke of his nephew and niece, the boy to rise up along with him in the world of property development, building and renovation, and the girl with the talent for flowers – 'Wonderful young people,' he said, 'and what have they done to deserve this curse?'

'Nothing at all, I'm sure,' she said. 'Just unlucky.'

'And your friend? Also unlucky?'

She would have passed over Hannah's situation with the usual opaque phrase, *a rather difficult war*, but as far as she understood, Hannah had led the other inmates to believe that she had been something or other on their side, probably to do with one of the listening stations. At least she had not dissented from this theory when it was put to her.

'She was in some rather hairy places,' Sarah said.

'Got you.'

She had no idea what he had taken from her statement but he seemed satisfied, had no further questions. He wiped butter from his mouth with a napkin. He had eaten three.

'A slice of cake, maybe? Would you like to see what they have? The selection is not bad, not bad at all, considering.'

'Oh, no. The teacake was more than enough.'

'And your friend is making progress?'

'Yes, in fact she's recovering, I think. Actually, the *rate* of recovery is quite extraordinary, faster than I had expected and faster, I think, than the doctor had anticipated, I mean the medical director, Dr Limb, do you know him?'

'No, I never had the pleasure.'

'Bit of an old fussbudget, and rather set in an old-fashioned view of the disease, from what I hear.'

'I don't care what he thinks, I only want for my boy and girl to be well again.'

'Of course, who wouldn't?'

'And how did she get to the top of the queue? Maybe she was at death's door?'

'Yes.' She had nothing to add.

For it had seemed to him all that week leading to the meeting with Sarah that there was something fishy about the German woman getting the stuff before anyone else and maybe he might in time get to the bottom of it, but she wasn't answering questions so this could only mean that she had something to hide. Which was not a bad thing at all, a good thing in fact, for anyone with a secret in their heart was a person you could generally do business with, whether they liked it or not.

'It is very nice that you are happy to take some things in for Miriam. It's just some clothes and magazines, and some perfume and creams and shampoos she likes. Me and their mother go every Sunday without fail, but tomorrow I have a difficulty, something I have to attend to.'

'I understand.'

'I'm going to give you money to take a taxi from the station.'

'Oh, no, really—'

'No two ways about it, you take the taxi. It's on me, *everything* is on me. It's a heavy case.'

And Sarah thought how funny it was, how amusing that tuberculosis should have brought the two of them together in Maison Lyons of all places, which she associated with people who came up from the provinces to take in a show and perhaps an exhibition; coming here because they were impressed by its potted palms, its chandeliers, the grandiose tea-urns and great quantities of chrome. And the hundreds and hundreds of people eating teacakes and scones and wiping the corners of their mouths and gossiping about such personal matters that they failed to notice, as Sarah had clocked, the covert smiles between the lady in the hat with the green feather sitting on her own in the corner, and the ash-blonde waitress whose uniform was slightly too tight around the hips. A girl whose ankles seemed finely formed to be admired from a horizontal angle, lying on a chaise longue. But no one noticed women, she thought, or not women in relation to each other, that is.

Manny walked out onto the street with her and hailed a taxi. He put the suitcase into it and handed her a five-pound note. 'Oh, no, that's far far too much, that's a fortune for a few taxis.'

'Then go first class on the train, stretch your legs, enjoy yourself.'

'No, I'll give the change to your niece when I get there, I wouldn't dream of anything else.'

The taxi took off and she looked behind through the rear

window to see him standing on the street, his hands in his trouser pockets, smiling. A fat Jew in a mohair suit with a dimple in his chin.

And how this suitcase clanked, she thought, when she got out at home. But it was locked and she hauled it up the stairs and put it next to the front door ready to take to Kent in the morning.

Manny posted the key to Lenny wrapped in a bit of newspaper. He rubbed from it his own fingerprints, handling it with leather gloves.

41

Lenny and Persky took Miriam into the wireless station and shut the door. Persky put a pile of platters onto the spool of the turntable, starting with his favourite of 1948, 'Chicken Shack Boogie' by Amos Milburn, a *peach* of a record that would disguise any commotion or sudden movements in the broom cupboard. Persky started singing.

> *They say it's the place where all the bad cats meet*
> *You'd better be mighty careful where you take a seat.*

'Up you go, baby,' he said, and kissed her on the nose.
'Are we ready?'
'All set.'
'Are you *sure* you know what you're doing?' Lenny said.
'Don't worry, my old ma has diabetes, I shot her up many times.'
She hoisted herself up on the desk and rolled up the sleeve of her dress and offered the inner arm to Arthur. He bent down and kissed the soft flesh inside her elbow. A vein ran blue and clear.
'Wait, that's not right,' Lenny said.
'What do you mean?'

'The shot isn't in the arm.'

'So where?'

'In the tush.'

'Oh! You better pull down your panties, baby.' He winked at her.

The broom cupboard smelled faintly of old dishcloths and foetid mops. The records rose in grooved black lines across the shelves, protected by their paper sleeves. A syringe had been stolen when the nurses' heads were turned. He unscrewed the cap and filled the glass tube.

There seemed to Miriam something eternal and everlasting in the three of them in this tight space together, giving her the holy water that came from the glass bottles, Lenny standing with his back to the door, his shoe raised and leaning against it, biting his forefinger as he watched them, plumper than she'd ever seen him, his shirt buttons straining round the stomach.

'You shouldn't watch,' she said. 'No! look away.'

'Why, darling? Why can't I see?'

'My bottom!'

'I seen it before.'

'Not now. Not since, you know.'

'Okay.' And he turned his head as he had looked away in the months when they had been resting at home and she had reached up to push her breasts into her brassiere. Now this intimate thing that was happening between them, this experiment to make her well, was being carried out by the man who was going to displace him – his friend, his sister's lover.

'I don't like injections,' she said. 'I'm not going to look either.' She put her hands over her black eyelashes, the mascara flaked onto her fingers.

'Ready?'

'Yes. Do it!'

And the streptomycin began to pulse through her whole system with its antibiotic properties, inhibiting protein synthesis and acting as a genocidal campaign against bacterial cells. It was as if both first and second world wars were being enacted inside her plump body, an orgy of death against malign forces. All this massive activity inside the human system was not visible to the three people in the room who only heard Miriam give a small squeal, an ouch, before rolling her sleeve down and looking round happily. 'I'm already starting to get better, aren't I?'

There was something of grandeur about what they had done, Lenny thought. These three outsiders who had kicked in the system. Who had done what none of the walking corpses would ever have thought of. Years ago Manny had pointed to an apple on a street-market stall. 'You want the apple, son? You really want it? Then *take it!*'

Miriam started telling Arthur to speak up. 'Your voice is going all whispery,' she said. 'You're like a ghost, I can see you but why have you turned quiet all of a sudden? Isn't he quiet, Val? And you, you need to speak up as well, I don't know what's got into everyone, turn up the bleeding volume on yourselves, will you?'

In their room Valerie turned the volume knob on the radio up to its highest setting until she herself was deafened, but Miriam still cocked a hand behind her ear and said, 'I *still* can't hear Arthur properly, will someone fetch him for me?'

Then everyone went quiet. Valerie was like a faint breath, Lenny the note on a very softly strummed guitar.

Lenny and Persky whispered together in the sound-proofed wireless station cupboard. 'What have we done to her?' Lenny said. 'What the fuck have we done?'

'I don't know.'

'You said you knew what you were doing.'

'I do, I know how to give injections, they went in clean, it wasn't that, there must have been something wrong with the stuff.'

'How come? It came straight from the hospital. The caps weren't tampered with. I went into Miss Spiegel's room and took a look at the bottles they were giving her. It was exactly the same stuff.

Exactly, I double-checked. She had some tablets to take as well, I don't know what they were for.'

'You think that could be it? She needed the tablets? They were part of it?'

'I don't know, maybe. Arthur, she's frightened. *I'm* frightened.'

'I know.'

'Are we going to talk? Are we going to tell anyone what we did?'

'No. We keep our mouths shut.'

'They're going to find out somehow.'

'Not if we hang together. Listen, we're buddies, we're in this thing, we just got to—'

'What have I done to my sister! Oh *Moses*, what the fuck have I done? I'm going to live with this for the rest of my life, I'm finished, I'll never—'

'Take it easy, we'll find a way out of this. Maybe her hearing will come back. We still don't know why it happened, anything is possible.'

'It is, but that doesn't include you doing a runner. You get me?'

'Yes, I get you.'

Nurse Chitty said to Valerie, 'Is she having problems with her hearing? But that's most peculiar, why would that happen? I am going to send for Dr Limb.'

Valerie watched his face turn the colour, she said, of ashes in the hearth, 'completely cold, you know, when the life has gone out of something'.

He started to ask Miriam questions, took off his glasses, gave a little mewing cry like a kitten and asked, 'Has anybody been giving you any medicine to take?'

Valerie said, 'I don't think she can hear you. Why don't you write it down?' He took out his notebook and fountain pen, unscrewed the mottled blue top and inscribed: *Has someone been giving you any medicine to take?*

Miriam paused, looked at him, thought that truth was a strange friend and could be an enemy. Shrugged. Turned away.

Valerie reached over the pad and wrote, *You've got to tell him, you must.*

Miriam shook her head with her mouth firmly closed like a child refusing a food she doesn't like.

'Why don't you come back later?' Valerie said to Dr Limb.

When he had left, Miriam wrote, *Worst crime is to be a blabber-mouth. You stay shtum. Might as well be a nonce.*

I don't know what any of that means.

Yes you do.

Well then, but we need to find out what's wrong.

Wrong. Miriam looked at the word. It had so many meanings. The teachers at school used it when they wanted to thwack you. But something was wrong. Everyone loved her, Uncle Manny, Lenny, Arthur, all wanted her to be better, not sick any more, and only the bitch in the next bed was after her to squeal, because when it came down to it, the middle classes stuck together.

You don't have to tell them the whole story.

I ain't got no story.

The girl's bravado, Valerie thought, she'll face everyone down, they do stick together, don't they? And where did sticking together get you?

Please, Miriam, tell them.

Nothing to tell.

But maybe I'll have to stay here for ever, Miriam thought, maybe I've stuffed myself. Oh, what's going to happen to me now? Whose fault was this? No one's fault. Love did it, and loyalty, and taking care of your own, but there had been a mistake. The doctor could fix it. Make the doctor fix it. They'd look after the consequences. They brought her lunch on a tray. She looked at the bread and butter and sliced boiled egg and salad and tinned fruit cocktail. He'd better fix me or I'll be eating this grub for the rest of my life.

When Limb reappeared, she wrote *Injections.*

Who gave them to you?

A friend.

Where did they get the medicine?

Miriam drew a large question mark. And smiled.

Were there any pills you had to take at the same time?

No.

Are you absolutely certain?

Yes.

No one had private supplies of streptomycin, it was under government control. Somehow it had to have been stolen and brought here – not by the American, he hadn't left the place apart from trips to the village, so a visitor.

The girl's uncle had to be the culprit but he had not been near the place in weeks. Of that particular crowd the only people who had come were Valerie's parents and Hannah Spiegel's friend and there could be no connection between that quiet, prim lady from the BBC and the racketeer who was the Lynskey relative.

It was all speculation and he had no idea how the streptomycin had got into the sanatorium but whoever was in charge of this crime had no idea at all what they were doing, what the correct dosage was and the nature of the combination therapy. They were shooting Miriam up in the dark.

It must be reported, to the Ministry of Health and to the police.

And that is the end for me.

He turned to Valerie. 'And how are you getting on, Miss Lewis?'

'Improving, thank you.'

'The operation—'

'The mutilation, you mean.'

'You won't complete it, have the rest removed?'

'No.'

'I see, I agree that we will be able to try you on the streptomycin very soon, within weeks; new supplies are arriving all the time.'

'Which was my point all along.'

'Well, I shall take my leave. We might not see each other again, so—'

'Why? Am I being transferred somewhere?'

'Oh no, we shall keep you on a little longer, be patient.'

"There is no longer any such thing as patience.'

'You young people, you—'

But he thought better of whatever he was going to say and left the room to make the telephone calls that would finish him.

Valerie felt a pale sweat evaporate in the air as he disappeared. A tired rotting darkness had gone. She righted herself against the pillows and picked up the notepad.

It was for the best, Miriam.

Always trouble for us, always bleeding trouble.

42

And it was the same ambulance driver who returned them to London, the brother and sister greatly changed, the brother filled out, less of a spiv, more of a man, that cocky air beaten out of him, and the girl silent, fat, frightened.

They looked back at the sanatorium. Inside were those who would be saved, those who would die and those who would continue to suffer, incurable. They turned their heads resolutely to the gravel drive and ignoring the woods focused on the exit.

'And how did you get on?' asked Joe Hart. 'Did they cure you?'

'I'm much better now,' said Lenny in a muffled voice, as if he was crying, and looking in the mirror Hart saw that he was wiping his eyes with his sleeve. A hare ran across the road.

'That's good luck, that is,' Hart said. 'Looks like the bluebells are out too. Did you ever find any ice cream in the end?'

'No.'

'And you, young lady? Feel the improvement?'

No reply.

'She's getting on all right,' the brother said, looking at her. She was, in the sense that she appeared the same, her make-up had been done, her hair styled for the return home. The Blustons costume was back on, her best outfit. In it, she looked like herself.

Miriam was feeling groggy, a dead weight of heavy air muffled the sound of the engine and the driver's voice. The air was blurry, thick, blocked. Her thoughts ricocheted round her head like a pinball table. Sounds did reach her, but as if she was hearing them underwater. High frequencies were out of range.

She had started to read her brother's lips, which wasn't difficult since she could normally read his mind anyway. But that thing he'd just said, that she was all right. Is this how it's going to be now, him talking for me? Me with the thoughts trapped in my head and no way of getting them out?

Arthur Arthur Arthur – two soft syllables, a name without much consonant definition, not like Persky, which was glass with jagged edges. She could hear that. But *Arthur* was a breath of air, a sigh. He'd gone. He was ahead of them, already in London, he was looking for a ship. He needed to see his momma and poppa in Brooklyn but then he'd turn right back again and come to her.

The place they were leaving was cursed, an enchanted castle she'd read about in a kids' book. The spell was going to be broken once they got out of here. In films there are only happy endings, she thought. I'll come through this, once we see London I'll be right as rain, I can hear better already. That fucking dump almost did for me. London will make me better. She thought of fried fish and a pickled herring and chopped liver on rye bread. Once I've got proper grub inside me, I'll be fine and dandy, look there's a—

They passed out of the village, watching the green, the fields, the hops, the animals, the birds. They would hate the English countryside for the rest of their lives. When they reached Rochester the river was dirty and ugly, they saw things they recognised – cranes, lorries, tankers, ships, ash-tips, rubbish, broken buildings, scarred streets, feral dogs and cats, women in hairnets standing in queues. This is more like it, Miriam said, in an echo in her head.

'So how long has it been?' Joe Hart was asking. 'Just over a year?'

'Yes, about that.'

'And was it what you expected?'

'No. Didn't you say you only brought people one way?'

'I didn't want to frighten you. Even a year ago a lot didn't come back at all. Of course everything's changed now. And you might say you've had the very best of it, a nice long rest *and* the cure. Not everyone gets the timing right. They'll be in and out of that place in no time soon. Look, here we are, dear old London, our good old Smoke.'

PART TWO

On the Beach

1953

43

None of their group had ever flown before, not even Sarah who before the war had got as far as Venice but that was by boat-train. The younger members of the party felt themselves to be pioneers of aviation up there in the gassy firmament eating a little meal from a tray and watching the contours of Europe spread below them, its borders their armies had defended or invaded a few years ago. But from above it was all dreamy, detached, affectless.

Other passengers, old hands who knew what to do when their ears grew painful, helpfully held out paper bags for the others to be sick in. No one actually disgraced themselves but as they approached the island they hit an air pocket, plunged a bit, a few people screamed and Lenny put his foot down on Spanish soil look-ing, Valerie said, 'white as a winding sheet'. Staggering. Holding shamefully on to his sister instead of her holding on to him, her hearing apparatus swinging on her chest like a plastic necklace.

Beyond the tarmac the aerodrome was nothing much compared to London, just a few shacks and metal prefabs. Soldiers in green uniforms roamed about with rifles over their shoulders wearing ridiculous patent-leather hats with the brims turned up at the back, making them seem, Valerie said, like characters from the lid of the Quality Street chocolate tin.

But they should not take this sight too lightly, Sarah warned them. For this was Franco's Spain and they must be careful. Did they know that the island's most famous resident, the poet Robert Graves, had once been arrested for having the wrong papers and worse – being in possession of a printing press? Valerie knew who Graves was, Lenny and Miriam did not. This holiday was, Lenny thought, turning out to be an education before they had even left the aerodrome.

'My pal Eggy Sitz's older brother was in Spain,' he said to Valerie, to assert himself as a person with knowledge and sophistication. 'He was with the International Brigades, came home with one arm, which was no good at all when you're a tailor and presser.'

'What happened to him?'

'He manages a bagel shop in Brick Lane, does the accounts, you only need one hand to write. What he's terrified of is typewriters.'

The country was a dusty residue of fascism, left behind after the great cataclysm of the world war, worn out, but still resistant to democracy. Valerie, waiting in the line to be processed, whispered to him that this was what all of Europe would be like if they had not won. Hannah, overhearing her, said under her breath that if Germany had conquered the world then Spain would have been swallowed up together with its timid neutrality into the greater project and not resembled *this*, a land of fancy-dress hats.

For Germany had an innate dislike of chaos and untidiness and this was why she had fallen in love with Sarah who was untidy, it was in her nature. Her flat was messy; after the severe order of the sanatorium Hannah found this surprising, exciting and enchanting. She *left her skirt on the floor*. Her one lipstick was put away without its cap screwed on tightly so it dried up or the stick got covered in hand-bag fluff and even biscuit crumbs. She had a stain inside the lining of the bag from a leaking bottle of cough mixture. Yet no one seemed to mark her down at work for these traits and she flew through life with hair in her eyes and scuffed toes on her shoes. Wasn't England *marvellous* to allow a being like Sarah to exist and even prosper? At home she would have been put away a long time ago.

In the spirit of the British there was, she felt, a kind of human glitch, the system could handle a sense of humour because it seemed to understand the essential unmanageability of things, this was her theory for why, to Sarah's surprise and dismay, Labour had lost the general election. Not everything needed to be subject to socialist planning and the people had understood this and rejected it. There were parts of the country, she'd heard, that still believed in their hearts in an Olde England of pixies and ghosts and magic and, privately, she thought that was a good thing, though obviously preposterous.

Sarah's messiness was a flaw she wanted to kiss and kiss.

A local government official was sitting at a desk flanked by two patent-heads. Lenny found it difficult to keep a straight face as the man examined his (new) passport. He had posed for the photograph in a studio on Tottenham Court Road a couple of months ago, looking, said the photographer's lady assistant, like a film star with his hair Brylcreemed into place and a jazzy yellow tie with a repeat pattern of fried eggs knotted round his neck. 'Do you think I look ill, at all?' he had asked.

'No. Why, have you had a cold lately? It doesn't show if you did.'

And that brief exchange made him think that perhaps the last traces of sickness had been erased from him, apart from the faint scars in his lungs. There was no question that in so many ways he was a different man, no longer his uncle's protégé and project but capable, he now thought, of being anyone he wanted, or at least of doing anything he liked, and he was helping Auntie Tessie wind up Manny's business affairs, get the books all straight, or as straight as the law would allow in their favour when he was in prison. But Manny had been cunning, that block of flats up Stroud Green, for example, had been put in Tessie's name. Lenny and Miriam were living there for the time being. From the kitchen window he could see the blinking mast of the Alexandra Palace transmitter and walked up there to be shown around by Sarah. The excitement of it got the better of him and he had to stand outside and smoke, his fingers trembling. Could this be him? Could he do *this*?

Miriam sat in the garden among real growing flowers, chewing American gum hard until she'd extracted all the flavour and kept the wad for ages pressed against her cheek. Plastic earpieces were in her ears. Her hearing wasn't as bad as it had been, she could get on all right in a shop, on a bus, as long as people spoke up clearly, and she could do a certain amount of lip-reading. The world wasn't exactly cut off.

She'd seen a film once, an American picture, where a car was driving along a road and suddenly a huge crevasse appeared, a mighty crack into which cars were falling and falling, the passengers screaming as they plunged to their deaths. As long as you stayed still and didn't keep your foot on the accelerator you'd be safe on one side, but still the cars seemed not to be able to stop themselves going forward. They were eaten up by the earth itself. When she saw it she'd laughed. She wouldn't laugh now.

I wouldn't even be able to hear myself laughing. A quiet life for me from now on. But that's not on. I'm not built for it. I've not got the qualifications.

Valerie had said, You've always got books. Yes, she always had those with their imaginary friends. Am I going to have to make do now with those paper people?

But here, on the hot tarmac, the air was much louder than in the garden. She sensed that there was plenty of noise all around her and she could hear some of it. And Arthur was on his way, he was right now on the deck of a cruise liner sailing from America, he was coming.

The official wore a suit and dark glasses and was the first representative of the Franco regime anyone had seen outside the newsreels. He seemed to Lenny very ordinary, like a clerk at the gas board. Sarah dealt with him briskly and authoritatively in that imperious manner that women of her class acquired at birth, with their accents and social poise and matronly bossiness. Valerie, it seemed, had not had time to learn this routine before she fell ill because she didn't behave that way at all, more open and egalitarian, talking to everyone as if they were the same.

'D'you *see*?' Sarah kept saying, as if the official was a backward child. (And Lenny thought, *Yes, I do, I just don't always bleeding agree.*)

The beauty of the island was mentioned as a significant issue regarding the purpose of the visit while the others stood around holding their pale faces up to the heat like sunflowers.

The sun! Sun they didn't need to be afraid of even slightly. Warm smells of paraffin, sweat, oil, flowers, cheap perfume, cooking oil, dusty dogs, the skin of others.

Evidently the official was satisfied and they were allowed to leave the aerodrome. Through letters and telegrams Sarah had arranged for a specially chartered bus to be waiting for them with a driver and a local interpreter who took them first to Palma to spend the night. Dusk gathered quicker than everyone had expected. Lives spent in watery light meeting for the first time the metal glare of the Mediterranean felt that it was impossible to believe that something so powerful could be extinguished simply by the earth turning away from it. Lenny thought it was easy to forget that winter was a product of the rotation of the planets, not some government policy imposed upon its citizens deliberately, like income tax and rationing. There were supposed to be countries where there was no winter at all. But now it was humid twilight and they drove through a wide shadowy avenue lined with palm trees. People were walking about. What they were doing out on the streets none of the English party understood. They passed women with large white handbags and two-tone high-heeled shoes arm in arm with dark men in double-breasted suits, hair shining with Macassar oil.

The interpreter told them the avenue was known by everyone as the Borne but the official name was Avenida del Generalísimo Franco and would remain so until – and here, under cover of darkness, she made the familiar gesture of a finger across the throat.

The next morning, after a hot, uncomfortable night in a fairly basic hotel, the bus took them to the north of the island and to

257

the village, a place known to Sarah through work as a spot where a bohemian population of artists and intellectuals lived a sybaritic life amongst the peasants. And why not a holiday, she had suggested, why not get away from it all to somewhere where the idea of freedom was the whole purpose?

It was an awful road (before the war it had taken a day to get there from Palma) but the scenes on either side were astounding – huge spiny plants, gaudy flowers, exotic unrecognisable smells, and the air becoming cooler with their ascent. Valerie was staring at a landscape she considered brutal and exciting. It was how she had imagined the terrible raging cataracts of Wordsworth's Lake District until she actually went there and found it surprisingly low-key, full of tea rooms and birdwatchers. Places did surprise you. One of the officers at the Gwendo had mentioned that while stationed in Italy during the war he had been startled to come across a road sign directing the traveller to Vallombrosa, 5 kilometres. 'That's from Milton,' he had said, 'and I'd thought until I saw it, that it was a made-up place like Atlantis.'

Spain to her was bullfights and Franco. She felt up to dealing with it. I am a stronger person than I used to be, she thought, and I can cope with this climate and topography. She didn't just mean in her health. The streptomycin had cured her lungs, but she had through her own force of will prevented them from sawing off any more ribs, she had stood up to the system, she had ceased to be the well-behaved, educated daughter of the Edgbaston suburbs and had screamed at Dr Limb, 'really quite like a fishwife', according to one of the nurses passing her room, under 'the appalling influence of that *very* common girl she's sharing with'.

She had thrown in her lot with this pair, who by Lenny's reckless actions on top of her father's dogged letter-writing on her own behalf had brought down the medical director, had him sacked from his job and the Gwendo placed under permanent Special Inspection by the Ministry. What they had done to Miriam was terrible, though they had not meant it to be. It was an action forced by love, the love of a brother for his sister.

She looked at the back of his head on the bus in front of her, the wiry black hair, the broad shoulders in his new light-weight silvery Italian jacket made of some material not tweed or any other fabric in Daddy's wardrobe at home, something new and modern and not necessarily originating wholly in the natural world, she remembered the way he came to life on the radio, and their post-Gwendo meetings in various cafés when he walked in and a smile cracked his whole face when he saw her – oh, she felt, he is *something*. But what exactly?

Miriam watched the passing landscape. Them plants were something, what were they even called? Look at that! Real lemons growing on a tree! She banged her brother hard in the ribs.

When they got off the bus from the city at the high village a procession of some kind was passing through which to Valerie seemed to have the aspect of an exuberant amateur ritual, such as a freshers' week parade.

To Hannah it resembled an unforced march of some kind by people evidently free in their spirits but nonetheless she still did not really like to see columns of people on foot. They gave her what she could only describe as 'a terrible feeling'. It came up from her stomach like acid reflux and spoiled everything. She did not want Sarah to know this so she pretended to laugh and clap in happiness at the sight of the carefree wanderers wherever they were going.

Sarah observed it as what it was: a leisurely walk by a group of holidaymakers down the steep escarpment to the beach.

At the front was a man wearing a pale shapeless linen suit of the type only Englishmen ever had in their wardrobes, being too pragmatic about the heat to mind the terrible creasing and bagginess of the fabric. He had made some gesture to artistic eccentricity with a multi-coloured waistcoat and a red bandanna tied round his neck. He did not notice the new arrivals fanning themselves in the dust with newspapers they had brought with them from the aeroplane for this purpose. All his energy was expended on pulling along a donkey, which, like a seaside attraction, had its head covered in a straw hat with holes cut out for its ears. The donkey's name was evidently Isabella because he kept on calling out to it when it dug in its hooves and refused to budge.

The donkey was trying to dislodge its passenger, a flamboyantly beautiful woman who stirred in the watchers a faint memory of having seen her face quite recently magnified a thousand times on the silver screen. It was infuriatingly tricky to be certain because she was shaded under a wide-brimmed hat held down by a tangerine-coloured silk scarf. Her mouth was slashed with a shade of lipstick which closely matched the scarf, bolting away from the conventions of red and rose pink, which was all Valerie had seen during her years in the sanatorium and precious little of that. To wear the colour of a citrus fruit on your face seemed to her to be a rather mocking reminder that here, on the island, there was all kinds of abundance (bushels of fruit, rivers of olive oil, but not much electricity). Miriam knew the name of the shade of lipstick, she could spot it a mile off. Tangerine Rapture. But she couldn't tell anyone and who, amongst her party, would be interested?

After the donkey came a tall thin delicate-looking Negro in tinted glasses, also wearing linen but with greater elegance due to his slender form, clutching a child's painted tin bucket and spade. More men strolled along behind in various degrees of dishevelment. One wore those heavy blue cotton trousers they had learned from Persky were called jeans. Being American and Australian and used to large spaces, they were talking loudly, as if they were trying to project their voices over the mountain down to the sea. Even Miriam could hear them and she brightened up. This lot are okay, she thought. Women appeared, striding along in rope-soled canvas shoes, and carrying bags of what looked like bathing things. Finally a gaggle of schoolchildren, robust boys and little girls, ran about screaming.

Behind the procession grey mountains flecked with red formed a massive wall on which olive trees hung precariously from stone terraces. The party was disappearing over the edge of the cliff along a winding track which when Lenny looked over it led down to huge flat rocks and beyond them, the beach itself. Pine trees precipitously clung to the fissures. None of them had ever seen a landscape like it, it was nothing like the vague rubbery outlines of Kent. It seemed to all of them infinitely savage, infinitely terrifying, infinitely exciting and a balloon went up in all of their hearts that here life was to begin, at last they would know that they were living, not just alive.

Apart from Sarah, they were all a little nervous, unacclimatised to the idea of the foreign holiday and with brand-new accessories such as sunglasses, suntan oil, sandals, cotton shirts and dresses and an absence of the familiar world of handkerchiefs, spittoons and thermometers which were already two years in the past, part of the old world in which George VI was king and none of them had yet seen television. Since then, they had all watched his funeral. Sarah had a minor part to play in the Outside Broadcast Unit and was a junior member of the planning team. Hannah was immensely proud of her.

Above, the sky was a high flat blue. What did you call it, Hannah asked Sarah. Azure. And not a finger of cloud. The heat throbbed in their faces and they turned to look at each other as if they had been transported not to a Mediterranean island a couple of hours' flight from London but to a place where they were not themselves, and glad not to be, hopeful of a permanent transformation.

At last the parade was gone by and their own party was left on the road. The dust raised by the pilgrims' feet started to settle, and then they were left with the hot silence of the village broken by the melodic jangle of sheep bells in the distance.

The spectacle of the gaudy procession down to the beach had rather jarred on Sarah. Yet wasn't she herself a pied piper with her collection of former inmates from the sanatorium, not just her beloved Hannah, but the cockney brother and sister, the nice girl from Somerville and the anticipated arrival of the American sailor in a day or two?

44

When Persky saw Mrs Dunte strolling on the deck with her husband before cocktails, the liner manoeuvring its way through the Straits of Gibraltar, he knew who would look a million times better in that dress.

The *gown*, as its owner would refer to it, had one of the new boned strapless bodices like a kid's drawing of a heart, the thing cupping the two breasts and narrowing to a wasp-waist held in by invisible bones beneath the satin. The skirt ballooned away in raspberry-coloured folds to a length around mid-calf and it was the most glorious bit of feminine frippery Persky had ever seen. The thing made his heart tune up an orchestra and put a soprano on the stage. Some song, some canary, some dress!

Mrs Dunte, who was one of those ice-blonde Grace Kelly types Persky only admired but who didn't do much for him in the menswear department, had with her a dozen gowns to wear in the evening, one for each night aboard ship. She was loaded yet still she seemed taut and slightly unhappy, with a Midwest accent and to him no one who came from that desolate flatscape could have any joy in their hearts – there was nothing there. Midwesterners grew up brooding over featureless terrain and Persky did not brood.

Maybe the dress looked different under artificial light, more enigmatic and shadowy, but in early-evening sunshine it blazed along the deck. Persky heard the salt wind blow the folds of the skirt, and the clack of her kid-leather shoes dyed to match the dress, and the light thwack of her husband's patent evening pumps. He heard and saw them clearly and sharply, while to the Duntes he was a white outline ready to be of service if they needed him. He was invisible even though his teeth were good and his sideburns black and glossy, tipped with salt spray from the spume.

They were cruising from New York down the boot of Italy to Palermo via the Balearic Islands. The voyage called in at the Mediterranean ports where several members of the crew once had taken part in the capture of the peninsula and were keen to revisit old fond-remembered sweethearts in the brothels of Naples, or if retired, try out their younger sisters. On board, several passengers were looking forward to pointing out to their wives the places where they had served in the US naval fleet, on destroyers and in landing craft. Italy was a place they were coming to sample the new pleasures of *la dolce vita* in a land of sunshine, lemons, oil, fruits, girls.

The next day Persky passed the Duntes' stateroom. The raspberry-coloured dress was in the rough teenage hands of a cabin boy called Mike Spellar, a college kid working his summer vacations in the merchant marine, holding it cloddishly, immune to the flamboyant fire of the satin, just something to add to a heavy canvas bag of soiled garments. This dame had spilt champagne on it the previous evening, she wanted the stains out in case they set in permanently.

The dress was Persky's for the taking so he was going to try to get it. It was free-floating in the space between him and the kid, and could be moved, as if by magnets, from one set of arms to the other.

'The dame sent me down to collect that dress.'

'It's for dry-cleaning.'

'No, she changed her mind.'

'Why?'

'Why should you care?'

'I don't know, it just seems weird to me.'

'You don't ask questions.'

'I'm in college, we're encouraged to ask questions.'

'This is a ship, you obey orders, I'm your superior officer.'

'What kind of officer are you?'

'The kind who fought a war so you could be inquisitive, that's who.'

'Well, I don't care, as long as it's legit.'

'Of course it is. What would I want with a ladies' evening gown?'

'How should I know?'

'Just hand it over.'

And the boy did.

Persky took possession of the dress and ran fast to his bunk below the waterline where he rolled it up and stashed it in his kitbag, throwing out spare shirts and two sets of socks to make room. It was going to be a creased mess when he took it out and gave it to Mimi but she would have an iron for sure, all women did.

Persky had come to an arrangement with the captain regarding his tenure on this voyage. Their relationship went back to a time just after the war when he had helped the Old Man out with a matter of extreme personal discretion, involving certain contacts and connections in the Bronx. He had received special dispensation to leave at Palma and find his own way back to his home port. It was an unusual arrangement but as Persky had persuasively explained, he was going to have to find a way to make it right with this girl.

The captain listened to this and said, 'So what's your plan?'

Persky said he was going to spend a week or so with her on the island and figure out what to do.

The captain said, 'Are you going to marry her?'

'Oh sure.'

But the captain didn't believe him and Persky didn't really believe himself. He had no idea how to get out of this situation, but there existed, implacably, this hard knot of uncomfortable morals he learned from his father which would not allow him to be a complete heel. What kind of ratfink would he be if he slunk off and abandoned her? And in the same breath, how could he spend his life shackled to a deaf chick?

Maybe he could, maybe marriage would be the minor part of his make-up – the wife at home, seldom visited, but with the name, the Persky name to comfort her – it could work, she maybe would be satisfied with that, he didn't know. Women were unfathomable, who would even *try* to figure them out? They were cute, they were not cute, they were clingy, they were free spirits, they liked a good time, they were mopes. But she had shown him her tush and he'd sunk the needle into the soft white flesh. 'Thank you, Arthur, thank you.'

Suppose I gave her a Paris gown. Wouldn't that be something?

Yes it would be something. She was a lovely girl, she was still lovely, but she was damaged goods. I broke her, I broke the kid. I didn't mean to. I feel terrible but no one can say it was my idea. They can't touch me on that one. He would go ashore, he would bring her the dress and then they would work something out.

The ship was having a wonderful run under sparkling skies. It sailed on along the villages of the Costa del Sol, white piles of houses lying low along the shore, passing the fishing village of Torremolinos, a huddle of small white houses along whose streets the first tourists in shaded glasses against the rays of the strong sun were discovering an undiscovered Spain. On board a visiting professor from Columbia University was giving a lecture about the novel *I, Claudius*. To preserve the privacy of Mr Graves there would be no visit to the village where he now lived but there would be a chance to explore the vibrant city of Palma with its magnificent Gothic cathedral built on the site of a Moorish mosque overlooking the harbour.

Mrs Dunte was looking for her dress. She called out to the cabin boy to ask where her dry-cleaning was, he said he hadn't taken it, he'd handed it over as per instructions.

'What instructions were those?'

'He said you changed your mind.'

'I most certainly did not.'

'Well, now I'm confused.'

'*Who* told you?'

'I don't know his name.'

'A passenger?'

'No, crew, like me.'

He had only seen Persky for a few minutes, he was sure he would recognise him if he laid eyes on him again, but there were plenty of swarthy young seamen in the crew – Jews, Italians, Puerto Ricans – and a simple description wouldn't be enough to pin him down.

Mr Dunte sent for the captain and told him that his wife's Dior gown, purchased last fall in Paris, had gone missing, presumably stolen. The captain listened carefully to the circumstances. It was in his mind that the kid might have taken the dress but this didn't seem likely. His uncle was a big shot in the union and had interfered to get him his seaman's ticket. So someone was framing him but he didn't want the kid to know that this was what he was thinking. Better he should feel under suspicion.

Mike backed away, frightened, in fact he was terrified. If he was accused of *stealing* on board ship, who knew what was going to happen to him, would they dump him off at Palma and let the local police arrest him? Or would he be put in chains in the hold and brought to justice back in New York? Either way he would probably not be able to return to Princeton.

On deck they played tennis and swam in the freshwater pool and felt that pleasure was rightly theirs. Persky lay low, avoiding the first-class passengers and the crew who served them. In a few hours they would reach Palma where he would go ashore. The dame had plenty of dresses and he thought she wouldn't miss this one once she'd accepted it was gone. He pictured Mimi's face when he handed her the garment. Mrs Dunte was a little flat-chested and didn't fill out the satin cups while Mimi had no problems in that department, she would *ooze* over the top.

She talked about flowers all the time. There was only so much a guy could hear about roses and irises and snapdragons and tulips and carnations and lilies but she rattled away indifferent to his boredom. He could set her up in her own store and leave her there, forget about her. His mom and she might start to feel for each other like sisters.

After dogged enquiries, because this was his life, his future at stake, the kid eventually tracked down Persky lying on his bunk.

'It was *you*!'

'Whaddaya mean?'

'You took the dress.'

'I never saw you before in my life.'

'My uncle is a big shot in the union, who are they going to believe?'

'Oh, go to hell, I'm busy.'

The kid came back with the captain.

'This is the guy.'

'Oh, really. You sure?'

'Certain.'

'Where's the dress, Persky?'

'What dress?'

'We're going to have to search you.'

When they found the dress rolled up in his kitbag and it came out like a bloody coiled baby from the canvas womb, Persky shrugged.

'I just wanted it for the chick I told you about, the deaf broad. Shouldn't she have a pretty thing like this?'

The captain turned to Mike. 'Do you know what the worst crime you can commit on board ship is?'

'Murder?'

'Sure. And then what?'

'I don't know.'

'Well, it's theft. And I'll tell you why, because theft interferes with the running of the ship and the running of the ship is a serious business. A thief until he's caught wreaks havoc on the functioning

267

of the crew as a cohesive team working diligently to keep the vessel afloat. Everybody hates a thief. Thieves at sea sow paranoia and mistrust until they're caught. You have to weed out the paranoia as well as the bad apple.'

'Wow.'

'You know I got to lock you up when we get to Palma,' the captain said to Persky. 'Don't take me for a nice guy.'

'You're kidding.'

'No. You've had it, son. This is your last run.'

'Wait! I know my rights. You can't blackball me, it's an anti-labour practice. The union won't—'

'You can find a job, they'll take you on in the union office.'

'I ain't going on the beach.'

'Tough. Find another way of life for yourself.'

The ship came into port, the passengers disembarked and toured the cathedral. They bought shoes of Spanish leather and other souvenirs. They were not the first cruise liner of tourists Mallorca had seen but they were among the early arrivals, the avant-garde for whom Europe meant the war and their memories of beach-heads and landings and battles to take a city. Mallorca was still an island of shoe-makers and olive-growers, Magaluf was a lonely bay.

Persky, locked in the dark of the brig, imagined that he could smell the lemons ripening on the trees and taste the crude wine and lift to his mouth a piece of fatty roasted lamb. He saw the sky through a slit in the iron of the ship's hold, not shackled, just locked up. There was nothing he could do, the captain was obdurate. The law of the merchant marine, an offshore jurisprudence, formed Persky's chains.

In the brig as the ship pulled out and turned eastwards to the Italian shore he thought fondly of Miriam as of an old bittersweet romance with a girl long dead and by whose grave in one's imagination you lay flowers. As the ship rolled slightly in the swell his mind turned to how he would live his life on land instead of sea and that took him far away from Miriam and the sanatorium to the radio stations and the rising tide of *beep-bob-a-loola rock and roll.* For after all, when the ship turned, at Palermo, he was going home, back to that big place, that endless land. He sailed on, to America, to the continent of Elvis Presley who was just then walking into the studios of Sun Records and laying down his first track.

45

In Deià the English party saw for the first time a bohemian colony of artists living in the sunshine on trust funds. The ex-pats did not seem to need jobs as any of the party understood the idea of work as a salaried affair or with a weekly wage packet. They painted, sculpted or wrote poetry (not novels, which were too time-consuming), they had parties, they had sex, and the three of these activities taken together were their occupation.

Valerie was enchanted. All the time she had been lying in bed subject to the Way of the Patient and painfully learning disobedience, on this island intellectuals had been living like this, without a care or a responsibility except to their art and their desires. It was absolutely marvellous.

Hannah was unimpressed. 'The people here,' she said, 'they think of themselves as rebels, but you know I don't think they really are, not after studying them. They are simply hedonists. It is quite boring, really. I doubt if any of them will ever do good work. They lack the discipline. In fact, in some ways this village reminds me of our former home in the sanatorium, a closed community living by its own special rules.'

'How interesting,' said Valerie. 'Perhaps you're right.' The two women, who had never met while they were both residents at the

Gwendo, had grown friendly since their release. They all felt the same complicity in Miriam's condition and though neither of them had played any part in damaging her hearing, they felt a moral responsibility not to abandon her. She sat, a silent heavy figure, cupping her hand round her ear, mouthing 'What's that? What's that?' She would laugh for no reason. Sometimes tears would roll down her face and she would try with a handkerchief to catch them before her mascara ran. Valerie hoped that Arthur was really coming. Lenny seemed sure he'd show up. He and Persky had had words, the contents of which were not known to the rest of the group.

Hannah had grown fond of Lenny, the little simpleton, and had encouraged Sarah to find him an opening in the television industry for he was, she sensed, having heard his radio programmes, a signpost to the future where fun and jollity would rule and social conventions would be relaxed. She felt for his poor sister, who had been damaged by nothing less than a brother's overwhelming love.

Valerie was an interesting young lady. She and Lenny made an odd couple. She could see that they were drawn to each other like faulty magnets.

They all made their way down the stony path to the beach for another morning of lying in the sun and bathing while the artists painted or performed impromptu modern dance.

Valerie was ahead, walking slowly and carefully. Lenny had dawdled to look at her from behind, and see how she got on on the steep path in case he needed to run forward and rescue her if she stumbled. She was still slender but no longer the skeleton with hair whose bed he had sat next to for so many months. She was wearing a long-sleeved cotton dress with a pattern of roses on it. Her waist was held in by a red leather belt.

He caught up with her and took her arm, 'Just so you don't fall.'

'I'm quite all right.'

'You never know.'

'Oh, *really*. But if you insist.'

They reached the rocky water.

271

'Can you swim?' she said.

'Yes. We used to go the baths on Hornsey Road but I don't know about now.'

'What do you mean?'

'This is the sea, it's rough, and I don't know if my lungs are up to it.'

'Well, don't go out too far then.'

'No, I won't. Are you going to get changed? You're not staying like that, are you?'

'Oh, I don't think—'

In the hospital she was always in her pyjamas, he had no idea what she looked like, the big scar, he supposed, the sunken chest. He didn't know what to say to her, he had no reassurance. He unbuttoned his shirt and took off his trousers. Beneath he was wearing royal blue swimming trunks, it was the first time he'd had them on since he was taken ill. Round the waist was a white rope belt tied in a knot.

He could not look at her. If he did, he might get hard.

'Well, I'm going in for a splash.'

'Okay.'

He walked in bare feet across the hot stones to the surf and Valerie watched him hesitate, look down at the water and up again at the horizon. He let the waves lap his feet. His hair was curling over the nape of his neck, the white rope was loose around his waist. He turned round and made with his hands an expression of helplessness, laughing at his own babyishness, she thought, and then she swatted a fly from her face and her hand obscured the sea and he was gone, just a head left and arms like slow rotors making their way out towards the horizon then turning prudently along the line of the shore.

This mutilation, this ugliness which would separate her off for the rest of her life from the human race – he will pity me, she thought, as Persky pities Miriam and feels an obligation he won't be able to live up to. So I will not permit him to let me down.

Sarah and Hannah returned from a stroll around the rocks.

'You look hot,' said Sarah. 'You must be boiling, why don't you change?'

'Oh, you see, I can't. Because—'

But Hannah said, 'Oh, I've seen worse, my dear, much worse.'

Valerie ignored her, for she could think of nothing more repulsive than her mutilated chest. She shaded her eyes and watched Lenny.

'Hasn't he come on?' said Sarah. 'When you think what he's come *from.*'

'I agree,' Hannah said. 'He could make his mark, that young man.'

'Doing what?' asked Valerie.

'The entertainment of the masses.'

'You make it sound a little like a fascist rally.'

'Do I? I don't mean to. Of course there will be a war of some sort between culture and populism, there always is, but I'm sure we will somehow manage to keep the upper hand. Well, I hope so.'

'You worry too much about the future.'

'And you can be a little placid, I feel.'

'Are you two quarrelling?'

'We have our differences,' Sarah said. 'Hannah feels that there must, in this world, be a true rebel and she is waiting to find one, a pure rebel in spirit, and she sits there quite passively looking on, watching to see if the next person is this defier of all convention.'

'Wouldn't that be Persky?'

'Oh, no. He is simply out for himself, he belongs heart and soul to the Persky party with a few traces left of his upbringing, a sort of weak moral undertow of communist ideas that are flaking away with every moment. A rebel disobeys for the sheer pleasure of disobedience, whatever the consequences.'

'And we were in thrall to the Way of the Patient, remember that?'

'Indeed. The poor doctor. I heard recently that he threw himself off – where was it, dear?'

'Beachy Head.'

'Yes, a cliff. A swift, tumultuous death. No patience, then, for the workings of, say, a poison.'

Lenny was getting out of the water. Valerie raised her arm and waved. He was shaking drops of surf from his hair and holding up the white rope round his waist.

Hannah watched his progress up the rocks to their beach towels. The heat, the heat! They all felt so hot and not a thermometer in sight, their bodies expanded in the warmth and the absence of danger, they were not coddled, they were free to catch colds or cut their feet or fall victim to an infection and be cured with antibiotics.

Lenny, observing the three women on their towels, reached them and took out the Box Brownie camera he had bought in London. He began to circle round, pressing the button, winding on the film, snap snap snap.

Hannah and Sarah put on their bathing caps, got up and waded into the water together. Valerie watched them bob up and down splashing each other's faces before swimming off.

The woman they had seen on the donkey approached Lenny. Her body was flawless, perfumed even in this heat with something that smelled of flowers and spices, from her neck and wrists.

'Hello, we haven't spoken, I'm Iris.'

'Hello there, Iris, I'm Lenny.'

'And what do you do here, your little group?'

Valerie, a few feet away, listened to him tentatively explain how it was a holiday after a period of incarceration, which he outlined in light detail. He identified the other members of the party.

'But you are all cured now?'

'Yes.'

She was an actress, a minor film star, he might have seen her name on the screen credits of a few films from the Ealing Studios. Better known, she agreed, in the theatre, but Lenny had never been.

'Oh, darling! How dreadfully deprived.' And she reached out and to his surprise laid a hand lightly on his bare leg.

274

Jesus, she fancies me, he thought, I don't believe it. She must be thirty if she's a day, probably older, and she fancies me.

Valerie said, 'I'm just going for a stroll, see you later.'

How stupid of me to come to a place where bare skin is de rigueur, she thought, and even Sarah and Hannah are wearing *shorts* of all things, and little blouses, and then running together, hand in hand into the sea and splashing each other and doing all the silly games, the horsing around of carefree individuals.

She looked back and saw Miriam enjoying the company of the painters who didn't want her to say anything or even listen to them. She was sitting, one leg extended, the other bent under her, like a starlet in a white ruched bathing suit, her hair rippling in carefully arranged blue-black waves. Her hearing aid apparatus which normally hung around her neck was lying beside her. Three artists were arranged around her, sketching. The old man they had seen at the head of the procession the morning of their arrival was pointing her out to a boy and saying something with a foolish smile on his face which the boy would always remember about his great-uncle, and decades later would wonder who the girl was who had appeared for a few days that summer and disappeared again, with no one able to explain what she was doing there, with whose entourage she had arrived or why she never returned.

Miriam felt the old man's breath on her shoulder. He was sitting down next to her and speaking in what seemed to her to be a whisper. She knew he was a famous person but he gave her the creeps. He was saying she was amusing. 'What makes you think I'm funny?' she said.

'No, my dear. A *muse.*'

The noise of the beach was a constant low roar, his voice was a drowned sailor blowing bubbles. The poet looked at her impassive face. She was always looking out to the horizon, she must belong with Poseidon. He wanted to bury his face in her breasts.

'Buzz off,' she said and turned down the dial of her hearing aid.

The beach was crowded now with Americans. Someone was prodding at a barbecuing sheep with a stick. His shining bald head was the bronzed dome of an ancient helmet. The sea smelled of brine and excitement and everyone on it seemed to Valerie to be doing exactly as they liked, apart from her.

She remembered something Persky had said to her on the day he left: 'You know, kid, you can be a free man anywhere, even this place.'

But she did not see how she was ever going to be free, she was dragging her sack of skin and a few bones round wherever she went. Her breath was always slightly laboured. She only had one lung to operate with. Life was always going to be what her mother called being careful.

She turned once again and saw the actress's body angling itself from the waist, the hipbones barely covered by the bikini and her hair down on her shoulders and her lipstick still indelibly imprinted on her mouth.

She moved her hand up to Lenny's knee and leaned forward to begin to delicately nibble his ear lobe with tiny white teeth and a pink darting tongue. Lenny allowed her tongue to enter the shell of his ear and lick it. He watched Valerie retreating towards the flank of the cliff face, a diminishing figure ignored by the boisterous party.

Valerie walked on. He's just a boy after all, she thought, and why on earth should I be interested in him anyway, for our lives are so far apart now despite all those conversations in London over tea. He's just an uneducated lout who in a few years' time will undoubtedly have gone to fat like his appalling uncle and be some small-time hoodlum, probably in prison himself, for they are all . . .

But how easily these prejudices come, she told herself. You turn them into an eternal race with eternal characteristics like Shylock and his pound of flesh and yet you know nothing about them, really. They surely aren't *just* a puzzle from novels and plays, how Dickens portrayed them, how George Eliot did, what T. S. Eliot said in *The Waste Land*, which was quite awful though Pound was much worse, and how they have suffered but then look at Hannah, and no one ever talks about that, about people like her, there's simply no conversation about it at all.

She had gone as far as she could. She stood with her back against the rock. Lenny was standing now, he was saying something to the woman, they were two miniature figures far away and they were obviously going to leave the party and go somewhere to do whatever it was adults do.

The actress was whispering something in his ear and was holding him by the upper arm as if he were an expensive handbag she had acquired in a Mayfair shop. Valerie looked out to sea.

A few heads bobbed in the water. Hannah and Sarah were swimming together in a line, their blue and white rubber caps rising and falling. Miriam was standing now with her hand shading her eyes, looking for Persky's ship. And there was a ship on the horizon, yes, moving slowly under the sun. Miriam jumped to her feet, raised her arms and waved at it as if she was performing semaphore, she was windmilling and windmilling. *Arthur*, she shouted into the wind.

Valerie watched the ship too. Somewhere on deck, if not that vessel then another one, Persky was about to lay anchor his heart. Everyone but her was sure he would come, why was she the one who was cynical, pessimistic?

When she looked back along the beach he was coming towards her. Oh, *look* at him, the hairy Jewish ape with the joined-up eyebrows, his outline wavering in the heat. What the hell does he want? Can't a girl get lost on a beach with her own thoughts, can you not be alone for a minute of your life without people crashing in on your privacy when they know better than anyone that you had *no* privacy at all, when they know perfectly well what you had to put up and put up and put up with – the hell of other people, then they come barging in when you want to be alone? It was tiresome, it was graceless, it was the way people are when they haven't read enough or thought enough or even looked closely enough at, say, a flower, not for its beauty but its structure, people who don't think, who—

'Let me look.'

'What do you mean?'

'I want to see what you're so keen to hide from everyone, what you're covering up with such a fuss like you're a nun or something.'

'My God, how *dare* you, it's none of your bloody business.'

'I told you, I want to see.'

He reached towards her and began to unbutton her dress. When he unfastened the second button he stopped and drew a finger across her skin, touched it with a hand damp with the sea and his sweat, then the bodice of the dress began to fall away and he saw the long scar, the uneven concavity of her chest.

'You don't understand,' she said. 'I'm not a woman, I'm a wooden doll brought to life. That's all. A doll.'

'Why do you always have to complicate things? I don't even understand you. And what are we even *doing* here amongst these people, and what have they got to do with us? They're all phonies and fakers and parasites. *We* suffered, they don't know the meaning of pain.'

'And so what?'

'Don't you remember, Valerie? Don't you remember how cold it was, always cold and no love, no love in there at all? The children without anyone to love them, just tie them down to the bed, put straitjackets on them. Me, I think you're beautiful. I don't care if you don't have enough ribs or that you have a scar, we all have scars, we all came out of there with bits of ourselves missing, but we're young, we can get over it.'

'I can't get my ribs back, I can't grow new ones.'

'No, I know you can't and what's more Miriam's still deaf but we can do something with our lives, we can make up for what we've missed. Are we going to carry that place around with us on our backs until we're dead and in a box? Are we not even going to free ourselves? *I won't take it.* I want to be loved, Valerie, and you do too. I want to be kissed and held.'

'Are you going to rape me?'

'How could you say such a thing? Don't you know me?'

'I know about your birds in Soho, Miriam told me.'

'They were nothing, little tarts.'

'And now you want—'

He pulled the dress above her head. She was standing in her

bra and pants, sensible smalls, she called them, and her sandals, and round her exposed chest a necklace of wooden beads she had bought from a woman in the village. The indented breast was held in by what looked to him like a surgical contraption in ointment-pink cotton.

He reached round and unfastened the bra, threw it across the rocks. She cringed, holding her arms across her chest. 'Don't look at me.'

'I'll look all I like.'

'Then to hell with you, see.'

'You're lopsided, that's all. It's nothing. And a pink line. It's fading. What a lot of fuss, honestly.'

'You can't diminish it like that.'

'We've *got* to live, Valerie, what choice do we have? I damaged my sister, I've still got to live, don't I? You're trembling, by the way.'

'What do you want?'

He was all sweat and salt-water getting down onto his knees. She laughed.

'Oh my God, a proposal of marriage.'

'No, not that.'

He reached up and pulled her pants down. '*Now* what are you doing?'

'Don't worry, it's something I heard about from Persky.'

PART THREE

The Dark Circle

46

'She called me her hairy Jewish ape, you know,' Lenny said, touching his wife's hand. 'She actually said that. Can you believe what this *shiksa* came out with and I still married her?'

'Well, darling, as you know, I was being ironic.'

'Get over yourself, sweetheart, you picked it up from your father who was the biggest anti-Semite that walked the earth.'

'Don't be silly, don't exaggerate.'

'Remember when you told him we were engaged?'

'Oh dear, well ... yes ... '

'Man, I was a total nogoodnik to him, come up from the slums, uncle in prison, no real job. And he said to her mother, "I told you, Phyllis, that we should have gone private." Of course, once I was working in television he bought himself an autograph book and was begging me to get signatures. "Do you know Richard Dimbleby?" No, I said, he's BBC, we're the other lot, and his face would fall. And you know what *she* said?' He jerked his thumb at his wife. '"Poor Daddy. Just his luck."'

Listening to Lenny being interviewed in the conservatory of their house in Hampstead Garden Suburb in 2002, the younger crew members were struck by the old man's voice, the remnants of that now-extinct accent of the East End they had heard in only wartime newsreels. Contemporary east London is composed of glottal stops making the speaker sound like they're swallowing their own tonsils. Lenny talked right at the front of his mouth as if he were shooting gumballs out of his lips, a slight lisp on certain words, overlaid with a veneer of Sixties posh (the Mayfair drawl) he picked up when he was hanging out with showbiz types like himself who had come up from the slums and made good and tried, ineffectually, to hide it.

Valerie, beside him on the cane sofa resting against seat cushions decorated with palm leaves, said, 'Well, you see he *was* terribly common, but when everyone is in their nightclothes you tend to notice less. We were all shoved together regardless of background and had to rub along as best we could. That was the NHS's doing, the world of charlatan private doctors with their fees in guineas just melted away and we actually and genuinely were all in it together. For a while we were, at any rate.'

A photograph in a silver frame on a coffee table next to them of the three women on the rocky beach at Deià reminded the director of the 1918 Picasso picture *The Bathers*. In the photograph as in the painting one woman is standing, drying her hair in the sun, one is lying on the sand sleeping, and one is resting and watching, her head turned to the right, as if she has seen something, or someone walking along, or is just generally curious about life on the beach and more self-consciously aware than the others.

'Is this you?' the director said.

'Yes, that was me, two years out from the sanatorium.'

'You look well.'

'She was fine,' Lenny said. 'Nothing the matter with her by then. Nothing at all. Strong as an ox. Me too.'

Neither of them were ever able to openly speak of the sanatorium as a form of hallucination. 'We all have our scars and our memories,' was all Lenny could say when asked about his time in Kent.

In the middle of shooting, when they were in the studio and the lights were hot and he was looking at his script and an actress was saying, 'Do I stand here or here?' then the apparatus which had inserted a needle into his chest would suddenly reappear in front of him, that nameless doctor with the elephant ears and a file of black hairs running from his forefinger to his wrist at the sink washing his hands, pulling on his rubber gloves, and Lenny would wince and the cameraman would ask, 'Are you all right? Not heartburn, is it?' 'Not at all, it's nothing, don't worry.'

They were being interviewed as pioneers of early commercial television, Lynskey and Lewis, names that everyone recognised from the rolling credits. After the holiday in Mallorca, revitalised by sunshine, Lenny got work on the televised *Sunday Night at the London Palladium* when ATV launched in 1955. Early in his career he worked on *The Army Game* (a British version of the *Phil Silvers Show*). The programme ran for four years from 1957 to 1961 and after that he went over to the hospital series *Emergency Ward 10*, the first British medical soap opera, where Valerie was already working as a junior script editor. From then on both were taken up by the TV impresario and boss of ATV, Lew Grade.

By the late Sixties Lynskey and Lewis were part of that glittering world of dinners at the Ivy, Lenny in his single-breasted midnight-blue Italian mohair suits, Valerie in one of her high-necked satin evening gowns with a matching bolero jacket, frequently pictured in the papers, both smiling broadly next to Joan Collins or Shirley Bassey. Valerie was the brains behind the outfit, she did character development, plotting, continuity, and Lenny was the huckster, the schmoozer who trusted his instincts, the brute ideas feller who knew from their own hard times in childhood what would make his sister crack a smile and what would make her weep rivulets of mascara down her face. He never worried about the schmaltz factor or considered it, as Valerie sometimes did, mawkish. From Persky he had learned the art of the pitch.

In the early Eighties they moved for a few years to Los Angeles, to work first on *Hill Street Blues*, then *The Golden Girls*. In California Valerie grew less inhibited about the body she still considered an ineradicable mutilation, swimming every morning behind a screen of bougainvillea in their pool then eventually undressing even at beach parties in Malibu.

One morning she thought she spotted Persky pulling in at a gas station. The same lean slightly cadaverous shape behind the wheel, the widow's peak far advanced but the hair as black as it once was with a suspicious high gloss. Ray-Bans hid his eyes. If it was indeed Persky he would be around sixty years old, grizzled by the weather, and the man getting out of the car had the sallow tan of someone used to being outdoors. The face was wrinkled but still handsome, the jawline had become jowly, but the outline of the lips was firm. Was it him? She pulled up. She had never seen him in sunlight, only in the clinical brightness of the sanatorium's fluorescent lights and once in the dimness of a hotel bar.

She felt, as Lenny did, that those who had been through the sanatoriums had an aura of darkness about them, that their past suffering had penetrated their skin. That there would always remain a breathlessness, a cautious attitude to danger or the opposite, a reckless disregard for it after the years of pent-up torment in bed, and the latter was undoubtedly what Persky would feel, already programmed as he was to rebel in his own self-interest.

The Camaro he was driving, a yellow fish in the sunshine, was a muscle car, a young man's vehicle, but bore a half-peeled-away Mondale sticker on the bumper. Had it been Reagan, Valerie would have been certain it wasn't him. The Persky she had known hated Republicans and phoneys and she had no reason to think he would have changed; for if it was true that he was out for himself, still, she could not imagine him taking his place comfortably in a prudish America cautioned against saying yes to everything he considered life-enhancing. People altered, she had herself, but surely not that much?

The driver was wearing blue jeans, but everyone in America wore them. A denim shirt held in its top pocket the outline of a package of cigarettes. Would Persky smoke? She and Lenny had not smoked since 1963. Would Arthur remain so defiant, so rebellious, that he would jeopardise his own health?

She watched him fill his car with gas, turn to admire a pretty thing walking in white high-heeled sandals towards the bathroom, then follow her until he veered towards the cashier's booth, paid, came out and got back into his Camaro. She had done nothing, had not tried to attract his attention, had concealed herself behind the wheel and her own sunglasses.

Then he turned to look at her. She was not the same, how would he have even recognised her after all these years when all she had ever been to him was a stick in a bed and later, recovering, a thin girl he had once joined (before the vanishing) with Lenny, for a drink at the bar of the Regent Palace Hotel?

There was a discrete section of time that day, a singular opportunity lasting about a minute and a half, when she could have got out of the car and walked across to him, said, 'Excuse me, is it Arthur Persky?' But to what purpose would she assault him with her own identity? To rebuke him for what he had done to Miriam, or simply to exercise her own curiosity about what he had made of his life? And then if it was not him, or he denied that it was, wouldn't that be worse?

So she still did not know if it was Persky when he drove off and she never told Lenny or her sister-in-law about the incident at the gas station. He remained what he would always be, a man lost at sea off the coast of Mallorca, carried away by the rushing waters to whatever life he was going to lead in Fifties America, an early hipster, some quality in him that would forever be ahead of its time.

By their teens Lenny and Valerie's children had understood how tight the circle of people who came out of that place were with each other. They observed the visits from their parents' oddball friends Sarah and Hannah, who would arrive, usually on a Saturday afternoon, wearing slacks and headscarves as if they thought that Hampstead Garden Suburb was, by virtue of its bucolic name, the countryside and they must dress for climbing over stiles. They were always laden with presents from Hamleys so the kids went wild when they saw this pair standing in the glass porch, made a rush at them and ran off with their new toys, and while they were preoccupied Lenny and Valerie would take them into the conservatory and close the door.

There *was* a dark circle and it was closed and opaque. These people had all come from a place of suffering and terror and Lenny and Valerie could always, with some second sight, instinctively recognise strangers who had been through the experience of the sanatorium, who had endured the futile boredom of the Way of the Patient, who had been made passive for years on end and had been cured not by deference to authority but defiance of it, and of course by a scientific miracle.

But it seemed to their children that something else was holding them together, more than a shared illness. When they asked, when they probed and even challenged, their questions turned their father evasive and guilty-looking, like a man terrified of being judged for some crime that had gone undetected.

It never occurred to them that it had anything to do with their aunt.

For Miriam was no Miss Havisham, she lacked the disposition to be a tragic heroine. The children remembered being taken to see her in Hendon in the early Sixties and dutifully answering questions about school and toys and of course television to which she was addicted, immensely proud of her brother and his wife who 'make the programmes!'

Their aunt seemed to them perfectly self-sufficient. Yet their parents spent every Sunday morning with her, brunches over bagels and smoked salmon and glasses of Russian tea drunk through sugar cubes. Every week Miriam would hand over bouquets of flowers for each room at home. She gave Valerie roses, gladioli, chrysanthemums, backed with fern. Valerie never succeeded in arranging them as well as Miriam. She did not have the eye for colour, proportion or choosing the right-sized vase. Lopsided and ungainly was how they appeared to her, as if she was expressing her own body, florally.

Miriam was still a good-looking woman, an Amazon with the strength of an archer in her arms, backcombing her hair into a high beehive decorated with butterfly bows and showing off her good legs in miniskirts, when she met Maurice. They started seeing each other after one of her deaf club holidays in Bournemouth. He was a book-keeper with his own house in Mill Hill, described by Lenny as a 'dull dog', a man in a trilby hat and elasticated metal armbands holding back his shirt cuffs. Miriam claimed he had more to him than met the eye. He'd turned up unexpectedly at the florist's shop in Hendon Manny had bought for her where she was standing amongst the flowers, her blue-black beehive rising above the peonies.

'Well, look what the cat's brought in,' she said, holding up a piece of yellow cellophane and looking at him through it so he appeared a high golden colour.

'I couldn't bring you flowers obviously so I bought you choco-lates.' He held out a box of Black Magic.

'Ooh, how did you guess they're my favourite? Much better than those sickly Milk Tray.'

'I had a hunch you'd like them because you're dark and sophis-ticated yourself.'

He *was* dull, Miriam thought. He would never live up to the promise of Persky who had written her a heartbroken letter all about the stolen dress, his confinement to the brig, his blacklisting from the merchant marine. He was locked in on the other side of the Atlantic. She had written back to tell him, 'But you'll find a way, I know you will.' Yet he hadn't and all the other letters she had sent him, sent him for years, went unanswered.

Now this Maurice. I'm not one to settle for second best, she thought. It's not in me. But Maurice picked up a long-stemmed rose and put it between his teeth. *Caramba!* he cried, sensing that he needed to appear more interesting. Miriam was the best-looking Jewish deaf woman he'd come across, and the pool you had to draw from wasn't exactly large.

Maybe I could turn him into Arthur, Miriam thought. There could be a spark there. I could *make* him interesting.

On their wedding night she gave him detailed instructions in the Persky way. Maurice, despite his trilby and armbands, wearing now a pair of royal blue pyjamas he'd bought for the occasion, was not surprised or shocked by this adamant request. He classified it under what he called 'the new freedoms', which covered a multitude of once-illicit or unspoken-of activities. For it seemed that he had some radical ideas such as supporting decimalisation and was interested in the potential for computers, buying and assembling from a kit the Acorn Atom. 'I like to be open-minded,' he said.

In Miriam's hands, Grecian Formula smoothed through his hair, a pink shirt from Marks and Spencer and new slip-on suede shoes on his feet, Maurice became what she called 'highly presentable'. The armbands and the trilby were eradicated with extreme prejudice. They took up golf and travelled together to links in faraway Scotland to play in tournaments. It was a full life.

After Maurice died in 1991 she moved to a seaside flat in Southend, a destination chosen, Valerie believed (though she was too tactful to mention it to anyone), so she could gaze out across the North Sea to look for Persky's ship on the horizon. He had begun to re-occupy her conversation. 'Oh, wasn't he something, Len? Wasn't he just the bee's knees?'

The house was airless and the TV always on, soundlessly. She never turned it off when visitors arrived and you could see her eyes straying towards the screen while Lenny fussed around with whatever household jobs they thought needed doing, making calls for her on the dusty phone and trying to find out if she understood what a certain letter from the Gas Board or the Rates meant. Valerie thought she probably would have been happier without their claustrophobic care and attention but Lenny's devotion to his sister only increased as the years went by.

For to him Miriam was left behind compared with his own advancement. He talked to Miriam every single day for over sixty years, even when he was in LA or New York doing deals for the network, he called her.

'As long as I hear her breathing at the other end, I know not to worry.'

*

In 1957 the government had enough streptomycin to cure everyone who could be cured, new combination therapies were developed and they embarked on one of the greatest public health programmes the country had ever known. They sent mobile X-ray units housed in bulky white ambulance-like vans out into all the big cities and got people to line up to be X-rayed. The sick – men and women and children who didn't even know they were ill, as Lenny hadn't known when he was X-rayed for his national service medical – were identified, sent off for treatment and the disease was on the verge of complete extinction. 'From a death sentence to a course of antibiotics in a decade,' Lenny said.

In a foolish moment he volunteered to be a driver, he said he'd do it for nothing. He would watch the white vans rumbling round the streets and wanted to help, but of course they didn't need him. So he would go and stand outside the queue of people waiting to take their turn and tell them his story – his, of course, not Miriam's – of how this miracle drug had cured him and cured his wife. The anxious, the paranoid (conspiracists who believed that the government was interfering with them in some way), the sceptical and the busy were all treated to his tale of the sanatorium and the lives that had petered out there and how now they just had to stand in front of the big machine for a few minutes and then they would know, and when they knew, then they could face a future not of ill-health but of cure.

To Lenny, the illness that struck them and their struggle to overcome it, the success and the failure and the violence of it, seemed a form of war. The ten-thousand-year conflict which still has its battles – he was always sending his children cuttings about the return of tuberculosis, particularly amongst the homeless or brought here by refugees fleeing wars and poverty, which impaled him on a certain contradiction in his thinking, knowing that he came himself from the body of a sickly foreigner and was what they called in those days 'immigrant scum'.

47

One afternoon in the mid-Nineties, he was driving through south London and remembering the long-ago ambulance journey when they saw for the first time the mirror city on the other side of the river, an impulse took him past his destination and he drove on through the outer suburbs into Kent. He knew that it was vanity: that he was driving his new silver Mercedes E-class coupé which he'd picked up only a week ago, his in-car phone ringing with people wanting his time, his ideas, his go-ahead, his imprimatur on their project, and if he kept going he'd be returning as a king, not a sickly teenage boy robbed of his future and his Italian birds.

He had no idea what he was coming back to. By the Sixties, all over the world the sanatoriums were closing down. Sarah and Hannah, on a skiing holiday, had observed their derelict carcasses clinging to the sides of Swiss mountains. In Britain genteel people with long pockets were no longer confined to institutions, the NHS treated its patients briskly and in hospital. Since then the Gwendo had been turned into a hotel and the name of the long-dead girl expunged, then a beauty spa where you went to have your spare tyre rolled away and live off lemon juice and hot water. Even this promising venture failed. There had never been much love in Britain for concrete Continental modernism and the building was fatally associated in the minds of visitors with institutions, council estates, council departments. The optimism of its form was at odds with the stained walls, the cracks in the structure, the unforgiving greyness of its materials.

Apart from some wind farms, white arms spinning, the Kent countryside looked no different to him. He saw the road-sign for the village and thought for the first time in many years of Mrs Kitson the art teacher who must now be an old lady if she was still alive. She had been one of the few who had come to say goodbye to him and Miriam on their last day, the day of their expulsion, to wish them well. 'I understood what you did,' she said. 'I'd have done the same if it could bring back my Trevor.' He tried to recall her in her Delft-blue smock, her rose-coloured lipstick, it was a faint, watery memory. But she had been real. On his way back he might ask in the shop if anyone knew her.

The village had changed in the way that everywhere had changed since the Fifties. Yellow lines marked the sides of the roads. Where an old fingerpost had marked the turnings to other villages, there was now a roundabout and a set of traffic lights directing the driver to a large fringe of executive homes extending out into the fields. The chemist shop was gone, replaced by a business which made bespoke curtains and blinds in Colefax and Fowler fabrics. The Singing Kettle remained, but under another name and with a Gaggia coffee machine spurting cappuccinos and lattes.

Lenny recalled his sister's long-ago wish for ice cream. Years later he had bought her her first tub of Ben & Jerry's. No doubt in the newsagent now you could buy anything you liked, frozen yogurt, ice creams on sticks. The Queen Anne houses in the centre of the village were shrouded by festoon blinds. Range Rovers were parked in their drives. He could see a small marquee being erected in a garden.

He turned the car up the road that led to the sanatorium. This is easy, he thought, I should have done it years ago, there's nothing to be frightened of. The woods to him looked the same, all woods looked the same. Woods were green or in winter brown, sparse, dry, abandoned nests visible in the branches, birds flying about. Whatever coppicing had taken place in the intervening decades, new species introduced in the undergrowth, the woods were to him as unchanged as the primeval forests of England and as intimidating as they had been when he tore his trousers and ruined his shoes. He was wearing a new Hugo Boss sports jacket. His neck gave off the odour of Acqua di Parma. His whole body was tanned from summers in the South of France, and to his hair, still bushy in his mid-sixties, his hairdresser discreetly applied something which imitated the appearance of the colour loss visible in a man twenty years younger.

The verandas appeared above the treeline. He could see the children's floor, the site of the agony of the kids' incarceration. The drive bent once more and he arrived at the boarded-up windows, the door barred by metal plates, keep-out notices screwed to the grey concrete walls. The place looked to him like a derelict home for rats and foxes, a stink of animal piss rose from where the benches had once stood.

I'm not a deep thinker, he told himself. That's Valerie's job, I don't know how to ... Was I once a kid who spent a year behind these walls, who read aloud to Valerie and my sister? Was I the boy who with the best intentions damaged her permanently? He didn't even feel like he was, so how come these memories? They seemed to him like recollections of a TV play or film he had once seen, starring Captain Jackson and the late Colin Cox. The Lenny he was now had long ago sloughed off the youth in the Italian drape and only shared his memories as if a stranger's brain had been transplanted into him. But if that was nuts, and it *was* nuts, and he was indeed the Lenny who knew Chitts and Arthur Persky and Mrs Kitson, the man who built cathedrals out of the matchsticks and the malevolent doctor, then it meant he was dead. That he was the ghost he had always feared becoming, haunting the ruins of his own life.

No, he couldn't face going any further.

They should pull this place down, he thought. It's too far gone.

And he walked back quickly to the car, drove to London and went straight to the Groucho Club for a stiff drink. Settled into an armchair, he thought, I've had a shot at life, my little portion, and it's not enough, is it? No, nowhere near enough. I want to live, I want to live for ever.

On his second glass he remembered he had not stopped to ask after Lettice Kitson.

Who was sitting in the Single Kettle drinking coffee when she saw the silver Mercedes disappear up the hill through the woods to the old sanatorium.

'Another old boy?' said the waitress.

'Probably.'

They were always returning. They would go for years thinking they'd never come back but something irresistible drew them to the site of their agony. Occasionally they brought wives or husbands or children. She had met Captain Jackson in the village once, thriving, with his family, on a vacation from Sydney Australia of all places. Moustache long gone. Almost unrecognisable out of uniform in summer slacks and an open-neck shirt, the picture of health. And he had of course remembered her, and told her all about his new life and everyone but him in his party had an Aussie accent. How odd it seemed to her, who had never got further than Brighton, had stayed on in the village where she had been born and her parents born, her grandfather coming from somewhere up country in the middle of the nineteenth century and remembering when the Downie house was built, before they bought it when the squire was a local man. It was now a banker's weekend retreat.

It was another England. The village was not in the same country it had once occupied. Everything was different, the money in your pocket was counted in hundreds not twelves, TV aerials had started to appear in the Fifties, now the walls spouted satellite dishes like white mushrooms. Tuberculosis was an old person's disease. The words for it – consumption, phthisis – had fallen out of use.

She knew of Lenny and Valerie's success, she saw their credits on the TV screen. 'They were here, you know,' she said to her second husband who had come to work as assistant manager when the sanatorium was turned into a hotel. 'I knew them quite well. There was a scandal, but I see they never mention *that* in their interviews in the paper. Well, good luck to them, is all I say.' For they had fulfilled longings for greatness she would never achieve.

Persky had never come back, as far as she knew. She still had something of him. A boogie-woogie record. He had bequeathed to her the appetite for rock and roll. Like Miriam, on her wedding night she had explained to her husband the American's special skill.

48

Oh, it is bleedin' boring like a month of wet Sundays when you are a widow looking out at the sea and for all they rave about it most of the time, it doesn't do much. And who'd believe you when you told them that once when you were very young and had no fear you swung a bouquet of flowers round the head of a fascist, stamped him into the gutter with your brown lace-up shoes, laughed your head off at him lying there. Because he was threatening to take a swing at your brother, all innocent as a lamb in his Italian drape, listening to the jaw-jaw in Trafalgar Square on a damp Monday lunchtime.

Those were the days, when everything was bad and no joke and you'd had enough and you kicked some prick in the goolies and ran away and no one caught you. And now it's come to this, an armchair by the window and bad knees, terrible hip, a lump in your chest which turned out to be nothing but terrified you that time in the bath surrounded by bubbles. Ridges in your fingernails that are just old age, says the manicure girl. Bleedin' cheek.

Meanwhile your brother, your twin, same birthday and you're always included though maybe he has another birthday with Val, just the two of them, some place where the waiters know them by name and they go à la carte because you don't always want a spare wheel, do you? He drives around in his silver Mercedes and you're just a lonely old widow looking at the sea, going on coach trips with other widows, turning up your hearing aid for the commentary. Seen castles. 'Castles, Len, with moats and everything.' 'Any sheep?' 'Coming out your ears.'

Going out to the charity shops looking for bargains, and Lenny says, 'What do you want with those old *schmattes*? Anything you need, just ask, you can have anything, anything!' But you want what you find yourself just for the thrills and you're tempted to hoist that skirt, just for the hell of it, because you're so bleedin' bored with your respectability and keeping up the Lynskey good name which is on TV or its arse on the sofa of his VIP club in Soho drinking martinis or some cocktail you've never even heard of with his telly pals and you've just got dust motes in the window and the unsurprising sea.

And why shouldn't you go and take a look at the old place yourself, but not tell him because he'd insist on driving you there and Valerie would want to come and they would start planning to make a day of it with lunch at a hotel on the way and a glass of champagne if you fancy it, like some old dame with a rug over her knees, when inside you're nineteen and coming downstairs in your Blustons costume and Arthur sliding across the floor on his knees?

At the hairdresser's. Having your roots done and your nails done.

'Going anywhere nice?' says the manicure girl who speaks up loud and clear like she's been told to, almost shouting to be heard above Radio One.

'Not a nice place at all, if you want to know. A horrible place.'
'Oh dear.'

Your hands like an old lady's, you can see the bones beneath the skin. Soon that's all there'll be of you.

The girl looks at you like you're something from another era when women wore those dead foxes round their necks and carried handbags with gilt clasps. She's taking you for one of those posters reminding people there's a war on, because you've put on your face that morning with the shaky bravado that can just about draw a straight line above your lids and outline a cupid's bow in rose pink which is bleeding into the cracks. Terrible. An old lady's face.

Life is leaching out of you, you can see it in the mirror. The absolute *sight* you just saw in the glass is like a trip in the street when you go down hard on your hands and knees and are foolishly trying to stagger up, your tights ripped, your skin bloody and abraded. Before and after. You've got to get up.

'I don't know what I think I'm doing, getting the idea that I could just go back like that, all dolled up, like my brother in his flash motor.'

'Sorry, dear? Where were you supposed to be going?'

And it comes up from your throat, an acid taste of anger and bitterness, and no one you can blame.

'I had a disease when I was young.'

'I'm sorry to hear that. What was it?'

'It was like Aids, but nothing to do with sex. They cured it in the end. You youngsters have never even heard of what I had.'

'What was it then?'

'Tuberculosis.'

'No. Sorry. Is it a cancer?'

She had been maimed by an illness that was so far out of fashion it might have been a wartime recipe for pink blancmange made from cornflour when everyone these days ate real chocolate mousse and tiramisu. TB was Spam fritters and two-bar electric fires and mangles and string bags and French knitting and a Bakelite phone in a freezing hall and loose tea and margarine and the black of the newspaper coming off on your fingers and milk in glass bottles and books from Boots Lending library with a hole in the spine where they put the ticket, and doilies and antimacassars and the wireless tuned to the Light Programme. It was outside lavatories and condensation and slum dwellings and no supermarkets. It was tuberculosis, which had died with the end of people drinking nerve tonics and Horlicks.

But I'll go, she thought. I'll tell nobody, I'll just go on my own.

And what a right schlep that turned out to be. Train to London,

299

Tube to another station, train to Canterbury, then two buses. She wrote away for the timetable because anything's better than staring at four walls, it'll be an adventure.

Since the day the ambulance driver brought them back she'd only been south of the river half a dozen times, it was still the mirror city, the moon in shadow. Then beyond there was Croydon and sheep. As soon as you left London it was sheep and cows and horses all the way. No pigs, she never saw any of them. A herd of an animal she didn't recognise raised their long necks and stared at the train. 'Alpacas,' said the woman opposite. 'They're getting very popular these days.'

'Speak up, dear, I'm hard of hearing.'

'I said ALPACAS.'

'Oh! Don't you make coats out of them?'

'You can do, yes.'

But like others had found, it was exhausting to talk to Miriam, to have to keep your voice raised almost into the shouting range, and she fell back into Miriam's companion, silence.

The fields slid past in the same green way. She was trying to remember what she had said when Lenny came to her and told her they'd got hold of the medicine and they were going to inject her. Arthur would put the needle in himself, and there was no point that she could recall when anyone *asked* her, because why would anyone need your permission to save your life? That wouldn't have made sense. And no one had explained if there were any risks, because how *could* they have known?

She'd walked into that broom cupboard like a sheep, like one of them out the window, she hadn't made any enquiries. She could have asked Valerie, she might have had more information, being educated. But Valerie would have told on them. She wouldn't have been able to help it, Edgbaston was still too strong in her, she'd have considered it her duty.

One time, Valerie asked her if she had forgiven Lenny. Miriam said, 'Forgive? What's that when it's at home? If you're ten minutes late meeting me for coffee and say you're sorry, I'll forgive you. But when you made someone deaf you never forgive, that's ridiculous. It's a silly little feeble word that people ask for to get themselves off the hook. Len and me have got our whole lives to live with this thing between us; he knows, he knows what he did and what he's guilty of and what not.'

'She's right,' Lenny said to Valerie.

'But forgiveness, surely you—'

'Darling, that's your religion not ours. Go to church and light a candle or tell the priest or whatever it is you do and your conscience is clear. It doesn't work like that.'

'So what's the alternative? Vengeance?'

'Never forgive, never forget, always bear a grudge.'

'Is that what she thinks?'

'Of course. We're built that way.'

'But you're her brother.'

'I know. And I'll get time off for good behaviour.'

'When?'

'Not yet.'

Miriam was his cross – not cross, wrong word. And she thought, Oh the Jews really are strangers after all. There was always another dark circle. They didn't even believe in hell, in the afterlife, just this one. Hell to them was death itself.

At Canterbury Miriam thought, Bugger it, I'll get a taxi, I'll come back in style. The taxi driver, who wasn't averse to bellowing, told her, 'It'll cost you, you know. Thirty quid.'

'I'll give you twenty.'

They settled on twenty-six.

He could see her hearing aid, he spoke up. 'Are you coming back today, love?'

'Of course, do I look like I'd live in a dump like that?'

'So do you want me to bring you back?'

They continued to haggle until they reached an agreeable price. He was to wait for her in the café. She'd cover him for a pot of tea and a cake if he fancied it.

A long time ago she had wanted ice cream. It had been March, it had been the era of austerity and rationing. Now it was July and ice creams were freely available in the shops but she didn't feel like one. The luxury of not even wanting what you could easily have, of being ferried around by your own driver while you lolled on the back seat looking at – 'What are they called again?'

'Oast houses, love.'

'That's right. Something to do with beer, are they?'

'Was. Not any more. All converted into luxury houses now.'

'Who'd want to live in a thing like that?'

'Rich people.'

'My brother's rich, he has a beautiful detached house in Hampstead Garden Suburb with a *swimming pool.*'

'How did he make his money?'

'Telly.'

'Actor?'

'No. What you call executive producer.'

'What's his name?'

'Lenny Lynskey.'

'I've heard of him, we used to watch—' They recalled lines and catchphrases from Lenny and Valerie's shows. 'As good as Hancock in its day,' the driver said.

'I know.'

The old fingerpost signs were still on the road leading to the village. The name caught in her throat like a fly.

'Here we are. Anywhere you'd like me to stop?'

'Drop me off at the café, I'll meet you back here in an hour. Have any cake you fancy, it's on me.'

The last time Miriam walked up the hill was after the day out at the races. She had struggled up on Persky's arm, her clothes soaked. Persky had said, 'Come on, baby, only a few more steps.' Lenny had encouraged her to stop and rest if she felt like it. Now she was on her own. The trees were heavily green and cow parsley waved in the heat. Her shoes, navy leather with gold snaffles and a low heel, struggled with the gravelly ground. Once, young men had strode through the woods with sticks, cravats at their necks, now there was no sound but unheard birdsong.

No vehicles passed her. Nothing to deliver, neither human nor supplies. This is a terrible lonely journey, she thought, alone next to the depressing trees.

Sweat patches appeared under her arms, and she took off her summer mac and held it over her arm.

'My knees, my fucking knees!' she shouted at the woods. No one heard apart from the worms slithering through the undergrowth and what did they know from knees?

It was hard going, harder than she remembered, every step a knife. And what's to become of me if I fall, she asked herself. The driver will come and look for me. You get what you pay for.

To the families that had once lived in the houses cleared to make way for the sanatorium, the hill was just a gentle slope. To the feebler patients it had been an insurmountable obstacle. I've left this too late, she told herself, I should have come back years ago when I was fit. A shaft of grey concrete appeared and the verandas rose in their terrible tiers. She stopped to look up at them, at where she had once been – second floor, third veranda along. The old place had taken a pasting from the weather and old age. Patches of concrete crumbled away into rubble and lay strewn on what had once been the ornamental flower beds. The whole place looked diseased by time and neglect and its architecture having fallen out of favour, and by concrete's natural old age, cracking and flaking like the human face. The signs cried WARNING KEEP OUT.

There was no obvious way to get in, just look up at the sad ruin which had kept a roof on thousands of suffering tubercular souls.

The monument to Gwendolyn Downie was still partly standing in the flower beds. Moss and funguses obscured the gold-lettered tributes to her youth and loveliness. Miriam could not remember anything about her. Poor little tart. Beneath fallen leaves the pointed top of the obelisk rested, knocked off by a chunk of falling concrete from a disintegrating veranda.

She had not come this far just to stand here and mourn, mourn

303

her own youth, mourn her hearing, mourn the loss of Arthur, her whole life, which could have been something completely different. You can't stand around and weep and have the taxi driver ask you if anything is the matter because your mascara is halfway down your face. No crying. Now isn't the time for tears.

She bent down and picked up the liver-coloured piece of marble. It was heavy, she could only carry it a few steps and she lifted it with all the strength she had and heaved it through the window of what had once been the day room. The entire pane, loose in its frame, fell out. The noise sent all the birds of the hill and the woods into a frenzy of fright and warning that even she could hear, a cacophony like the applause of an audience at a momentous stunt when all she'd wanted was to give the old place a bloody nose, take its lights out. She could actually step inside if she wanted, could haul her leg over and put her foot down and drag the other leg over to join it being careful on the other side not to cut herself. Her hip might not like it, her knees would protest, she could fall over in there and nobody would hear her cries for help. She'd seen enough. The place had taken a battering and no one loved or wanted it and this was the last laugh.

But was that enough? No. For Arthur was in there somewhere, and herself in the radio cupboard perched on the desk, her knickers round her ankles, Arthur snapping at her suspender belt.

Her shoes crunched on broken glass, she stepped in tiny mincing motions out of its way. Little beads of blood rose around her ankles and seeped through her tights. She didn't feel the pain, she should have, maybe I've got diabetes, she thought. That does in your feet, doesn't it? For she ate enough sweets and cakes these days, a whole packet of biscuits on a Saturday afternoon watching an old film with the subtitles on.

Inside, strenuous attempts had been made to efface all signs that this had once been a hospital for the sick and dying, a place of spittoons and thermometers. The spa retreat made the well even healthier through mineral water, fruit teas, a very light diet and plenty of exercise. Lenny had once booked a weekend at

Champneys in an effort to slim down and get back into his Hugo Boss suit but came home after two nights. 'It reminded me of you-know-what.'

Gold-framed mirrors still hung from the walls, which had been papered over in vinyl sheets of lilac, mint green and lemon. Low off-white leather sofas had replaced the adjustable medicinal chairs on wheels. A noticeboard propped on an easel announced the final day's activities, the massages, aerobics classes, t'ai chi, yoga, self-improvement talks. There was a pleading tone to it, as if the last guests already knew that when they left they would slacken off, eat cream cakes, the pounds would come back on, and they gave themselves permission to laze in their rooms with a magazine.

To Miriam, it was simply pathetic. Once you took away the nurses in their uniforms and the doctors in their white coats and the knowledge of the surgical block along the ramp, it exuded the faint memory of tears. To think she had been here, to think Arthur of all fellers was here. It was ridiculous. The ghosts of the officers' table and the Mothers' Union with their Knit and Natter Club, of the very posh bird always dressed in silk and cashmere who had been making it up the whole time, all these characters returned to her as cards in a deck, shuffled faces back and forth. Whatever happened to the little nurse, and to the art teacher? And where was Arthur now, *where was he?* What was he doing while she stood there in the ruins of a concrete world – the bacteria still infecting the walls or how could you account for the building's sickness?

The lift had been turned off. The electrical systems had all been disconnected. Her knees lumbered up two flights of stairs. The smell of damp concrete. God this place stinks, she thought, gone to rack and ruin like we went to rack and ruin and is there a cure for it? Hope not. And here I am inside the old room, where me and Valerie lay beside each other and read each other stories and did our hair and our make-up and froze together out on the veranda, the snow falling on our blankets and listening to what – an owl hooting, and sometimes seagulls lost from the coast. The trees much taller now, the village hidden, not a spire or a chimney but on the opposite hill an estate of houses for people who hadn't been born when she and Valerie slept out here together.

And you had to confront it, the truth, that you had been sick, very sick, and you had been given an injection and made to lose your hearing, not stone deaf like some in the deaf club, but your brother and your boyfriend did this to you. They did it out of love and whatever they say, whatever the songs and the greetings cards tell you, love is not enough or all you need, you need your common sense.

But who to visit justice on? Her brother prayed every year, waiting for the Day of Atonement when his name would be written down in the Book of Life, he *hoped* the Book of Life, but God would take his moving finger one day and inscribe the words Leonard Lynskey and he would be gone. The doctor jumped off the cliff. Manny ended his days in the prison hospital, his liver eaten up with cancers.

She stood out on the veranda where once she and Valerie had read and chatted and talked about love and film stars and harder ideas tentatively suggested by her future sister-in-law (who'd have seen that coming, and a long and happy marriage as far as she knew, though she'd had her doubts when she saw them walking back down the beach hand in hand – Valerie all flushed in the face, not her pale self at all – that it would last, they were so different). She could go and find the broom cupboard, probably wasn't there any more, or stay here and make her mark. It's not something a nice girl does, is it, Mimi, she said to herself, using the old name, the special name that Arthur used when his hand touched her breasts.

She pulled up her skirt, rolled down her tights and her pants and standing as close as she could to the edge of the veranda squatted and took a long wee, which dripped down onto the veranda below then onto the windows of the day room and onto the flower beds and onto the remains of poor Gwendolyn's marble memorial.

'Ain't I the piss artist?' she said aloud to the trees.

49

In their retirement the Lynskeys sold the house in Hampstead Garden Suburb and moved permanently to their second home near the Côte d'Azur, taking delight in their olive trees and the oil that was pressed from the fruit, swimming towels draped over the chairs, the smell of salt rising from the damp threads, the sea around them, the heat.

When Valerie died, Miriam came out to live with her brother.

'Look at us,' he said, and she scarcely had to listen or watch the movement of his lips to know what he was saying.

She lay on a sun lounger, eighty-one years old, in a ruched black and silver bathing costume, her toenails painted silver, a slash of lipstick, not caring any more about the red mess in the deep lines round her mouth. Lenny in shorts, bronzed withered bare chest, white espadrilles on old painful feet. He could not reach his toenails any more to cut them. Miriam clipped away those horns for him.

He thought of an old saying, a half-remembered line, what was it? That there was nothing so whole as a broken heart? It had made no sense when he was young. But now she seemed to him to be nothing less than the sister he had always had before she was maimed.

'Will there ever be a statute of limitations, darling?'

'On what?'

'What I did to you.'

But she did not speak. And why *should she*, he thought.

For always in the heat, the shimmer of the sun on the surface of the pool, the cicadas in the trees, the smell of suntan oil, the rustling of the maid in the dimness of the kitchen preparing lunch, as if seen from the corner of the eye, a deserted half-ruined building in Kent, a remnant of an old disease, now undergoing a revival. Stealthy, lying low, waiting for a point of weakness in the human race, then lodging in the lungs of humanity to make its sluggish progress through the body, the magnificent shape of our temporary wholeness, until we die and other species take us on.

Acknowledgements

I would like to offer my deepest thanks to Margaret Morris, who after receiving a scholarship to study history at the University of Birmingham in 1949 was X-rayed, discovered to have tuberculosis and sent to a sanatorium where she endured the horrors of both the icy veranda and the thoracoplasty operation before she finally received the streptomycin cure. Her great generosity in telling me this story in her kitchen over two enthralling mornings was the genesis for this novel. Alan Simpson, one half of the writing team Galton and Simpson, creators of some of the greatest comedy radio and television (*Steptoe and Son*, *Hancock*) very kindly told me about his incarceration in the same sanatorium a couple of years earlier and the birth of his and Ray's broadcasting career on hospital radio. Thanks too to Isabelle Grey, who told me of her mother's experiences.

I am hugely grateful to Helen Bynum, author of *Spitting Blood: The History of Tuberculosis*, my desktop bible throughout the writing. She answered all my dumb questions with such enthusiasm and energy (though any errors are mine and mine alone).

The Gwendo is an imaginary sanatorium, the architecture of which I have based on Paimio Sanatorium, Alvar Aalto's modernist masterpiece in Finland. The staff and patients are also a work of fiction and are not based on any individuals.

My thanks to my agent Jonny Geller, who read the completed manuscript while in bed with flu and related to the poor patients' plight.

Finally, my editor Lennie Goodings has proved, yet again, to be the most, most intelligent, ruthless and relentless pursuer of narrative consistency and the bond between text and reader. Bravo to her!

Credits